FOLLOW MY LEADER:

OR,

LIONEL WILFUL'S SCHOOLDAYS.

WITH NUMEROUS ILLUSTRATIONS

By "PHIZ,"

(HABLOT K. BROWNE.)

VOL. II.

Publishing Office:

HOGARTH HOUSE, 32, BOUVERIE STREET,

LONDON, E.C.

ILLUSTRATIONS.

FOLLOW-MY-LEADER.

PART II.

CHAPTER I.

THE blow that had fallen upon Lionel had come with such crushing force that for the time it stunned him, and deprived him utterly of the power to reason.

"Ruin!" That one dreadful word in his mother's letter kept sounding in his ears, as if some mocking devil was whispering it; and when the train dashed with a scream and a roar into a tunnel, Lionel fancied that he could see it written in blazing characters in the thick darkness.

It is no exaggeration to say that the journey from Cheetham Hall to the Great Southern Terminus was a dream to our hero. If he had awakened suddenly, and found himself in his own little bed at Cheetham Hall, he would not have been in the least surprised—but, ah, how unutterably glad!

Even the noise, bustle, and confusion which followed the arrival of the train at the terminus failed to arouse him.

He got out of the carriage in a slow, mechanical way, and was moving along the platform in the track of the other passengers, utterly forgetting his luggage, when the guard ran after him, shouting, "Hi!"

Poor old Noodles, the odd man, had given the man his last shilling to look after Lionel, seeing how dejected and miserable he was, and the guard being unusually honest that day, earned the money.

"You're going away without your portmanty," he said. "Here it is."

Lionel said, "Thank you," and opened his purse. There was very little in it—only one half sovereign and sixpence. The guard got the sixpence in defiance of the company's by-laws, touched his cap, and was off again.

Just then a shabby little man, with a white, unwholesome-looking face, and a very red nose—which looked like a pimple of abnormal size—came up to Lionel and whispered confidentially in his ear.

"Goin' to take a keb, sir—long four, sir? Allow me to carry your portmanty, sir."

These questions aroused Lionel's attentions. He was at his journey's end. To-morrow his mother would be at the Terminus Hotel, and he made up his mind to go there at once.

"I am going to the Terminus Hotel," he said to his very shabby but very polite acquaintance. "Is it far?"

"No, sir; close by," replied the shabby man, hitting the nail he wanted on the head by accident, as he added, "But it's most awful dear!"

Lionel instantly thought of his own and his mother's slender purses, and he drew back.

"Dear, is it? Do you know how much they charge for a bed for one night?"

"Well," replied the shabby one, thoughtfully tickling a pimple, "it ain't the busiest time, and you *might* get one for ten shillings."

"That won't do," said Lionel, hastily; "but are you sure that it is so dear?"

"I was waiter there for three year," said the shabby man, "and I think I orter know how they sticks it on. 'Alf-a-crown for a cup o' tea and a slice or two of bread-and-butter, so thin that if you leave the winder open the draught carries 'em out; and eighteenpence every time you speaks to the waiter. Now, if a young gent like you wants a really cheap, clean, and respectable lodgin' for a night or so, I can show you one. It's close by—only round the corner."

Lionel nodded assent, and the shabby little man picked up the portmanteau, and, shouldering it, started off.

At any other time Lionel would have thought twice before trusting himself to the guidance of a stranger, especially such a man as this, who bore "thief" stamped on every square inch of him; but just then our hero would not have noticed any great difference between the archangel Gabriel and Bill Sykes, if they had been placed side by side before him.

He might have noticed, too, that the shabby little man had a remarkably keen eye for a policeman, and whenever he saw one of these minions of the law, dodged with such surprising agility, that he seemed to become suddenly invisible; but Lionel, more by chance than anything else, stuck close to him, and in a few minutes they had left the station, and were proceeding at a sharp pace down a narrow, dirty, but exceedingly noisy street, containing some dozen or two of public-houses, all of which were doing literally a "roaring" trade.

Down that street, up another, then through a labyrinth of grimy courts and alleys, the shabby little man led Lionel, till at length he came to a halt in front of a small public-house of a modest and unambitious character so far as regarded its consumption of gas and paint.

The man, without stopping for a moment, butted open the swing-door with the portmanteau, and entered the bar, which was agreeably flavoured with the odour of bad rum and stale tobacco.

"Here we are," said the shabby man, speaking very quickly, as if to anticipate any objections Lionel might make. "I'll just run upstairs and pick out the best room there is for you. I may have to pay in advance, though. *Have* you got a little change in your purse?"

Lionel just then had got Mr. Grubbe—mentally—into chancery, and was giving him the sweetest kind of a hiding, and so absorbed was he in his fancied revenge, that, without considering the folly of the action, he handed his purse to the shabby man, who, catching up the portmanteau again, sailed off down a dark passage beyond the bar, and was seen no more.

Our hero sat down, and was soon deep in thought again upon the subject of his mother's ruin and Grubbe's villainy.

How long he sat there he had not the least idea himself; but it was really more than half an hour, when a rough voice called to him, and he saw that a square-built man, in his shirt-sleeves, and with only one eye and a broken nose, was looking at him over the counter.

"Now, young un, what's your lay?"

"I'm waiting for the man who went to get a room for me. Hasn't he came back?"

I don't know nothing about no man, nor no rooms," growled the landlord. "There ain't no rooms to let here."

"What!" exclaimed Lionel, starting up, and with all thought of Mr. Grubbe driven out of his head.

"There ain't no lodging to let here, I tell you," repeated the landlord, raising his voice.

"Then where's the man gone who took my portmanteau and my money?" demanded Lionel. "He went down there into the house."

"And you may go down there, too, if you like. That's the back way out, only, if you valleys your life, I wouldn't advise you to, unless you're on the cross."

"I've been robbed, then," said Lionel, flushing scarlet, as much with shame as anger, at the way in which he had allowed himself to be fooled. "That vagabond has got every penny I have in the world."

"More fool you to trust him," was the landlord's complimentary reply. "I didn't see you come in, or I might have given you the office. And now you take my advice; I see you're a young un and a green un. You get out of this as soon as you can; the air ain't 'ealthy for sich as you."

Lionel was half inclined to accuse the landlord of being an accomplice; but his senses had come back to him, and, without another word, he passed into the street, and walked rapidly along it on the look-out for some trace of the robber.

"Confound it!" thought our hero. "What an ass I have made of myself! I ought to be kicked. Only let me get hold of that red-nosed chap for five minutes, though; I'd redden him somewhere else. Shall I go back to the terminus?—he may be there on the look-out for another fool with a portmanteau to give away."

So, alternately abusing himself and the shabby man, Lionel wandered round and round about the scene of the robbery until afternoon gave place to evening, and the blaze of gas flared in the darkness of the coming night.

"Here's a pretty go!" muttered Lionel, savagely. "Here's the night coming on, and I haven't got a penny to bless myself with! Where am I to stop, and how the deuce am I to get anything to eat?"

Lionel was just becoming aware of the fact that he was very hungry; and the more he was forced to realise the impossibility of satisfying that appetite, the more ravenous he became.

But for that dreadful letter he would have gone to the hotel and ordered whatever his fancy suggested, leaving his mother to pay the bill in the morning. But he could not do that now; every shilling was of consequence.

"Dash it!" thought Lionel, suddenly. "I'll ask a policeman. Why didn't I think of that before?" Lionel had not thought of it before, probably because the neighbourhood bore such an evil reputation, that no constable in his senses ever ventured into it alone, and not then unless there was special duty to be done.

But by good fortune our hero stumbled across one —a new member of the force, literally a "green" hand, for he was a splendid young Irishman, nearly six feet high, and strong as a horse, and full of health and pluck.

"I say," said Lionel, catching him by the arm, "I've been robbed."

"Faith, and what else did ye expect when ye kem into this divil's hole?" said the policeman good-humouredly, as he turned up Lionel's chin the better to see his face. "Ah—and ye a young gintleman too! But who's robbed you, and where?"

Lionel soon described the circumstances and gave him a vivid verbal photograph of the shabby man, the public-house, and the landlord.

"Faix, it's lucky it is that ye wasn't murthered entirely! It's in the very pick of the biggest blagguards in London that ye were. There ain't half a dozen men in the constaburalee that 'ud go there alone at night."

"Then I must go and look after the thief myself, I suppose."

"Divil a bit, young gintleman. Wait awhile; it's thinking I am where we can discint deep down upon him."

"Do you know him, then?"

"Every baste of the lot that kennels in this hole is as well beknown to us as our own sisthers alanna. This chap they call Leary Moss, the pieman, and I'll stake a month's pay agin a pratee that he's at Mangle's this blessed minnit."

"Let's make haste, then. Which is the way?"

"Stop thin, me lad; it's not afther coming wid me that ye are."

"I am, though," said Lionel resolutely. "I want to lay hold of that red-nosed chap who boned my portmanteau. I'll give him what for."

"Bedad, ye've got pluck in ye. Kem along harrum shan't happen t'ye while Dennis Sullivan, X 94, is wid ye."

Now Mr. Dennis Sullivan, of the metropolitan police force, was, by going to Mangle's single handed, doing as wise an action as if he had crawled unarmed into the den of a set of hungry tigers.

There were men there stained with every crime that disgraces human nature—past masters in the devil's arts, who would have disgraced the lowest savages by claiming kin with them. In short, Mangle's was the very core of one of those foul plague spots, so many of which, to the shame of our civilisation, still exist in London.

Our hero of course knew nothing of this. He thought all thieves were mean, sneaking curs, whom the very sight of a policeman would cause to run yelping away. He was to learn a different lesson this night, a lesson which he never forgot

Constable Sullivan was so uncertain, too, about the locality of Mangle's, that he lost his way more than once, but at last he stopped at a house at the end of a dark deserted street.

"This is the place alanna," he said in a low voice to Lionel, "and well I remember it by the same token that inspecthor cursed it all over whin he showed it to me, for he rickened on nabbin' Wilson, the forger, that there's a thousand pound out for; but, by jabers, whin he got there the bird was flown?"

"And so will this one if we stand talking here," said Lionel; "how do you get in?"

"Faith, I believe we'll have to knock at the door civilly, and if they haven't got the manners to answer, sure we'll break it open for 'um."

There was no knocker to the door, but X 94 supplied its place with the toe of his heavy blucher.

Silence for a few minutes, then a shuffling footstep in the passage, and a sliding panel in the door was shot back, through which there peeped for a secon or so the dark cunning eyes of a small jew boy.

"Now ye young divil's spawn," said Constable Sullivan, "open the door, will ye, or I'll be afther breakin' the ugly little neck of ye and savin' the hangman the throuble."

The panel had closed long before the policeman had finished his speech, and he was about to apply the toe of his boot again when the door was suddenly opened.

"Hould back a bit alanna," said X 94, "them divils is up to all manner of thricks, so by your lave I'll go first."

He turned on his "bull's-eye;" the passage was

empty, but from the farther end there came the sound of voices, and light streamed through a partly open door.

Sullivan strode forward in his best official manner. He was a young hand in the force, but he had head enough to know that to take a prisoner single handed out of Mangle's was a deed as daring as any for which the Victoria Cross was ever given.

"Kape close beside me alanna," he whispered to Lionel, "and if there's a bit of a scrimmage get under the table."

Lionel made no answer, and the next moment X 94 had thrown open the door and walked in.

There were four men there, seated at a table, playing cards. They were all well dressed and were drinking wine—champagne—and smoking cigars which, judging by the fragrant odour they gave forth, were of a first rate brand; but the man they had come for was not there. Lionel saw all this in his first glance, and felt convinced that X 94 had made a mistake. These men could not be thieves.

Now, as to X 94, though not one of the men had taken the slightest notice of this intrusion, he marched up to the table, said in his most abrupt, official manner—

"Now, I'll throuble you to attend to me. It's Leary Moss, the pieman, I'm wanting, and he's in the crib at this blessed minnit; so hand him over, or it'll be the worse for ye."

"Two trebles and the rub," said one of the men—they were playing at short whist. "I'll trouble you for twenty pounds."

The man addressed pulled out a pocket-book, took from it four five pound notes, and passed them across the table. The other loser paid his losses, too, in the same cool, unconcerned fashion, but none of them took the slightest notice of either X 94 or Lionel.

It was exasperating; the constable felt it to be so. His Celtic blood got warm, and taking the nearest man by his shoulders he shook him till his teeth rattled.

The next moment the barrel of a revolver was in a direct line with the right eye of X 94; but one of the other men, the best-looking and best-dressed of them all, made a quick, imperative gesture with his hand, and the pistol was placed on the table.

"You are too hasty with your firearms," he said. "Recollect, for our sakes if not for your own, that you are not in California, and that the explosion of a revolver makes a disagreeably loud noise."

X 94 was himself beginning to think that he had made a mistake, but the next words of the quiet-speaking, well-dressed man settled the question.

"Well, my man, and what do you want at Mangle's?"

"I want," said X 94—not yet knowing what to make of his customers, but keeping a wary and resolute eye on them, "a thief o' the world who's stole this young gintleman's portmanty. Leary Moss, the pieman—that's the blaggaird!"

The soft-spoken, well-dressed man sat down again and laughed heartily.

"My good fellow," he said, "you must be a green hand! Who ever put you on this beat? Is it possible you are so ignorant that none but the very highest class are admitted to the hospitable shelter of Mangle's, that you come here to look for an airey-sneak, a gutter loafer?"

The others laughed, too; but Lionel, who had been watching their eyes, began to get uneasy, and he whispered to the policeman—

"Come away. These men mean mischief."

"Look ye here now," said X 94, "no more of your blarney; for, *mona mon dhiaoul!* if ye don't give up Leary Moss in five minutes I'll run you all in!"

"Thank you for your benevolent intentions, my

friend," said the soft-spoken man, coolly unwiring another bottle of champagne; "and as you will want our names when you make the charge to the night-inspector, suppose I introduce myself and these other gentlemen."

"Don't be a fool," began one of the men, half rising out of his chair; but was stopped by an imperious gesture from the other.

"That gentleman in the grey suit is Mr. James Weston, who left his employers, Messrs. Ephraim and Co., Clerkenwell, in a hurry, and forgot to return some ten thousand pounds' worth of unset jewels. They are sewn in his waistcoat at this present moment, and two hundred pounds are offered for his apprehension."

"Are these men mad?" thought Lionel, bewildered. "He can't mean what he is saying."

"Next is Mr. Milford, late cashier to the Timbuctoo Banking Company, Limited. He is worth five hundred pounds to any one who arrests him. The third gentleman is only a mutual friend, not worth your official attention; but now do you know who *I* am?"

He paused, and having looked X 94 full in the face, X 94 made no sign of recognition, but Lionel noticed that his hand was feeling for his staff, when suddenly there sounded through the room three sharp, clear strokes of a bell.

In an instant three of the men were on their feet, their faces white with terror; the fourth muttered, "D——n!" between his clenched teeth, and seizing the champagne-bottle, hurled it at the constable, who fell like an ox in the shambles.

The next moment he fell, too—his arm shattered at the elbow, and Lionel, with a leap like that of a tiger, stood with his back to the door, holding the other three at bay with the muzzle of the still-smoking barrel of the revolver pointed at them.

They were desperate men, and only hesitated for a second—then all three rushed upon him. He heard the report of the pistol as he pulled the trigger, then a crushing blow descended on his head, and all was darkness.

CHAPTER II.

MR. BELLERS AND LONG JEM HOLD A DISCUSSION RELATIVE TO THE PROVERBIAL INEBRIETY OF THE ENGLISH ARISTOCRACY, WHICH RESULTS IN A TERRIFIC COMBAT OF TWO—THE WAITER GETS RATHER MORE MELTED BUTTER THAN HE KNOWS WHAT TO DO WITH—SAM'S REMEDY FOR A SCALDED FACE, AND HOW IT OPERATED—BAD NEWS—ON THE ROAD TO LONDON.

THAT profound and dreamless slumber in which Mr. Bellers, Long Jem, and Sam indulged at the hostelry of Mr. Nopples was the last comfortable snooze they had for many a long day.

But they were very happy for the time. Mr. Nopples himself had gone off to the county town on business, but he had left strict orders that his friends were to be well looked after. So, when Mr. Bellers awoke about midday and roared for more soda water, it was brought with lightning promptitude. Similarly, when Long Jem insisted on having strong green tea and dry toast in less than five minutes, under penalty of skinning the waiter alive, his orders were executed as promptly as if the tea and toast had been waiting ready for him outside the door.

About four in the afternoon they began to feel hungry, but still indisposed to rise. The fumes of the wine still clouded their massive intellects, and invited them to slumber.

"This is proper," said Mr. Bellers, punching up his pillow to make it easier for his head. "I feel like a lord, Jem."

"So do I," growled Jem, "if a lord's 'ed feels like a balloon with a steam-engine at full work inside of it."

" Lor bless you! they gits used to it," said Mr. Bellers, with the easy confidence of one who was on familiar terms with the whole peerage. "Wot do that werse say, Jem—I aint sure it don't come out o' the Bible?"

" Wot werse?"

"Why, 'as drunk as a lord,'" said Mr. Bellers. "It's all nat'ral and proper, you see, Jem, for there's Scripter, or werry nigh as good, for it. But there, you've seen 'em at the races as well as me—"

"How do you know they was lords?" growled the obstinate Jem. "That's open to argyment."

"How do I know they was lords!" repeated Mr. Bellers, sarcastically. "Why, the same way as I knows you're a old fool, Jem—by hinstink."

"I'll give yer a taste o' this 'ere soda water bottle if yer calls me names," growled Long Jem.

Mr. Bellers fortified himself behind h's pillow, and called him a fool, and worse.

Whiz came the bottle—a full one—hitting the wall just above Mr. Bellers's head, where it burst like a shell, deluging him with its contents.

It was like a shower-bath; and a shower-bath ceases to be a pleasure when it comes upon you in bed, where you have tucked yourself up snugly, with the full intention of stopping there for another two hours.

Mr. Bellers uttered a considerable quantity of bad language; then, scrambling out of bed, he picked up one of his double-soled Wellington boots, and rushed upon his foe.

Long Jem was a practised acrobat, and he intended to spring out of bed after the manner of a harlequin; but there was an unlucky hole in the sheet, in which his foot got caught, and Mr. Bellers had him at his mercy.

Jem was hanging over the edge of the bed, so that when Mr. Bellers caught him by the leg he had the victim in a fine position for punishment.

"Whack!" came the heel of the Wellington boot, bringing forth a moan of anguish from Long Jem.

"You'll chuck soda water bottles at me, will you?" said Mr. Bellers, holding firmly on, and dealing a fresh blow with every word. "And not content with heavin' of a empty one, you must go and spile a man's snooze by drenchin' of him and his bed. Take that—and that—and that."

The last blow was a particularly painful one, the heel of the boot having come in painful contact with that small bone or rudimentary tail, which terminates the spine, and is called by anatomists the *os coccygis.*

Jem gave a tremendous howl of mingled pain and wrath, and, making a desperate effort, wrenched himself, and, catching Mr. Bellers in his long arms, staggered out with him into the centre of the room.

Wrestling is, we believe, a most healthy and invigorating sport as exhibited, say, at the Agricultural Hall; but when two middle-aged gentlemen in short-tailed shirts indulge in it in a bedroom, it becomes decidedly comic.

They were pretty well matched, and both had been good wrestlers in their younger days, so now, hugging each other with the affectionate grip of a grizzly bear, they tried trips, hitches, and falls, after the most approved method, much to the admiration of Sam and the waiter, who had just come in with a nice boiled chicken for their dinner.

"Go it!" roared Sam, clapping his hands; " go it Bellers, go it Jem!"

But Mr. Bellers felt that his wind was going, and that now or never was his time, and, collecting all his strength, he bent Long Jem's back in, and treated him to a first-class "cross-buttock."

Now no particular harm would have resulted from this but for the fact that the waiter got in the way just as Long Jem was trying to butt a hole in the door with his head.

The waiter went down with the tray on top of him, and, painful to relate, the whole sauce-boat-full of scalding melted butter and parsley was shot into his face.

The language of that waiter when he arose—which he appeared to do as if he were in a hurry—we empathetically decline to reproduce in these pages—the very ink would blush and turn red.

But then it must be owned that he had some excuse—to have seen him at that moment dancing wildly about the room trying to scoop hot melted butter out of his eyes would have moved any man to pity.

"Here, hi!" said Mr. Bellers, running after him, utterly forgetting the scandalous state of undress he was in; "stop a bit and have some water. Stop him, Sam, he'll be scalded to death."

Mr. Bellers made a clutch at the waiter, one of whose arms, which were whirling about like flails, struck the showman in the wind and doubled him up on the floor, where he sat gasping like a frog whose supply of water has been stopped.

Sam was seized with a happy idea for securing the unfortunate waiter, who still danced frantically about the room, still pouring forth volumes of that language which we have already declined to repeat.

The long youth seized a bottle of soda water, and, unwiring it, waited till the waiter came opposite and then let fly in his face, in the hope that the water would cool him a little.

Sam's theory was an excellent one, but unluckily the cork was in front of the water, and as the waiter's mouth happened to be wide open to let out an oath of extra profanity, the cork was propelled into his gullet.

The waiter fell on his back across Mr. Bellers' bed, he didn't swear any more, but there was a dreadful kind of rumbling sound somewhere inside him, and he turned so deep a red in the face that it showed even through the melted butter.

Sam was horrified, a creepy feeling went up his back, and his short crop of red hair seemed to stand on end.

"Bellers," he roared—"Jim, help! run and fetch a corkscrew somebody."

The two showmen were still on the floor, apparently absorbed in the contemplation of some object of deep interest, for they looked extremely vacant and paid no attention to Sam.

Meanwhile the waiter had turned a brilliant purple, his eyes stood out like hat pegs, and his arms and legs were jerking spasmodically like those of the childrens' toy which are worked by a string.

Sam put his fingers in to feel for the cork, but the waiter shut his mouth with a snap, and made Sam howl dismally, but he bawled for help too.

In the midst of all this there entered Mr. Nopples, in a state of the extremest agitation and alarm.

"Get up, Bellers—get up Jem," he said; " while you've been lying snoring here you've been ruined."

"He's black now," roared Sam. "Help! won't nobody fetch a corkscrew?"

"Hallo! what's the matter here?" demanded Mr. Nopples.

"Chokin'—I shot him with a soda water corkscrew," muttered the bewildered Sam, faintly.

Mr. Nopples' remedy was prompt. With one hand he raised the unlucky waiter into a sitting position, and with the other he gave him such a mighty thump in the middle of the back that the cork flew out like a rocket. Then he gave him a good shaking to settle things down into their proper place again, and stood him on his legs, which appeared to be very shaky.

Then he went to Mr. Bellers and Long Jem, and administered part of the remedy to them—that is, he shook *them* and stood them on *their* legs.

SAM'S EXCITEMENT AT SEEING LIONEL WAS SO GREAT THAT HE RUSHED TO GREET HIM,
REGARDLESS OF THE ACROBAT ABOVE.

No. 17.

"Now," he said in a low, solemn tone, "you three chaps get on your togs at once; suthin very serus has 'appened."

The showmen had recovered sufficiently now to comprehend Mr. Nopples' words.

"What's gone wrong?" they said all three at once.

"Get on your togs, I tell you, and come down to me in the private parlour."

And away went Mr. Nopples, soon followed by our three friends in such a hurry that they had to complete some portion of their toilet in the passage.

"Now, wot is it, Nopples?" said Mr. Bellers.

"How's the nerves?" said Mr. Nopples.

"Mighty shaky, and you've made 'em worse."

"Have a nip. Take one all round; you'll want it."

Mr. Nopples' idea of a "nip" was a quarter of a pint, or thereabouts, of old brandy. But they drank it, and seemed to feel better.

"I'm ready for anything now," said Mr. Bellers defiantly.

"Well, then," said Mr. Nopples, "you're bust up."

"Wot!"

"Your tent's tore down; your carryvan's broke open; everything that was worth takin' away is took, and everything that wasn't is smashed. Is that strong enough for you, Bellers?"

The showman sank back in his chair, looking ghastly pale.

"You're jokin', Nopples," he said, faintly. "Say you're jokin'."

"I wish I was, old chap. But put on your hat and come along o' me. If I hadn't been away to town to-day about my license this wouldn't ha' happened."

There was a gaping crowd about the wreck of the show, and Mr. Bellers, elbowing his way fiercely through, saw that Nopples had not overdrawn the picture. Everything was destroyed or taken away, and, above all, the cash-box containing every penny he possessed in the world was stolen.

He did not say a word until they all got back to the inn. Then he spoke.

"Now, Nopples, I want to know who did this for me?"

"You're an old friend o' mine, Bellers, and I'll tell yer all I do know, which ain't much arter all; but when one thing and another is put together it looks bad. You know a chap called Barney Bailey?"

"The chap as used to come the thimble-rig and three-card dodges?" said Mr. Bellers. "I ought to, for I hid that chap away for a month when the perlice was arter him, and give him a pound to'rds a fresh start when it blew over."

"Ah! that's the way o' the world," said Mr. Nopples. "If you want to make a enemy, do a man a good turn. Well, Barney Bailey is square now, and is gone parcners with a chap as has some performing dawgs."

"It can't be him," said Bellers; "I never did the chap a haporth of harm in my life—quite contrary, as I've told you."

"Well, hear me out, and then think what you like," continued Mr. Nopples. "This show of Bailey's was behind yourn, and quite early he came in with his pardner—furious—'Cuss that 'ere Bellers!' he ses. 'We shan't clear a penny out o' the blessed town while he's here——'"

"Go on," said Mr. Bellers; "I see wot's comin.'"

"I didn't hear no more, for they began whisperin', and I didn't take any pertikler notice of wot I did hear, thinkin' it was only jealousy; but my boy Jem, who's got ears like a cat's, he heard a good deal besides; and when I found that Barney Bailey and his mate had left the town directly after your show was bust up, I settled the thing in my mind."

"And I've settled it in mine," said Mr. Bellers, putting his hat on, and fixing it there with an emphatic thump, "that Barney Bailey set the mob on to bust up my show, and I'd lay a pound, if I had one to spare, that the vagabone nailed my cash-box. Which way did he go when he struck his tent?"

"He took the London road. My boy Jem watched 'em sneakin' off whilst everybody else was busy at the fair."

"Then London's my way, and, by all that's holy, I won't rest till I've had that rascal by the throat. Come on, Jem; come, Sam. You can sell wot's left of the old carryvan, Nopples, and the old mare. I'll come back and settle accounts afore long. But I must reckon up with Barney Bailey first."

"You won't do anything rash, Bellers!" said Mr. Nopples, alarmed.

"I'd pound him to a jelly, if you call that rash," was Mr. Bellers' reply. And so it came to pass that on the morrow of the day which had been so bright and jovial, the two showmen and Sam were trudging back to London, with light purses and heavy hearts.

CHAPTER III.

LIONEL FINDS HIMSELF CONSIDERABLY MORE OF A HERO THAN HE THINKS AGREEABLE—SHOWING WHAT THE "DAILY DELIGHTER" THOUGHT OF THE MATTER—THE ARRIVAL OF OUR HERO'S MOTHER, AND HER OPINION OF THE STATE OF AFFAIRS—A STRANGE MEETING.

WHEN Lionel recovered his senses he found that he was lying on an improvised bed of rags and great-coats in the room where the fight had taken place.

Two men were bending over him—one a handsome, middle-aged man, in what looked like a military undress uniform and a cap with a straight peak to it. This was the inspector; the other, X 94, with his head tied up in a towel, and his honest face all aglow with joy when he saw Lionel open his eyes and stare round him.

"Are you better now, my boy?" said the inspector, putting down the sponge with which he had been bathing Lionel's head.

"Yes, thank you; I feel a little giddy, that's all."

And our hero, with a little assistance, rose to his feet and looked about him wonderingly, not yet quite sure whether or no he had been dreaming.

The first glance told him that he had not. The room was full of police, and there, in a corner, securely handcuffed, were three of the men he had seen playing cards—the fourth, the one whom he had shot in the arm, was lying on a sofa, while a surgeon was dressing his wound.

"Yes," said the inspector, following the direction of our hero's eyes, "we've got them all; and a precious good haul it will be," he added, with a slight chuckle at his own little joke, "close upon twelve hundred pounds. You may consider yourself in luck, youngster."

Lionel failed to understand him; his head was still giddy from the effects of the blow, and he was faint with hunger too, for he had touched nothing since his breakfast.

"Ah, I see! you're a bit faint, poor lad, and no wonder. You'd better go home and go to bed; but give me your name and address first, for we shall want you in the morning."

Then Lionel had to tell his story for the second time, and to confess that he was penniless and with nowhere to sleep. He nearly broke down in the telling, for he was worn out, but he bore himself bravely to the end.

"Poor boy! who'd have thought that?" said the inspector, gently. "Here, Sergeant Coppem, I want you; your place is the nearest. Take this young gentleman home with you, call a doctor to see that his head is all right, and let him have anything he takes a fancy to. Bring him with you to the station in the morning. I relieve you from duty till then."

"But," said Lionel, holding back alarmed, "my mother—I have to meet her to-morrow."

"We'll see to that, my boy," said the inspector in the same gentle, yet firm, voice; "I'll tell off a man to wait there till your mother comes, and you shall go to her at once. You mustn't forget, you know," he added, with a smile, "that you have a public duty to perform. If you begin thief catching you must go through with it. Don't say any more now, but be off."

And ten minutes afterwards he was in a cab with the sergeant, being driven away, goodness only knew where—he didn't.

    *   *   *

Lionel went to bed at the sergeant's, feeling more comfortable in the region of the epigastrium—vulgarly styled the bread-basket—than he had done for a long time.

The doctor had prescribed a cooling lotion for the exterior of his head, and some roast chicken, jelly, grapes, and other delicacies for the interior of his stomach, after discussing which, with such an appetite as few but schoolboys are favoured with, he went to bed and slept like the proverbial top.

He awoke in the morning to find himself famous. The capture had taken place early enough in the evening to enable the reporters to embellish the dry facts they managed to pick up with a few flowers of fiction of their own peculiar sort, and the sergeant had a specimen in his hand when he came towards his youthful charge.

"Eight o'clock, sir," said the serjeant. "Your breakfast will be ready at a quarter-past, and we must be at the station by nine. Would you like to see the paper?"

"No, thankee," replied Lionel; "I'll get up."

"There's a deal about last night's affair in it," said the serjeant.

"What, already?"

"Lor bless you, yes. Them newspaper chaps are like the vultures you read of, they smell out a murder or a suicide, or anything else that's likely to get 'em a dinner, as soon as it's done."

Our hero was a little curious now. He took the paper and read there such a version of the affair as made his eyes almost start from their sockets.

He was there adorned in all the majesty of type, that it was he who had tracked the four villains to their lair—the worst and most dangerous hiding place of the worst and most dangerous villains in England—that he had entered the den alone, and making sure that the men he wanted were there, he had given the signal—that the villains, getting suspicious, had rushed upon him, and that in conclusion, he had held them all at bay for a quarter of an hour, until the police came.

"What an awful lot of lies," said our hero aghast, "and yet they've mixed up the truth with it so that even I can hardly tell which is which."

"That's their bisniss, you see, sir," replied the serjeant; "the public like things spicy, and if a newspaper didn't give it the public hot now and then, why it might as well put the shutters up."

As they neared the police-station Lionel saw a crowd about the doors, and knew at once that he was going to be made a hero of again, and very uncomfortable indeed it made him feel.

"You're quite a celebrity," said the serjeant. "'Tain't many young gentleman of your age as 'ad get so many people to look at 'em. Only wait till the cases are tried, and you'll see what a fuss they'll make of you."

"What, shall I have to go to the trial?"

"Of course you will—you won't have to say much—for your evidence won't bear on what they're charged with—but you know, I suppose, that if it hadn't been for you they wouldn't have been took

for they'd got the artfullest hiding place at Mangle's as ever was, and would have escaped to it if you hadn't stopped 'em at the door. We've searched the crib a dozen times for 'em, with our sharpest men, too, and never found it out. But here we are—jump out."

As it is not our intention to plague our readers with the details of the trial, at which Lionel very unwillingly assisted, we may as well dismiss the subject in as few words as possible.

The men were all convicted, and at the trial the judges paid Lionel such compliments on his bravery that he blushed to the very roots of his hair, and felt rather more uncomfortable than if he had been the prisoners in the dock.

Of the rewards he would not touch a penny; he would have done so for his mother's sake, but she shrunk from the idea. "Her boy could do his duty manfully," she said, "but to take money for doing it would degrade him and her. It was blood money, and no good could come of it."

The inspector had kept his word—and more. When the preliminary examination was over, he found that gentleman waiting for him at the door of the court, where a cab was standing.

"Your mother has arrived," he said, "and there is something in the cab which I think belongs to you. Do you identify it?"

It was Lionel's portmanteau, with his purse laid on the top, half-sovereign and all.

"You caught the vagabond, then?" said Lionel; "I'm awfully obliged to you."

"That was nothing," said the inspector; "we could catch him fifty times a day if we wanted him. You're the boy for the warm concerns, I only wish you were old enough for the force; you'd be an inspector in six months. Good-bye."

And away rattled the cab, Lionel's heart thumping almost as loudly as the wheels. In five minutes he had forgotten all about his last night's adventure, and was thinking of his mother—in fifteen more he was clasped to her breast, where for the present we will leave him.

    *   *   *   *

Mr. Bellers and his faithful friends arrived in London by easy stages, following as early as possible in the track of the rascally Barney Bailey, of whom they here and there picked up news.

They were spending money freely, Mr. Bellers was told, eating and drinking of the best at the hostelries where they put up, and the honest showman went nearly wild as he thought of his hard-earned coin being converted into luxuries to tickle the felonious Barney's throttle.

All trace of him was lost as they neared London, but there was little doubt but that he had gone on to the great city. If he had, Mr. Bellers knew that he should soon find him out, and then——

Mr. Bellers would grind his teeth and shake his fist when he thought of the meeting, in a way that augured badly for the safety of Barney Bailey's health.

Sam was equally vengeful. Was it not owing to this Barney Bailey that he had been compelled to use his long legs instead of riding comfortably in a caravan? Was it not because of Barney Bailey that his requirements as to food were limited to a supply which fell little short of actual starvation? Sam was ready to wring Barney Bailey's head off, and would have done it with pleasure.

"Now, while we're in London looking arter this wagabone," said Mr. Bellers, "we can't afford to be idle. I've been talking to old Bobbles, and he can set us up in a line."

"Wot line?" asked Jem.

"Hackeryback! He's got two soots o' tights, as'll do you and Sam, and a pole, likewise a drum and pipes for me."

"Busted if I thought I should have to chuck sumersets at my time o' life," growled Long Jem. "I'm out o' practice—stiff as drill sergeant——"

"It's no use growlin', Jem," said Mr. Bellers. "It's a come down, I'll allow; but we've got to put up with it till me meets Bailey."

"Wot good 'll that do? He'll have spent all the money by this."

"I'll make him swallow the big drum, and run him through with the pole—dash me, if I don't."

And so it happened that in something less than a week afterwards the three friends were tramping the streets of London with a two-fold object—one being, of course, to pick up all the stray halfpence they could, and the other to encounter Barney Bailey.

Sam had a third, which he had never forgotten or relinquished, and that was to see his young master. He thought him still safe at Cheetham Hall; he little knew that he was at that moment in London, poorer than Sam himself.

It was about four in the afternoon, and they had struck a "pitch" which promised remarkably well, for the preliminary banging of the drum and the feeble wail of the Pandean pipes attracted a large audience—not ragged little boys and girls, with hardly enough clothing to make one respectable packet, but people who looked as if they had halfpence, and didn't mind giving them away.

They had gone through the first part of the performance, and the grand finale—the pole trick—was to come.

It was Sam's turn to balance the pole, and support the weight of Long Jem at the top. He was wonderfully strong in spite of his bony development, and could do it easily, as Long Jem had proved, or he would never have trusted his "precious carcase" in such a position.

All was ready. Mr. Bellers was banging the drum, and making a very brave attempt to coax "Pop Goes the Weasel"—the only tune he knew—out of the pipes. Long Jem had raised his feet, got on Sam's shoulders, and was at the top of the pole, when, unluckily for him, the long youth, whose marvellous squint enabled him to look two ways at once, caught sight of a well-known face and form walking along the pavement opposite.

Sam forgot in an instant all about the pole and Long Jem at the top of it, and, darting forward, he roared out—

"Master Lionel! Master Lionel! Here I am! Don't you know me?"

CHAPTER IV.

TUMBLING EXTRAORDINARY—LONG JEM BREAKS HIS FALL UPON A STOUT LADY—STOUT LADY OBJECTS—INSERTION OF CLAUSE NOT PREVIOUSLY IN THE AGREEMENT—A FRIEND IN NEED IS A FRIEND IN—— THE METROPOLITAN POLICE FORCE—RE-UNITED.

LIONEL looked round at the sound of Sam's familiar voice, just in time to see that youthful acrobat jerked on the flat of his back by the pole, while Long Jem, descending like a meteor, broke his fall upon a middle-aged, stout lady, who was trying to cross the road, and "dratting the tumbling."

The crowd, which had recoiled like a wave of the sea, was swept back again, closing in upon the central point of attraction, where Long Jem and the stout lady were clasped in each other's arms, engaged apparently in mortal combat.

She had been deprived of her wind by the shock, but not of her strength or of her temper. Her left hand was twined in his back hair, which was long, and, with her right, she clawed at his face with the ferocity of six tom-cats on the war-path.

"Go it! let 'im 'ave it!" bawled a respectable working man, a carpenter, who was on strike, because his bloated capitalist employer had refused to pay him and his mates twice as much as they were worth, and who had religiously spent his strike-money in getting drunk, and the spare time in kicking his wife.

"I'll lay a pot the old gal licks," said another.

"Look out!" said a third; "here's the slop."

And the policemen elbowed their way through the crowd scientifically, separated the combatants, stood them upright, and gave them a shake to bring them to a fitting state of comprehension.

Mr. Bellers had sufficiently recovered from his fright to use his voice, and began to give evidence at once in the most bewildering manner.

"You shut up, will you," said the constable; then, giving the old lady another shake, he added, "now then, what's the row?"

"He knocked me down, the wretch, he did!" screamed the old lady, who was fast working herself up to the hysterical stage of feminine wrath.

"What did he knock you down with—his fist or a himplement?"

"He fell on me, off the top of a pole," was the reply, delivered in gasps. "Oh, let me get at him—I'll flay him!"

As the stout lady had already under her finger-nails enough of Jem to make a slight lunch for a cannibal of moderate appetite, the policeman held her fast.

"It was all a haxident, policeman," said the unfortunate Jem. "I was on the pole, when my mate give a slip, and down I come on top of her, and she began clawing at me like a wild beast. Just look at my face!"

"And serve you right; you hadn't got no business in the road at all, obstructin' the traffic. Do you charge him, mum?"

"Charge him! I just wish you'd let me!" snarled the old lady, with a vicious glare at Jem. "I'd charge him into the middle of next week, the brute!"

"Come on," said the policeman, transferring his attentions to the unlucky Jem. "You'd better explain your haxident at the station."

The other constable instantly took Mr. Bellers by the collar as an aider and abettor of the assault, and the procession began to move on, when Lionel came pushing through the crowd and whispered a few words to one of the policeman.

He was one of those who had been at Mangle's on the memorable night described in our first chapter. He recognised Lionel instantly, and became as mild and affable as any ordinary mortal.

"All right, sir," he said, in reply to Lionel. "They shan't be run in. We'll turn 'em loose at the corner, and jacket the old woman."

Lionel waited, and, sure enough, at the corner of the street Long Jem and Mr. Bellers were liberated, despite the very violent objections of the stout lady, who, with no fear of the majesty of the law before her eyes, shook her fist in the faces of the constables, and, in the end, so far forgot what was due to her sex as to serve one of them as she had done Long Jem, whereupon she was herself conveyed to the station comfortably strapped down upon a stretcher.

"Much obliged to you, young gentleman," said Mr. Bellers. "We see it was you as done it for us."

"It was nothing," replied Lionel, who hated, above all things, being thanked. "Let us go back to Sam; he's in the chemist's shop yonder, poor fellow. He got a nasty cut."

"Wot!" said Mr. Bellers, "you know Sam, do you?"

"Ever since he was a baby. He was brought up in my mother's house."

"Why, you don't mean to say you're the young gen'lemen he was always a talking about to us. You're not young Master Wilful, surely?"

"Yes, I am, indeed."

"Then I'm proud to make your acquaintance," said Mr. Bellers, heartily. "For 'cordon to wot Sam ses, you must be a hangel, and nothink under."

"That's open to argyment," growled Long Jem. "*I* don't see no wings on the gent."

"Can't there be hangels without wings, you old idyot?" retorted Mr. Bellers. "Warn't I speakin' in a metaflooragal way?"

"I've floored one gal to-day, and that's quite enough for me," growled Jem again. "P'r'aps you'll say she was a hangel next."

"Metaphorical, you mean, Mr. Bellers," laughed Lionel; "but here's the chemist's shop. Hallo! that unlucky Sam's in another mess."

It looked indeed very much like it; for, as they entered the shop, Sam, armed with a large marble pestle, appeared in the background, defying the chemist and his two assistants, who barred the way to the door.

"You won't let me go, won't you?" Sam was saying, wrathfully. "I'll pound you into pills, the ole biling—so I give you fair warning. Do you think I'm a goin' to lose my young master, just as I've found him?"

"Pay the eighteenpence, then, for dressing your head, you young scamp!" said the chemist. "Do you think I'm going to lose my time over such as you, and then get nothing but insult for it?"

It was at this juncture that Sam caught sight of Lionel entering the door. In an instant he dropped the pestle, charged the enemy, driving one assistant into the perfumery case, and the other into a case of soda water, and then began such a frantic pantomimic dance around Lionel expressive of his joy, that the whole shop was in danger of destruction.

"Oh, lor'!" he exclaimed, in jerks, between the steps of the dance, and shaking both hands vigorously the while, "at last. My, ain't I glad! This is prime! Strike up 'Rule Britannia,' Bellers."

Here he kicked out behind in the fulness of his joy, and caught the pale assistant in the wind as he was vengefully creeping up behind Sam to drop him one with the pestle.

The chemist plainly thought that he had got into company with a few first-class lunatics, and, retiring to a back window, put his head out and bawled, "Police!"

"Don't, Sam, don't," said Lionel—"don't, old fellow. I'm as glad to see you as you are to see me, but take it a little more quietly. Look, you're getting a crowd round the shop."

"I beg your parding, Master Lionel," said Sam, checking a last wild attempt to fling his legs up to the ceiling, "but if you only knew how glad I was!"

"And so am I, Sam," said Lionel, hastily; "but there's something to pay before we go. How much is it?"

"Nothing, if you'll only go," said the pale chemist, who had returned from the back window as soon as he found there was nobody to hear him but the cats. "Do go at once, there's good people!"

"That's lucky," said Lionel, as soon as they were clear of the shop and the crowd; "I had forgotten for the time that I had no money."

"And we ain't took much," said Sam; "arf a crown at the outside, I should—— But lor' bless my art! wot am I a doing of?—walkin' alonger you in this dress! Why, your mar would faint, and as for Miss Mariar——"

"Stop, Sam," said our hero, quietly. "I hope I should never have been fool enough to have been ashamed of you in any dress, but there is less reason for it now. Sam, I am as poor as you!"

Sam turned pale, and clutched a neighbouring lamp-post for support. He noticed now for the first time how pale and thin his young master looked, and how shabbily he was dressed, but he could not speak.

"Yes, old fellow," Lionel went on, in the same quiet voice, trying to speak cheerfully, while his heart was so heavy, "we are, to put it in one word, ruined!"

"But not your mar?" said Sam, speaking in a low voice, and with eyes wide open.

Lionel nodded.

"And the viller—the dear old house at 'Ampstid?"

"All gone, Sam," Lionel forced himself to say, with a trembling lip. He could hardly keep the tears from his eyes, but Sam's next question drove them back, and dried them up with the hot fury of anger.

"Who done it?—I want to know who done it," said Sam.

"That oily rascal, Grubbe," explained Lionel, with a shudder of hatred and repugnance.

"Wot! him as we chevied from Hendon Bridge?"

Lionel nodded.

"Then I'll have his life!" said Sam.

"Stop, Sam. I say you mustn't talk like that," said Lionel; for Sam spoke so earnestly, and looked so pale and fierce, that our hero thought him quite capable of carrying his threat into execution.

"Don't make no herror, Master Lionel," said Sam, proudly; "I ain't agoin' to go behind old Grubbe and stick a carvin' knife into the small of his back. No; I'll fight him fair with pistols or swords, it's all the same to me, for down he goes. You'll be my second in the jewel, Master Lionel, won't you?"

"You'd make a pretty jewel of it," replied our hero, who, despite his distress, could not refrain from laughing at the idea of Sam and Mr. Grubbe engaged in mortal strife. "But don't talk any more about this in the street; your friends are waiting."

"Ah! and good friends they've bin to me, Master Lionel," said Sam, warmly. "Bellers is a brick out and out, a reg'lar lib'ral cove; and as for allowancing a chap in regard to wittles, why he'd scorn it. And Long Jem, too, though he's surly, ain't arf a bad sort."

"You shall tell me all about them directly, Sam. But where are you going now?"

"Up to our place, o' course," was Sam's reply. "We can't perform any more to-day. Long Jem's face is too bad, and my 'ed ain't in a state to let me pitch flip-flaps."

By this time they had come up with the showmen, who were waiting at the end of the street.

"Beg pardon, sir," said Mr. Bellers; "but me and my mate thought as 'twasn't quite the right kind o' thing for you to be seen walkin' along with us in this here costoom——"

"Not a bit of it," interrupted Lionel. "Sam and I have been friends too long for me to be ashamed of him in any dress."

"Well, if you *reely* don't mind, sir," said Mr. Bellers, highly pleased, "we shall be werry glad o' your company at our poor little place. You shall be welcome, sir; we're rough, maybe, but we're 'arty. Let him try it."

"That's open to argyment," growled Jem. "How can a man be 'arty with a face as pale as if it had bin 'arf roast and then stung all over with wapses?"

But Mr. Bellers unceremoniously shouldered him off with the drum before his ungracious speech could reach the ears of Lionel.

"Wot a aggravatin' chap you are, Jem!" said Mr. Bellers. "Always a puttin' your oar in when it ain't wanted. Now, when a real young gentleman like him——"

"That's open to argyment," growled Jem again. "How do you know he's a gent? Look at his clothes and his boots, a-bustin' out at the sides!"

"Well, you do surprise me, Jem," said Mr. Bellers. "The idea of a man o' your hage judgin' a gentleman by his clothes! Now, I'll just tell you a little thing as happened to me once when I wasn't 'arf your age, as'll p'r'aps open your eyes a bit——"

"That's open to argyment," growled Jem.

THE PAPER WAS SNATCHED FROM HIS GRASP, AND A POKER, WIELDED BY NO LIGHT HAND, DESCENDED ON HIS SKULL,

"Never you mind; you listen. "Well, I were goin' along the Byford road on my way to Laxham fair, with my little moke, Topper, and a barrer-load of sticks and cocoa-nuts. I were only about six miles orf, and were whistlin' to Topper to cheer him up, when I see a smart pair-oss broom pulled up in the road ahead, and the coachman sayin' somethin' to a queer, shabby-looking old chap as were sittin' on the bank.

"'So, my man,' he ses to the coachman, 'you see that I've sprained my ankle, and that there's a storm coming on, and still you refuses to give me a lift as far as Haverly'?

"'In course I does,' ses the coachman. 'I ain't goin' to put sech as you into my carridge. Who's to know wot wermin you ain't got about you—though if you'd tip a shillin' for your ride I'd chance it.'

"And with that he drives orf, just as I got up and jumped orf the barrer.

"'Do you want a lift, sir?' I ses. "I'm goin' into Laxham, and I'll set you down. 'Taint such a smart affair as that surly chap's broom; but I'll put you where you wants to go afore the storm busts.'

"He ses, 'Spoken kindly!' And I ups with him, and settles him in the barrer as comf'tble as I could, with my coat at his back, and then I whistles up Topper, and away we goes, the moke keeping on at a smart trot for a good five mile, when I stopped him oppersite Haverly Wood, where there was a lodge.

"'That'll do, my friend,' he said, when I lifted him orf. 'The porter here knows me.' And he began fumblin' in his pocket, when I stopped him.

"'Excuse me, sir,' I ses; 'but I don't want nothin', and I can't take nothin' from a gen'leman—if you excoose me sayin' it—as has seen better days.'

"'You're a good man,' he says, 'and have probably saved my life, for I'm old, and lyin' in the wet would have killed me. But promise one thing. Laxham ain't fur orf. Come and see me; ax for Mr. John at this here lodge.'

"I said I would, and he fixed me down to a day and a hour quite precise, and I kept the appointment, thinkin' I were goin' to hev a blow-out of beef and beer in the servants' 'all.

"The porter were crusty at first, but when I said I'd come to see Mr. John he gets remarkable civil, and showed me up to the house himself.

"'Hallo!' thinks I, 'the old chap is somebody arter all,' and it were more so in the passidge, where about a dozen six-foot flunkeys passed me on one to the tother till I found myself in a tremenjus big drawin'-room nigh as large as a two-acre field, with hundreds o' swell ladies and gen'lemen standin' about, and him in the middle on 'em."

"Wot, the old chap as you picked up?" asked Long Jem, getting interested in the story.

"The werry same," said Mr. Bellers, gravely; "him as called himself Mr. John. Well, Jem, I were all in a blaze from head to foot; I'd never see sech a sight afore, it beat all the waxwork; and I was reg'lar giddy, till the old gen'leman he came for'ard, and shakes me 'arty by the 'and, and tells the swells all about it.

"Then I heard some o' the gen'lemen say that I was a 'good feller,' and one o' the ladies—a pretty gal she was, too, Jem—called me a 'dear.' She did really, Jem; and I got so confused and flabbergasted at sech a fuss being made out o' nothink, that the old gen'leman see it and rang the bell for one o' the Johnnies.

"'Now,' he ses, 'take this young man away and treat him well. Let him have the best of everythink,' he ses, 'or I'll sack the lot of yer.'

"And they did, too. I never had such a feast before or since. If I had had forty stummicks they'd ha' filled them all; and as for wine, there, I don't believe as anybody since the days o' Noah

was arf as drunk as me; but my head was pretty good in them days, so a turn under the pump in the mornin' put me right for breakfast, and arter that the dook sends for me."

"*The wot?*" demanded Long Jem.

"The dook!" repeated Mr. Bellers; "didn't I tell you as the old gen'leman turned out to be the Dook o' Bayswater; a nobleman nigh as great as the Queen, but peculiar, so the Johnnies told me, sech as dressin' shabby, and goin' out for miles quite alone, jist as I found him. The greatest lark were, Jem, that the werry coachman as wouldn't give him a lift were one o' the dook's servants as hadn't sense enough to know his master in a shabby dress."

"He got the sack, I s'pose," said Jem.

"You may take your oath of that," replied Mr. Bellers. "Well, to cut a long story short, the dook were remarkable affable and perlite; couldn't hev been more free if I'd been a dook as well as him; and first he wanted me to give up strollin' and come into his sarvice, but I said I'd been used to ramblin' ever since I was a babby, and I knew it wouldn't come out of me now. Then he wanted to know how he could help me, and I said I wouldn't take anything, and he said positive that I should, till we got nigh quarrellin'.

"'Well, then, you distant man,' he ses, 'will you take a hundred pounds as a loan, on conditions?'

"I jumped at that, for I knowed Willis's team was for sale for eighty pounds, and I could pay the hundred orf in a year, if I had luck.

"'There it is, then,' he ses, handin' me two fifty-pun notes from a lot as was in his desk. 'Now write me out on this here paper, "I O U one hundred pounds,"' which I did, and signed it all proper.

"'Now,' he ses ag'in, 'the conditions on which I lend you the money is these 'ere. Fust you're not to pay me back till I ask you; and second, you're to come here once a year, on this werry day, till one of us is dead.'

"'I will,' I ses; 'but your grace has stole a march on me in respect of this here money, becos you never mean to ax me for it, and so I shall never be able to pay it back.'

"'Never mind that,' he ses; 'you've promised, and you keep your word. Good-bye, till next year.'

"And so, Jem, to make an end on it—for here we are at our crib—I got my start in life through being able to tell a gen'leman when I met one, though he had got a shabby soot o' clothes on him."

"H'm," grunted Long Jem; "and when is it that you go to see this precious dook o' yourn?"

"The first o' June," replied Mr. Bellers, somewhat incautiously. "Three days from now."

"Then blow me if I don't go too," said Jem.

"And I'm blowed twice over if you do," retorted Mr. Bellers, as he elbowed Long Jem up the passage, dropped the drum on his toes, and prepared to usher Lionel with due ceremony upstairs.

CHAPTER V.

MR. BELLERS' HOSPITALITY—LIONEL TELLS HIS STORY—AND MR. BELLERS' COMMENTS THEREON—ADVICE GRATIS BY J. BELLERS—LIONEL TAKES SOME OF IT—AND HOW IT AGREED WITH HIM—SAM DISAPPEARS MYSTERIOUSLY—AND THE OLD SHOWMAN RE-APPEARS ACCORDING TO PROMISE.

M. BELLERS' notion of hospitality was comprised mainly in making his guests eat and drink until they were uncomfortable; when they had reached that stage of repletion at which breathing becomes difficult, Mr. Bellers was content, and considered that he had done his duty.

At this time his affairs were far from flourishing,

as our readers know, but Mr. Bellers' credit was good for twenty pounds wherever he was known, and in honour of Sam's young master he was ready to make use of it.

"You're used to peckin' later than this, sir, I dare say," he said to my hero; "but you'll try a mouthful o' summat—a pound o' rump-steak and a few hysters, or a chicken, till your own dinner's ready."

"I'm sure I don't know when that will be," said Lionel, with a smile. "I have to dine where and how I can, Mr. Bellers. A dinner will soon be a startling novelty to me."

"Bless me, sir! I hope things ain't so bad as that," replied the showman. "Sam hev just told me as you'd met with a misfortant, which I ax your pardon if I've offended in mentunin'.'

"Not at all," said Lionel. "On the contrary, Mr. Bellers, I wanted to ask your advice."

"And you shall have it, sir, and welcome," replied Mr. Bellers, heartily. "But first and foremost is wittles. My adwice ain't worth a penny till I've had a good tuck out; so, by your leave, I'll see to a little bit o' dinner being got ready."

Mr. Bellers' notion of a little bit of dinner was very liberal. The steak and oysters and roast chicken were all procured, and, besides that, a huge bowl of lobster salad, with some ham and tongue for anyone who had a delicate appetite and preferred fancy dishes.

In the way of drinkables, he offered for Lionel's acceptance almost every kind that is distilled or brewed for the laudable purpose of "making glad the heart of man"—pressing champagne particularly, as being, what he called a "swell's tipple."

But upon Lionel declaring positively that he would neither eat nor drink if Mr. Bellers even hinted again at such expensive luxuries, the showman contented himself with ordering from below some very choice old bottled ale, as clear and bright as sherry, and nearly as strong.

This "little bit o' dinner," as Mr. Bellers styled it, seemed, when it was placed upon the table, to be sufficient to satisfy the appetites of a dozen sharpset navvies; but when our four friends relinquished their knives and forks the dishes were empty, and only the skeleton of the fowl remained to tell the tale of what had been.

"Now, sir," said Mr. Bellers, "if noways disagreeable to you, I'll put on a pipe, and then, if you're in the same mind about my adwice, I'll let out as much as you want; for, blow me! if the dinner's left any room inside me for it."

"It is a painful story to me," said Lionel, in a low tone, "and I'll make it as short as I can."

"Ay, sir; quite nat'ral," said the showman, nodding his head.

"Well, my mother was persuaded to invest all the money she had in some company—a sort of bank, it was, I believe—which was to pay her twenty per cent. instead of the three and a half she got from the Bank of England."

Mr. Bellers puffed solemnly at his pipe and shook his head, as if he, too, could say something upon the subject of high interest carrying bad security.

"This was owing," continued Lionel, "partly to my dear mother's wish to leave me a rich man at her death, but principally to the persuasions of my aunt Maria, who knew that Mr. Grubbe was one of the promoters of the bank, and believed, or pretended to believe, in his sham piety."

"Miss Mariar? Oh, lor'!" gasped Sam.

"She persuaded my mother not only to invest all her money, but to sell her houses and land, our own dear home at Hampstead as well, and invest the capital in this confounded bank—in spite of the warnings of her lawyer, who at last declined to act for her at all."

"That Miss Mariar!" interrupted Sam, "she'd worrit a party into anythink!"

"All went on well for a little while. The twenty

per cent. was paid, but before my poor mother, who was in Italy, had touched a penny, the smash came, and she heard that she was utterly ruined."

Lionel paused. Mr. Bellers and Long Jem looked gravely at each other, while Sam, with his mouth tightly shut, and his eyes staring at the ground, seemed to be meditating whether roasting Mr. Grubbe alive, or flaying him an inch at a time was the most adequate punishment for his crimes.

"When the terrible news reached my mother, she had only little more than enough to pay her bill at the hotel and her travelling expenses to England. When I met her at the Great Southern Terminus Hotel she had only five pounds and a few shillings left; that was a fortnight ago, and a few days more will reduce us to our last penny."

"Hanged if it shall!" said Mr. Bellers, rising up and striking the table a tremendous blow with his huge fist; "not while I've a shillin'."

"Here, none o' that," said Sam, suddenly starting up and joining in the debate. "I know you means well, but it had better be understood at first that no one but me sarves my old mistress and young master. I won't have it, I tell you."

"You're right, Sam," replied Mr. Bellers, with a peculiar wink at the long youth. "And I axes young Master Wilful's pardon for havin' said what I did in the 'eat of the moment."

"Mr. Bellers, you're a thoroughly good fellow. I understand you, and I thank you heartily, though, of course, I can't accept what you offer. I'll take your advice all the same, if you'll give it me."

"Name the pint, sir, and I'll do my best endeavours."

"In a week or less, then," said Lionel, setting his teeth hard, and trying to speak calmly, "we shall be destitute unless I can get some work to do which will maintain my mother and myself. The only relative she knows, except Aunt Maria, is somewhere in India. They have not corresponded for years. My aunt, under pretence of a quarrel, has left my mother to her fate, and the few friends she had have done the same."

"Just like 'em," said Mr. Bellers, in a low voice.

"Oh, don't I wish Miss Mariar was a man?" said Sam between his teeth.

"Day after day, Mr. Bellers," Lionel continued, "I have tramped the streets trying to get something to do, but I am fit for nothing but a clerk, and I soon found that there were thousands of grown men eager to jump at situations which offered a pound or at the most twenty-five shillings a-week for ten, or even twelve, hours daily drudgery. If I had only learnt to be a blacksmith or a carpenter, no matter what, I could earn bread for my mother and myself, but, God help me, I am fit for nothing but a porter or an errand boy."

"Cheer up, sir—cheer up!" said Mr. Bellers, and his bluff, weather-beaten features brightened up with the sunbeam of a happy thought. "You axed my advice; here it is—but, fust, can you hold out till the second o' June—four days from now?"

"Yes," said Lionel. "We have enough to last a week."

"Then, sir," said Mr. Bellers, "you take my advice and go 'long home, and comfort your lady mother. I'll hev good news for you by the second o' June."

"But——" Lionel began, when the showman interrupted him.

"'Xcuse me, Mister Lionel, but I knows you wouldn't like to ax me questions, as I can't answer —for fear, may be, of disappointin' after all. You can depend upon me, sir, not doin' anything on your account which a young gentleman like you wouldn't approve on. I'm rough, sir, but you can depend on my word. Ask Sam."

"I know I can," replied Lionel, shaking the bluff showman's hand with the frank candour natural to his age, "and I do, Mr. Bellers. I will wait the four days, and even if nothing comes of it I will thank you just as heartily. When shall I see you again, for I must go now, my mother expects me?"

"Not afore the second o' June, sir," replied Mr. Bellers. "I starts orf to-morrow on the bisness, and some of my own, too. It's nigh a two days' journey from here."

"Good-bye, then, and God speed you," said Lionel, shaking the showman's hand as heartily as if he had known him for years—he felt as if he had. "Good-bye, Mr. Jem. Good-bye, Sam."

"Good evenin'," returned Jem shortly, "and if you wouldn't mind recollectin' of it, my name's Jem—or Long Jem, which you likes—but no mister afore it."

"I'll remember," said Lionel good humouredly. "Good-bye, Sam."

"Wot's the use of sayin' good-bye Mister Lionel, when I'm goin' with you," replied that worthy.

"What nonsense, Sam. I have told you how poor we are. Where are you to sleep? You know, old fellow," he went on, "if you had nowhere else to go you should share my bed and my last crust, but you have a comfortable home here."

"My home is where you and your mar is," replied Sam, doggedly. "I've been away from you too long to lose you again, and if you won't let me into the 'ouse, Master Lionel, I'll sleep on the door-step, I will."

"Let him have his own way, sir," added Mr. Bellers. "He's right. His dooty is to go along o' you. As for his peck and a doss, he'll always find 'em here if taint convenient at your place. 'Sides," he continued, with an almost inperceptible wink at Sam, "here's his wages. I've been a savin' up for him, and well he's earned 'em."

And, taking a five pound note from out of a greasy leather purse, he passed it to Sam.

"The right account is four pound fifteen, but you've been a good lad, Sam, and I makes you a present o' the five bob."

"Thankee," said Sam, returning Mr. Bellers' wink. He guessed what was actually the truth, that the good-hearted showman had borrowed the note from his friend, the landlord, knowing that Sam would use the money for his young master's benefit.

There was a vacant room in the little house at Camberwell where Lionel lived. This, not without violent objection on the part of our hero, Sam engaged, and paid a week's rent for it in advance, and then settled down to his old duties with a resolute obstinacy it was useless to contend against.

This went on for two days, but on the morning of the third Lionel missed Sam's accustomed knock at his bed-room door, but the breakfast things were laid as usual in the little parlour, and on his plate Lionel saw a curiously-shaped note, something like a triangle trying to believe that it was square. It was in Sam's writing, and was as follows:—

"Dere Mr. Lionel,

"I have gon' aweigh for a wile, as the song ses in 'Pore Mari An,' butt don't yer be frit—you wil se me sonen as yer expeck.

"Yors trooly faitful,
"SAM."

"Here's a go," muttered Lionel, after reading the letter over a dozen times, and making no more of it than he had done at first. "Where the dickens has he gone, and what has he gone after?"

Then he thought ot Sam's blood-thirsty threat when he first heard of Mr. Grubbe's villanous conduct, but Lionel shook his head.

"No, no, he wouldn't be such an ass as that. At the most he would only wait for him somewhere and give him one or two hot 'uns. And I don't know that I should be sorry if he did. He'll come back safe enough, that's one comfort, so we'll let him have his own way for a day."

Directly breakfast was over there came the first of a series of little surprises, which lasted at intervals throughout the day.

First, the baker called, left his bill receipted, and ith the usual quantity of bread, a large pound ke, and a plum ditto of luscious richness. In swer to inquiries, he stated that Mrs. Whiffet's ge had called that morning, paid the account, d also for the cake.

Then the butcher came with a fine piece of sirin, and the same story as the baker. The grocer ollowed suit, and after him the cheesemonger, the fishmonger, and the milkman, until it became evident that Sam had been round to every one of the tradespeople, preparing the little surprise.

But the crowning one of all was reserved for the last, when two parcels arrived for "Lionel Wilful, Esq.," and were found, upon examination, to contain a neat suit of clothes and a pair of boots.

"Confound that Sam!" said Lionel, half laughing, half angry. "See what the foolish fellow has done, mother! He must have spent nearly twice the five pounds Mr. Bellers gave him, and now he's stopping away so that we shan't be able to give him the money back."

"He has a true, good heart, my boy," said Mrs. Wilful. "How many of the friends who flattered us when we were rich would do a thousandth part as much as poor Sam! It almost makes me content with poverty, dear Lionel, when it brings to the light such faithfulness as his."

"I hope we may be able to reward him as he deserves, mother. To-morrow, you know, Mr. Bellers is to come, and who knows what good news he may bring!"

The morrow came, and with it Mr. Bellers, actually riding in a cab. He had on a handsome suit of mourning, but there was no sign of grief in his beaming, good-humoured face as he dashed out of the cab, plunged at the knocker, and nearly knocked a hole in the door with the first rat-tat.

CHAPTER VI.

IN WHICH SAM UNDERGOES AN EXTRAORDINARY METAMORPHOSIS ON HAMPSTEAD HEATH—MR. GRUBBE ENGAGES A SERVANT, AND FINDS, WHEN TOO LATE, THAT HE HAS CAUGHT A TARTAR.

SAM'S mind squinted, if we may be allowed to use the term in such a connection, as much as his organs of vision—or, to explain ourselves more fully, it was as difficult for any one to be certain of what Sam had made up his mind to do as to determine the particular object at which he was gazing.

It was so in this instance, for while Lionel believed that the long youth had returned fully resolved never to quit him or his mother, Master Samuel had concocted what he thought a neat little plan whereby the villanies of Mr. Grubbe might be laid bare, and that oily and slippery gentleman justly punished.

"I don't like leavin' of 'em, but I must," thought Sam on the morning he levanted. "Master Lionel would larf at me if I told him wot I was goin' to do, and, as likely as not, stop me. No; here's the note that'll tell him I'm all right. And now here goes to bust up that 'ily old willin, Grubbe."

First paying those visits to the tradespeople the result of which subsequently astonished our hero, Sam turned away from Camberwell, and steered due north in the direction of Hampstead, only stopping once at an old clothes shop to negotiate for certain articles of female attire, which, from their shape, colour, and flavour, might have been worn by the immortal Mrs. Gamp in the days of her youth.

With these purchases, tied up in an old handkerchief, Sam trudged through Camberwell, crossed Blackfriars-bridge, passed up Fetter-lane, and, taking a short cut through Holborn, found himself in the apparently interminable road which has its birth in Oxford-street and terminates its chec-quered career in Hampstead Fields.

"I must get on the heath by the back way," thought Sam, "or the old chap will drop on me. He always comes down the middle of the 'Igh-street as if it belonged to him, and he was ablessin' the people he let live in his 'ouses for nothing."

There were very few people in the street, and Sam, who knew every inch of it, found no difficulty in selecting a sweet, secluded spot, screened by clumps of furze.

Behind these bushes Sam disappeared, and in ten minutes there issued forth a tall, bony female, attired in such a comically hideous caricature of a "slavey's" costume, that it alone would have made the fortune of a comic actor if he had worn it on the stage.

"I wish I could get a peep in the glass," thought Sam, as he strode along with very unfeminine strides. "I ain't quite certing about this 'ere gownd. I hope it's all right at the back—but the look of it don't matter so long as old Grubbe don't know 'ose in it."

Now, it so happened, luckily for the success of Sam's plot, that Mr. Grubbe was in want of a slavey who would do the work of a horse, be con-tent with food at which an Irish pig would turn up his snout, and accept an infinitesimal amount of wages therefor.

Sam arrived just in the nick of time. The old housekeeper and Mr. Grubbe had just dismissed the last of a batch of applicants for the situation, the most moderate of whom demanded twelve pounds a-year, "Sundays out" without number, leave to have her "young man" in to tea, wanted the wash-ing put out, and knives, forks, and boots cleaned for her, with sundry other trifles hardly worth mentioning.

"Do you want a servant, mum?" Sam squeaked to the housekeeper, who still stood in the gravel path, shaking her fist after the "dressed-up hussey" who had laughed at the offer of eight pounds a year and "find herself."

"'Want a servant?' Yes, I do want a servant," snarled the old woman, eying the new-comer up and down with a critical eye, "and, instead of 'em, a pack of dressed-up dabs, no better than they should be, come alaughing in my face."

"I ain't alaughin', mum; and as for being dressed up, I'm sure no one can say as I'm anyways too smart."

"Well, come in, and don't stand chatterin' there," said the old woman; "come and see the master."

Sam's heart beat rapidly, and the blood tingled in his veins, as he stood within a few yards of the rascal who had reduced his dearly-loved mistress to poverty, but he controlled himself, and his huge flapping cap hid his features.

"How much wages do you want?" was Mr. Grubbe's first question.

"I'd rayther leave it to you, sir," replied the sham slavey, in a squeaking whisper.

"Ah!" said he, "rubbing his fat hands in a satisfied manner. "You'll come for a month on trial, then, and I'll pay you according to the way you do your work."

"I'm agreeable, sir."

"Very good. Now what's your name?"

Sam hadn't thought of the question, but at length, after a wheezy cough, said—

"Mariar——"

"Maria what?"

"P—Pecker, sir."

"Oh, Maria Pecker, eh? Well, where did you come from?"

"The workus, sir."

"You're a parish child, then, eh?"

"Yes, sir; Laxham parish."

"Ah—now, are you strong?"

"Oh, yes, sir, I could lick Betsy Baker, and she were two year old 'n me."

"Try if you can lift that chair."

Mr. Grubbe pointed to a heavy arm-chair, to lift which would have tried the muscles of an average man, but Sam hoisted it on his shoulders in a trice, and nearly put Mr. Grubbe's eye out with one of the legs.

"That'll do—that'll do. You're strong enough. Now, about your meals. You mustn't expect to gorge here, you know."

"I never was used to it, sir," said Sam, alias Pecker.

"And as to sleep, now, you'll have to get up early."

"I don't want no sleep, sir, unless it's convenient. I used to be up a week at the time, when I were nuss in the sick ward o' the workus."

"Well, I think you'll do, Maria. Go with Mrs. Corkum, and she'll set you to work at once. I can't bear idle people about my house."

"Can't bear idle people, can't you," thought Sam, with a triumphant chuckle. "I think, old chap, as you'll find me a trifle too busy for you afore I've done."

And now poor Sam's troubles fairly began. He was strong, as my readers know, but that strength was taxed to the uttermost by the old house-keeper, who seemed to pass the whole of her time in finding work for Sam.

When, in addition to this, we record that he passed nearly the whole of the night in listening at Mr. Grubbe's door, and hunting in likely places for any documents that might prove his guilt, and that the scraps he got to eat would hardly have kept life in a middling-sized dog, our readers may get some faint idea of what the faithful Sam suffered in his endeavour to right his master's wrongs.

It would have been impossible for anything composed of flesh and blood to have endured such an ordeal for long. Sam was on the point of giving up, when he discovered that Mrs. Corkum was extremely partial to gin, but that, owing to Mr. Grubbe's economy, she seldom had the chance of getting any.

Sam had still some money left—nearly a sovereign. He invested in a pint of the precious cordial, the strongest old tom he could buy, and invited Mrs. Corkum to the carouse.

In half an hour the dear old lady was singing comic songs, and trying to dance, while Sam tripped her up with a broom handle every now and then, to keep her lively. In another fifteen minutes she had emptied the bottle, with the exception of a taste Sam had, to keep his spirits up, and, rolling into the corner, began to snore.

"Hooray!" cried Sam, executing a fantastic pas seul in honour of his triumph; "I've got the old girl now. I've only got to give her gin enough, and I can do what I likes. Hallo, there's the bell, and old Grubbe going to the door himself."

Sam shot out of the kitchen, and, running up the stairs, was just in time to see Mr. Grubbe shaking warmly by the hand, a sharp-nosed, ferret-like little man, habited, like his host, in a semi-clerical costume.

"So you've come at last," Sam heard Mr. Grubbe say.

"Yes. Better late than never. It isn't safe for you and me to be seen together too soon after our little smash—one of the best managed things I ever was in, by Jingo! Let's see: this was Mrs. Wilful's place, wasn't it?"

Mr. Grubbe nodded.

"You were precious hard upon her, though, weren't you? Never left her a sixpence to bless herself with."

"No, nor did I mean to. You'll laugh, Santy, when I tell you that I organised that company with the sole object of ruining a boy."

"Eh?" said the little, ferret-like man, staring at Mr. Grubbe as if he doubted his sanity.

"I did," continued the oily hypocrite; "I swore

SOKER SEIZED THE HANDLE AND SET THE FLOGGING MACHINE IN MOTION, AMID THE STRUGGLES AND YELLS OF THE VICTIMS,

that young Wilful should be reduced to beggary and rot in gaol. I have accomplished the first part of my oath; the second will follow, as surely as the night the day."

"Will it?" chuckled Sam to himself; "you don't know who's a-listening, old feller."

"That boy—that brat," continued Mr. Grubbe, raising his clenched fist, while a spasm of hate made his face absolutely hideous for a moment, "thwarted me, injured me, ridiculed, held me up to be the laughing-stock of my sect; but I've turned the tables now. He and his mother are starving in a hole at Camberwell; another week of it will make the boy turn thief for her sake. I know how fond he is of her."

"Oh, you wiper," murmured Sam, turning hot and cold at this confession of villany; "oh, you precious black-hearted, murderin', schemin' scamp; to actooly reckon on Master Lionel's love for his mother makin' him a thief to save her from starvin'. He ain't a man; he can't be."

"How about the papers and books?" said Santy, who, though he was rascal enough in all conscience, yet seemed disgusted with his companion; "I've no time to spare."

"They're all safe upstairs in a little back room, which I always keep locked."

"What, *all*?"

"Every one."

"That's very dangerous; you should have burnt them at once. By the lord, Grubbe, if any one got hold of those papers we should be booked for fifteen years' penal servitude as sure as we stand here. Who have you got in the house?"

"Only old Mrs. Corkum and a girl I got out of a workhouse; she's as strong as a horse, and costs next to nothing to keep."

"Don't she?" chuckled Maria Pecker, otherwise Sam; "her keep 'll cost you a pretty penny afore she's done with you."

"Is she's safe?"

"Lord, yes! She's a born fool, or she wouldn't stay here and work as she does for the wages she gets."

"All right, then; we'll go up and look the papers through—I've just got time; and mind you destroy all those I mark. They ought to have been burnt long ago."

And together Mr. Grubbe and his accomplice mounted the stairs, leaving Sam nearly petrified with wonder at what he had heard, and joy at the discovery.

But how was he to act?

"Let me see," thought Sam; "the little chap's agoin' away directly, and old Grubbe is to destroy the dokiments directly arterwards. Now my way is to wait till I hears him go out, and then drop in on the old 'un."

It was the best plan Sam could hit upon, and, first possessing himself of a poker, he waited till the ferret-like gentleman and Mr. Grubbe came down together.

Sam watched his opportunity, and while their backs were turned, ran lightly up the stairs to the little room, which he saw at a hasty glance contained a quantity of legal looking documents, letters and huge ledgers.

There was another room leading out of it, and fitted up as a study. Behind the door of this Sam posted himself and waited.

In a few moments Mr. Grubbe came towards the door hurriedly, and entering the room where the papers were, took up a roll of paper and began to tear it.

The rent was not half an inch long, when the paper was snatched from his grasp, and a poker, wielded by no light hand, descended on his skull.

I keep well within the bounds of moderation in describing as the proudest moment of Sam's life that in which he beheld the ruthless enemy of his young master grovelling on the ground, with all his crime and rascality laid bare.

Mr. Grubbe had only been slightly stunned, and before Miss Maria Pecker, alias Sam, had time to execute the first step of a vigorous pas de triomphe, he struggled into a sitting posture, felt his wounded head with one hand, and stared vaguely around him.

Maria had the poker ready for him in a minute.

"Who—who—where—I say, didn't some one knock me down?" said Mr. Grubbe.

"Somebody—certingly—did," replied Sam, slowly and with much emphasis.

"Who was it, then? Where is he? What the devil business have you here?" getting angry and suspicious as his senses recovered their activity.

"He's safe enough, and so air you, old cock," replied the triumphant slavey. "As for my bis'ness, s'pose we has a chat about it."

And Maria Pecker flourished the document and the poker over Mr. Grubbe's head as if bestowing an animated kind of blessing.

Mr. Grubbe flushed red, and then the deeper colour faded out of his features and left them a pale ashen gray.

"By ——, this is a conspiracy," he said, with a fearful oath. "You cursed jade, I'll strangle you!"

He made a furious effort to arise and fly at Sam's throat; but the long youth had the poker ready, and again it descended on the very apex of Mr. Grubbe's bald head, stunning him in earnest this time.

"I hopes I didn't drop it *too* heavy," thought Sam, as he looked into the pale, flabby, villanous face. "I'll tie him up, though, and gag him, in case he's shamming, while I get these 'ere books and papers together."

There was plenty of strong thick cord lying on the floor, and in five minutes Sam had bound Mr. Grubbe in such a complication of knots as would have defied the efforts of Maskelyne and Cook to untie.

"Now, for the papers," thought Sam. "My eye, wot a lot of 'em. I think the old trunk is big enough. How about the old gal, though; it won't do to have her wakin' up and spilin' the game."

Five minutes, and a couple of yards of the stout cord sufficed to render the tipsy old lady incapable of interference with Sam's "little game."

With all the haste he could, Sam then set to work to pack every book and scrap of paper he could find into a shabby leather portmanteau that was in a corner of the room; but before he had half finished, he heard an inarticulate sound—half-groan, half-choke—proceeding from the spot where he had stunned Mr. Grubbe.

"Wot!" said Sam, turning about to look at his prisoner; "you've come to life agin, have you? Oh! you 'oary-'eaded old sinner, it's plain as you ain't to come to your end by means of a poker."

Mr. Grubbe was almost black in the face through his efforts to speak; but Sam's dirty pocket handkerchief was rammed too tightly into his mouth to allow of anything but a feeble groan to come out.

"Ah!" said Sam, folding his lean arms tightly across the bosom of his slavey's dress; "I know wot you want. You wants me to take that there hankercher out of your mouth. Eh?"

Mr. Grubbe nodded violently.

"And p'r'aps you'd like me to cut them cords," Sam continued in an ironical tone, "and fetch a cab, and let you drive away comf't'ble with all these 'ere little dokyments as I'm packin' up. Eh?"

Again Mr. Grubbe nodded his head.

"I should think you would. What would you give me if I did it. Eh?"

Again Mr. Grubbe grew crimson with the vain effort to speak through the gag.

"A thousand pound, p'r'aps," said Sam; "or maybe, two thousand. Eh?"

Mr. Grubbe made a desperate effort, and forced out a grunt that was meant for "yes."

"Well," said Sam, "afore we comes to terms, p'r'aps you'd better know who I ham. It'll be a satisfaction to you. Look here!"

And Miss Maria Pecker, with a shameless disregard for propriety, pulled up the skirts of her "gownd," drew that garment over her head, and stood revealed as Sam Scarecrow, minus his jacket, and with the bottoms of his trousers rolled up to the knee.

He had altered wonderfully since their last meeting at Cheetham Hall; he was taller, and looked older; but Mr. Grubbe knew him. His face turned livid, and his jaw fell as if he were dying.

"You've got a good mem'ry for faces, old feller," said Sam, drawing a chair close to Mr. Grubbe and sitting down upon it. "Yes, I'm Sam Scarecrow, I am—him as was page here afore you swindled my missus out of her property—him as you were kind enough to send to the lunatic 'sylum, and who out o' gratitood for them there ax o' benevolence is goin' to perwide you with a snug crib in Newgate. That's me, old feller."

And Sam—squinting horribly—grinned at Mr. Grubbe in such an amiably ferocious manner, that the oily gentleman recoiled as far as his bonds permitted.

"You thought you'd got hold of a nice cheap slavey, didn't you?" said Sam, determined not to lose such a chance as that presented for torturing his enemy. "Six pound a year and all found. Aha, you little thought, old feller, wot it was I'd come to find—and I've found it. Hooray!"

Sam had cheered as loudly as if he had been in the open air, charging Mr. Grubbe over Hampstead Heath again; and he saw the oily gentleman's eyes light up with a gleam of hope as he glared towards the door.

"No fear of that, old feller," said Sam, who had seen the look and guessed its meaning; "there's nobody to hear us. I made your precious house-keeper as drunk as a biled owl, while I listened to the interestin' conversation of you and your mate; and now she's tied up as tight as you are."

Mr. Grubbe bestowed a glance on Sam, which, if looks had power to kill, would have slain him on the spot.

"Now," continued Sam, "as time's gettin' short, and I'm rayther in a hurry, I'll just tell you wot I'm goin' to do, and do it. First, I'll finish packin' up these here dokyments; then I'm goin' to carry you and the old gal into the coal-cellar and tie you back to back for company's sake, then I'm goin' to tell a perliceman, a frend o' mine, to keep his heye on any frend o' your'n as may happen to call; and finerly, to conclood, I'm goin' straight up to young master's with the portmanty. *That's* the programmy. How d'ye like it?"

Mr. Grubbe did not like it at all, to judge from the expression of his face. In truth, the passions of hate, fear, rage and baffled avarice, all strong within him, made his face so hideous, so repulsive, that for a moment Sam hesitated to approach him.

But as he had said, time was short, and in a moment he had Mr. Grubbe by the collar, and was dragging him towards the kitchen stairs.

"I hope I don't bump you too much," said Sam; "but you're too heavy to carry. Yer see, if you *will* steal widders' and orphans' money, and get fat on it, you must take the consekences. Down you go!"

And with a "bump—bump—bump," that sorely tried the strength of the stairs, Mr. Grubbe rolled down, and lay swearing and cursing soundly at the bottom.

The rest of Sam's task in his old home was soon accomplished. Mr. Grubbe and his housekeeper were fastened back to back, securely locked in the cellar, and then, Sam shouldering the portmanteau, made his way out of the house and ran to the nearest cab-stand.

"Station-road, Camberwell," said Sam, pitching the portmanteau into a hansom. "'Arf-a-sov. if you do it under a hour!"

"Jump in," replied cabby, and in another minute Sam was on his road to his young master, with the lightest heart in all England beating in his breast.

CHAPTER VII.

THE RIDE TO CAMBERWELL—SAM'S PLAN FOR "MAKING THE MARE TO GO"—THE DRIVER'S OBJECTION THERETO—SAM ARRIVES AT CAMBERWELL, AND CONSIDERABLY ASTONISHES A SELECT PARTY OF THREE—MR. RIGHTSON, THE LAWYER, AND WHAT HE THOUGHT OF IT—SAM ON GUARD AGAIN.

STIMULATED by Sam's liberal promise, the cabman, setting the traffic regulations at defiance, picked out one or two tender places that were yet left on his horse's hide, and tickled them with his whip-lash till the poor beast sped along at racing pace.

But even this seemed slow to Sam's impatience, and taking out his scarf-pin—a splendid affair, price ninepence, warranted all brass—he stealthily stabbed the cab horse, until that over-tortured brute lifted up his hind-legs and nearly kicked the splash-board in two.

Then the cabman shrieked a blessing through the little trap in the roof, and Sam, blushing guiltily, put the scarf-pin in its proper place.

The old horse, though, what with the whip and the scarf-pin, did the journey in less than the stipulated time, but the cabman growled as Sam tumbled out.

"A nice young gal you are to sit be'ind a 'oss. A donkey on 'Amsted 'Eath is more in your line. You orter stand a bob extry for the pin."

But Sam never heard a word. He was out of the cab almost before it had stopped, and lifting up the portmanteau, he charged at the door with the dash of a Zouave at the Malakoff.

The door was not shut close, and in consequence Sam and the portmanteau turned somersaults together in the passage, so startling the landlady, who was just coming up the kitchen stairs with a tray full of tea-things, that she fell backwards upon five of her off-spring, who were holding on to her skirts, or one another, just as they found it convenient.

There was a scream, a crash, and then wails of agony from youthful throats made the house hideous. They were promptly put to bed, but even then the muffled sounds of woe were heard far into the night, at each fresh discovery of pieces of crockery or glass embedded in their tender limbs.

But Sam heeded this not. He had no ears even for that sound so sacred to every true Briton, the cry of a female in distress. He had peeled a long strip of bark off his nose, too, against the lock of the portmanteau, but what cared he for that? He was up again directly, mounting the stairs four at a time, and nearly knocking down Lionel and Mr. Bellers, who had come out to see what was the matter.

"Why, it's Sam!" exclaimed our hero, after a prolonged stare at the strange object.

"Dash my buttons, so it is," said Mr. Bellers. "But lor', where have the lad bin? He looks like a ghost."

"Never mind wot I looks like," said Sam, perfectly radiant with delight at the surprise he was about to give his young master. "Get out o' the way, Bellers, and let the portmanty pass. Ok, Master Lionel, I've got sich noose!"

"And we have news for you, too, Sam," replied our hero with a laugh; "but go in and beg my mother's pardon, you villain, for running away without notice."

"Which I do most 'arty, mum," said Sam, making an elaborate bow to Mrs. Wilful with the portmanteau still on his shoulder, thereby chucking Mr. Bellers smartly under the chin with the corner.

"Dash that 'ere portmanty," said Mr. Bellers; "all my teeth is loose. Put it down, Sam, will yer."

"No, Mr. Bellers, I will not," replied the long youth, sternly. "I'd sooner part with my life than that 'ere portmanty."

"Hallo, Sam," laughed Lionel, "you must have got something valuable there. Is it full of diamonds? Have you been privateering on the Spanish main?"

"Master Lionel," said Sam, in a solemn tone, "and missus. In that portmanty Heath End Willer is contained; likewise a lot of other valuable prop'ty; also a forty years' penal servitood for a certing party as I will give a name to presently."

"The boy's mad!" exclaimed Mr. Bellers.

"Oh, no, I ain't," retorted Sam, loftily. "Don't you be in sich a hurry; you wait till I've done."

"All right, Sam; no offence. Only when you come to talk of puttin' willers in portmantys, it's rayther strong, you know."

Just then a neat little maid-of-all-work put her head in at the door.

"If you please, the cabman ses how long is he to wait for his 'arf soverin', and he ses, please, it's a extry shillin' for stickin' pins in the 'orse."

"There you are, my dear," said Sam, handing out the money with the easy indifference of a millionaire; "and tell cabby he should have had another bob if he hadn't been so cheeky. Now, Master Lionel," he added, becoming once again grave and even solemn in his manner, "we'll proceed to bisness, and as this is a pertickler private matter consarnin' you and missus, p'r'aps Bellers 'll wait outside."

"That isn't necessary, Sam, I'm sure," said Lionel. "Mr. Bellers has been so good and kind a friend, that whatever you may have to tell you can say before him."

"Werry good, Master Lionel, it's for you to decide; I'm willin'. And now," said Sam, all aglow with excitement and enthusiasm, "prepare for a staggerer!"

Not having the slightest idea of what his eccentric follower meant, Lionel laughed lightly, and seated himself close by his mother. She was gazing at Sam with a rather alarmed expression, for she really thought that he was a little mad.

"Now, first of all, you'd like to know where I've been. Well, I've been at Heath End Willer, actin' as a slavey to old Grubbe."

"Wot?" said Mr. Bellers, staring aghast at Sam.

"Well," added Lionel, as much astonished as the showman; "that is a staggerer—as you call it."

"Wait a bit, Master Lionel, and missus. When I went away from here—sudden—I had an idea in my mind, which I knowed you'd larf at, if I told you on it. That idea was to go to old Grubbe in disguise, and keep a strick watch on the old willin', hop'n' as I might find out where he'd hid missus's money."

They were all listening now, gravely and attentively. Sam's story, which at first seemed so ridiculous and incredible, evidently had a serious meaning. Of how much importance, though, they little guessed.

"So I went," Sam continued; "sayin' nothin' to nobody. And for nigh a fortnite—wot with being worked like a nigger, drove and worritted all day, watchin' old Grubbe at night, and lookin' out for the place where he'd hidden the prop'ty, I do assure you that I was nigh made a corpse on. And as for grub, why the werry black-beadles was a starvin', and they can live as cheap as anyone I knows on."

"Poor old feller," murmured Mr. Bellers in sympathy. He knew the range of Sam's appetite, and pitied him.

"I was pretty nigh worn out, and I hadn't discovered nothin', for the old woman, she was arter me all day, when I hit on her weak p'int. She was fond o' gin. I got some immediate. She drunk herself blind quicker'n ever I see anybody do it; and that werry arternoon old Grubbe had a wisitor. I lis'ened, and wot I heard, Master Lionel and missus, is enough to make your blood bile, and your werry marrer stand on end!"

Then Sam, with great animation and abundance of gesture, repeated the conversation that had taken place between Mr. Grubbe and his accomplice, while Lionel, pale with excitement and astonishment, listened eagerly to every word.

But when he took the poker from the fire-place, and told how he had knocked down the oily vagabond and snatched the evidence of his guilt from him, Mr. Bellers uttered a wild "Hooray," and danced round Sam in a manner quite unbecoming, a man of his age and respectability.

"I can hardly believe what I hear," said Lionel. "Sam, for my sake, for my mother's sake, don't deceive me. Is all this true?"

"And d'ye think I could deceive you, Master Lionel," said the long youth, reproachfully. "But here's the papers—you can believe them."

In a minute he had unfastened the straps of the trunk, and revealed to Lionel's gaze the confused mass of parchments, papers, and books which he had brought from the villa.

Lionel eagerly turned them over, and looked through some; but disordered and confused as his mind was by Sam's story, he could make nothing of the contents.

"What is to be done?" he said, hopelessly. "I can't understand them."

"My dear," said Mrs. Wilful, quietly; "Samuel has done us an immense service; but a lawyer must finish the work he has so well began."

"You are right, mother," said Lionel. "I'll go to Mr. Rightson's office at once. Fig Tree-court, Lincoln's Inn, isn't it?"

"But Mr. Rightson would not care to have me for a client again, Lionel. Remember that I treated him very badly when I was foolish enough to yield to your aunt Maria's advice."

"Nonsense, mother. He has been your friend for years. I've heard you say so, and he'll only be too glad to do anything which will put salt on Grubbe's tail."

And without giving his mother time to make any further remonstrance, Lionel hurried off, took the first cab he could catch, drove to Mr. Rightson's chambers, almost dragged him into the cab he kept waiting at the door; and in an incredibly short space of time was back at Camberwell.

"My dear madam," said the old lawyer, shaking Mrs. Wilful warmly by the hand. "What is all this which your scapegrace has been driving into my ears in the cab; but, pardon me, had this not better be a private consultation?"

"Not unless you think it necessary, Mr. Rightson," replied Mrs. Wilful. "Sam, you know well——"

"Sam—what your page? Really, my dear Mrs. Wilful, I don't see him."

"Oh, I forgot, he is disguised. That is Sam in the—the—gown and cap!"

Mr. Rightson burst into a hearty peal of laughter.

"Ha, ha! I recognise him now; but I own he rather startled me at first."

"Mr. Bellers," continued Mrs. Wilful, turning to the showman—who had backed against the wall, and stood bowing in his politest manner to the lawyer, of whom he seemed to stand in great awe —"is a——"

"A regular brick," said Lionel; "a friend of

Sam's and a friend of mine, Mr. Rightson. There's nothing that must be kept from him."

"Very well, my young friend; if your mother coincides, let us get on."

"Sam," said Lionel, "just tell this gentleman all that you told me."

Sam was ready enough to tell his story a hundred times, and the keen old lawyer was soon listening, with knitted brows, to the adventures of the long youth and Mr. Grubbe.

A short search amongst the papers in the portmanteau convinced him that Sam's story was not only true, but that there was evidence of a gigantic conspiracy to defraud, implicating not only Grubbe but numerous others.

"And what has become of this rascal, Grubbe? Escaped by this time, no doubt, and on his way to one of the sea-ports, after warning his accomplices."

"Oh, no he ain't, sir," said Sam, with a knowing shake of his head.

"What!" exclaimed the lawyer, "you didn't bring him here, too, in the portmanteau?"

"No, sir, I left him safe enough," replied Sam. "He'll bide where I put him till he's wanted."

"Where is he—what have you done to him? You didn't kill him with the poker, did you?"

"No, sir," said Sam, a little regretfully, "I didn't kill him, because I wasn't quite sure whether it was right or not."

"Lucky for you you had a doubt, my lad," said Mr. Rightson gravely; "as it is, you've gone quite against the law. You have taken away documents and other property to which you had no legal right, and you have committed assault and battery against this man Grubbe without lawful authority."

"Blow the legal authority!" said Sam. "He thieved missus's prop'ty, and I got it back the best way I could."

"Sam," said Mr. Rightson, shaking the long youth by the hand until his teeth rattled, "you don't know anything about law—but you're a fine fellow."

"Hear, hear," growled Mr. Bellers.

"And so say all of us," sang Lionel.

"Now, first of all," began Mr. Rightson—— "but stop—you haven't yet told me where Mr. Grubbe is."

"In the coal cellar of the willer," replied Sam, with a grin. "I tied him back to back with the old housekeeper. They won't starve ayther, for I give 'em each a old hankercher to chew while I was away."

"Gagged them, I suppose you mean?"

"That's it, sir. Agin the law, too, I spose, sir."

"Of course it is. I don't suppose you could do anything lawful if you tried, and here am I, like an old fool, aiding and abetting you."

"I hope, Mr. Rightson, that Sam has not incurred any danger by what he has done?"

"We shall see, my dear madam, we shall see," replied the lawyer. "But there is not a moment to lose, for these papers are, if I mistake not, of great importance, not only to you, but to many others whom Grubbe and his accomplices have robbed."

"Heaven grant that the villains may be brought to justice."

"Little doubt of that, madam; but very much depends upon the next few hours. In the first place, all this must be kept a strict secret, but that he will understand. In the second, Sam must go back to Heath End Villa—but no more of that poker business mind."

"I'll take care, sir," replied Sam; "but suppose he should want to cut away again."

"Then you must use your own discretion, Sam, I suppose; but don't hit him hard."

"I won't, sir. Am I to go now?"

"Yes, you had better go at once. If any of Grubbe's friends call, and no one is there to answer them, suspicion might be aroused, which would spoil my plans. I will send a private detective to watch the house, so you will have help near. Sam."

"I don't want no help, sir; I could tackle old Grubbe easy, with the old woman chucked into the bargain."

"Very likely, Sam, but in my profession we are accustomed to take every precaution. And now, my dear madam, I must go, for it will take me all night, probably, to examine these documents."

"How shall we ever thank you sufficiently, Mr. Rightson?"

"By not thanking me at all, madam. Thank that lad, Sam, if you must thank somebody, for he has accomplished that which would have defied the whole power of the law to do, though he has done it in a most illegal manner. Why, where is the boy? Gone already?"

The long youth, still adorned in the primitive gown and cap with which he had concealed the manly beauties of his figure, had indeed gone, and was well on his way to Hampstead.

"I saw him go," said Lionel; "but he signed to me not to notice him. He was afraid that somebody was going to thank him, and he can't bear that."

"To take a quotation from you, Master Lionel," said the lawyer, "he is a regular brick; and I think I may say that, thanks to his fidelity, you will soon again be master of your fortune and your home."

CHAPTER VIII.

IN WHICH SAM ENJOYS TO THE FULL THE SWEETS OF REVENGE — MR. GRUBBE'S THREAT — MR. RIGHTSON PAYS A VERY SATISFACTORY VISIT TO CAMBERWELL — THE RAT IN THE CAGE AT HAMPSTEAD — AT BAY — A DASTARDLY SHOT.

THE lawyer could not have given Sam a task more congenial to his feelings than that of keeping watch and ward over the oily villain who had been so neatly trapped.

But in the midst of his delight at having to go back to the villa, he did not neglect any precaution which suggested itself to him.

He had hired a four-wheeler at the bottom of the road, the driver of which had just had Mrs. Giacommetti Prodgers for a fare, and who, having as a matter of course been what he called "done" by that estimable lady, was in a state of mind which rendered him careless as to whether the Old Gentleman himself was his next fare.

The cabman drove at a pace that threatened to shake the crazy old rabbit-hutch he called a cab to pieces; but it landed Sam safely in the High-street, and then, by sundry devious ways, to the back of Heath End Villa, which he entered by the pantry window—a mode of entrance well-known to Sam in the old days.

"I'll jest take a peep out o' the drawin'-room winder," thought the supposed "slavey." "They've been waterin' the road in front, and if anybody's been the steps 'll be mnddy."

But there were no traces of foot-marks visible, and then Miss Maria Pecker, lighting the handsomest lamp she, or rather "he," could find, went to the cellar straight.

Mr. Grubbe and his housekeeper were still in the position in which Sam had left them, tied back to back, and propped up in a sitting attitude against a heap of coals.

The sudden glare of light caused them to turn their heads away from a light so painful to their eyes, whereupon Sam began—as he phrased it—to "chaff" them.

"Ah, well, you may turn your heads away. Oh, you sinful old man! Courtin' the housekeeper in the coal-cellar! And at your hage, too! Well, I am surprised."

Sam set down the lamp and betook himself to a closer inspection of the happy pair, first stirring

Mr. Grubbe up with the poker he had brought with him, to let him know he was at home.

"You hardened old sinner," he continued, after a pause occupied by the poker. "Not a word to say for hisself. If he's been insultin' of you, mum, jist let me know, and I'll give him a taste o' this. He knows the flaviour."

Mr. Grubbe slowly turned his head, and fixed a look upon Sam which made that young gentleman clasp the poker more tightly.

The features of the defeated rascal were very pale, only his eyes were so bloodshot that they seemed more like the glaring orbs of some hunted wild beast than those of a man.

"How de do, sir?" said the undaunted Sam. "I thort I'd jist step back and tell you that everythink is a-goin' on as well as can be expected. Them there papers as you were so kind to give me to take care on, is in werry good 'ands. Mr. Rightson, of Lincoln's Inn—p'r'aps you know him? Oh, you do—well, *he's* got 'em."

A hideous scowl darkened Grubbe's face at these words. Had he been free at that moment Sam would have had need of his weapon and all his strength, too, to have kept his brains from being dashed out against the brick walls of the cellar, but he could only look, and Sam cared nothing for that.

"But lor' bless my 'art," the disguised Sam went on; "here am I a doin' all the talkin', and forgettin' that you can't speak in consekens of the 'ankercher I tied round your mouth to keep the cold out. There now, is that better? Don't be afraid to speak out loud; nobody 'll hear you but me, if you'd got the lungs of a steam ingine."

This was a gentle way of intimating to Mr. Grubbe that it was no use shouting for help, but the oily gentleman was as well aware of that fact as Sam, and the first use he made of his recovered speech was to utter the word—

"Water!"

"Now, dear me," said Sam, affecting to be quite shocked, "I know you don't mean that; it's only your modesty, ain't it? Some shammy, the real sparklin', foamin' shammy's your sort; or p'r'aps you prefers buggandy, or 'ock. Give it a name, now; tell me where the key o' the wine cellar is, and I'll fetch it."

"Water, I tell you," repeated Mr. Grubbe, hoarsely; for his throat and lips were parched with the fire of hate and anger.

"Say beer, now," pursued Sam; "I really couldn't go any lower than beer. I should blush to bring sich a gentleman as you anythink less. There's a bootiful tap on the premises; p'r'aps you've tasted it? I have."

And away went Sam, chuckling at a happy thought which had just occurred to him, which was that he would force his captives to swallow the unsavoury fare upon which they had starved him while in the character of Maria Pecker, ex-workhouse drudge and slavey.

"My eye, won't it be fine to see old Grubbe makin' faces over the grub he give me to eat. I know he's fond o' good livin', for I've seen him in the hold times peckin' away at the wenison and partridges, and snipe and sich. And then the swipes—oh, lor', it's enough to kill a fellow to think of."

Sam hurried away into the now dingy, dirty kitchen, and selecting the largest dish he could see, heaped upon it all the most unsavoury scraps he could rake out of the cupboards or find lying on the dresser.

Then he drew off a large jugful of the flat stale table beer, and providing himself with a fork and a funnel, he returned to the cellar.

"Hope I ain't kept your long, sir," said Sam, cheerfully. "If I has, why never mind, your appetite 'll be all the better for it."

"The water—the water," gasped Mr. Grubbe, eyeing the jug with a fierce wild glare of a caged tiger when it scents its food.

"Now that ain't perlite," said Sam. "That ain't manners, you know. Wot you orter say is, 'If you please, Mr. Sam'l, will you be so good as to 'blige me with a drink o' water, or beer,' as the case may be."

"Curse you!" said Grubbe, hoarsely. "It's your infernal young whelp of a master who has set you on to do this. He's got the whip-hand now, but my time will come again some day, and then let him look out, and you too, for by —— I'll not spare you."

"Wuss and wuss!" said Sam, affecting to be dreadfully shocked. "I never thought to see you come down so low as to go cussin' and swearin' like any low street feller. I'm afraid, Mr. Grubbe, you've fallen away from the ways of grace, as you used to say when you came to pray along of Miss Mariar, in the hold times."

"Go on—go on," said Grubbe, with the fierce, angry light smouldering like a spark in his evil eyes, "but I tell you, and you tell that cub, Wilful, that if it's fifty years hence, I'll have my revenge for this."

"Only hark to him," said Sam, appealing to the coals. "Only listen. He talks of wot he'll do fifty year to come, and he's fifty year old hisself if he's a day. Oh, he's Methoosalem the Second, that's wot he is—and now I'm going to give to Methoosalam his dinner."

With a malicious grin Sam placed the dish on the ground, and selecting a piece of most unsavoury fat, which looked as if it had enjoyed a lengthened stay at a marine store dealer's, held it under his victim's nose.

"Rich, ain't it?" said Sam, with a chuckle; "full o' flavour; reminds you o' wenison, or them delishus bits as swims about in turtle soup. Open your mouth now—don't be shy."

And catching Mr. Grubbe dexterously by the nose, Sam forced him to open his mouth, and then popped the choice morsel into it.

The miserable man shuddered with repugnance, the taste was horrible, but he was obliged to swallow it.

Sam followed the first tit-bit with a second, then a third and a fourth, picking out the nastiest pieces he could find, and each time allowing his victim to sniff the fragrance, until a curious wavey motion of Mr. Grubbe's waistcoat denoted that the stomach beneath was on the verge of a revolution.

"Gettin' thirsty? Better have a drink o' beer afore you goes on with the eatin'. You reklect how they give me the medsine that time I was at Cheetham Hall, and you was so kind as to have me sent to the lunatic asylum, don't you?"

Sam saw by the look on Mr. Grubbe's face that he did remember that incident.

"This is the way," continued the long youth, producing the funnel. "They puts the end of it between the teeth, just as I'm puttin' the end o' this between yours, and then they pours the stuff in atop."

And Sam gave his victim a practical explanation of the method, by pouring about a pint of that horrible beer into the funnel, which Grubbe, helpless, was forced to swallow to the very dregs.

"There now, don't you feel better? Isn't that prime? Better than all your shammy and sich stuff as that. Nothing like good old English beer to cheer a feller up. Will you have a little more now? Don't say no, there's a plenty more in the barrel."

But Mr. Grubbe could not reply. In fact he was too ill—the beer had finished what Sam's tit-bits had so well begun, and with a few convulsive gasps and groans, Mr. Grubbe's dinner was shot among the coals.

"Now blow me if that ain't downright ungrateful," said Sam, with affected indignation. "Arter spendin' all that time gettin' you a good blow-out and actorally feedin' of you myself, you goes and chucks it out agin in that disgraceful fashion. I must waste no more time on you."

And first putting the dish of scraps where Mr. Grubbe could not avoid smelling their exquisite perfume, Sam stalked away, chuckling with delight at the way in which he had retaliated upon his enemy.

*　　　*　　　*　　　*

Early the next morning Mr. Rightson was at Camberwell—so early, indeed, that our hero and his mother had not yet finished breakfast.

"Good news, Mr. Rightson," exclaimed Lionel. "I see it in your face."

"Good indeed, my boy—beyond what our utmost hopes could have expected," replied the lawyer, seating himself, and placing a leather hand-bag on the table. "Pardon me, Mrs. Wilful, if I interrupt your breakfast, but time presses."

"Pray make no excuse to us, Mr. Rightson; we are too heavily your debtors already."

"I proceed then. You gave this scoundrel Grubbe a power of attorney to transfer the money you had in the funds, and to sell out certain shares."

Mrs. Wilful bowed assent.

"You also empowered him, always in the name of this swindling bank, to sell your villa at Hampstead, and your other house and landed property?"

"I was foolish enough to do so."

"Then he," said the lawyer, passing a packet of papers to Mrs. Wilful, "has been more foolish still, for he has made no use whatever of the rights you gave him. The power of attorney has never been executed—your shares and stock still stand in your name—and, in a word, you are as much mistress of your fortune as if you had never seen this Grubbe, or he had never existed. Good Heaven! I have been too hasty. Look to your mother, Lionel, she has fainted."

But Mrs. Wilful revived in a few minutes, sufficiently to thank Mr. Rightson in trembling tones for his great kindness.

"Pooh, pooh. Don't thank me, ma'am," said the honest old lawyer. "That lad of yours, Sam, has done it all. A fine fellow; if he only had a little more respect for the law, I'd take him into my office without a premium. But I must go now, and relieve him of his charge."

"What, are you going to the villa, sir?" said Lionel.

"Why, yes, my boy. I found enough in those papers to enable me to apply for warrants against Grubbe and four of his co-swindlers. The police are out after the lot, and I daresay, by this time, a sergeant and four constables are ready at the Hampstead police office."

"Let me go with you, sir? Don't stop me, mother. I must see this villain who tried to ruin you without any cause, run to earth, and trapped, like the skunk he is."

Mrs. Wilful said no more, beyond a whispered caution to be careful. Mr. Rightson's carriage was at the door, and in another minute was whirling them swiftly towards the doomed man.

The sergeant and his men were ready at the station, and there Mr. Rightson and Lionel got out, and walked quickly towards the villa.

The two detectives, one at the back and one at the front, reported all quiet. No one had entered the house, and no one had left it.

"Good," said Mr. Rightson, as he rang the bell. "Now for our bird."

They waited a few minutes, but no Sam appeared. The bell was rung again, this time violently, but with the same result.

"Great Heaven!" said Mr. Rightson. "What if the villain has got free from his bonds, and—and done some desperate deed. Burst in the door."

"There's an easier way than that, sir," said the detective who had watched at the back. "Come this way."

Two of the men were left to guard the front, while the rest hurried to the back, and, guided by the detective, crawled in through the pantry window.

"The coal cellar—quick," said Mr. Rightson, in an agitated voice. "You know the house, Lionel."

The place was reached in a moment. One of the policemen had lighted his bull's-eye, and flashed it round the cellar. Mr. Grubbe was not there, but lying on the coals was a huddled heap of clothes, which a moment's glance showed to be poor Sam, bleeding and insensible—perhaps dying.

Mr. Rightson raised the head upon his knees and cried hoarsely—

"He cannot have escaped, men. Fifty pounds, to the one who captures him."

The hunt was hot now, for there was blood upon the track. The police began to scatter to strike the trail, when Lionel called out—

"He is here. This way—quick!"

The two who were nearest hurried to the door, and there they saw him standing at bay, blood upon his face, blood upon his hands, and murder in his heart, for at the sight of Lionel he, with the grin of a demon on his lips, snatched a pistol from his breast, and fired it point blank at our hero's head.

CHAPTER IX.

A NARROW ESCAPE—MR. GRUBBE IN THE TOILS —THE THREAT—THE SENTENCE—AT HOME AGAIN —MRS. WILFUL'S GRATITUDE AND SAM'S OBSTINACY—MR. RIGHTSON TAKES HIM IN HAND— THE RESULT—VISIONS OF SCHOOL-LIFE ONCE MORE.

ONLY one little inch of space intervened between Lionel and death at that dread moment.

Quick as the flash of the pistol itself he bent his head—he heard the sharp "ping" of the bullet as it whistled past his ear, and a lock of his hair fell floating to the ground. Then, while yet the last wreath of smoke curled upwards from the muzzle of the pistol the policemen hurled themselves upon Mr. Grubbe, wrenched the weapon from his grasp, and snapped a pair of handcuffs on his wrists.

"Whew!" whistled one of the policemen, keeping a tight hold of Mr. Grubbe's collar the while. "That was a narrow squeak for you, young man!"

Lionel saw that now. His face went pale as marble, his teeth clenched, and his eyes lit up with fierce anger against the villain who had tried to ruin him, and then sought to take his life.

The fighting element was very strong in our hero's nature when he felt himself wronged or injured, and, but for the policeman, Lionel, boy as he was, would have flown at his throat and pulled him down, much as a mastiff pins a bull.

Mr. Grubbe had changed too. The last time that Lionel had looked upon him at Cheetham Hall he was still the bland semi-clerical gentleman, portly of figure, oily of speech and manners —a man looking as incapable of any deed of violence as a pound of fresh butter; now he seemed to have shrunk within his clothes, his face was white and haggard, and his eyes gleamed with that hateful wild-beast glare which had already startled poor Sam.

He had uttered a bitter blasphemous oath when he saw that his shot failed, and felt himself powerless in the strong grip of the police. At that moment he would have given his own life to have seen Lionel stretched dead before him.

But suddenly the dark scowl of baffled hate cleared from his features, and a faint shadow of the old cruel smile curved his lips.

"A moment ago," he said, "I was sorry my bullet missed you, but now I rejoice at it. You have the best of the game now, but I have a card or two to play yet. Remember my words, Lionel Wilful; I will revenge myself a hundred fold for this day on you and that cunning abortion of humanity, Sam Scarecrow."

"Thanky; don't put yourself out o' the way," said a faint voice behind him, and, turning, he saw Sam, supported by Mr. Rightson, standing in the doorway.

Mr. Grubbe turned that evil glance on him for a moment, but he did not speak.

"You're a nice old party, ain't you?" continued Sam; "a gratefool Christian kind of cove—the sort of stuff they used to make saints of in the old days. —Yah, I'm ashamed of you."

"Let him alone, Sam. Let us go; the very sight of him is poison to me."

"I'm willin'. But only fancy a chap like that callin hisself a 'shepherd,' and a 'guider of the blind,' and a 'elected leader of the faithful,' and all that kind o' gammon, when he sarved me like this. Why I treated that chap as if he'd been my father; I tied him up comf't'ble, picked out a nice soft place for him among the coals, brought him his grub, and actoolly fed him with all the tender bits, and poured his beer inter him to save him the trouble. Was he gratefool?—not a bit on it. While my back was turned he gets loose, and fetches me a whack on the 'ed with a lump of coal."

"Never mind, Sam," said Lionel. "It will be many a long day before he has the opportunity of giving you another."

"Ah, that's true," replied the lanky one, with a chuckle of satisfaction. "There's somethink in that. Besides, twenty year of skilly and hard labour will pull him down a bit, summut near my weight, and then I can have a fair go at him. I'll teach him to knock chaps down with lumps of coal when they ain't lookin'."

"Let your parting wish be a more gentle one than that," said Mr. Rightson. "When his term of punishment—and it is certain to be a long one —is over, he will emerge from his prison a broken down and ruined old man. Hope for him that he may be brought to see not only the wickedness, but the folly, of sin, and——"

"Stop," said Grubbe, with a harsh, contemptuous laugh. "Do you think that I have talked that canting rubbish to fools for twenty years to wish to have it repeated to me now. I know its value as well as you do, for I have grown rich and fared sumptuously by it. Ay, and shall again."

"I believe you," said Mr. Rightson; "for there is no more thorough-going scoundrel on this earth than a hypocrite unmasked."

"As for you," Grubbe added, turning to our hero, "you will be a man before we meet again. Think of me sometimes, and when you do, remember that David Grubbe is your Evil Genius, and will work your ruin yet."

He was led away between the two policemen, his eyes fixed to the last upon Lionel. As he had prophesied, it was many years before he and our hero met again, and when they did, Lionel had cause to remember his ill-omened words.

* * *

It would be out of place in a story of this nature to enter into the long and somewhat dry details of a criminal trial, so we may as well dispose here of Mr. Grubbe, until he is again wanted to play his part in this drama.

He was tried, with four of his accomplices, at the Old Bailey, and there—thanks to the proofs that Sam had found—all four were pronounced guilty of gross and shameful fraud upon the public; not only in the bank which had so nearly swamped Mrs. Wilful's fortune, but in others of those swindling companies which were launched for the sole purpose of robbing too confiding investors.

The four minor thieves were sentenced each to ten years' penal servitude; David Grubbe, who had been shown to be the prime mover in all, got twenty for his share, and a shout of applause confirmed the justice of the sentence.

Thanks to Mr. Rightson's careful and judicious arrangement, Mrs. Wilful, Lionel, and Sam were saved the trouble of giving any evidence at the trial, and the discovery of the proofs of guilt was scored to the "active and intelligent" members of the force.

This was greatly to Sam's disgust, who longed to go into the witness-box and give the learned judge and jury a piece of his mind respecting Mr. Grubbe; but when Mr. Rightson pointed out that this course would infallibly end in dragging his mistress's name into public notoriety, the long youth gave way at once.

It may well be supposed that the day on which our hero entered his old home was, indeed, a happy one; not alone for him, but for all who had passed through, or had any part in the startling events we have faithfully recorded in the preceding chapters of the second part of our story.

Sam, in particular, was so elated, so much inclined to dance and leap high from the earth at the most inopportune moments, that he really seemed more allied to the baboon family than the human race.

"We shall have to tie you up in some corner, Sam," said Lionel, when his faithful but eccentric follower had, for the second time, kicked over the luncheon tray. "You've been to some gas-works and got yourself filled with gas."

"'Tain't gas, Master Lionel," replied Sam, "it's joy, that's wot it is. Hooray! Be it never so 'umble, there's no place like 'o-o-ome."

"Don't sing, Sam," said our hero; "shout 'hooray,' and talk as much as you like, but don't sing any more—till you've had some lessons."

"I won't, Master Lionel. I knows my woice ain't ekal to my feelin's; but I say, wot a pity your mar won't have some fireworks, and a band, and make a reg'lar tryangrunt pursesshun of it."

"A triumphal entry, eh, Sam? Well, you know, my mother is not strong, and any excitement might make her very ill. Ask for anything else, Sam, and I'll go bail that you shall have it. You don't know how grateful my mother is to you."

"Don't, Master Lionel—don't, now, please. None o' that."

"None of what?"

"Why," replied Sam, in a confused way; "none o' that there—that thankin'. I ain't done nothin' to be thanked for, and bust me, Master Lionel," he added, with desperate energy, "if anybody does it any more, I'll bolt again, I will."

Lionel burst out laughing.

"Why, what a queer fellow you are, Sam. But there, I promise that nobody shall thank you against your will."

This dread which Sam entertained was a serious obstacle to one thing which Mrs. Wilful was desirous to accomplish—namely, the suitably rewarding of Sam for what he had done.

Several times she had endeavoured to question Sam as to what his wishes were with regard to his future; but the lanky youth, who had insisted on resuming his livery, seemed to know instinctively what Mrs. Wilful was aiming at, and invariably "bolted," and hid himself for an hour or two.

"Really," said Mrs. Wilful to the lawyer, whom, as a last resource, she had called in as an aid, "I do not know how to deal with Sam. He will not listen to me—he won't even let me begin what I want to say to him."

"Leave him to me, ma'am," said Mr. Rightson. "I'll get him in a corner; but by your permission, I think I had better see him alone."

So the lawyer proceeded to the library, and, ringing the bell, was presently waited upon by Sam, who held Mr. Rightson in great awe and affection.

"Now, Sam," said the lawyer, "I want a word or two with you."

Sam ducked his head, and grinned amiably.

"You know who I am, don't you?"

"'Deed I do, sir, and perroud I am on it. You've been a good friend to missis."

"Enough of that, my boy. I dislike being thanked as much as you do, especially when I have done nothing. You know I'm a solicitor, don't you?"

"If that means a lawyer—yes, sir."

"It's one branch of the law, Sam. Now, would you like to be a lawyer?"

"No, sir."

"Ah, don't care for it. It's just as well, perhaps. I don't think you'd make a good lawyer myself. You haven't sufficient respect for its formulæ. How would the sea suit you?"

"No, sir."

"The army?"

"Likewise no, sir."

"You wouldn't do for the church," said the lawyer, meditatively. "I don't think there's the stuff for a country curate in you, Sam. How would you like to be a doctor, now?"

"Not at all, sir. I can't abear fizzic."

"Well, that settles all the professions," said the lawyer. "Now we come to the trades. Come now, Sam, choose a business. You've only to say the word."

"And I ses it to you now, sir," said Sam, becoming all at once very red in the face, and very excited. "I knows wot you're a drivin' at, sir, and werry grateful I am to you and to missis; but my last words is this, sir: I wus picked orf that there 'eath when I were a baby; missis, she's been like a mother to me ever since; Master Lionel he've been a brother—my bisness is to stick to 'em, sir. I left 'em once, and see wot come of it, and leave 'em I never will again—if I do I'm d——."

And for the first time in his life, and in the height of his excitement, poor Sam clenched his assertion with an oath. Let us hope that, like the famous one uttered by Uncle Toby, a tear of the Recording Angel blotted it out as it was written.

Mr. Rightson leaned back in the arm-chair, looking at Sam with mingled amusement and admiration.

"Sam," he said, at last, "you're an extraordinary fellow. Here is your mistress positively hungering to do you a service, and you won't allow her. But there, I see you're obstinate—shake hands, and I'll say no more."

Sam carefully polished his right hand on the leg of his trousers, and then, with a relieved countenance, shook hands with Mr. Rightson and departed.

"That boy is a treasure, madam," said the lawyer, when he rejoined Mrs. Wilful. "Faithful as steel, and true as gold. I'd give half I possess to have a son with such a nature as Sam."

"You cannot say a word in his favour with which I will not heartily concur, Mr. Rightson. But how did you succeed?"

"I didn't succeed at all, ma'am. He beat me at every point. You will never get that boy to leave you and your son—the Koh-i-noor wouldn't tempt him."

"What can be done for him? Think, Mr. Rightson, I could never enjoy my recovered wealth, and know that Sam, to whom I owe it, was no better off than he was before."

"The only plan that I can think of is this. Invest a sum for him—good security, consols, I should suggest—and let the interest accumulate. Then, in the second place, I presume you are going to send Lionel to school again?"

"Yes. It will be hard to part with him, but it will be for the best."

"I agree with you, ma'am. No preparation for the battle of life is so valuable as school to a boy, and, by the way, I can recommend a capital one."

"Your recommendation is sufficient, Mr. Rightson. Lionel shall go."

"And Sam also. He will follow Lionel anywhere. You remember, of course, that mad trick of his when he ran away to join him at Cheetham Hall?"

"Indeed I do," replied Mrs. Wilful, smiling.

"Of course his position at the school will have to be defined. He had better go as a confidential attendant upon your son. I will arrange with Mr. Stiffback for his receiving such instruction as may be necessary."

"But why can he not go to the school on an equality with the other pupils?" said Mrs. Wilful. "I wish to raise him above his present condition."

"And that is what you will never succeed in doing, for the best of reasons—that Sam himself does not desire it. If he went to the school, as you suggest, on an equality with the other pupils, poor Sam would become the most wretched boy in England in a week—his ways, his speech would be ridiculed, and the matter would infallibly end in his having to leave the school."

"I suppose you are right; but I wished to do so much for him, and he will let me do so little—"

"The little, as you call it, may turn out a great deal by-and-by. He is a sharp lad, and is certain to pick up more refined manners and better ways of speech from contact with the youngsters at Stiffback's, and as he gets older and sees more of the world, he will learn to appreciate and take advantage of your kind intentions towards him."

"I hope so."

"Of course he will. Sam is no fool," said Mr. Rightson, rising to take his leave. "This is Mr. Stiffback's address; you can write to him at once, and Lionel can go to him as soon as the midsummer holidays are over. Good-bye."

CHAPTER X.

ON THE ROAD TO SCHOOL AGAIN—DELIVERHAM JUNCTION—THE MEETING OF THE CHUMS—TOMMY CODLINGS TELLS THE STORY OF HOW HE MALTREATED THE CATS AND GOT HIS FREEDOM—SOME OF MR. STIFFBACK'S YOUNG GENTLEMEN—THE SHINY HAT AND WHAT HAPPENED TO IT—TOMMY CODLINGS AVENGES THE INSULT OFFERED TO HIS FAMILY, AND WIPES OUT THE STAIN IN BLOOD—A NEW ARRIVAL—LIONEL GIVES A PRACTICAL ILLUSTRATION OF THE OLD SAYING, "THE CART BEFORE THE HORSE."

THE intelligence that he was once again destined to enter the little world of school-life soon reached the ears of Lionel and Sam, and formed the subject of a long and animated discussion.

"Take it all round, I'm glad enough to go, Sam, for school is a jolly place; but I wish my old chums were going to this new place. It is not always you can find fellows you like."

"Why don't they then?"

"Why don't they—what, Sam?"

"Go to the new school alonger you and me, Master Lionel."

"They'd come, Sam, but they've got fathers and mothers and that sort of thing, you know, and they mightn't see it in the same light as we do."

"Ax 'em," was Sam's laconic advice.

"'Pon my word, that isn't a bad idea. I've got Charlie Drummond's address somewhere, and I'll write to him at once."

So Master Lionel took possession of paper, pen, and ink, and employed a couple of hours in giving his chum a summary of the adventures which had befallen him since they parted, and winding up with a suggestion that Charlie should persuade his father to send him to Mr. Stiffback's, instead of to Cheetham Hall.

It was posted in company with a note from Mrs.

Wilful, addressed to the pedagogue himself, and two days after the answers arrived, both of which being to the purpose we here transcribe.

The first is from Mr. Stiffback.

"Madam,—I had already received a communication from my personal friend, Mr. Rightson, of Lincoln's Inn, when your letter reached me. His explanations regarding the course to be adopted towards your son, Master Lionel Wilful, and his attendant, Samuel Scarecrow, meet with my complete approval. I enclose a prospectus, in which you will find detailed the method of instruction, &c., pursued in my establishment.

"I have the honour to be, madam,
"Your very obedient servant,
"ARCHIMEDES STIFFBACK.
"Principal of Lake Island Academy.

The second epistle was from Charlie Drummond.

"My dear old Li,—Your letter is the jolliest thing I've had all the holidays. I was pleased to get it, and no mistake. You've no idea how dull the school got after you were gone. Pretty well every day I was bothered half out of my life by them coming and asking me whether I'd heard from you, and, of course, as you never answered the letters I sent to your crib at Hampstead, I couldn't tell 'em anything, for I didn't know then that old beast, Grubbe, had done you out of anything. Poor Tommy wasted away to a shadow, and from being the good-tempered, jolly little chap he was when you knew him, became as surly and spiteful as a pet lap-dog. He was awful with the masters; he said flatly that he wouldn't do any work, and he didn't. They tried caning, and he stood that for a while, till one day Crocklejack was paying him, and Tommy gave him such a buster on the shin, it sounded all over the school, and we thought his leg was broke by the way he howled, and he had to go on crutches for a week. The next day de Bewty pulled Tommy's ears—you remember how tender they always were—and Tommy ups with a ruler and fetches de Bewty one over the nose that made him see stars, and he had a pair of black eyes for a fortnight. Then old Styngy took him in hand, and said he must be a little out of his mind, so he had the doctor in and they physicked Tommy, and kept him on bread and water in a dark room, till he was as weak as a wet towel, and then they let him out and said he was better. Poor old Tommy was awfully white and thin, but didn't he look vicious? Well, about a week after Tommy was missing again, and we heard that he had tried to murder old Styngy, and that Styngy had telegraphed for Tommy's aunt. She came the next day, such an awful old lady, Li, six feet high if she was an inch, and dressed all in black velvet and bugles, and a long parasol with a spike at the end like a spear. 'Where,' she says, marching straight up the schoolroom, 'is this wretched nephew of mine?' Old Styngy was taken aback and wanted her to go in the library, but she wouldn't, so Tommy was fetched up from the coal-cellar, I fancy, for he was precious black, and then the old 'un let out at him. I won't tell you all he said. I couldn't remember if I tried, only the last bit was good. 'Madam,' he said, 'I have treated the degraded boy like a father. My ushers have been his guides, philosophers, and friends, and you have heard how he has treated them. Despite that I bore with him, hoping that a mild and gentle course of discipline [good that, ain't it? Precious mild and gentle, eh?] would wean him from the error of his ways. But, madam, there are limits to human forbearance, and when a boy puts two pounds of gunpowder in connection with a slow match under my bed, I cast that boy off.' 'What,' says the aunt, 'did he do that?' 'On my honour, madam,' says old Styngy. 'Then,' says she, 'the boy's a born fool; he ought to have known that two pounds was no use for a man of your weight.' And then, without

another word, she collared Tommy, gave him a shake, and marched off with him. What do you think of that, old fellow? I wish I could see you while you read my letter. And now I come to another bit of news. About a fortnight after Tommy had gone one of the chaps was taken ill, and the doctor said it was a cold, and physicked him. But in two or three days all the chaps in the dormitory were laid up. Another doctor was sent for and he said it was typhus fever. My eye, weren't we packed off in a hurry! School was broken up, and all the fellows who hadn't got the fever were sent home. I believe it will ruin old Styngy's school, and serve him right, I say, for the way he treated you, Li. Of course, I'm not going back, and I shall begin to worry the governor directly about sending me with you. Tommy is pretty sure to come as well, as we write to one another, and he says that his aunt doesn't care where he goes so long as he gets out of her sight. I must shut up now, Li, as John is waiting to take the letter-bag to the post. Good-bye, old fellow, and good luck.

"Your affectionate chum,
"CHARLIE DRUMMOND."

"Well, that is good news," said our hero to Sam, as soon as he had mastered the contents of this somewhat lengthy epistle. "It will be prime having Charlie for a chum, and poor old Tommy too—fancy his turning out such a desperate character. I should like to have seen old Styngy when he found the gunpowder under his bed."

"He's a young gen'leman I shall be perroud to know," replied Sam. "I only wish the powder had gone off. That 'ere Styngy, in my 'pinion, was as bad as Grubbe, and wuss, for he hadn't got so much pluck."

"Hush, Sam; it won't do to say Mr. Styngy had anything to do with the swindling affair, you know."

"I ain't so sure o' that, Master Lionel. He were a friend o' Grubbe's, and that's quite enough for me. I hopes his school is busted up, that's all the harm I wishes him."

"Sam, you're getting malicious, and I shall have to cut your acquaintance, if you don't behave better."

"That ain't no use; you'll never get rid o' me any more so long as you live, Master Lionel."

"Behave better and don't be so spiteful, or I'll run away from you, Sam; and what would you do then?"

"You try it on and you'll see," replied Sam with a grin.

"Be off, you long-legged son of a sauce-box, and get me the pen and ink. I'm going to write to Charlie directly."

The letter was written and posted, and then Lionel gave himself up to the delights of preparations for his departure.

Everything was to be new—Mrs. Wilful insisted upon that. Her boy, she said, should take nothing with him which had ever been in that hateful Mr. Styngy's school, neither clothes, nor books, nor playthings.

So our hero revelled in new clothes of the very best, and adapted for all possible occasions. There was a suit for school work, a plain suit for every day out of door use, a cricketing suit, a swell equipment for Sunday wear, and one of extra beauty for extraordinary occasions. His linen—shirts, collars, handkerchiefs, and so on—were of the finest and whitest that money could buy, and the shapes and colours of his neckties were legion.

Sam was not forgotten, our readers may be sure. In its degree his outfit rivalled that of his young master.

The purchase of what Mrs. Wilful, much to her son's indignation, persisted in calling "toys," was entrusted to Lionel himself, and three happy days did he and Sam spend in the selection and purchas of cricket-bats, balls, and stumps; fishing-rods, gut lines, hair lines, floats, and all things appertaining to the "gentle craft;" a wonderful knife, with a whole set of carpenter's tools cunningly hidden in the handle; a lancewood bow and a dozen arrows; and so on, until only eighteen pence remained out of the five-pound note Mrs. Wilful had bestowed upon our hero.

We regret to say that Master Lionel did not follow the example of the good little boys in the Sunday school books—he did not put the eighteen pence into his money-box, neither did he bestow it on the Society for the Propagation of Four-post Bedsteads among the South Sea Islanders; no, he did nothing half so virtuous, for he marched with Sam into an ice-shop in Oxford-street and spent the one-and-sixpence in those seductive but chilly delicacies.

And now there remained but three short days before that on which our hero was destined to depart for school. Charlie Drummond had written to say that he had worried his papa out of an idea he had entertained of sending him to Eton, and that he (Charlie) could be at Lake Island Academy almost as soon as his chum.

There was also good news of Tommy. That enterprising young gentleman had managed to tie an old saucepan lid to each of the tails of her favourite cats, and then start them through the drawing-room, where all the best china was. After that, as Tommy wrote hopefully, his aunt would send him anywhere.

The three days passed, and then came the parting with his mother, which we will not describe, firstly, because this is not a sentimental story, and, secondly, because it is just possible that Lionel cried a little, and that Sam blubbered outright, and what would a hero's character be worth if he were found guilty of such foolishness?

Let our readers, then, imagine the carriage "scrunching" the gravel on the drive, the last "good-byes" said, the last waves of the handkerchief exchanged, and our hero and Sam borne swiftly on their way to Ludgate Hill Station.

It was reached, with a quarter of an hour to spare, which interval Sam and the footman spent in getting the luggage labelled and safely placed in the train, while Lionel visited the refreshment room, and laid in a stock of toothsome delicacies for consumption on the journey.

Deliverham, which as everybody knows is in Dumbledowndearyshire, is reached by the 10.40 express from Ludgate in one hour and a quarter, and the engine drivers on that line being, as a rule, conscientious men, generally manage to keep time, unless an obstinate coal or goods train gets in the way.

On this occasion the train and its contents arrived whole, instead of in fragments, at Deliverham Junction, and almost the first object on which our hero's gaze alighted was Charlie Drummond, running up the platform, looking into every carriage as he passed.

"Charlie!"

"Lionel, old boy."

And then they made pump-handles of one another's arms for the next few minutes, and looked at each other with brightened eyes and real happy faces.

"This is jolly," said our hero. "I suppose Tommy hasn't turned up?"

"Yes he has. He came with me but ten minutes ago; with his usual luck, he got in the way of a porter, and got a box dropped on his toes. Come on, he's in the waiting-room; there's a lot of other chaps, too."

"What, going to Stiffback's?"

"Yes. I don't know what to make of 'em, though. I asked one fellow if he was going to Stiffback's, and he said he really couldn't speak to me, because we hadn't been introduced."

Tommy was on a seat in a corner nursing his wounded toes, but otherwise looking fatter and rosier than ever.

His features were screwed up into a most dismal expression of pain, but as he saw Lionel hurrying towards him, his face became one huge grin, and he hopped off the seat like a sparrow, and seemed to forget all about his injured toes in a moment.

"So you did the trick, eh, Tommy?" said Lionel, when the first greetings were over; "and how did your aunt like it?"

"Oh, the cats, you mean," chuckled Tommy. "My eye, that was a game!"

"Tell us all about it, Tommy."

"There ain't much to tell, for the affair was short and sharp, I can tell you. Well, my aunt she's got half a dozen favourite cats, and as she's a bit of a politician, and goes in for women's rights, you know, she named 'em after Gladstone, and Goschen, and Bright—that's the three toms; and the three shes are called Miss Becker, Miss Tod, and Dr. Mary Walker. There was another she called Mrs. Prodgers, but that turned out to be a low-minded cat who was always having kittens, so she gave it away."

"Never mind the names, Tommy. Drive on."

"Well, you know, my aunt always sees these cats fed herself, and in the afternoon they're all put in a room by themselves, while my aunt has a nap herself. This was my time, so I got the saucepan lids from the kitchen, and tied 'em firm on to the cats' tails, and then shot 'em out one at a time into the passage, leaving the door open so that they could go in and tell my aunt what the matter was."

"And they did, eh, Tommy?"

"I believe you," replied that young gentleman, with a wink; "you never heard such a row in your life, as they dashed up the passage, with the saucepan lids clattering behind 'em. Then they flew into the drawing room, and I heard the china going, and my aunt squeaking, and the bell ringing like mad."

"Where were you all the time, Tommy?"

"Oh, I tucked myself away behind the big umbrella-stand in the hall—it wasn't very safe where those cats were. It took the two footmen, the coachman, and the gardener half an hour to catch 'em, and it took all the sticking-plaister out of three chemists' shops to mend the servants."

"Was it as bad as that, Tommy?" laughed Lionel.

"It just was, and they all threatened to give warning unless the scratching was considered in the wages. My aunt got off pretty clear, for when she saw the cats coming she popped her head under the sofa cushions. Of course, when things were quiet, she began to think who'd done it, and of course she decided it was me."

"Which you meant her to do, Tommy?"

"Just so; but she said I shouldn't stop in the house another day; and I said I didn't want to, and asked if she'd send me to Stiffback's school. She said I might go to Jericho if I liked—and here I am. Hooray!"

And Tommy, quite forgetting his injuries, arose and executed the first few steps of a fantastic dance of triumph, in the course of which he knocked off, by accident, the glossy pot-hat of a gloomy young gentleman of about his own age, who was regarding the dance with an air of disgust.

The gloomy young gentleman was one of a group of half a dozen others, who all had the appearance of being discontented with life in general, and they glared in a strong way at the culprit who had dared to insult one of them.

"Pick my hat up, you low fellow."

"Tum, tum, tumtilly tum," sang Tommy, as he executed a fresh step, and trod on the gloomy young gentleman's toes. "Confound you, why don't you get out of my way, you feller."

WITH A VIGOROUS SWEEP OF HIS PADDLE, LIONEL PROPELLED THE PLANK FORWARD, AND HURLED HIS OPPONENT INTO THE WATER.

This was awful. The gloomy young gentleman flushed red. He had not only had his sacred hat knocked off but he had actually been "confounded" and told to get out of the way by a dreadful low boy who danced. He was speechless.

"Here's a lark," whispered Charlie. "It's Stiff-back's lot that I told you of. The chap whose hat Tommy knocked off is the one who said he couldn't speak to me because he wasn't introduced."

"What a starchy lot of beggars. I wonder if they're all like that."

"Dashed if I know. Let's see what they're made of, Li. Tell Tommy to punch that chap's head."

"He'll do it without telling," replied Lionel. "The other's at him again."

And at that moment the gloomy one repeated in a louder voice—

"Do you hear, you fellow? Pick up my hat instantly."

Tommy stopped his dance and looked at the gloomy one, first winking at Lionel slyly.

"Did you speak to me, sir?" he said, politely.

"I did," said the gloomy one. "Pick up my hat."

"Would you be so good as to say that again?" said Tommy. "I'm rather deaf."

"Pick—up—my hat," squeaked the gloomy one, in his shrillest tones.

"Oh, certainly, if you wish it," said Tommy. "I don't mind if you don't," and walking up to the fallen tile, Tommy bestowed upon it a kick which sent it flying to the other end of the waiting room.

"You—you—low, common fellow," gasped the morose young gentleman. "How dare you?"

"Call the police," suggested the other gloomy young gentlemen.

"Hallo, Tommy," said Lionel, affecting to perceive the row for the first time; "what's all this fuss about?"

"Why," said Tommy, with an air of the most aggravating innocence, "that chap, who looks as if he couldn't help himself, told me to kick up his hat, and I did."

"I did not; I told you to pick it up," screamed the injured one.

"You said kick," Tommy insisted.

"How dare you contradict me?" said the other, white with wrath at the sight of his beloved "chimney-pot," which was ruined for ever. "You low, common boy!"

"Here, I say, none of that," said Tommy, looking monstrous fierce, and swaggering up to the owner of the injured tile. "Who are you calling low and common?"

"You must be," shrieked the grief-stricken mourner, "or you wouldn't have done it."

"That's an insult," said Tommy, tucking up his jacket sleeves, "and a Codlings always wipes out an insult in blood! Take that."

That was what Tommy called a rum 'un on the nose for the gloomy one, from which organ there instantly trickled forth a supply of the ruby fluid which the representative of the Codlings' family deemed essential to obliterate the insult offered to him.

"Come on!" vociferated Tommy, revolving his podgy little fists in front of him, and skipping about from one foot to the other; "I'll show you what it is to call one of my family 'low and common.' Come on!"

The six gloomy young gentlemen looked gloomier still, as Tommy became more valiant and appeared anxious to punch all their heads, when the door of the waiting-room was opened, and they exclaimed in one breath—

"Oh, here's Vansittart!"

Vansittart was a tall, fair-haired, blue-eyed youth of seventeen, rather good-looking, and having in his expression and carriage the unmistake-

able air of an aristocrat. Lionel and Charlie were content with one glance him; they decided that he was a "good fellow."

"Hallo!" he said, stopping at the door and calmly surveying the scene; "fighting already! and *you*, too, Bobbles! Why, I should as soon have expected to see a mouse tackle a bull-terrier."

In a moment all the six gloomy young gentlemen were clustered round Vansittart and jabbering their version of the story.

Then Tommy shouldered his victim out of the way and gave his version to Vansittart; and finally Lionel and Charlie added their testimony, seeing that Tommy was quarrelsome, and longed for more blood.

"It's all your own fault," said Vansittart, when he had heard the evidence. "If this young gentleman chose to dance you had no business to get in the way, and if he knocked your hat off I'm sure he is ready to apologise."

Which Tommy instantly did with a grin.

"Much good that is," growled Bobbles the gloomy. "Apologies won't get me a new hat, or stop my nose from bleeding."

"It's all you're likely to get," said Vansittart, sharply; "you and the others had better be off with the waggonette, or you'll get into more trouble. Those shiny hats of yours are enough to aggravate a saint."

"I suppose, then," said Lionel, "that you belong to Stiffback's?"

"Yes; are you fellows going there?"

"All three of us," replied Lionel.

"I'm glad of that, for I like the look of you."

"And I of you," replied our hero. "I hope there ain't many chaps at the school like those who have just gone out."

"Not many," said Vansittart. "Stiffback's a queer character, and tries hard to model us all after one pattern. Those fellows are all relations, and as like one another as peas in a pod. He had an easy job there; but there are plenty of fellows you'll like."

"I'm glad of that. Hallo, here's Sam!"

"And who's Sam? Another new pupil?"

"Yes and no," said Lionel, with a laugh. "He's my servant, or, I should say, companion, and he's to be a sort of pupil as well; and a first-rate fellow he is."

"You'd better have kept him away," said Vansittart. "There's plenty of stuck-up youngsters who'll make an awful fuss if your companion pretends to any sort of equality with them."

"There's no fear of that; I'll look after him."

"And I'll back you," said Vansittart. "Hallo! here's the waggonette; but where's that lazy beggar of a driver? The horse isn't put to."

After a short search the driver was discovered helplessly drunk in a public-house.

"Con-found it; here's a nuisance. We shall have to walk."

"Not a bit of it," said Lionel. "We'll have some fun out of this. Do you mind a little sky-larking?"

"I'm good for anything," said Vansittart.

"All right. We'll shake the Bobbles fellows up a bit. Tie the driver on to his seat and let's drive ourselves."

No sooner said than done. The luggage was already stowed away, the six gloomy ones mounted into their seats, the driver was lashed in his place, and Sam soon returned bringing up the horse.

"Turn him round, Sam," said our hero. "Head towards me. By George! we'll illustrate the old proverb, and have the cart before the horse in reality."

"That's a good idee, Master Lionel," chuckled Sam; "as I always said, you can do it, bar none."

Vansittart burst into a hearty laugh at the queer spectacle the poor horse presented, with his tail where his head ought to be.

"But I say, Wilful, how on earth are you going to drive?"

"Oh, I'll ride him postillion fashion."

"All right, fire away. It's a straight road through the town. I'll guide you."

The Bobbles family looked on in wonder and disgust at this breach of the proprieties, and even ventured to remark that the general appearance was not gentlemanly; but as they were peremptorily desired to shut up, or get out and walk if they didn't like it, they held their tongues.

There was some little difficulty in getting the horse to start, as he had no previous experience in pushing a load; but Lionel got him into a steady trot at last, and as the road was broad and level, they got along with only two or three narrow escapes from being spilt in the ditches, until the busy little town of Deliverham was entered.

And now the troubles, or as our hero termed it, the "fun," began in real earnest.

CHAPTER XI.

LIONEL AND THE WAGGONETTE CREATE A LITTLE SENSATION—THE COUNTRYMAN AND THE EGGS—"TOMMY, MAKE ROOM FOR YOUR UNCLE"—THE PUMP IN THE MARKET-PLACE, AND WHAT HAPPENED TO THE DEAF GENTLEMAN—THE CATASTROPHE—RUBBISH SHOT HERE—HOW TOMMY CODLINGS WAS CAUGHT—SAM SCARECROW AND THE BEADLE—MR. STIFFBACK MAKES HIS APPEARANCE ON THE SCENE.

"LOOK out now, Wilful," said Vansittart. "We're coming into the town and you can't guide the horse, you know."

"Never mind," laughed Lionel, knocking a double knock with his heels against the horse's ribs. "If there's anything in the way it'll have to get out of it. 'Tain't my affair."

"All right," said Vansittart. "There'll be a first-rate smash directly."

"Anythin' for a lark, as the burglar said when he set the fat gen'leman afire, to see to play cards with," added Sam, cheerfully.

"I say, you let us down," said the gloomy young gentleman upon whom Tommy had bestowed the 'rum-un,' and who, in common with his five distinguished relatives, was remarkably pale.

"What's that?"

"You let us get down. That's not the proper way to drive, and I know there'll be an accident. Besides, Vassittart said so."

"There will be presently if you don't keep still," replied our hero. "You'll all get pitched out, and then there'll be a nice little job for the coroner."

"I'll make my father bring an action against you," whined Bobbles; "and so will my cousins."

"If you don't hold your noise," said Vansittart, "I'll come and stop it for you. Hold hard, Wilful; there's a trap just ahead."

"Let him know we're coming," replied Lionel. "Strike up a song, and make the Bobbles family join in."

"I know 'Tommy make Room for your Uncle,'" said Codlings.

"That'll do. Out with it, and if those beggars next you won't sing, run a pin into 'em and make 'm howl."

Tommy did both, and instantly such a hideous wail of mingled melody and anguish poured forth from the waggonette, that the stout countryman who was jogging sturdily to market, with a trap full of eggs and butter, pulled up, looked behind him, and saw the astounding spectacle of a waggonette load of youthful maniacs, coming, full tilt and hind-side before, upon him.

"Hi! hi!" shouted Vansittart.

"Get out of the way!" roared Lionel.

"Tommy, make Room for your Uncle," sang Tommy.

"Well, oi'm darned!" said the countryman; and

that was as far as he got for a little while, as, just then, the waggonette caught his off-wheel, and shot him backwards into the midst of his eggs and butter.

But that was not the only misfortune that occurred, for the collision was sharp and sudden, and as the gloomy young gentlemen were holding on for dear life to the rails or the seats, every one of the shiny hats was jerked into the roadway.

"Stop, stop! our hats, our hats!" yelled the agonized Bobbles family, as they saw those precious ornaments rolling into the ditch or being trampled on by the horse.

"Get out and pick 'em up if you want them," replied Lionel, coolly, "or if you stay where you are, keep on singing. Stir 'em up with the pin, Tommy."

"You'd better stir the horse up with the pin too, Wilful," said Vansittart. "There'll be the dickens to pay when that lout gets the eggs and butter out of his eyes. Straight across the market-place, and mind the pump."

Now, the fact was that our hero knew no more how to guide the horse than Dammerkopf Leiningen how to handle a steam yacht.

The waggonette was in front—where that chose to go the horse had to follow, and as it happened that the ground sloped a little towards the pump, away they went for it at a rattling pace.

Leaning against the trough of the pump was a stout, jolly looking old gentleman, with a very contented expression of face, as if he had just driven a first-rate bargain. He had both hands in his pockets, and the money therein gave forth a pleasant chink, as, all unconscious of the approach of the waggonette, he jingled it.

"Hi!" shouted Vansittart; "get out of the way."

"Look out! look out!" roared the crowd, scattering here and there in dire confusion, for the waggonette dodged from side to side in a most perplexing manner.

But it was all of no use—the jolly old gentleman was as deaf as the pump itself. The waggonette dashed on, and the next thing he knew was that he was being flattened out against the trough, turned round and round, and finally deposited on the ground with not an atom of breath left to swear with.

"Is he hurt?" said Lionel, anxiously.

"No. Don't stop. There'll be a deuce of a row, Wilful. Make him go."

Our hero, thus urged, drummed on the horse's ribs with his heels, pushed him with his left hand, and with his scarf-pin tickled him in the hind quarters.

This was the most unwise thing he could have done, for the tickling not being to the horse's liking, he kicked up behind, nearly unseated Lionel, and drove the waggonette full against a row of stalls.

The wood and canvas gave way as if they had been paper—apples, gingerbread, nuts, toys, and crockery were scattered over the pavement. Five of the unlucky Bobbles family were shot out amidst the wreck, and immediately collared and spanked by the injured proprietors.

Lionel tried to pull the horse up, but in vain. The poor brute was frightened by the noise, and making a convulsive leap forward, spoilt the plate-glass front of an enterprising tradesman, and deposited the last remaining Bobbles in the shop, where he was instantly made prisoner.

"Cut!" said Vansittart to Lionel and Charlie, hastily. "Follow me; dodge where you can, bit out when you can't."

So saying, he sprang from the waggonette, and, clearing a path for himself by knocking over two market men and the beadle, ran at the top of his speed down the High-street.

Lionel, Charlie, and Sam, followed like three

flashes of lightning, but Tommy, the unlucky, hooked the slack of his pantaloons on a nail, and hung there helpless, until the wrathful beadle arose, and marked him for his prey.

"I've got 'un!" he gasped, as he grabbed Tommy by one leg and pulled it like a bell-handle.

The beadle, keeping faithfully to the traditions of his class, was fat, red-faced, short-winded, short-tempered, and a mortal enemy to all boys.

"You let go my leg," roared Tommy.

"Oh, I'll let it go, when I've got ye by the scurf o' the neck, you darned young wampire," said the beadle, giving a fresh tug, which pulled Tommy's boots off.

"Let me alone," yelled the wrathful but helpless Tommy. "What are you stealing my boots for. I'll call the police."

"Ah, you'll have enough o' the perlice afore you've done with 'em," said the beadle. "Catch holt on his tother leg, and pull him down."

"Yah! you brutes—let go—the nail's running into me."

But, regardless of the unlucky youth's cries, the beadle and his assistant brought Tommy down with a last vigorous effort, which not only tore his breeches in a very inconvenient place, but took off a long strip of his skin, whereat poor Codlings howled dismally,

"I'll give 'e sumat to 'owl fur," said one of the market men, whose stall had been converted into matchwood by the waggonette.

And with a hand about as broad and hard as the bottom of a well-baked country loaf, he "fetched" Tommy a spank under the ear which spun him round like a top.

Then such of the other victims who were not lucky enough to have one of the captured Bobbles family to maltreat, fell upon the unlucky Codlings, and so clouted his head and pulled his ears, that by the time he was hauled into the damaged shop and shoved into a corner with the other six trembling culprits, he was so red and steamy that he looked as if he had been boiled.

It was the doctor's shop that had been so ruthlessly treated by the errant waggonette, and just where the Bobbles family were standing were a couple of dozen bottles with some particularly evil smelling liquid in them, and all the gloomy young gentlemen were holding their noses and looking dreadfully unhappy.

"One, two, three, four, five, six," mused Tommy, his features lighting up with an unholy joy. "I don't care so much now these beggars are all in for it. I wonder how Li and the others are. Safe by this time, I'll bet."

And now an animated discussion began as to what was to be done with the boys, and who was responsible for the damage.

The culprits being strangers to the town, it was plain that the information must be got from themselves, and the beadle, as the representative of the law, undertook the cross-examination.

Just as he had given his laced hat a dignified tilt to one side, and pulled his cape well over his shoulders, there was a scuffling as of many feet at the entrance, and half a dozen voices united in making the following statement—

"Here be anoother on 'em !"

And our old friend Sam made his appearance, not gloomy or downcast, but with a cheerful smile upon his countenance. The moment he had seen his young master beyond the reach of capture he had returned to look after Tommy, for whom, on account of his exquisite rendering of "Tommy, make Room for your Uncle," Sam had conceived a strong affection.

"Bring him forrard," said the beadle, majestically; "a dreadful defiant lookin' willun."

"Come now, stow them compliments," retorted Sam; "I ain't a relation o' yourn."

Some of the spectators, whose stalls had not

been injured, chuckled at this biting sarcasm, and the beadle turned red.

"Don't you be sassy, young gallus-bird. We knows a way to take the cheek out o' you."

"Hadn't you better hev some o' yer own took out?" retorted Sam politely. "You're the fatest."

There were more chuckles this time, and one man laughed aloud. The beadle was getting the worst of it.

"Silence!" vociferated the beadle. "Hold that there noise, or I'll have the court cleared. Now, young feller, wot's your name?"

And the great man, with much show of importance, produced a very greasy pocket-book and a stump of lead pencil.

"How much room hev you got in that there book o' yourn, old un, as mine's a precious long name?"

"It hain't too long for the Newgit Calendar," retorted the beadle, and got a laugh on his side.

"Nebuchadnezzar Jeremiah Issachar Zebulon," began Sam, pouring out the long Hebrew names with a rapidity that did infinite credit to his memory. "Put them down fust, and will one o' you gents be kind enough to see as he spells 'em right. I don't want my names took down wrong, for they're first-class harticles."

A perfect roar of laughter rang out now. Even the sufferers by Lionel's last practical joke chuckled at the beadle, who tried hard to preserve his dignity, while he was choking with wrath.

He was debating in his own mind whether or no he should cast his dignity to the winds and punch Sam's head, but just then a very tall thin gentleman hurried into the shop, and pushing the beadle aside, gazed at the boys with a look of mournful reproach, and moving his head slowly from side to side as if some one had hooked it on to some invisible pendulum.

"Can it be?" he said at last. "Do I, indeed, behold six of my pupils, *the* six of whom I was so hopeful, reduced to this disgraceful position. I can hardly believe the evidence of my senses."

"Hallo," thought Sam. "Here's a go. It's old Stiffback."

The Bobbles family uttered a low moan, expressive of the most abject misery, and each member screwed the knuckles of his right fist into his right eye.

"I heard something of this shocking affair as I passed through the town, but I little thought that it was true, and that some of *my* pupils were the disgraced culprits."

Another chorus of moans, and the left fists screwed into the corresponding eyes by way of an appropriate change.

"And who," added Mr. Stiffback, after a pause, "are these boys?"

"My name is Codlings, sir," replied Tommy, who wished himself in the cellar, under the shop, or anywhere out of the reach of the schoolmaster's eye.

"And yours?"

"Scarecrow, sir. I come along of Master Wilful,"

"And where is Master Wilful?"

"He've gone on in front, sir, along of Master Funnystart, and left me to look arter the luggage."

"Vansittart, I suppose you mean," said Mr. Stiffback. "But I will postpone further examination until we reach the school. You will oblige me, beadle, by directing all persons who have sustained damage by reason of this disgraceful freak to send in their claims to me."

Mr. Stiffback was evidently well known, for a murmur of respectful applause arose, and several who had not suffered at all went out and broke something. They knew that Mr. Stiffback would pay them, and well, too; but then it was not his money that he parted with, which made a difference.

His quiet way of speaking, too, had a most comfortable effect upon Tommy, who from his youth upwards had been accustomed to be bullied. He was always being screamed or roared at, according to the sex of the scolder for the time being, and even when spanked he was always howled at first.

"I say," whispered Tommy to Sam, "what's he up to—what do you think he'll do?"

"Don't know, Master Codlings. These here quiet uns is always the worst to get over. When you see a chap wot flusters and blusters about, you can pretty well tell as there ain't much in him, like some bottles o' ginger-beer, all froth and no flavour."

"Ah," said Tommy, thoughtfully. "Then Stiffback is all flavour and no froth."

"That's it azackly, and I think as how we shall find the flavour pretty strong when he gets us 'ome."

Tommy shivered with the anticipation of his impending doom, but a look at the six unhappy Bobbles reconciled him. It was balm of Gilead to him; if he suffered, so would they—and they seemed to be aware of the fact.

Outside the waggonette had been set in order, the horse re-harnessed—this time in the orthodox way—while the tipsy driver was being held under the pump by half a dozen vigorous hands, and a big lout, who much enjoyed the fun, worked the handle with all his might.

"Get in, young gentlemen," said Mr. Stiffback. "I will drive you myself, to prevent the possibility of any further mishap."

Tommy and the others obeyed, but a deep silence and gloom seemed to have fallen upon all except Sam, who cheerfully remarked that he was reminded of a "furneral percesshun where nobody had been remembered in the will."

CHAPTER XII.

A TWO-MILE SPIN—VANSITTART AND LIONEL EXCHANGE CONFIDENCES—WHY VANSITTART LEFT ETON—THE NEW SCHOOLMASTER'S THEORY RELATIVE TO TALE-BEARERS, COMMONLY CALLED SNEAKS—THE ACCOUNT OF THE WAGGONETTE—LAKE ISLAND SCHOOL—DISTANCE LENDS ENCHANTMENT TO THE VIEW—THE EMBARCATION.

OUR hero, Charlie Drummond, and their new acquaintance, Vansittart, did not relax their speed for an instant, until they were fairly compelled by want of breath to pull up, and by that time they were nearly two miles from the market-place of Deliverham.

"By Jove," said Vansittart, "you fellows run well! I'm nearly beat myself."

Lionel was too short of wind to make any reply just then in speaking. He was seated on the bank by the road side, feebly feeling for his pocket handkerchief wherewith to wipe his face, while Charlie lay down flat on the turf, too utterly weak to do anything at all.

"I'm precious glad we got off for your sakes," added Vansittart, after a long pause. "Old Stiffback's a queer card to deal with."

"It don't matter much," replied Lionel. "Those shiny-hatted chaps are sure to peach."

"Not they," said Vansittart. "It wouldn't be of any use, and they know it. There's one good thing about old Stiffback—he never encourages sneaks. If a fellow's caught out doing anything against the rules, he catches it, and severe too, let me tell you."

"That's fine," said Charlie, breaking into the conversation. "When the master discourages sneaking, it's sure to be put a stop to."

"Yes. There are sneaks at Lake Island of course, or fellows who would be sneaks if it was any use, but it is not. Stiffback won't hear a word."

"He can't be a bad sort of a fellow then."

"Neither is he, when you come to know him, but

he's difficult to understand, because he is so different to other masters."

"How?"

"Oh! in lots of ways. The whole school's different to anything you ever saw before, I'll wager."

"Are there any other masters?" asked Charlie.

"Oh, yes! Five altogether, with the French and German ones. If either of you fellows feel inclined to be a sap, you'll find this a first-rate shop."

"A sap! What's that?"

"Oh! don't you know? It's a bit of Eton slang, and means a fellow who grinds at his books, and is never swished for bad lines or construing. I was at Eton for a year."

"I wonder you left Eton for a private school," said Lionel.

"So did a good many others," replied Vansittart, with a laugh; "and the life there is easy enough, for a fellow can do almost as he pleases, and half the time is spent at cricket, foot-ball, or boating; but the fact was, I got toadied out of the place."

"That's a queer thing," said Charlie; "I thought most fellows liked being flattered."

"A little's all very well," replied Vansittart, "and I don't mean to say that if I gained the prize for Latin hexameters or kicked the winning goal in a foot-ball match, I should quarrel with any fellow who cried, 'Bravo! well done.' But at Eton it was different. You see, added Vansittart, "I had the misfortune to be born with a title."

"What a queer fellow you are," said Lionel, with a laugh. "I never heard any one complain of such a thing as that before."

"I'm serious, though. My father, Earl Vansittart, died when I was quite a little fellow, and but for my mother—God bless her!—I believe that injudicious relatives and bad servants would have turned me out the most consummate snob that ever had a handle to his name."

"I say, you know this won't do," laughed Lionel. "The idea of you, a born aristocrat, running down your own class like this. You're worse than Odger."

"Lord forbid!" said Vansittart. "But come, we're getting prosy, and I must cut my story short. Well, at Eton, I found that things were worse than at home."

"But I thought that at a swell public school like Eton, where there are so many noblemen's sons, no difference was made whether a fellow had a title or not."

"It used to be so, I believe, but things have altered. At any rate, I found it so. I was the highest in rank there that year, and I had a couple of hundred a year for pocket-money. Nothing could go wrong with me. My tutor was always willing to find an excuse for me, if I wasn't up to the mark in class, while out of school I had all the toadies—and there's sure to be a good many amongst over five hundred boys—swarming after me like flies after treacle."

"Ah, I see!" said our hero; "I should precious soon get sick of that myself."

"So did I! One year was more than enough. I tried all sorts of ways to get rid of 'em, but they were too many for me. If I gave 'em money, they came back for more. If I punched their heads, they took it meekly, as a mongrel takes a kick; so I left Eton, fished out old Stiffback by accident, and came to him."

"But don't you find yourself worse off?" asked Charlie.

"No. Stiffback allows no favouritism of any kind, and that's why I was rather astonished when you told me you'd brought a servant with you. What's he going to do? You're not dandy enough to want a valet?"

"Not exactly," laughed Lionel. "I've got him here because he refused to keep away from me. He ran away from home not very long ago, to come to the school where I was."

And then Lionel narrated the episode of the Japanese Prince, with which our readers are already familiar.

"He must be e queer card," said Vansittart with a laugh. "I thought so when I saw him."

"And he's one of the truest-hearted, staunchest fellows, too, that ever lived," added Lionel; and then followed the story, condensed, of Mr. Grubbe's villany, and Sam's detection thereof and recovery, of the stolen deeds.

"By Jove," said Vansittart, "such a fellow as that is worth his weight in diamonds. Can't you make anything better of him than a servant."

"That's the difficulty. He won't let us do anything for him. He actually swore at the lawyer when he tried to coax him to better his condition. The only thing my mother has been able to do was to put some money in the funds in his name, but we're afraid to let him know of that even."

"Well, he is an oddity," laughed Vansittart. "I've been called odd and eccentric, on account of my whims, but he beats me. Hallo! here comes the waggonette, and—yes—it *is* old Stiffback himself driving."

Lionel and Charlie got up in a hurry with the intention of making another "bolt," but Vansittart stopped them.

"Stay where you are," he said, "we may as well ride as walk; it can't make any difference in the end."

Mr. Stiffback pulled up the horses, and the boys took off their caps politely.

"Vansittart, and the two new pupils, Wilful and Drummond, I presume."

Lionel and Charlie acknowledged that such was the fact.

"Will you ride, or do you prefer to walk?"

"We'll ride, with your permission, sir," said Vansittart. "We were waiting here for the waggonette, expecting that it would overtake us."

"Ah!" was Mr. Stiffback's short, but expressive remark.

He felt quite sure that Vansittart and the others were concerned in the little affair in the market place, but it was against his rule to make any boy criminate himself, so he asked no questions.

The waggonette rolled on for about a quarter of an hour, through a narrow lane, well wooded on either side, and terminating suddenly on the shore of a lake, in the centre of which a small island sloped upwards from the water, and in the centre of the island, partly hidden by the dense foliage of a plantation of young trees, was a large white house.

It was a pretty scene—so pretty as to call forth a murmur of admiration from our hero, Charlie, Codlings, and Sam, who now saw it for the first time.

"That is Lake Island School, young gentlemen," said Mr. Stiffback, pointing across the water with his whip. "Vansittart, oblige me by telegraphing for the boat No. 2."

There was a white post on the shore of the lake, exactly like a railway signal post, but taller.

Vansittart worked a lever at the foot, and a long red arm shot out from the upper part, moved up and down twice, and then resumed its former position.

The signal was hardly made, when a large boat, manned—or I suppose I should say—boyed by six youngsters, left the island, and was rapidly pulled towards them.

"My stars," whispered Lionel to Charlie; "this is jolly—fancy living on an island."

"Prime," said Charlie.

"I wonder if there are any fish in the lake?"

"Sure to be; and won't we have some swimming, too, old fellow?"

Vansittart listened with a smile.

"Don't you fellows count your chickens before they're hatched," he said.

Before Lionel could reply the boat grounded, and the boys had to take their places.

It was evident that there were mysteries about Lake Island School which had yet to be seen into.

CHAPTER XIII.

THE LANDING IN LAKE ISLAND—THE MATHEMATICAL TREES AND THE UNMATHEMATICAL STUDENTS—MR. STIFFBACK'S NEW METHOD OF TEACHING GEOMETRY—THE SCHOOLROOM—THE FIRST NIGHT IN LAKE ISLAND SCHOOL—THE FIRST MORNING—AN INTRODUCTION TO THE NEW PATENT FLOGGING-MACHINE.

THE situation of Lake Island was as utterly unlike anything which the new arrivals had ever seen or heard, except—perhaps, in a picture or book—that their curiosity kept them silent as they neared their future home.

There was one peculiarity about the island which struck Lionel at once, and that was the mathematical regularity of everything.

The trees were all as much alike in size and shape as those seen in a Dutch landscape, and were, besides, arranged in curious lines and curves, the object of which puzzled him very much, especially when he saw five or six boys marching in and out among them, each one following his own track, advancing and retiring as if they were practising some new kind of quadrille without the music.

At sight of this strange performance Lionel could no longer restrain his curiosity, and he whispered to Vansittart—

"What the dickens are those fellows up to there among the trees?"

"Hush!" was the reply. "Don't talk now; I'll tell you by-and-by."

A moment or two after the boat grounded at the foot of a neatly-paved causeway, where all alighted except the six rowers, who, Lionel fancied, cast a mute, appealing glance at Mr. Stiffback's cold, inflexible visage.

"I say," whispered Charlie to our hero, "these chaps don't seem to like their job much. How glumpy they look. Now, I should just fancy a row on such a day as this."

"So should I," replied Lionel; "but the further we get the queerer things seem to be. Look at those chaps among the trees."

"It *is* queer," said Charlie; "they don't look as if they were enjoying themselves."

"Perhaps it's the way they take exercise," suggested Lionel.

"Can't be. No fellow would be such a fool as to walk about in that sort of way."

"Then it's a game of some sort."

"Not it, Li. Who ever saw fellows playing any game with such miserable mugs as they've got?"

"Then this must be a lunatic asylum for boys," said our hero, with a laugh. "What on earth can it be else?"

"We shall find out all about it in a little while. Hallo! here's Tommy and the Bobbles family."

"Look at the one Tommy propped. He's got a beautiful black eye already."

"Yes, hasn't he! I wonder if Stiffback knows how he got it?"

"If he doesn't he'll find out. There's a queer look about him that I don't fancy much. We shall have to mind what we're at, Charlie."

"It's lucky we made a chum of Vansittart, then. He'll put us up to the dodges."

"I expect we shall have to find the dodges out for ourselves," replied Lionel; "we're green here, you know, and green hands always have to pay for experience."

And indeed before long our hero found that his guess was unpleasantly correct.

Further conversation was now checked by Mr. Stiffback himself, who, approaching our hero and his friends, smiled benignly upon them.

"Well, young gentlemen," he said, "what do you think of Lake Island?"

"I like what I have seen very much, sir," said Lionel, "but ——"

"But!" repeated Mr. Stiffback. "What is there behind that 'but,' Wilful?"

"I was only going to say," replied our hero, a little confused, "that—that there are—some things which I can't quite make out."

"Aha! Those young gentlemen yonder, for instance?"

"Yes, sir."

"Now, tell me what you thought when you first saw them walking amongst the trees in that manner."

"I couldn't account for it at all, sir. Neither could Charlie. So we set them down as lunatics."

Mr. Stiffback very nearly laughed. He never did quite by any chance, but this time he was very near it.

"Come with me," he said. "I will explain to you in some measure the practical system of education pursued here. You too, Vansittart."

Lionel and Charlie looked inquiringly at their new chum, but that young gentleman was as grave in appearance as Mr. Stiffback himself, in whose wake they followed until the first supposed lunatic was reached.

He was slowly plodding along the sides of some saplings, neatly arranged in the form of an equilateral triangle, and he looked as though his situation didn't agree with him.

He stopped at a sign from Mr. Stiffback, and looked at the schoolmaster with a gloomy expression.

"Well, Jinkleberry," said Mr. Stiffback; "are you fully impressed with the signification of the word equilateral?"

"Quite, sir," replied Jinkleberry. "I'd take an oath that all the sides are equal."

"Tut, tut, tut, Jinkleberry, you mustn't speak in that way. You are too excited, and you will please to continue studying the equilateral triangle till dinner-time."

A short groan escaped the wretched Jinkleberry, but Mr. Stiffback took no notice of it, and marched on to the next victim.

This unhappy youth was staggering unsteadily round the circumference of a circle of saplings, bringing himself up wish a jolt against the trunks at every third step.

The casual observer might have supposed him to be drunk, but he was not, he was only giddy.

"This boy," Mr. Stiffback proceeded blandly to explain, "was utterly unable to understand the proportion which the diameter of a circle bears to its circumference. He is now making himself practically acquainted with the subject."

"He is certainly making himself practically acquainted with the bark of the trees," thought our hero, as the giddy youth pursued his weary round.

"Well, what do you think of my system?" asked Mr. Stiffback.

"I have no doubt it's a—a capital one, sir; but I'd rather learn my geometry out of Enclid."

"So would these boys, I have no doubt," said the schoolmaster; "but if their intellects are too dull to comprehend the diagrams, they must learn in this way. Mr. Vansittart, I leave Wilful and Drummond in your charge. It wants an hour to dinner-time, and during that hour you will explain as much of the ways of the place as you can."

"I beg your pardon, sir," said Charlie, as the schoolmaster turned to go away; "but Codlings and Sam, they are strangers too. Aren't they to come with us?"

"They are not," replied Mr. Stiffback, emphatically. "They are under arrest, and you may consider yourselves fortunate that you are not similarly situated."

A cold chill crept down Lionel's back.

What did "under arrest" signify at Lake Island School?

Vansittart was the one to answer that question, and to him our hero applied.

"What's up? What's going to be done to them?" he said.

"I don't know yet, neither does Stiffback himself yet; you see this is what he would call a bad case; as the pupils were known to be his, it is likely to create a scandal about the character of the school."

"And what will he do, then?"

"Well, he may have 'em welted."

"Caned, I suppose you mean?"

Vansittart nodded.

"Well, that don't matter much. Tommy don't mind it any more than a door-mat, and Sam 'll take it quietly if I speak to him."

"Oh! that's all very well. You're thinking of an ordinary welting, when the master lays it on himself, but old Stiffback does it by machinery."

"What?" ejaculated Lionel and Charlie together.

"Ah! I thought that would startle you. Everything in the place is done by machinery that it is possible to do; but you'll see the affair yourselves."

"I don't half like this place now I'm in it," said Charlie; "eh, Li?"

"Oh! it'll turn out all right when we've got used to it," replied our hero. "But there are, certainly, some queer games about the place though."

"Queerer than you think," said Vansittart, with a laugh. "But come, I've got to show you the island, and explain the rules, and there's not too much time between now and luncheon, or dinner, as Stiffback calls it."

What these rules were, and how they impressed Lionel and his chum, we shall show as this story progresses; for the present it is enough to say that what they heard made them exceedingly curious to hear more, and rendered stronger than ever their belief that Mr. Stiffback was an exceedingly queer customer, and with those ideas impressed upon them, they went to dinner.

Mr. Stiffback had luckily not carried his eccentric liking for improvement into the kitchen, possibly because of the well-known obstinacy or conservatism of all cooks, who dislike nothing so much as being interfered with.

It was a much better meal in quantity and quality than the generality of school dinners, and our hero ate with an appetite.

The only thing that disturbed him was the absence of Sam and Tommy.

"They peck by themselves," whispered Vansittart; "all the fellows do who are in disgrace for anything."

"I almost wish I'd been caught in the waggonette now," said Lionel. "It seems mean that Tommy and Sam should suffer, and we get off."

"Not a bit of it," replied Vansittart. "Our luck to-day may be theirs to-morrow, Wilful. Never put your nose into more hornets' nests than you can help."

"Well, I suppose you're right. What shall we have to do this afternoon?"

"There's a quarter of an hour's leave after dinner with which to do as we like. Suppose I take you into the school-room; you'll get an idea of the place, and it won't be so strange to you when you go in for good."

"When will that be?"

"Not till to-morrow. Stiffback will put you through your exam. to-day, and he'll name the class he thinks you're fit for."

The school-room was a large, airy, well-ventilated place, lit from the top by an arched skylight, like that of the nave of the Crystal Palace in miniature. At one end of the room was a raised platform, whereon was Mr. Stiffback's stool and desk.

The boys forms and desks were arranged in semi-circular rows in front of the platform, and the whole place had that orderly mathematical aspect which our hero had already noticed in the arrangement of the trees on the island.

Lionel shrugged his shoulders.

Charlie shivered, as if he felt cold.

"How do you like the look of the place?" said Vansittart.

"It don't look very lively," said Charlie.

"Reminds one of a penitentiary," added Lionel.

"It will be lively enough presently, Wilful, when all the masters are at their desks, and the classes busy; but come, it's time for you to go to the governor."

The examination was soon over, but to the disgust both of Lionel and Charlie, who were rather proud of their scholarship, Mr. Stiffback assigned them a very low place in the school, giving as his reason, the opinion that the knowledge the boys had acquired, was in great part utterly useless, and that they would have to begin all over again.

"You will take your places in the school this afternoon," said Mr. Stiffback; "but you will not be required to stand up in your class. You will also have an opportunity of observing the system of punishment I have adopted. It may serve as a useful lesson to you."

"Hallo!" said our hero, as he and Charlie left the library. "That means poor Tommy and Sam are to be introduced to the flogging machine."

"Looks like it. I say, Li, there's something precious cold-blooded and uncomfortable in the idea of being welted in that way."

"You're right. It makes one think of the torture chambers of the Inquisition."

The school-room did indeed look lively enough, as Vansittart had predicted, when Lionel and Charlie entered it.

The boys, to the number of nearly a hundred, were seated on the forms, and the under masters at their desks, which were behind the pupils, were keeping a sharp look out for any breaches of discipline.

They took their places, and directly afterwards Mr. Stiffback entered, followed by the Bobbles family and Tommy.

Sam was nowhere visible.

"Hallo, he's let Sam off," whispered Lionel. "I say, don't those chaps look down in the mouth, all except Tommy; he looks as if he expected a gold medal?"

"He's been slipping into 'em again," replied Drummond. "Don't you see two more of 'em have got black eyes?"

"So they have. What a vicious little beggar Tommy is getting; when I first knew him he had no more fight in him than a cold dumpling."

"There's the coachman behind, the one who was tight on the waggonette. I wonder if he's going to be flogged by machinery, Li?"

"Not much—I expect he's the executioner."

And so it proved, for the coachman, mounting on the platform, opened the door of a sort of cupboard, and hauled out and wheeled out first a wooden apparatus resembling the stocks or pillory used in England a century or so ago, and then the famous flogging machine, looking like a gigantic cotton reel mounted on a stand, and bristling all over with long flexible canes.

Mr. Stiffback looked upon this apparatus with an eye of affectionate admiration, and then unfolding a paper he held in his hand, read aloud—

"The four elder Bobbles and Thomas Codlings, caught in the commission of riotous and disorderly acts in the town of Deliverham, whereby not only

were they disgraced, but the character of the school imperilled, are adjudged to be flogged. They will endure the flogging during twelve revolutions of the handle; the two younger Bobbles will endure each six revolutions of the handle. Soker, do your duty."

The coachman advanced with a grin, and laid hold of Tommy by the arm.

Poor Tommy was limp and horror-stricken.

It was like going to be hung, and when he felt his head and hands imprisoned in the pillory, he gave a yell of terror—he couldn't help it.

CHAPTER XIV.

TOMMY HAS HIS FIRST TASTE OF THE PATENT FLOGGING-MACHINE, AND DOESN'T LIKE IT—HIS AGONY, AND SUBSEQUENT REVENGE UPON SOKER—MR. STIFFBACK'S OPINION UPON THE VULGARITY OF FIGHTING, AND HIS CURE FOR THE VICTIMS OF THE VICE.

THERE was a curious expression visible upon Mr. Stiffback's features as the first victim was imprisoned in the pillory—an expression of pleasure and of a grave kind of joy, which induced one to think at first that the schoolmaster was one of those inhuman creatures to whom the infliction of pain is a keen gratification.

But to do him justice, Mr. Stiffback had no such thought in his head—he was a scientific man to the core—the flogging-machine was his pet invention, and it was for that, and not for the victims, that his smile of pleasure was intended.

In fact, if the question had been put to him, we doubt whether he would not have thought it rather nice than otherwise to be caned by an instrument of such perfection.

We need hardly say that his pupils disagreed with him upon this point.

"Handle them gently, Soker," he said to the coachman, who probably felt bad after his dissipation; "do not be s rough.

"Wot did he kick me in the shin for?" growled Soker, as he flopped the last of the Bobbles into the pillory.

And he brought down the top bar of the structure with a crash, as if it had been the knife of a guillotine.

"Ow-ow—yah!" yelled Tommy, "he's pushed some of my skin in. Let me out?"

But Soker only grinned malevolently, and Mr. Stiffback, thinking, no doubt, that our hero and Charlie, as new boys, would greatly enjoy the sight of such a piece of mechanism in operation, called them to take their places in the front row.

"You see the advantages which my system possesses," said Mr. Stiffback to Lionel, while Soker was adjusting the flogging-machine.

"The ordinary way of administering chastisement to a refractory pupil is merely a brutalising exhibition of the superior physical power of a man over a boy. The pupil kicks and struggles not unfrequently, and the master consequently becomes red in the face, and disordered in his costume, presenting an unseemly spectacle. By my method all that is avoided, and mind triumphs over matter."

Lionel and Charlie listened as gravely as they could, but it was no easy matter, for the sight of that row of heads sticking helplessly out of the pillory was inexpressibly comic.

The Bobbles family had evidently undergone the ordeal before, for they only looked miserable; but Tommy was fairly scared—his mouth was wide open, his little round eyes were about starting out of his head, and his colour was a pale green.

"All ready, Soker?" said Mr. Stiffback, as if he were in command of a battery of artillery, and about to give the order to fire.

"Yes, sir," replied Soker, hoisting his hands and grasping the crank.

"Then proceed. Twelve revolutions, Soker."

Soker went at it with a will, for the Bobbles family were his special aversion, as they never "tipped" him at the end of the half, and always grumbled about the polish of their boots.

Round went the instrument of torture, and "Swish—smack!—Swish—smack!" down came the limber whalebone upon the tightly stretched trousers of the victims.

"Poor old Tommy," thought Lionel; "it must be awful. The whacks all come on the same place."

Round went the crank again, this time with greater rapidity, for Soker had got way on.

The whalebone struck with a sharper sound, and five pairs of youthful legs began to jerk in agony.

"Bear up, Tommy," whispered Lionel; "be plucky—show 'em you don't care for it."

Tommy heard the encouraging voice of his chum, and tried hard to play the hero.

He shut his mouth and clenched his teeth, but he was getting very red in the face, and at the third round the tears began to lay the dust upon the floor.

Soker was in full play now.

He ground away like a mad organ-grinder, and at the fifth revolution music began.

The Bobbles family were too genteel to howl in a vulgar way, but they all groaned miserably in a minor key, while Tommy shrieked an ear-splitting alto.

He had held on as long as he could, but this new flogging by machinery was more than a plump boy could be expected to bear.

"Dear me," said Mr. Stiffback, placidly, "what a noise that boy makes!"

"So would you," muttered Lionel, "if you were fixed up in that confounded machine. Hang it, I'd like to give you a taste."

"Poor Tommy'll have a fit," whispered Charlie. "He's black in the face now with howling."

"Enough to make him. Look at the way that beggar's turning the handle! We'll pay him out for this, Charlie."

"Right you are, Li. Thank goodness it's over, though. There goes the last turn."

The last turn, as Charlie called it, was made by Soker, who threw all his energy into it, and brought from Tommy a yell of unparalleled power and shrillness.

Then Mr. Stiffback gave the signal to stop, and Soker, with the satisfied air of a man who has done his duty, and done it well, mopped his face with a snuffy red cotton handkerchief, unfastened the staple, and released the victims.

The moment he was set free, the smarting Tommy clapped both his hands upon that portion of his frame which had suffered most, and danced a double-shuffle expressive of intense agony.

"Oh, my! Oh, dear! Oh, lor! How it smarts! Oh, you brute! I'll serve you out for this!"

And just then, catching sight of Soker with a particularly aggravating grin on his countenance, Tommy danced up to him and gave him one on the shin.

It was Soker's turn to roar now, for he was like a nigger, very sensitive in the region of the shin, and he danced vis-à-vis to Tommy, holding his injured leg with one hand, and shaking the other at his assailant.

Mr. Stiffback raised his eyebrows, and looked at the new pupil with mild surprise.

"Really, Codlings," he said, "this is most ungentlemanly behaviour."

"Ungentlemanly be blowed!" roared the reckless and wrathful Tommy. "How do you think anybody can behave himself when he's smarting as if he'd been mustard-plastered all over?"

"Tut, tut, tut!" said Mr. Stiffback. "I fear you have been very badly trained, Codlings. Your language is most gross, and quite unbefitting the station which I presume you are intended to fill. Soker, you will put him in the machine again, with the two younger Bobbles."

"I won't!" roared Tommy. "Just you lay a finger on me."

But the revengeful Soker had expected the order, and when it came, he pounced on his victim like a spider on a fly.

Tommy only had time to give him one more "shinner," and then he was lifted up and pilloried again in company with the two youngest of the Bobbles family.

"'Pon my word it's a shame," whispered Lionel. "A dozen from that machine's enough for a nigger."

"Let's groan?" suggested Charlie.

"No, we'd better not; it might only make it worse for Tommy. But I say, Charlie."

"What old boy?"

"I'll spoil that machine for old Stiffback, before long."

"I'll lend a hand, Li, for I've got a strong suspicion that if we don't you and I will be tucked up in it before long."

Lionel shrugged up his shoulders as if something cold had gone down his back, for he was much of the same opinion as his chum.

Tommy took his last half-dozen in the gentlemanly manner prescribed by Mr. Stiffback—that is to say he did not yell, and when he was set free he made no further attempt on Soker's shins.

"That is much better, Codlings," said the schoolmaster, approvingly. "We shall improve you in time, but there is one most ungentlemanly vice of which you must instantly get rid."

Tommy was aware of a most ungentlemanly pain from which he was suffering and with which he would gladly have parted.

"Napoleon Bobbles and Julius Cæsar Bobbles stand forward," said Mr. Stiffback.

Napoleon Bobbles was the gloomy young gentleman whom Tommy had "propped" in the waiting room, and Julius Cæsar Bobbles had been similarly decorated in the privacy of the prison chamber of Lake Island school.

"That," continued Mr. Stiffback, waving his hand in the direction of the two black eyes, "is your handiwork, Codlings, and it is evidence of a low tendency to fight, or, as it is vulgarly styled, punch your fellow-creatures' heads."

Tommy smiled a gratified smile as he looked upon the closed peepers of his adversaries, and he was about to express his readiness to serve the remaining four of the family in the same way, when it occurred to him that he had better hold his tongue.

"You do not deny it, I suppose, Codlings?" said Mr. Stiffback.

"Oh, no, sir," replied Tommy, cheerfully. "I punched their heads."

"Ah, you punched their heads, and both in the course of the same day. Now, Codlings, that goes far to prove that you are fond of fighting, and as I will admit that the exercise itself is healthy, I will allow you to have enough of it. Soker, bring out Magog, but first put away the machine."

CHAPTER XV.

MAGOG—TOMMY HAS A FEW ROUNDS WITH A TOUGH CUSTOMER—FIRST KNOCK DOWN BLOW TO MAGOG—A TOUR OF INSPECTION—IN THE DORMITORY—MRS. CITRON AND THE HAMPERS—VANSITTART MAKES AN INTERESTING COMMUNICATION—A SHORT ACCOUNT OF SLOGGING STINGER—IN TRAINING FOR THE FIGHT—VANSITTART'S PROMISE.

"WHAT on earth is he going to do with Tommy now?" whispered Lionel. "Who's Magog?"

"I don't know," in the same cautious tone, "except that Magog's one of the Lord Mayor's giants, and kept in the Guildhall."

"Yes, I know. But it can't be that Magog, Charlie."

"We shall see. There goes old Soker to fetch it."

And the coachman, or footman, having first carefully put away the machine behind the door of the recess, opened another, whence he dragged into the light of day a queer looking figure, about four feet high, bearing some distant likeness to a boy with his arms extended at right angles to his body.

Suspended to each of its wrists was a bag as large as a man's head, and evidently containing flour or some similar substance.

"Of all the cribs I ever heard of this is the queerest. What in the name of wonder is he going to make Tommy do with that?"

But Lionel's wondering were soon satisfied by Mr. Stiffback himself, for, pointing to the figure, he said—

"There, Codlings, is your opponent. Since you relish fighting so greatly, you shall fight that till tea time. Take off your jacket and begin."

Poor Tommy looked stupefied, and glanced vacantly first at Mr. Stiffback and then at Magog. If there had been a live boy put up for him to punch, Tommy would have gone in for him with a will, especially if it had been one of the Bobbles family; but this wooden image—it was too ridiculous.

"Go on, Codlings," said Mr. Stiffback, in the same bland tone; "take off your jacket, I say, and begin to fight; you are really remarkably slow for a boy who is so fond of that sport."

Slowly and reluctantly Tommy peeled, rolled up his shirt-sleeves, and put up his hands.

"Go on," said Mr. Stiffback, encouragingly; "you have courage enough to fight two living boys, and surely you are not afraid of a carven image."

"Fire away, Tommy," whispered Lionel, as loudly as he dared. "Show a little science, and put your left well in on his conk."

"Dash the thing!" thought Tommy; "if I am to practice boxing I may as well go in a buster. I wish I could knock him over."

So saying, Tommy feinted with his right in the most scientific manner, and then landed a beauty on the right eye of the image.

The result was startling, for no sooner was the blow struck than the figure swung round on a pivot, its right arm catching Tommy full on the side of the head, while a cloud of white dust flew out of the bag, powdering him from head to foot.

A roar of laughter went up from the youthful spectators—Lionel and Charlie, to whom this spectacle was quite new, being specially amused.

Tommy sat on the floor, rubbing his head with one hand, and blinking in a wondering way at Magog. Was it alive? he thought; could it be a real boy made up to look like a dummy? At all events, the pain in his head and the flour in his eyes were real enough, and scrambling to his feet he felt as angry as if he had been facing an antagonist of flesh and blood.

"Go on, Codlings," said Mr. Stiffback, "you will please to fight with Magog until tea time; you need not be afraid of tiring your opponent."

Another roar of laughter followed the schoolmaster's little joke, but Lionel, as soon as he had his laugh out, whispered to Charlie—

"I say, do you think Stiffback can be right in his head? Whoever heard of making a fellow do such a thing as that?"

"He's a rum one, that's certain," replied Charlie,

"but he can't be mad, you know, Li, or he'd never be allowed to keep a school."

"Well, we shall see. Ha, ha! There goes Tommy down again; he's no match for the dummy."

"Silence, young gentlemen," said Mr. Stiffback; "the classes will resume their respective studies. Codlings, go on with your fighting; if you desist for an instant, until I give you permission, I shall have you flogged again. Now Soker, I want to have a few words with you."

"Hallo!" thought Lionel, "he's going to catch it for getting tight. I wish old Stiffback would put him in the flogging-machine and let me turn the crank."

"Now, Soker," continued the schoolmaster, "I am grieved that all my exhortations to you to abjure the filthy vice of intoxication have failed, and that my advice has been utterly thrown away upon you."

Soker, abashed, murmured a feeble negative.

"But it is so. I place you in charge of a waggonette, and entrust you with the lives and limbs of a number of my pupils—a most responsible charge—and you show your sense of the responsibility by getting helplessly drunk. It was necessary to pump upon you for fully a quarter of an hour before you showed a sign of animation."

"I certainly were wet," murmured Mr. Soker.

"So, as advice fails, and to discharge you would in all probability only drive you to worse, I will try a course which will, I think, prove effectual."

"Thankee, sir," murmured Soker, rather timidly, for he stood much in awe of Mr. Stiffback.

"You wish to be cured of your bad habit, of course?"

Mr. Soker replied that he did, but his expression said that he didn't.

"What liquors do you prefer, now, when you indulge in this degrading vice?"

"Well, sir," said Soker, smacking his lips thoughtfully, "I ain't wery pertikler."

"Any kind of beer?" suggested Mr. Stiffback.

"Well, beer ain't bad, but it in gen'ral takes such a lot, that a man gets uncomf't'ble afore he's swipy."

"Swipy—that means drunk, I suppose?"

"It do," said Soker, with an evident knowledge of his subject.

"Spirits answer the purpose better, then?"

"Wery much so, sir," said Soker, wondering what on earth his master was driving at.

"And what particular spirit has your preference, Soker?"

"Well, in my 'pinion, sir, there ain't nothing to ekal good old meller whiskey."

"But I suppose you can drink other kinds—gin, for instance, or brandy?"

"Oh, yes, sir," replied Soker, warming with a subject on which he was so well qualified to speak, "I don't say nothink agin 'em. They're wery good in their way."

"You shall have an opportunity of trying them all, then, Soker. You will come here punctually to-morrow morning, at nine o'clock, and every day after, for a week, and get drunk if you please."

Never was a man more startled than Soker. He stared up at his employer wide-eyed and open-mouthed. He had expected at the very least a severe reprimand, but instead of that here was Mr. Stiffback encouraging him to indulge in his favourite vice.

"Thankee, sir," he said, as soon as he had satisfied himself that his ears had heard rightly, "I'll be punctual, sir."

And away he went, the grin widening upon his face as he thought of the treat in store for him on the morrow.

"There's another go," whispered Charlie. "'Pon my word, Li, I begin to think that he must be cranky."

"Not he. He's wide awake in this case. He means to make this chap drink such a lot that he'll get sick of it."

"Ah, I see, just as the grocers do when they take a new apprentice—let him have the run of the shop, till in a week the sight of a fig makes him ill."

"That's it, and we, you know, are supposed to take example as the Spartan youth used to do when the Helots were made drunk on purpose to show 'em what a beast a tipsy man looks."

"Here, blow all that, Li. We ain't in class to-day, and Greek history at second-hand isn't amusing. Look at Tommy, that's better fun."

"I wish we could get out again with Vansittart. I want to get put up to the rigs of this place."

"I don't half like it, Li."

"That's because you don't understand it yet. I'll bet that we'll get some splendid fun out of this crib."

"Oh! oh! how about being caught and tucked up in that dashed machine?"

"You won't mind that when you're used to it, Charlie."

"If ever he offers to have me flogged with it I'll shy a ruler at him and bolt."

"No you wouldn't, Charlie; you can stand a whacking better than Tommy, surely?"

"I don't know that. Tommy was always plucky enough at old Styngy's. The torture must have been something dreadful to have made him howl like that."

"It wasn't the pain, Charlie. He funked the machine just as you're doing now."

"Funk or not, I'll do something to Stiffback and bolt, if he attempts to flog me in it."

"It's all very well to talk about bolting, Charlie; but how are you going to do it? You forget you are on an island."

"I can swim."

"You can't do half-a-mile with your clothes on."

"I'll try."

"Besides, if you could, there's the boat."

"That isn't always on the look out."

"Yes, it is. Don't you remember Vansittart told us that those fellows who rowed us over were there as a punishment, and when their time's up there'll be others to take their places."

"Not at night, though."

"Oh, shut up, Charlie! Don't let's think about getting off Lake Island when we've only just got on. What's made you so funky?"

"I'm not funky, Li; but I don't understand these goings on."

"Then wait till you do," laughed Lionel.

"Wilful and Drummond, you are talking and interrupting the classes," said the voice of Mr. Stiffback. "I excuse you to-day, as you are new arrivals, but to-morrow be careful, or you will be punished."

Our hero and his chum were silent as mice.

The sight of the flogging-machine in operation had produced a profound impression on them.

"Vansittart," continued Mr. Stiffback, "you can take the new pupils out and show them the house. They are doing no good there, and may as well familiarise themselves with their future home."

Vansittart arose from his seat, winked slyly at Lionel, and led the way out of the school-room.

"You're in luck, young fellows," he said, as soon as they were fairly out of hearing.

"How's that? Charlie here was just saying he'd run away as soon as he could."

"What for?"

"Because of the flogging-machine. He's frightened of it."

"I'm not, Li; and it isn't fair of you to say so. I said I thought Stiffback was mad."

"There's method in his madness, young Drummond," replied Vansittart; "and a precious deep method, too, as you'll soon find out. His queer ways startle a new fellow at first. But when you get used to him he's prime fun."

"That's just what I told Charlie," said Lionel.

"And that's what he'll find out for himself if he only has a little patience. But come along, and I'll show you the dormitories."

They were situated on the third floor, and reached by a well staircase.

From the landing at the top of the staircase, a number of passages branched out like the spokes of a wheel from the hub, and in these passages were the doors leading to the dormitories.

"What a queer way of building a house!"

"It is rather. It's Stiffback's own idea. Some ventilating dodge or another. You see the numbers over each passage? That's the number of the class."

"What's yours? Number one, I suppose?"

"Number seven. We begin to count from the bottom. You're both in number three. This is your passage. Don't forget it when you come to bed to-night."

"Why? Are there any larks played on new boys?"

"There might be," said Vansittart, meaningly, "especially if you get into the wrong passage."

He pushed open the door as he spoke, and our hero and Charlie following, found themselves in a large, well-lit, well-ventilated room, provided with some fifteen small iron bedsteads, and the usual furniture of a bedroom.

Everything was exquisitely clean and neat, and a stout, matronly-looking woman was bending over the contents of two trunks, which Lionel and Charlie instantly recognised as their property.

She stood up and nodded pleasantly at Vansittart, and then at our young friends.

"Glad to see me back, eh, Mrs. Citron?" said Vansittart, with a smile.

"Yes, I am, and that's what I couldn't say with a clear conscience for too many in this school. Ah, if you boys only knew what a worry and a nuisance you are to grown people, you'd never be born at all."

"Come, Mrs. Citron," laughed the young aristocrat, "you must have a better opinion of my friends here than that. Two first-rate fellows, I assure you."

"Oh, I daresay they are!" replied the matron, with a doubtful shake of her head, as she looked kindly, even good-humouredly, at Lionel and Charlie. "But if I know anything of boys, and I ought to by this time, they're a couple of as saucy young imps as ever plagued a body's life out!"

"Thank you for the compliment," said Lionel, with a laugh. "But you might have waited till you found us out."

"It won't be long before that happens, I'm thinking," said Mrs. Citron. "But if you two young gentlemen's names are Wilful and Drummond, there's two hampers downstairs which mustn't come into the dormitory."

"Hampers, eh?" said Vansittart; "and something good inside, Mrs. Citron?"

"Something bad, I should say," replied the matron; "something that'll bring the doctor here with his pills and black draughts, and give me another job of nursing. If we may judge by the weight of 'em, there's enough in the hampers to spoil the digestion of a good twenty of you."

"I say, that's promising," said Vansittart, who, though he felt the manly pride of eighteen, had not relinquished the wholesome appetite for jam and such-like toothsome delicacies in favour of tobacco and beer. "You'll invite me to the feast, eh, Wilful?"

"Rather. But what's the rule here about prog?"

WITHOUT A MOMENT'S WARNING THE MATTRESSES, SLEEPERS, AND BED CLOTHES WERE SHOT UP IN THE AIR.

No. 20.

"Oh, Stiffback's a good fellow in that way. There's a strict rule against buying anything in the town, but if a new boy brings any prog from home, he may do what he likes with it. We'll have a picnic to-morrow."

"Is it a half-holiday?"

"There are no regular holidays. Stiffback's plan is to give 'em when the fancy takes him. We generally have one, though, a day or two after new fellows come, for he likes the pupils to get acquainted and chummy."

"All right; but I must get you to make up the party; and suppose we have a look in the hampers, and see how far they'll go. It won't do to invite too many."

"A sensible thought, young Wilful. I remember a fellow last half inviting nearly the whole school, and when they came, expecting no end of good things, he'd only got a stale cake and half a bottle of currant wine—not enough for a crumb apiece."

Motherly Mrs. Citron led them down to the store-room, where the hampers were, and soon the treasures of cakes, candied fruits, jars of preserves, guava jelly, Chinese ginger, packets of sweets, and sundry bottles of wine, delicious to the palate, but innocent of any intoxicating property, were unearthed.

"My dear boys," said Mrs. Citron, "it's fortunate for you that Mr. Stiffback doesn't look into these matters himself, or he'd certainly order Soker to sink all that in the bottom of the lake."

"We'll bury it in a better place, matron," laughed Vansittart. "You have got a heap of good things, young fellows; but there is one thing I advise you to do."

"What's that?"

"Ask Mrs. Citron to take care of a portion of that guava jelly and the preserved ginger for you. You won't be able to get such stuff down here."

"I don't like keeping anything back," said Lionel, doubtfully; "it looks greedy."

"Not at all. If you were only to share half with the fellows, it would be the best tuck-out this half. Better do as I tell you."

So it was done, and the kind-hearted matron readily consented to take charge of a portion of the choice delicacies.

"Suppose we have a taste now," said Charlie, whose mouth had been set watering by the sight of the eatables, though it was not long past dinner-time.

"You can if you like," said Vansittart. "I'll wait; I mustn't touch anything of that sort for awhile."

"Why not?"

Vansittart looked round to see that Mrs. Citron was not within hearing distance, and then said, in a low tone—

"I'm in training for a fight!"

The boys' eyes sparkled as the eyes of English boys' will do at the prospect of a fight, and both said, eagerly—

"Who with? When is it coming off? You'll let us come?"

"Hush! I'll tell you more about it directly. Peg into your cake first."

But Lionel and Charlie had their appetites taken away by Vansittart's communication, and they both declared that they didn't want any, and showed a readiness to hurry away from the "good things," which Mrs. Citron, who had now come back armed with a carving knife, quite failed to understand.

"Well," she said, "you boys are a puzzle as well as a plague. I can't make you out, and I'm not going to try. There, go along with you!"

And they did go along, one on each side of Vansittart, eager to hear more news of the coming fight.

"I didn't mean to say anything about it, but I've taken a fancy to you fellows; I know you're true-blue, and won't split."

"You may be certain of that. But who are you going to fight?"

"A fellow who belongs to the town. He's the son of a man in the pig-jobbing line. He's about two years older than I am, and built like a bull. I shall have a precious tough job, I expect."

"But you'll lick him, of course?" said Lionel, looking with admiration at Vansittart's lithe, active frame, to every sinew and muscle of which judicious exercise had given the strength and elasticity of steel.

"I hope so," laughed the young champion; "I shall certainly try hard, for the conceit and bounce of the fellow are past bearing."

"Is that why you're going to fight him?" asked Lionel.

"Yes, partly. You see he's a quarrelsome, bragging chap, and up to now he's thrashed everyone who stood up to him. Well, when he found that he had pasted or bullied everybody till no one dared come near him, he began to brag, and whenever any of the Lake Island School went into the town he'd drop on them, fight them if they were big enough, or steal their caps, and drench 'em with water if they were young 'uns."

"What a confounded bully!" said Lionel, his face flushing. "I should like to have a go at him myself."

"That would never do, Wilful," said Vansittart, laughing. "You're a good plucky 'un to say it though. Well, to go on with my story, all this that I'm telling you happened before I came, and the school was in such a state of funk, that no one ever dared go into the town, as, just before my arrival, he'd pitched into one of our masters—an Oxford man he was, too, and no bad hand with his fists—and knocked him about so that he was laid up for a fortnight."

"The dickins he did!" exclaimed Lionel, beginning to feel his confidence in the young champion's chance of success a great deal weakened.

"So I resolved to see if I couldn't put a stop to what was getting a regular nuisance, and more than that, a disgrace to the school."

"That was plucky of you, Vansittart. Bothered if I should like to challenge a chap who was able to lick a man."

"Oh, but you see I'm eighteen, Wilful, as strong as most fellows of my age, and as to science, I ought to be a good boxer, for I was taught by the best light-weight in London; but don't think I'm bragging in my turn. I only want you to understand all about it."

"There's no brag in you," said Lionel. "Don't fear that we shall think that of you."

"Well, I went over Deliverham the first chance I could get, but Stinger wasn't there, and after a bit I found out that his father had sent him away for a while, thinking that his son would get into trouble for licking our Latin master."

"Was the Latin master going to lock him up?" asked Charlie.

"Not he. He was too much of a gentleman to bear malice for a licking got in a fair fight, though he felt the disgrace so much that he left the school as soon as he was able to go."

"It was hard lines to be thrashed by a lout."

"Wasn't it. Well, I must cut on, or I shall never get to the end of my story. So when I found that the son was gone, I went to see the father, and a nice old party he is."

"Like father like son," said Charlie.

"'Tis so in this case, for he's as proud of young Stinger as if he was Commander-in-Chief of the army. 'Well,' he says, looking at me as I went in, 'and wot do you want?' 'I wished to see your son,' said I. 'And who be you? and wot do 'ee want to see Bill for?' 'I want,' said I as politely as possible, to give him a thrashing.' You should lave heard the old man laugh when I said this. 'Wot!' said he, 'thee wollop my Bill? why he'll eat thee. Be 'ee one 'o the Lake Island bwoys?' 'Yes,' said I, 'I'm a new pupil, and I want to try my luck with your Bill.'"

"I should like to have seen the conceited old beast. I hope you'll lick young Stinger, Vansittart."

"Don't interrupt, there's a good chap," said Vansittart. "Somehow the old man was suspicious of me, and fancied that we wanted his son back in order to charge him with assaulting the Latin master, and he managed somehow to keep Bill away till the end of last half, when I dropped on him in the town."

"Why didn't you fight then?"

"He'd poisoned his right hand, and had got a fist as big as a summer cabbage; but, to do the fellow justice, he was as eager to fight as I was, and we arranged that the fight should come off the first week in this half. I shall send a note to him this evening, and make the appointment for Monday."

"Will that be a holiday?" said Lionel, eagerly. "Shall we be able to go?"

"The fellows in our form are allowed to take a day once a month, for a free holiday, and I'll try and bring up a couple of passes for you."

"How can you do that?"

"Easily enough. If a fellow doesn't want his holiday he can transfer it to anyone else he likes. I daresay there are a couple who will sell their day for five shillings apiece."

"I'd give a sovereign sooner than miss it," said Lionel, producing his purse. "I've got plenty of money."

"So have I," said Charlie, pulling out a handful, and dropping half of it in his eagerness to secure a chance for a view of the great fight.

"Then keep it, and take care of it," said Vansittart. "I'll arrange matters for you. Hullo! there's the tea bell already, and I haven't shown you the house yet."

"Blow the house!" said Lionel, "we'll find out all about that for ourselves. Don't forget your promise, Vansittart, or I'll never forgive you."

Vansittart smiled and nodded, and the next moment Lionel and his chums were mixed up in the throng of boys, hurrying tumultuously towards the tea-room.

CHAPTER XVI.

LIONEL'S PIC-NIC PARTY, AND SUNDRY IMPORTANT EVENTS WHICH FOLLOWED IT — THE RIVAL SCHOOL—CAPTURE OF THE ENEMY'S BAGGAGE— THE CHASE—A BATTLE IN THE WATER.

THE intelligence that the new boys were about to give a "spread" soon communicated itself to the hundred or so of units who made up the great total of Lake Island School, and the number of new friends who desired the honour of Lionel's and Charlie's acquaintance was great indeed.

"Confound it!" said our hero; "if I'd known, I'd have brought twice as much. It looks mean to invite some and leave the others out."

"Don't see it," said Charlie. "We didn't contract to feed 'em, Li. Hang it! they can't expect us to do more than give 'em all we've got!"

"No, I s'pose not, Charlie."

"I'm glad we kept some of the best things back, Li. Several of the fellows have got such mouths —when they open 'em their heads are half off!"

"Well, it don't matter, the prog'll have to go, and the larger the mouths are the sooner it'll be got rid of."

This little dialogue occurred on the morning after the events recorded in our last chapter, and related of course to the proposed picnic, Mr. Stiffback having, as Vansittart anticipated, granted a holiday for the purpose.

There was a pretty little hollow at the back of the school, specially devoted to picnicking purposes, and which had in consequence been unpoetically named Grub Hole, and at this famed spot, about five p.m., the merry party assembled.

The hampers and all things fitting were carried to Grub Hole by the picnickers themselves, who, probably fearing the intrusion of uninvited fellows, prudently declined all help from the outsiders.

We need hardly say that there was very little ceremony at our hero's dinner party.

If a guest saw anything that he fancied, he grabbed it and ate it, unless captured in transit by a stronger grabber than himself.

Similarly, if a guest had a knife, he used it; if he had not, he used his fingers, and wiped them afterwards upon the grass table-napkin so plentifully provided by Dame Nature.

Neither were corkscrews in fashion, for the necks of the bottles were neatly knocked off by Vansittart, and so handed round to the guests, who took as long a swig as the patience of their next neighbours would allow.

One boy had provided himself with a tin mug, but he was unanimously voted a dainty epicure, and deprived of his share of wine for being "over particular."

Lionel and Charlie, to do them justice, had a far smaller share than any of their companions, which, from a sanitary point of view, was all the better for them.

As for Vansittart, he, as our readers know, was, by the rules of training, forbidden to touch anything in the shape of pastry.

When, at last, there was nothing left but crumbs, and not many of them, a young gentleman, who was perfectly rosy with excess of raspberry jam, uprose and proposed that they should sing, by way of grace, "For they're both Jolly Good Fellows," a proposal which was carried uproariously, and sang in the same way.

Lionel returned thanks in a brief speech, the pith of which was that he was glad they had enjoyed themselves, and sorry that the prog had not held out a little longer.

Tommy, who had come off uncommonly short, grunted at this last sentiment, and muttered something uncomplimentary relative to chaps who were like pigs, and never knew when they had enough.

This remark, calculated to provoke a breach of the peace, was pointedly addressed to a very wide-mouthed young gentleman who had feasted to such an extent that he was already yielding to the influence of an apoplectic slumber.

He was in far too blissful a state to heed either Tommy or the flies which had settled like a moustache around his mouth, and Codlings, promising himself a full measure of revenge, as soon as he had got over the soreness of knuckles and other portions of his frame, started after Lionel, Charlie, and Vansittart, who were making for the shore.

Suddenly Vansittart uttered an exclamation, and catching Lionel and Charlie by the arms, drove them back.

"Here's a bit of fun," he said. "Look over there—do you see anything?"

"There's a lot of fellows bathing on the other side of the lake."

"Well, they're old Growlagain's boys, and they're trespassing, for no one has a right to bathe or fish in the lake without Stiffback's permission."

"What shall we do? They're too far off to pelt."

"Can you fellows swim?"

"I can," said Lionel.

"So can I," added Charlie.

"Yes, but can you swim well? Could you cross the lake and back?"

"Twice over, if you like."

"That'll do," said Vansittart. "Come down here and strip, then we'll swim quietly across, and while they're in the water we'll bag their clothes."

"We're on," said our hero. "Hallo, here's Tommy. He'll mind our things while we swim across; won't you, old fellow?"

Tommy consented, and the next moment the three boys had slipped silently into the water, and were swimming steadily in the direction of the enemy.

CHAPTER XVII.

VANSITTART'S MANŒUVRE IN THE LAKE—STALKING THE ENEMY—LIONEL SUCCEEDS IN CAPTURING THE SPOILS OF THE FOE—THE WAR-CRY— THE ATTACK—COMPLETE ROUT OF THE TRESPASSERS—WHERE ARE THE CLOTHES?—A LITTLE CHAFF FOR AN OLD BIRD.

THE cool, clear, fresh water was so deliciously invigorating that Lionel felt greatly tempted to turn on his side and sweep through the water at full speed.

But caution was necessary.

Sound travels far over water, and it was necessary to keep up the steady, noiseless breast-stroke, lest an untimely splash should alarm the enemy.

Vansittart was ahead, moving through the water with an easy, yet powerful stroke, that told our hero and his chum at a glance that he was a first-rate swimmer.

He was heading for a point some distance below that where the boys of the rival school were disporting themselves.

Lionel wondered at his being so cautious, but for once he was content to take the second place, and follow *his* leader without remonstrance.

In little more than ten minutes they had reached a sweet secluded spot, where, once upon a time, some one had commenced to erect a landing-stage, but the attempt had been abandoned, and logs of wood and half-hewn planks cumbered the shore, or lay floating in the water.

"Now, you fellows," said Vansittart, "shove a few of these in. Take the biggest."

"What on earth are you going to do with 'em?" said Charlie.

"You'll see directly, young 'un. That's it, Wilful. Easy. Don't splash."

"Another one, and that'll do," said Vansittart. "Now don't you see the dodge?"

"Can't say I do."

"Nor I."

"Why, we'll shove these into the water, and, getting behind 'em, swim towards those fellows till we get to the creek. Then one of us must creep up and bag the clothes, bring 'em back, tie 'em to these logs, and shove them out into the middle of the lake. If we do it quietly they won't be missed till they go to dress."

"And then?" laughed Lionel. "Ha! ha! I fancy I can see 'em."

"Hush! No laughing yet. Out with the logs. Steady!"

The approach of the pieces of floating timber occasioned no alarm or even surprise amongst the trespassers, for there was always some in the lake, and indeed more than one of the timid swimmers were using stray logs as aids to their defective powers.

Lionel was nearest the shore, and to him fell the difficult task of collecting the clothes of the enemy.

"Be careful, Wilful," whispered Vansittart from behind the shelter of his log. "If one of 'em sees you it'll spoil all the fun."

Lionel smiled and winked as he crawled stealthily up the bank, and creeping, Indian-fashion, on his stomach, and taking advantage of every depression in the ground, he soon reached the clothes.

Luckily they had all been piled close together at the bottom of the slope, so that they were hardly visible to the owners.

"There's a precious heap of 'em," thought our hero. "I can't take all these at once. Ah! I know."

A happy thought had occurred to him, and rapidly picking out all the waist-straps and belts, he fastened them together, and then tied the clothes into a bundle, which he rolled on before him down to the creek.

"Here they are, all safe," he whispered to Vansittart. "It'll take a biggish plank to bear the weight."

"This one will do it. Make haste and hook on the end. Some of those fellows are coming out of the water, I think."

The bundle was rapidly, but not very securely, fastened to a log, and pushed out into the lake, our three friends following up behind, and urging it gently onwards until it was in the deepest part of the water.

In five minutes the clothes had soaked up so much water that the log was sunk a little way below the surface, invisible indeed to anyone who was within a yard of it."

"That's prime," chuckled Charlie. "Are we to wait here and see the fun?"

"No, better than that," replied Vansittart. "We'll give 'em a scare."

"How?"

"Swim down towards 'em, and as soon as we're near enough, jump up on the logs and shout as loud as you can."

"There are some of them on these planks, and out of their depth too," said Lionel.

"Upset them then. If they're so fond of the water, they won't mind taking a little away with 'em."

Another minute or two and our friends were upon the unsuspecting enemy.

Vansittart gave the signal by giving a tremendous shout and vaulting upon his log.

In an instant Charlie had followed his example, while Lionel scrambled upright upon his plank, and using a smaller piece of wood by way of a paddle, rowed full tilt against a lubberly youth, who was affectionately cuddling a log, and upset him into the water.

"Lake Island School for ever! Down with the trespassers!" shouted Charlie.

"Drown 'em all!" cried Lionel. "Look out, Charlie, there's a fellow making a grab at your leg."

Charlie promptly administered a kick under the chin to his foe which rolled him over into shallower water, when he scrambled to his feet, and yelling "Murder!" at the top of his voice, made for his clothes, or rather the place where he had left them.

About a dozen others joined him, and only three or four, who were being fairly soused by Vansittart, our hero, and Charlie, remained to splash in the lake and endeavour to dodge their active foes.

"So you'll come here trespassing, will you?" said Lionel, giving one a gentle tap on the head with his paddle. "You try it on again, old fellow, and we'll take you out into the middle of the lake and tie an anchor to your legs."

"Give 'em pepper!" shouted Charlie, who had got hold of his victim by the hair, and was ducking him every other minute.

"Let 'em go," said Vansittart; "there's two of their masters coming."

"And," added Charlie, "there's old Stiffback and another on our side. We shall get it warm for this."

"Not a bit of it," replied Vansittart. "He hates this opposition school like poison, and it's understood that we can clout the trespassers whenever we catch 'em. Hallo! there's the old 'un opening fire."

The "old 'un," by which irreverent appellation Vansittart intended to designate the head master of the rival school, now marched to the edge of the lake.

"Hi! you low boys; come here."

"You've got 'em all on shore," shouted Lionel, in reply.

"Come here at once," screamed the stout gentleman, getting very red in the face.

"We'd rather stay where we are if it's all the same to you," replied Lionel, politely. "It's cooler, don't you see?"

"I'll—I'll—'cool' you for this, you—you—infamous young blackguard."

"You'd rather 'warm' it, in my opinion," laughed Charlie.

"Don't give us any more of those rich compliments, old fellow," said Vansittart; "we've just had a heavy lunch, and they might make us bilious."

"I'll send for the police unless you tell me this instant where you have put my boys' clothes," roared the master, fairly dancing with rage.

"What?" said our hero, in feigned astonishment.

"The clothes. You know very well what I said, you rascals! Where have you hidden them? You had better confess."

"Do you see their clothes, Van?" said Lionel, turning innocently to his companion.

"Not I."

"Or you, Charlie?"

"Not a rag. I don't believe they've got any."

"You hear that, sir?" shouted Lionel. "We can't see your boys' clothes, and our private opinion is that they haven't got any."

The stout master's wrath was unutterable.

He stamped to and fro on the shore, shook his stick, and even swore; but our hero and his chums only smiled sweetly, and "chaffed" him again.

"It's a shame to put such boys as them into togs at all," said Vansittart. "Their elegant figures were never made to be hidden by jackets and trousers."

"Certainly not," assented Charlie.

"I say, governor," said our hero, "if you're so very particular about decency, there's a fig-tree in the plantation, where you can get a few leaves."

"Or send 'em over to our place," said Vansittart, "and we'll tattoo them for you."

"I wish I had the tattooing of you, you dashed young blackguards. But you shall pay dearly for this outrage, you and your rascally master too."

"Hallo! that's libel," said Vansittart. "You heard what he said, you fellows?"

"Yes," replied Lionel and Charlie, in a breath.

"Then there'll be an action brought against him."

"Dash the action!" roared the master. "Will you bring those clothes?"

"Really, sir," said Vansittart, affecting to be shocked, "your language is so coarse that we cannot stay to hear it any longer. Come on, boys."

And Vansittart paddled his log a little further away.

"Here, I say," shouted the master, "remember, I warn you; these young gentlemen may catch a fatal illness if their clothes are not restored. Give them up, and I promise to say nothing about the matter."

"Exceedingly kind of you, sir," replied Vansittart; "but if you *will* persist in trespassing on other people's property, and then libelling them, you must take the consequences. Good afternoon: it's a beautiful day for a walk."

"Ta-ta," said Charlie.

"Adieu, my friends," added Lionel.

And then, we regret to add, that all three, before paddling away, indulged in a gesture which, from time immemorial, and by all nations, savage and civilized, has been, and is held, **expressive of con-tempt and derision.**

CHAPTER XVIII.

MR. STIFFBACK'S OPINION UPON TRESPASSING— WHAT'S TO BE DONE WITH THE CLOTHES? RETURNED WITH THANKS—SHAMEFUL WANT OF GRATITUDE ON THE PART OF THE STOUT GENTLEMAN—THE CARTE DE VISITE, AND WHAT BEFELL IT IN THE MARKET-PLACE OF DE-LIVERHAM.

"BUT I say, Vansittart," said Charlie, "don't you think we'd better give up the clothes. If any of them poor beggars should catch cold and be taken ill?"

"What, this weather? Besides, don't you see that the togs are soaked now, and they couldn't put 'em on if they wanted to."

"It would take an hour to dry 'em," said Lionel. "But they must be sent back some time, or that spiteful old chap will set the police on us."

"That wouldn't be of much use. Country policemen are a thick-headed lot and they'd never find the clothes where we've put 'em."

"Don't you mean to send them back, then?"

"Yes, by the carrier, but they won't be able to prove that they were sent by us. But put on steam, we haven't had all our fun out yet."

"Let's get off these logs then, and race in," said Lionel. "I'm getting chilly."

"All right," said Vansittart; "I'll give you a start."

"No, start fair. It's only a hundred yards."

"Ready then. Off."

Like three flashes of flesh-coloured lightning the boys dived into the water, a minute after three heads bobbed up, Lionel's a yard in front, for he had taken the longest dive, Charlie's next, and Vansittart's last.

Lionel put on the side-stroke, and shot like a fish through the water, and at such a pace, that Vansittart, who was taking it easily, with a breast-stroke, was compelled to put on the screw.

He was a first-class swimmer, as more than one cup and medal could testify, and he naturally expected that he could go two yards to one in a trial with a boy so much younger and slighter than himself, and he actually felt a little humiliated and even hurt when he found that, with his utmost efforts, he could not recover the advantage which he had lost, and that Lionel touched the shore first by half a dozen yards, Charlie a bad third.

He could not express his disappointment then, however, if he had intended to do so, for Mr. Stiffback and the second master were waiting for them on the shore.

"Vansittart," he said, "you are bathing against the rules."

"I am aware of that, sir, but there were some trespassers and we went to warn them."

Mr. Stiffback was perfectly well aware of this, but according to rule he felt bound to put the regulation question.

"Trespassers, eh?"

"Yes, sir."

"What were they doing?"

"Bathing sir; you can see them now on the shore yonder."

"Oh, yes, you warned them away then?"

"We did, sir," said Vansittart, with a wink at Lionel and Charlie, which sent both those young gentlemen into fits of ill-repressed laughter.

"They do not seem to be dressed yet," said Mr. Stiffback, peering through his spectacles at the group of naked boys on the opposite shore of the lake. "I hope they are not going to bathe again."

"I don't think they'll do that, sir," replied Vansittart. "I think they said something about having lost their clothes, as we were going away."

"Lost their clothes? Dear me, that's very unfortunate for them," said the schoolmaster. "I hope you have nothing to do with the loss, Vansittart."

"Nothing can be lost, sir, as the Irishman said, if you only know where it is."

"Never mind the Irishman, Vansittart. Do you know where those clothes are? It will never do to give such a person as the conductor of that school a just cause of complaint against any of my pupils."

"Well, we do know where they are, sir," replied Vansittart. "They're in the middle of the lake."

"Bless my soul! you don't mean to say that you have sunk them! The water is fifteen feet deep."

"No, they're not sunk. We tied them to a log of wood to save them from drowning, sir."

"Then have the goodness to get them at once. Stay, I do not wish you to swim again. Finish your dressing and take the boat."

This was exactly what Vansittart wished. In that space of time indefinitely called a "twinkling," the boys were dressed. The key of the boathouse was handed to them by Mr. Stiffback, and a couple of dozen eager volunteers offered to help.

"No, stay here, all of you," said the schoolmaster. "Three will be quite enough, will it not, Vansittart?"

"Say you want another, and take Codlings," whispered Lionel, who saw his old chum making frenzied gestures to be taken on.

The request was made and granted, for Mr. Stiffback had great confidence in his senior pupil, and usually let him have his own way. Perhaps his title had a little to do with it, for schoolmasters are but human after all.

The boathouse was close at hand, and Vansittart selecting a neat gig which would just hold four comfortably, launched her, and leaving Lionel and Charlie to row, and Tommy to steer, took his place in the boat to look out for the log.

It was some time before his keen eyes fell upon the missing object, for it had sunk below the level of the water, and when at length he laid hands on it there remained the difficult task of attempting to haul it into the boat.

"Confound it!" he said. "It's so soaked with water that we shall be swamped, and those fellows are longing to move."

"Tow it behind," suggested Tommy.

"Bravo fat 'un!" said Vansittart. "There's something in you besides pudding, after all."

"I say, none of that, you know," and Tommy got very red in the face. "If I ain't built like a darning needle, I'm not going to put up being told of it—now then."

"Shut up, Tommy," said Lionel, "and look out for the bundle. Tie that rope to it, and mind you don't let it slip, or it's all up with the togs."

Tommy grumbled, but obeyed, as he generally did when our hero spoke to him; and when all was ready, Lionel and Charlie bent to their work and headed the boat for the creek.

"Hi!" shouted Vansittart. "Hi! you sir, we've found the clothes."

The schoolmaster, who had gathered his naked, forlorn pupils together, and was driving them before him like a flock of plucked geese, halted and gazed towards the boat.

"Ah!" he said majestically, "you have thought better of it, I suppose, and fortunate indeed it is for you that you have done so."

"I suppose it is," said Lionel, with affected terror. "I suppose you would have done something very dreadful to us, wouldn't you?"

"Boiled us alive like lobsters at the very least," said Charlie.

"You can hold your tongue," said the stout schoolmaster, wrathfully.

"Thanky," replied Charlie, "but I prefer to let it jolt about, if it's all the same to you."

"Where are those clothes?" bawled the angry master.

"Towing behind our boat," replied Vansittart. "They are in an awfully dirty state, but we shan't charge you anything for washing."

And as the boat grounded Vansittart jumped ashore, hauled up the bundle, and dropped it with a "squash" at the stout gentleman's feet.

His language when he saw that heap of shirts, jackets, boots, caps, trousers, &c., soaked through and through with water, was really dreadful, and could only be vaguely hinted at means of suggestive blanks and dashes.

Vansittart put his fingers in his ears, Charlie laughed, and Lionel began feeling in his pockets.

"There, now," he said, after a hurried search. "What a pity; I had some beautiful little tracts this morning that would have done you a world of good. There was one especially, called "The Wicked Quaker, who swore at his grandmother," which would have cured you of that bad habit in no time."

Several more "blank" and "dash" remarks were made by the stout gentleman, and making a rush at Lionel with the amiable intention of knocking his head off, he fell over the bundle of wet clothes, and pitching on his hat, reduced it to the semblance of a concertina out of repair.

"'Let not your angry passions rise,'" sang Lionel, quoting from Dr. Watts, the immortal water-gruel poet.

"Keep cool, governor," said Vansittart, "or if you try that game on you may find yourself in the lake."

The stout gentleman arose, and wrathfully straightening his hat, glared at Vansittart, but there was something in the fearless blue eyes, and lithe, muscular form, that showed Vansittart to be a "nasty customer." Besides, Lionel was shouldering one of the sculls, and Charlie had a boat-hook in his right fist, so the stout gentleman thought discretion the better part of valour, and getting out a few more remarks of the blank and dash order, called the boys to come and pick up their clothes.

Miserable enough they looked as they obeyed the order. They were nearly dry and had been keeping up their circulation by playing leap-frog and touch, and now the contact of the wet, sloppy clothes was particularly uncomfortable.

"What a pity there isn't a photographer here," said Vansittart, laughing. "What a pretty picture those chaps would make to be sure."

"Wouldn't it? such elegant attitudes."

"I'd put you in an elegant attitude if I had got you at my school," growled the stout gentleman.

"I dare say you would," retorted Lionel. "Bless you for an amiable christian."

"Isn't he?" added Charlie, with a laugh; "and then his language too, how flowery!"

"Blank and dash you," roared the stout gentleman. "Will you hold your blanked tongues? Make haste, you boys, or I shall forget myself, and shed the blood of those dashed young imps."

And with a final shake of his fist at our young friends, the stout gentleman kicked a boy or two to ease his mind, and marched away in a red-hot rage.

"Now, I wonder how he is going to manage," said Vansittart. "His school is nearly three miles away, and he must pass through Deliverham to get to it."

"He can't walk the boys in that state."

"Perhaps he keeps a carriage."

"He has a ricketty old trap which he drives to church on Sunday, but that wouldn't hold more than half-a-dozen," said Vansittart. "Ah, now I guess what his game is. He had one of his ushers with him, hadn't he?"

"He had a chap with him who was ugly enough for anything."

"Then he's sent him into the town to get a cart,

or something of that sort. Come on you fellows ; game enough to follow 'em up ? "

" Game for anything," said Lionel.

" Let's pelt 'em," added Charlie. " Hallo, where's Tommy."

" Fast asleep in the boat. Let him alone, he's better there," said our hero.

" Then on we go. We'll take this short cut through the plantation, so as to strike the road before they do."

" They can't go very fast if it's gravelly," laughed Lionel.

Ten minutes' sharp walking brought them to the road, where, sure enough, stood a cart, and the usher by the side of it, in conversation with the driver.

" You're a prophet," whispered Lionel. " How the dickins could you tell what he was going to do ? "

" Reasoning by analogy," replied Vansittart. " You'll know fast enough if ever you study metaphysics. Hallo, I hear the old 'un coming."

And the next moment the stout gentleman emerged from the lane, driving his little flock before him, at sight of which the carter indulged in a hearty " Haw, haw, haw ! "

" Now, what are you grinning at," demanded the master, sharply. " Help these youngsters into the cart, and keep a quiet tongue in your head, or I shan't pay you."

" Be 'em all to get in ?" asked the driver.

" Of course, and make haste about it."

" 'Twill be a rare tight-fit, measter."

" That isn't your affair," said the stout gentleman, sharply.

" Well, if one or two on 'em be smothered afore I gets to school, 'twon't be my fault."

And with his mind thus eased, the carter grabbed a couple of the youngest and pitched them in as if they had been hay, and shrieks of agony instantly arose from the injured ones.

" Confound you, what do you mean by that?" roared the stout gentleman.

" Wot do 'ee mean by badgerin' of a man loik this ? First 'ee tells oi to make haste, and when I does it, 'ee swears at me."

" Dash you," growled the master, in an agony of terror lest any one should pass along the road, and see the condition of his pupils. " Go on, anyhow, only make haste."

It was almost more than Lionel and his chums could do to refrain from bursting with a hearty fit of laughter, and so betraying their position. Fortunately for them the packing did not last long. The tail-board was fastened in its place, with the linch-pins, and the stout gentleman, leaving the usher to accompany the cart, and see that it was driven gently, stalked on ahead.

The carter cracked his whip, the horse moved on, and as soon as it was a few yards away, the three friends cast themselves on the turf and had their laugh out in the grass.

" Oh my, those poor chaps in the cart ! " said our hero, faint with excess of merriment. " How happy they must feel—tight as sardines in a box—and with their wet clothes to keep 'em from spoiling."

" Come on," said Vansittart ; " we haven't done with 'em yet."

" You can't do anything with 'em now," said Charlie. " That big carter's there, and I shouldn't care much for a taste of his whip."

" No fear of that. Come along ; the cart's turned the corner."

And so, following the cart, but keeping a respectful distance behind it, the boys moved silently on, until the High-street of Deliverham was reached.

" Now, be ready you fellows," said Vansittart. " Is old Gruff-and-Grim still in front of the cart?"

" Yes, about twenty yards ahead."

" That'll do. Now, the minute the cart's in the middle of the market-place, where the people are

thickest, you two run to the off-side and pull out the linch-pin. I'll do the same for this side, and you'll see some fun."

Deliverham was a busy little town which had sprung up some forty years ago, at the touch of the railway enchanters. There was a great deal of traffic that afternoon, and more than once the cart was brought to a stop.

The third time it happened the master, who was in an agony of fear lest any accident should reveal his secret, turned back to hurry the carter.

It was at that moment that our hero and his chums darted across from the pavement and paused for a moment behind the cart.

As quickly as ever aching tooth was extracted by the dentist's forceps, the linch-pins were drawn out, the tail-board fell with a crash just as the cart moved on, and fourteen unhappy youngsters, naked as they were born, were shot out upon the stones of the market-place, as if they had been coals !

CHAPTER XIX.

RUBBISH MAY BE SHOT HERE !—THE USHER IN A FIX—HORRIBLE SUGGESTIONS MADE BY THE CROWD AS TO THE USHER'S IDENTITY WITH SWEENEY TODD—OUR HEROES MAKE THEIR ESCAPE—THE REWARD OF MERIT—VANSITTART'S WARNING—" GETTING UP " IN THE MORNING.

THE fourteen small boys so suddenly transferred from the darkness of the cart to the light of the day, and the hard cobble-stones of the market-place, set up fourteen shill, ear-piercing yells.

They made up their minds that something very dreadful was going to happen to them, and so they howled with all their might.

The Deliverham folks were not much accustomed to novelty.

Each day they rose at the same hour, did the same work, took in the usual amount of provender, and snored in the same key when bed-time came.

Their amusement came at fair time, and whenever there was an election, but here was a treat ab extra, and with one accord every man, woman, and child stopped in what he, she, or it was doing, and stared at the strange spectacle.

" Hi ! wot be they ? " said one, gazing open-mouthed and eyed.

" Why bwoys, be'nt um ?" said another.

" Any fule can see that," retorted the first, " but wa'at be 'um doin' 'ere wi'out ne'er a clout ?"

" They be toombling bwoys, I recons," said the second yokel.

" That be for sartin ; but oi say, Gearge."

" Well, Billie."

" 'Taint quite roight, be it, for 'em to be toombling wi'out ne'er a rag. Wa'at would pa'ason say ?

Meanwhile another section of the crowd had hit upon a theory much more romantic and blood-thirsty than that of the two first rustics, and, headed by a butcher, whose stalwart frame and rubicund face testified to the nourishing properties of his beef, surrounded the carter and the usher.

" Noo, I tell 'ee wa'at, lads," said the butcher, " these 'ere chaps were a gooin' to burke they lads. Ha'nt none on 'ee heeard tell o' th' sassidge factories i' Lunnon ?"

" Ah," said another, " Sweeney Todd—him as shoved men into pies."

The name of the ghoul-like barber of Fleet-street passed through the crowd, first with a threatening murmur, and then with a fierce voice.

" Sweeney Todd ! Sweeney Todd ! Duck 'un, lads ! Pull 'un to pieces !"

The carter stood leaning against the wheel scratching his head, trying probably to stir up an idea.

The usher turned very pale as he saw hundreds of angry eyes staring at him.

"My good men," he said, faintly, "you are mistaken, I assure you."

"Wa'at be 'ee doin' wi' all them naked boys in that there cart?" demanded the butcher.

Another angry roar arose from the crowd.

The usher looked round for the head-master, but that gentleman, when he saw what had happened, had cast his hat upon the ground, trampled on it, and then bolted out of the town till he came to a hay-rick, into which he stuck his head, and moaned in the bitterness of his despair.

"We'd better be moving," said Vansittart. "The crowd may take it into their heads to duck that fellow, and it won't do for us to be seen too near."

"Confound it! I should like to see him ducked," said Charlie.

"It won't do, my boy. We've been too long away already, and if we stay longer, and Stiffback hears of this—as he's sure to—we shall get in for it. I shall have my holiday stopped, and you'll get a taste of the flogging-machine."

"Not for me, thank you," said Lionel. "I'm off."

And at a swinging trot the three friends made for the shore of the lake, where they found the boat, and Tommy still fast asleep in the stern.

It was past tea-time when they reached the house, but Mr. Stiffback, in consideration of the service they had rendered in driving away the trespassers, invited the friends to tea with him.

"What a chap you are to sleep, Tommy," said Lionel, in the course of a hurried toilette to fit him for the presence of the head-master.

"You've missed no end of fun," said Charlie, polishing his face vigorously with a towel.

"I had a jolly good nap," replied Tommy, contentedly, "and such beautiful dreams."

"What were they, Tommy? About the flogging machine?"

"Not exactly, and yet it had something to do with 'em, too. I thought there was a machine—like the tickler, you know—only when the handle was turned there came out of it all sorts of lovely things—cakes, sweets, toffee, jam, fruit—everything a chap could wish for, only just as I was going to begin you fellows woke me up."

"Never mind, Tommy, you can realise your dream presently. I daresay old Stiffback will have something good for tea."

"I hope so, for I'm precious hungry," said Tommy.

"And I feel as if I could peck; the swim, the row, and the run on the top of 'em both, has sharpened my appetite."

"And mine," added Lionel. "Come along, here's Vansittart."

Mr. Stiffback was a capital host. He set the boys quite at their ease at once, and by the time the meal was over, our hero, as well as Charlie and Tommy, had conceived a strong liking for him.

"He's a brick, that's what he is!" said the tender young gentleman. "His apricot jam can't be beaten."

"What!" said Lionel, with a laugh. "Have you forgotten the flogging-machine already, Tommy, and the little turn up you had with Magog?"

"That apricot jam wipes out a multitude of sins," said Tommy, gravely. "I forgive him all. I'll take a flogging once a week if he'll only invite me to tea afterwards."

"Well, you are a good natured chap, Tommy. There's no malice in your composition."

"I'd forgive a man for poisoning me if he did it with apricot jam," was Tommy's truly christian reply, and then he went away to have another quiet little nap till bed time.

When that time came our hero and Chrlie welcomed it like a friend, for they had eaten a good

deal and taken no small quantity of exercise, both of which are excellent soporifics.

Vansittart noticed this, and called Lionel aside.

"I say, yon seem tired, Wilful."

"I am, and sleepy, too."

"Then take this bit of advice. Don't oversleep yourself in the morning, but directly the gong awakes you jump out of bed."

"But why? I thought there was half an hour allowed for dressing."

"So there is, but don't stop in bed a minute after the gong strikes. I oughtn't to tell you this for it's against the rules; but I don't want to see you laughed at. Good night."

*　　*　　*　　*

From a sweet and dreamless slumber, Lionel was awakened the next morning by a terrific sound which in his semi-conscious state he at first imagined was the bombardment of Lake House School by the rival master, but when it had been repeated the third time he recognised it as the unwelcome sound of the "getting up" gong.

"Dash it," thought Lionel. "I'll have another ten minutes. I'm a quick dresser."

And utterly forgetting Vansittart's warning, Lionel closed his eyes again and was fast asleep in a minute.

Charlie and Tommy had done precisely the same thing. Five minutes passed, and a group of boys collected, with grinning and expectant faces, round the beds where all three lay snoring.

Suddenly, and without a moment's warning, the mattresses, sleepers, bed clothes and all, were shot high up in the air.

CHAPTER XX.

OUR HERO AND HIS CHUMS MAKE THE ACQUAINTANCE OF MR. STIFFBACK'S PATENT—"SLUGGARDS' BEDSTEADS"—WARRANTED TO WAKE THE SOUNDEST SLEEPER IN FIVE SECONDS—A SCRIMMAGE IN THE DORMITORY—TOMMY FINDS THAT HE IS ACQUAINTED WITH THE FRENCH LANGUAGE—AND LOSES HIS BREAKFAST IN CONSEQUENCE.

WE take it for granted that no human being likes to be awakened from a sound refreshing sleep in a hurry, especially when the awakening is accompanied by violence. We think, too that animals might be included in this remark, for we know of our own knowledge that cats will scratch and dogs snap spitefully if aroused with the toe of a boot or other such gentle stimulant, and we dare not imagine the fate of the rough mortal who should venture to intrude upon the slumbers of a full-grown lion or tiger.

The first impression of anyone awakened in this way is that the house is on fire; the second, that thieves have broken in; and the third, an impulse to curse the disturber with all the profanity with which nature and education has endowed him.

But the manner in which our three friends had been aroused was as unpleasant as peculiar. First, there was a tremendous jolt in the small of the back, followed by a sensation as of flying in a perpendicular direction, then a rapid descent, terminating in the contact of their lightly clad frames with the hard deal boards of the floor, or the harder iron of the bedsteads.

Lionel escaped with a shaking, for he fell into the bed again. Charlie tested the solidity of his head by contact with the floor; but Tommy, with his usual luck, came down upon one of the knobs of the iron bedstead, which would infallibly have impaled him had it only been sharp enough.

All this happened amidst a shrill chorus of laughter, and when Lionel, red and indignant, got right end up again, and had got the tail of his night-shirt from off the top of his head, he saw the other occupants of the dormitory standing in a row, and laughing as if for a wager.

No one likes to be placed in a ridiculous position and then laughed at for the misfortune. Lionel was especially tender on this point, and getting off the bed he looked savagely at the laughers. He thought, and naturally enough, that meant some trick had been played upon him, and he to take it out of somebody.

"Now then," he said, "when you're done grinning there perhaps you'll say who did this."

No answer, only a fresh burst of laughter.

"I'll make some of you laugh in the wrong place," said Lionel, getting redder and angrier. "Here, Charlie, get up and help me give these fellows toko. Confound it, they're not going to have all the grin on their side."

But Charlie was "out of it:" the bump on his head had confused his intellect, and at that moment he was seated on the floor, engaged in trying to remember what had happened to him, and where he was.

Lionel, as our readers know, cared little for odds, when his blood was up; so grasping a pillow and a bolster he hurled them into the midst of his enemies, and then picking out a boy with a very large mouth, who had been grinning most aggravatingly, pitched into him right and left.

It was the same boy whose gluttonous consumption of jam had so aroused Tommy's indignation on the day of the pic-nic, and our plump friend heard the "smack, smack" of Lionel's blows with peculiar satisfaction.

"Go it, Li," he said, trying to shout, but only getting out a faint whisper. "Let 'em have it. I'm coming."

And Tommy, spying his old foes, the Bobbles, rushed into the thick of the fight, seized two by the hair, and knocked their heads together, while with all the wind he could muster he sang the chorus of the "Postman's Knock."

It was long odds, though, against Lionel, for besides the wide-mouthed boy, who, to do him justice, could fight as well as eat, our hero had three others hammering away at his back, while a fourth stood by with a bolster and put in a whack with the implement whenever he saw an opening.

Tommy was soon in as bad a plight, as the four remaining Bobbles, armed with boots and nice sharp-cornered squares of yellow soap, took shots at him from a safe distance, and as he was very tender in certain quarters, by reason of his late introduction to the flogging-machine, soon caused him to release his first victims in order to chase his new attackers.

But of course Tommy never could go through a scrimmage like anyone else. At the first step he fell over a pillow, and then his fate was sealed, for his foes pressed upon him, and by force of numbers held him down, whilst a torture, known by the name of "cobbing," at school and on board ship, was inflicted on him with the aid of slippers.

The combat was at its height.

Our hero was pounding away at random, for he had so many to tackle that there was no time to pick them out.

Tommy was kicking and struggling in vain to get on his legs, while Charlie Drummond was just beginning to be dimly conscious that there was a row somewhere, when the door of the dormitory was flung open, and Vansittart, half-dressed, came in.

"Hallo, here!" he shouted. "What the deuce is all this about? Stop it, you fellows."

The big boys of the upper form were expected to keep order in the dormitories, which duty they generally performed by thrashing the offenders, for "reporting," or, as it is better termed by the youngsters, "sneaking," was not allowed.

So the mere sound of Vansittart's voice was enough to make the combatants scatter, except Lionel, who now had the wide-mouthed boy in chancery, and Tommy, who had got one of the Boobles down at last, and was practising the drum on his ribs.

"Is that you in this scrimmage, Wilful?" Vansittart said, as he laughingly pulled Lionel away. "Stop, or his head will be only fit for a jam pot. What's it all about?"

"Why, some fellows got playing larks with us in bed this morning. Shot us out like so many shuttlecocks, and, as no one would own who did it, I pitched into the lot."

Vansittart burst into a hearty fit of laughter, whereat Lionel grew angry again, for the wide-mouthed boy and his assistants had made him tolerably sore about the ribs and the parts thereby adjacent.

"I don't see much to laugh at, Van, and if you'd been first pitched out of bed, and then pitched into into by a dozen fellows, you wouldn't grin so fast."

"What a fellow you are, Li. Why, don't you remember what I told you last night?"

"What was that?"

"To get up directly the first gong sounded. You didn't, of course?"

"Well no, I didn't," replied Lionel, recollecting how he had turned over for another sweet little nap.

"Nor the other two fellows?"

"No. But what has that to do with our being pitched out of bed?"

"Everything," laughed Vansittart. "They're called the 'sluggards' beds,' and every new boy has a turn in one of 'em until he's learned to turn out sharp at the first stroke of the gong."

"Some invention of old Stiffback's, I suppose?" said our hero, savagely.

"Yes. It was his pet idea till he invented the flogging-machine," replied Vansittart. "There's a very strong spiral spring below each mattrass that's let loose by clockwork a couple of minutes after the gong sounds."

"Blow old Stiffback and his inventions!" said Lionel. "I've got a pain in the back that I sha'n't get over for a week. Hallo! Charlie, how are you?"

"Dashed if I know," replied that gentleman, who was holding on to a bedstead to steady himself. "Everything's going round, and you look twice as big as you were yesterday."

"Very likely," grumbled Lionel. "I've been pitched about so that I've begun to swell. Why didn't you come and help me with those chaps?"

"What, have you had a mill?"

"Ah! I should think so. Half a dozen on to me at once."

"Couldn't help it, Li. I didn't know where I was till just now. But I can take it out of some of 'em by-and-by."

"You'd better not," said Vansittart. "Take warning by Codlings."

"Does he treat all the chaps who 'mill' like that?"

"Nearly all. Stiffback has a great objection to fighting, not for its sake, for he's sensible enough to know that a fight now and then encourages pluck in a school."

"What is he down on it so for, then?"

"Because the fellows get damaged—black eyes, and so on, and when parents or guardians come to visit, or there's a general walk out, the bruises look bad."

"That isn't much of a reason," said Tommy. "I'd as soon have a black eye as not. I've given that Bobbles one, I think."

"What, again?"

"Not the same one. One of his brothers."

"My eye, Tommy," said Lionel, "you'll be in for another spar with the dummy."

"Blow that!" said Tommy, aghast. "I'd forgotten that dashed Magog."

"I wouldn't stand in your shoes for a trifle," added Charlie.

"If you fellows don't make haste you'll all be marked for punishment," said Vansittart. "The second gong will sound directly."

Not knowing what awful punishment Mr. Stiffback might have invented for the crime of being late at prayers, our three friends completed their toilettes with magical rapidity.

Tommy, who was as usual short of buttons, and without time to hunt for pins, had to hold together certain portions of his attire with his fingers.

Fortunately the lynx eyes of Mr. Stiffback did not observe the deficiencies of his toilette, and Tommy slipped into his place, which was next to Bobbles senior.

"I say," whispered Tommy to his late antagonist, "how's your eye?"

Bobbles, whose dexter optic already showed symptoms of adumbration, or, in plainer English, was turning black, and was developing a perfect wink preliminary to shutting up, looked sternly before him, but made no reply.

"I say," replied Tommy, touching him up with his elbow, "how's that eye of yours?"

Master Bobbles still maintained a severe silence.

"If you don't speak," said Tommy, in a ferocious whisper, "I'll punch the life out of you, and then drop you in the lake."

This awful threat produced some effect upon Bobbles, who regarded the new boy as a desperate ruffian, capable of any wickedness, so this time he spoke, but haughtily, as if to warn Tommy from taking any more liberties.

"My eye is quite well, thank you."

"Glad to hear it," said Tommy. "You're a good sort of chap, after all; but there, a black eye's nothing to make a fuss about, is it?"

Master Bobbles was silent. He had already compromised his dignity by speaking to a low boy who was always fighting, and he resolved to say no more.

But Tommy was not to be so easily baffled.

"I say," he whispered, after a pause, "got a pin?"

"A-men," said Bobbles, in a loud voice, and arose stiffly from his knees, as did all the others, for prayers were over, and more than four score healthy young appetites longed for breakfast.

But Tommy seemed strangely pious that morning. When the final "amen" was pronounced he arose half way and then sank down upon his knees again, with an alarmed expression upon his plump features.

"Come, Tommy," whispered Lionel, as he passed his chum, "up you get. Prayers are over."

"It's all up with me too," replied Tommy. "Here, stand close to me, Li."

"Why, what's the matter? What has frightened you?"

"The last button's gone off my trousers, and my braces are broke as well."

"You'll have to bolt upstairs and change 'em."

"Oh, ah, and lose my breakfast. Oh, yes, and get into a row with Stiffback, too. Not for me. Li, lend me a couple of pins."

The pins were produced, and Tommy managing with their aid to supply the place of the missing buttons, shuffled into the breakfast room with a hungry eye.

Mr. Stiffback himself did not preside at the boys' breakfast table; that duty was confided to the under masters, and very well they performed it, as Tommy soon found out.

Just opposite him was seated the French master, Monsieur de Vinaigre, a little, brown, thin man, with a remarkably wide awake expression, and whose complexion seemed to indicate that Monsieur de Vinaigre had been made out of compressed snuff.

He stared at Tommy, and Tommy returned the look with interest, for he was just thinking how very much a monkey he had seen at the Zoo resembled M. de Vinaigre.

"Pourquoi me regardez vous de cette manière là?"* demanded the French master, when he found his attempt to stare Tommy out a hopeless task.

It was the rule for the French and German masters always to speak to the pupils in those languages, but Tommy's knowledge of those languages may be set down as nought, but fancying that probably the native politeness of the foreigner had induced him to inquire after his health, he said in an off-hand way—

"Quite well, thanky, mossoo; how do you find yourself?"

A universal chuckle passed round the table at Tommy's impromptu reply. Even Mr. Jilk, the second classical master, condescended to smile, and Herr Kobblersvax, the German master, and a deadly enemy to Viniagre, laughed outright.

"C'est bien. On ose m'insulter à table. Mais nous parlerons de cela tonte-à-l'heure. Quel est votre nom?"†

Tommy had not the least idea that anything was going wrong. He thought he had made a good hit with his first answer, so he tried another, putting on an amiable smile to give it effect—

"I think I'll take coffee, if it's all the same to you."

Chuckle number two passed round the table. Mr. Jilk tried to look severe, but failed. Herr Kobblersvax exploded in a series of cachinnatory grunts, and the French master, looking more like a monkey than ever, in his anger, inquired Tommy's name of one of the upper form boys, and entered it in his note book.

Poor Tommy thought he was getting on beautifully, and wondered whether he had made a joke unawares, since everybody seemed so amused, but he was too hungry to waste much time on thinking, and looked eagerly round for the neat-handed Phillis to pass him the bread and butter, but the spiteful little French master was "down upon" him.

"Vous ne dejeunerez pas ce matin, Monsieur Codleens. Levez vous et mettez vous là au corin."*

This time Tommy had the meaning practically explained to him by Monsieur de Vinaigre, who led him by the arm into the corner, and bade him stay there, with a gesture more expressive than words.

"But I say, mossoo," Tommy began to expostulate.

"Silence!" said Monsieur de Vinaigre, with a sibillation of the "s," like a forest full of rattlesnakes.

Tommy almost burst into tears—he was so hungry, and the breakfast smelt so nice; but he swallowed his tears and vowed a vow of vengeance against Monsieur de Vinaigre.

CHAPTER XXI.

THE FURTHER MISFORTUNES OF MASTER THOMAS CODLINGS, SHOWING THE IMPORTANT CONNECTION EXISTING BETWEEN PIETY AND BUTTONS—OUR OLD FRIEND SAM MAKES HIMSELF AT HOME IN THE KITCHEN, AND NARRATES A MARVELLOUS AND VERACIOUS TALE OF A TUB, DEDICATED TO SIR WILFRED LAWSON.

"WHAT a mean beast that Frenchy is," whispered Lionel to Charlie. "Look at poor Tommy, done out of his breakfast, and all because he didn't understand the lingo. I believe he'd rather have had another taste of the flogging-machine."

"So do I," said Charlie, with his mouth full.

---

* "Why do you stare at me in that way?"

† "Very well; you dare to insult me at the breakfast table; but we will talk about that presently. What is your name?"

"But, lor, it's no use saying anything, Tommy can't help being unlucky. It comes natural to him."

"Such a stunning breakfast too. Why it's as good as a fellow gets at home."

"And as much as you like of it too—no stint," added Charlie, as he passed his cup for some more coffee.

"I wonder if old Stiffback would let us have some of my guava jelly?"

"Ask—they can't say much if it isn't allowed," replied Charlie. "We're new, you know, and can't be supposed to know all the rules."

"I don't like howling out before all these fellows. We'll ask that pleasant looking old lady, Mrs. Citron, and have some for tea."

"By-the-by, there'll be a good lark this morning, Li."

"Where?"

"In the schoolroom, to be sure. Don't you remember about Soker?"

"Oh, ah, Stiffback's going to make him get tight for a week, to cure him of being drunk."

"Queer kind of cure that, eh, Li?"

"Homœopathic, Charlie—similia similibus curantur."

"Stow that, Li. If you'd been at Styngy's you'd have had to pay a fine all round for quoting Latin out of school."

"I wonder what's become of him?"

"Who—Styngy?"

"Yes."

"Can't guess. The fever breaking out at his school settled that, and my father said that he'd been persuaded by Grubbe to invest all the tin he had in some of those precious banks that bust up."

"He must be hard up then, Charlie," said Lionel, thoughtfully.

"Con-foundedly, I should say. But blow him. It all serves him right for having such a rascal as Grubbe for a friend, and for treating you as meanly as he did. That's my verdict, old chap."

By this time breakfast was over, the gastronomical joys of eating had become things of the past until dinner time, and the stern reality of the schoolroom lay before the pupils.

Just as they had risen and were filing out Mr. Stiffback appeared, and at once spotted Tommy in disgrace in the corner.

"Who is that boy there, Mr. Jilk?"

"Monsieur de Vinaigre will explain, sir," replied the classical master.

And thereupon the Frenchman, with much of dramatic gesticulation, explained how he had been insulted.

Tommy listened mournfully, but holding tightly to the waistband of his breeches all the while, and every now and then giving a sailor-like hitch to that garment.

"Stand up properly, Codlings," said Mr. Stiffback, "and tell me what you have to say in your defence. Leave your trousers alone, and put your hands behind you."

"If you please, sir," began Tommy, holding on tight to his pantaloons, for a very good reason too—the pins had given away.

"Do as I tell you, sir," said Mr. Stiffback, sternly. "Put your hands behind you this moment."

"Oh, lor!" thought Tommy, "if I must I must; here goes."

His faltering fingers relaxed their hold of the waistband, and—but why dwell on the indecorous scene? Our readers already know that his braces were broken and that the pins had given away.

"Tut, tut, tut! Dear me!" said Mr. Stiffback. "This is disgraceful. How dare you come here with your clothes in that condition, Codlings? Pull them up directly."

* "You will have no breakfast this morning, Master Codlings. Get up and stand over there in the corner."

There was a roar of laughter from all the boys who were behind the head master, but when he looked angrily round, there was not half a smile to be seen amongst the four-score-odd mouths of his pupils.

"It's the tailor, it is, indeed, sir," pleaded Tommy. "It's his fault. He never *will* sew the buttons on tight. They're *always* coming off."

"I cannot allow you to blame the tailor or any one else," said Mr. Stiffback. "If it was not for the possible injury to public modesty, I would make you walk through the town every day for a week in your present condition."

Cold drops of perspiration started out on Tommy's forehead. He was naturally a modest boy, and the thought of so appearing in public was truly awful, to say nothing of the youthful population of Deliverham, and how they would revile and pelt him.

"You have other trousers, I presume, Codlings?"

"Oh yes, sir."

"Are they in a similar condition with respect to their buttons?"

"Not so bad, sir," replied Tommy. "But some of 'em may be shaky."

"Go to your dormitory, and I will send Mrs. Citron to examine into the condition of your clothes. Your friends should have seen to that before they sent you."

"They were all new, sir," said Tommy. "But the tailors *won't* sew the buttons on tight, and prayers are a great trial to them, sir."

"*What!*" ejaculated the astonished Mr. Stiffback.

"I mean the kneeling down, you know, sir," Tommy hastily explained. "It's a strain unless they're sewn on very tightly, sir."

"There, there, get along with you. I will take care that you shall have no excuse of that kind for the future."

And away Tommy shuffled, feeling as shamefaced as if he had been discovered stealing a halfpenny from the tray of a blind man's dog, than which we suppose no meaner crime exists.

While this little episode was passing in the breakfast-room, another culprit, also bending beneath the weight of Mr. Stiffback's displeasure, was awaiting the hour of execution.

It was Mr. Soker—Swipy Soker, as his intimate friends called him—and he in company with the other domestics of the house, and our old friend Sam Scarecrow, were discussing their breakfast and Mr. Stiffback's strange cure for habitual intemperance.

Sam had already made himself a favourite in the servants' hall, with the female element, while he had gained the respect and even awe of the male portion by his marvellous tales of London and his adventures therein.

"Now," Sam was saying, "here we find Mr. Soker, a wery nice man, and a wery respectable man, though hardly fit for the company of sich angels as I see at this 'ere table."

"Lor now, Mr. Sam—do adun," said the cook with a giggle. "Angels, indeed! Wot next?"

Here Mr. Bunglebottle, the butler, who was supposed to entertain matrimonial designs upon the youngest housemaid, leered at that damsel until he nearly gave himself a squint as crooked as Sam's.

"But, as I was a goin' to say with regard to this 'ere go of Mr. Stiffback's, he should have tried it on a man I knowed once—his name was Wilks, but they called him the Sponge, and well he earned his name, for he soaked up everything to drink as he could come nigh, and it never took no effect on him."

"That's the sort of man I likes," said Mr. Bunglebottle—"one as can carry away his liquor on his own two legs, as a man ought for to do."

This was a home thrust at Soker, who shuffled his feet and looked guilty.

LIONEL STRUCK THE MATCH, AND APPLIED IT CAUTIOUSLY TO THE HEAP OF POWDER,

No. 21.

"Well," Sam continued, "a lot of chaps what had knowed Wilks a long time made up their minds to see if 'twasn't possible to make him tight. So ten of 'em clubbed together ten bob each, that were five pounds, and invited Wilks to a hevenin' party.'

"The wretches," said the pretty housemaid.

"So they would have bin, Mary," said Sam, "but you see this were done in the hinterests of skyence. Well, the first two of the ten was ready for Wilks when he came, and they started on cribbage and hot whiskey-and-water. In a hour the first two were under the table, and two more was fetched in, and in hour a arf they was cuddlin' one another in the fireplace, and so they came in twos, till by one in the mornin' the whole ten was insensible drunk, the whiskey gone, and Wilks as fresh as a lark."

"They never tried that game again, did they?" said Mr. Soker.

"Not they," said Sam. "But you ain't heard the rummiest part o' the story yet. This 'ere Wilks had been a cooper at a wine merchant's ever since he wos a boy, about forty years that were, and everybody had got wery fond on him, but one day he were missin' for the first time — he never would take a holiday. They sent to his lodgings to see if he were ill, but no, he'd started off to his work at the regular time; then they searched the place all over, from the cellars to the top attic, but there wasn't a sign of him; they advertised, and offered fifty pound reward; 'twasn't no use; and arter a month they guv him up."

"Had he got a wife, Mr. Sam?"

"Not as anybody ever heard tell of."

"A man of his convivial disposition weren't fit to marry," said Mr. Soker.

"That's just my opinion," said the pretty housemaid, sharply. "Women is thrown away on such low fellows."

"It was all in this way of bis'ness, Mary," said Sam. "He was in the wine and spirit trade, and he done his duty by his employers, and set a hexample to the public as can be ekalled by few and hexcelled by none. But to make a end of my story, the head gem'men about two months arter Wilks' disappearance, went over the cellars to take stock o' the wines, and arter he and his managers had, as they thought gone through the lots, the guvnor he see a hogshead stuck up agin the wall.

" 'Wot's that,' ses he?

" 'Oh, that's a hempty one,' ses the manager. 'Poor Wilks was at work puttin' new staves to it the day afore he disappeared.'

" 'Ah!' ses the guvnor, rappin' his knuckles agin it in a melancholy sort o' way, 'what a man that was! This werry cask, was it?'

" 'That werry one, sir.'

"And the manager he give it a tap too with the 'ammer.

" 'Hullo!' ses he, 'that don't sound 'oller.'

"Then the guvnor takes the 'ammer and taps the hogshead.

" 'Blow me if it is,' he ses. 'Get the ladder and we'll see into it.'

"They got the ladder, and the guvnor got up, but the moment he got his nose over the top, he began sniffing away like old boots.

" 'It's poor Wilks tumbled in,' ses the manager. 'He smells rayther high, don't he, sir?'

" 'No it ain't,' ses the guvnor, 'it's port, I think; yet there's a flavour o' sherry about it, and now I take another sniff, it might be rum. But no, it's more like good old whiskey now I come to—— Dashed if I know what it is.'

"Then the manager got up and sniffed, but he couldn't make no more on it than the guvnor, so they took some out and looked at it, and tasted it, and then the wine merchant he invited a lot of old gents as was up to everything in that way, and they smelt it, and tasted it, and was puzzled in a similar manner.

"But at last they all agreed that it must be some rare old wine as had been left there and forgot a hundred years or more ago, for it was pertikler delishus, and so strong that the old gents wot tasted it had to be took home in cabs.

"Well, the wine was drored orf, and bottled, and sold at a rare price, for there warn't nothink else like it to be got anywhere.

"So when they got nigh the bottom, the wine merchant he ses to his manager—

" 'There ain't much left, and I've made enough money out of it, so I'll keep the rest for myself. Dror it orf, and see how much there is.'

"A little while arter the manager comes up to his guvnor's orfice, pale as death, and with three pearl weskit buttons in his 'and.

" 'Hallo!' ses the old gent, 'wot's the matter?'

" 'Look 'ere,' ses the manager, holding out the buttons, 'the tap wouldn't run free, and we fished these out. Don't you reklect 'em, sir?'

"The guvnor turned pale.

"He remembered 'em. They was the weskit buttons Wilks had worn.

"He bolted into the cellar, and had the hogshead turned over, and there, at the bottom, they found all Wilks' clothes, his silver watch, and the bad 'apenny he used to toss with, but not so much as a little toe of Wilks himself.

"The guvnor was pretty nigh wild, for he didn't know wot to make of it.

"The perlice was called in, and took the clothes into custody, but that warn't much comfort. But at last a skyentific gent, who heard of the matter, and knowed Wilks, took away some o' the wine, and anerlized it to see wot it was made of, and then he came to the wine merchant, and he ses—

" 'My friend, do you know wot you and these other gents have been a drinkin' of?'

" 'No,' ses they.

" 'You've bin imbibin' essence o' Wilks,' he ses. 'That unfortunate man had so soaked hisself for nigh forty years with all sorts of licker, that at last, bein' completually satoorated, he melted down in the bottom o' that cask, and you're nothin' less than cannibils.'

"They all fainted away on the spot, and when the guvnor came round, he had a crowner's quest on all the bottled Wilks as hadn't been sold, and they do say that the jurry, arter givin' their verdic' got hold o' the bottles aud drank all the flavoured Wilks there was left.

"As for the old wine merchant, he took to hankybilious pills to get Wilks out of his system, and brought hisself down to sich a shadder that there warn't enough of him to die."

"Come, Mr. Sam," said the cook, as our long friend brought his story to a conclusion, "you don't expect us to believe all that?"

"It's true, every word," said Sam, gravely. "I tasted a drop of the poor chap myself, and wery good he was. I know one old gent who wos made a infidel of through the story, for he couldn't make out how Wilks would get along at the Resurrection."

"I believe you're a infiddle yourself, Mr. Sam," said the pretty housemaid; "or you wouldn't say such things."

"I believe in one thing, Mary," said Sam, with a winning smile.

"What's that?"

"Why, that you're the puttiest gal for twenty mile round," replied Sam, squinting affectionately at her.

"Here, young man," said Mr. Bunglebottle, "don't you go too fur."

"You be blowed!" said Sam. "Who's agoin' too far?"

"What!" ejaculated the butler. "Have I lived to be blowed by a red-headed boy who squints?"

"Squint, do I?" said Sam. "I can see the way

straight enough to your nose, and I'll find it too.
I'd rayther hev a red head than a red nose any
day."

Mr. Bunglebottle grew crimson with wrath, and
looked round for wherewith to smash Sam, and a
battle royal would have ensued, but for Mary, who
threw her arms around the long youth, and the
cook, who fainted up against the butler, and thereby upset him.

Just then the clock chimed forth the hour of
nine, and simultaneously the schoolroom bell
rang.

A sweet smile stole over the features of Soker.
The signal was for him to appear, and intoxicate
himself in Mr. Stiffback's presence. He was a
victim, but never went forth victim to the sacrifice
with a more serene and happy countenance.

CHAPTER XXII.

HOW MR. STIFFBACK TRIED TO CURE SOKER OF
GETTING TIPSY, ON THE HOMŒOPATHIC PRIN-
CIPLE, AND THE RESULTS THEREOF—THE HEAD
MASTER'S ELOQUENT LECTURE UPON THE DE-
BASING EFFECTS OF INTOXICATION, ILLUS-
TRATED BY SOKER—END OF THE FIRST ACT,
AND BEGINNING OF A LITTLE FARCE BY
LIONEL WILFUL & CO.

MR. SOKER, attired in his holiday costume to
do full honour to the occasion, presented
himself at the class room door severely
erect, like a man conscious that he was
about to perform a public duty.

"Oh! is that you, Soker?" said Mr. Stiffback,
blandly. "Come up here."

On the dais or platform, where stood the head
master's desk, were a table and chairs, and on the
former a neat array of bottles, a tumbler, a sugar
basin, and a spirit lamp, with a small kettle of
water simmering merrily away.

Soker fixed his eyes upon the tempting sight,
licked his lips, and then slowly passed the back of
his hand across his mouth.

"Sit down, Soker, and begin," said Mr. Stiffback again. "There are brandy, gin, rum, and
whiskey; you can manage to intoxicate yourself by
dinner time, I hope?"

"Lor bless you, yes, sir," said Soker, with a pity-
ing smile at his master's simplicity. "A man who
knows wot's wot can get tight and begin again in
three hours."

"Then get tight, as you call it, and begin again,"
said Mr. Stiffback. "There is no stint, Soker;
when you have emptied those bottles they shall be
refilled."

"You're very good, sir," said Soker, taking his
seat at the table, and singling out a bottle with a
red seal and pink labels, the distinctive marks of
the genuine and only Kinahan, he mixed himself a
stiff glass of toddy.

It was a rather embarrassing position to sit there
in solitary state, the cynosure of so many merry,
mischievous eyes; but having disposed of his first
tumbler and filled it up again, his bashfulness departed, and its place was filled by a strong tendency
to harmony, very much out of keeping with the
studious decorum of a schoolroom.

"He's getting buffy already," whispered Lionel.
"I wish I had a pea-shooter."

"I've got one," said Charlie.

"Hand it over, and just cover me, will you? I
don't want old Stiffback to catch me out."

Our hero had no peas, but a piece of paper
neatly manipulated did as well, and the first shot
struck Soker on the tip of the nose and bounced
off into his glass.

Soker audibly "cussed" an imaginary fly, took
a drink, and was instantly choked with the pellet of
paper.

He turned red in the face, a spluttering kind of

growl seemed to proceed from some region very low
down behind his waistcoat, then he clutched his
throat with one hand, got up and stamped, and
after a minute or so of this eccentric exercise he
heaved up a sigh of relief and the piece of paper,
"cussed" the flies more loudly than before, and
swallowed the remainder of his grog at a draught.

"Silence, Soker," said Mr. Stiffback; "you must
get intoxicated quietly. I cannot allow you to
disturb the school."

"Wot did the flies want a gettin' in my licker
for?" growled Soker, who was fast approaching
that republican stage of intoxication, when every
man is as good as another, and better too.

"I'll have a shy now," said Charlie. "I've got
such a buster ready for him."

"Right you are," said Lionel. "Take aim under
my arm."

The "buster," which Drummond had prepared
occupied nearly one half of the pea-shooter, and
was indeed such a portentous missile that Drummond blew himself nearly black in the face before
he could get it to start.

It was well aimed and soft, and spread all over
Soker's right eye, striking with a "plop" that was
quite audible throughout the school.

Soker thought that he was attacked by a blue-
bottle of the first magnitude, and brought his hand
down with a smack upon the paper.

"I've got him," he exclaimed.

"What is it, Soker?" demanded Mr. Stiffback,
angrily. "You really must intoxicate yourself
with less noise."

"It's these here dashed blue-bottles," said Soker,
"but I've settled this chap anyhow."

And carefully scooping out the wet paper, he
threw it away, and, feeling satisfied that his enemy
was done for, mixed another tumbler full of grog.

"He must be getting groggy, Charlie, to take that
for a blue-bottle," said Lionel. "Hallo, he's going
to sing."

In fact Soker, who had nearly finished the whiskey now, gave sundry preliminary growls, and
suddenly burst forth into song, leaning back in
his chair, shutting his eyes, and opening his mouth
so widely that a curious man might have been
able to see what he had had for his breakfast.

"Be quiet, Soker," said Mr. Stiffback, raising his
voice to an unusual pitch.

"For my love she's crossed the wide blue sea,
Ten thousand miles awa—a—a—a—ay."

"Silence," thundered the head master, shaking
Soper vigorously by the collar. "Dear me, Mr.
Jilk, I had no idea that tipsy persons were noisy
unless they were in congenial company. Oblige
me by shaking him a little on your side."

The classical master, who had been a powerful
athlete in his college days, and had rowed stroke
in the Oxford eight, gave Soker such a shaking
that his singing was instantly stopped, and one
of the legs of the chair came off.

"Who di' that?" shouted Soker, staring at Mr.
Stiffback with a glassy eye.

Mr. Jilk relieved his mind of any doubt upon the
subject by shaking him again. Mr. Soker glared
strangely at the master, and then making a supreme
effort to stand upright, commenced to pull off his
coat.

Mr. Jilk just gave the warlike Soker a push with
his forefinger, and he rolled over amidst the ruins
of the broken chairs.

Mr. Stiffback looked down upon the fallen Soker,
who was making frantic attempts to rise, and
pointing at him the finger of scorn, thus addressed
the boys:—

"Oh see, young gentlemen, some of the evil
effects of that fatal vice, intoxication! It was not
without a purpose that I have caused this odious
scene to be enacted before you, even as the
Spartans brought their sons to look upon the filthy

debauches of the Helots. ("I thought he'd bring that in," growled Charlie.) In after years may this picture of a man reduced to the level of the brutes by drunkenness dwell upon your memories, and cause you to shun that abhorrent Lethe. Rather submit to the direst adversity—rather suffer the most cruel blow—— Oh !"

It was a dreadful anti-climax to Mr. Stiffback's touching speech, but just as he had reached this pathetic adjuration Soker succeeded in balancing himself, and hitting out, struck his master, with singular exactitude, on the very tip of his nose.

Mr. Stiffback went over as if he had been shot. Mr. Jilk revenged the insult offered to his chief by bestowing on Soker a back-handed slap, sending that gentleman once more amongst the ruins of the chairs, where he made the acquaintance of several splinters of colossal magnitude.

"How do you feel, sir—are you much hurt ?" inquired Mr. Jilk, as he hauled the head master to his feet.

"Not much," gasped Mr. Stiffback, trying to smile, but looking as if he would very much like to punch Soker's head.

"Take my handkerchief, sir ; one of you boys get a little cold water."

"Put a key up his nose, sir," suggested Tommy, with some hazy idea of a popular remedy for such accidents.

It is needless to say that Tommy's advice was not adopted, the cold water soon stopped the bleeding, and Mr. Stiffback improved the occasion by pointing out to his pupils how the vile habit of intoxication changed quiet men into wild beasts, who under its baneful influence delighted in shedding the gore of their fellow creatures.

"That's all very fine," whispered Lionel, "but I'll bet he don't like his own gore shed. He'll give up trying to make Soker sober by making him drunk."

"Not a bit of it," said Charlie. "He's an obstinate old chap, and he'll try the game for a week."

"If he does we'll have some fun with Soker. Did you ever have a lark with a tipsy man, Charlie ?"

"Why, yes, you know we have. With Noodles, at Styngy's."

"Oh ah, I'd forgotten that. Well, if we get a chance at dinner time we'll take it out of him for turning the handle of that dashed flogging-machine."

"Tell Tommy, then. He'd like to be in that."

"He's behind somewhere. The French master's got hold of him, by jingo."

"Has he ? So he has. That's a venomous little beast."

"He's all that. By the way, I wonder what became of that French chap I had the duel with."

"Why, I told you when I went to Hampstead."

"You never mentioned him."

"I meant to, then. Poor beggar, he was one of the first who caught the fever, and he died."

"I am sorry," said Lionel, regretfully. "There were the makings of a thorough good fellow in him, only those confounded notions they stuffed into his head about rank and birth damaged him a little. See what a different chap Vansittart is."

"Ah, isn't he ? But I say, Li, haven't you heard anything more about his fight ?"

"It's all right for Monday, you know, and I'm going to spar with him this evening."

"That's prime ; you'll let me come and look ? "

"I'll ask him ; but you'll have to keep it very quiet, for if Stiffback gets wind of the fight he'll stop it."

"That wouldn't do."

"Not at any price," said Lionel, emphatically.

Here the conversation was brought to a full stop by the class in which our hero and his chums were being called up for examination.

About an hour after, Soker, who had gone to sleep on the platform after an ineffectual attempt to wrestle with the splinters, woke up a little sober, but very thirsty, and demanded something to drink.

"There is the brandy bottle, Soker," said Mr. Stiffback, blandly. "Help yourself."

After awhile, Soker managed to extricate himself from the wreck of the chairs, and mix himself a stiff dose of brandy and water.

That made him feel better, so he had another, then a third, then a fourth to keep the other three company, and by dinner time he was as helplessly drunk as any respectable publican could wish to see a man.

Mr. Bunglebottle and the footman were summoned to carry him away, having strict orders to bring him back to the class-room at two o'clock ; and so the helpless Soker was borne, being heavily bumped at all the available corners, and finally deposited in the outhouse, where the gentle exercises of boot and knife cleaning, and such other domestic gymnastics were performed.

He reposed for awhile peacefully on the mat where he had been laid, but in the course of half an hour, three demons, who looked like boys to ordinary mortals, and who called each other Lionel, Charlie, and Tommy, entered, and then his sleep began to be troubled by visions of boots and blacking brushes and saucepan lids flying about his head, and occasionally alighting upon his body, much to the inconvenience thereof.

"Wa' th' dooshe's matter ?" he said, struggling into a sitting position, and glaring wildly about the room.

Everything seemed to his muddled intellect to be ten times its size, things which ought to have been stationary were moving about in the most eccentric manner, and inanimate objects were strangely endowed with life.

Soker was in an incipient state of delirium tremens, and the belief that he was haunted by a legion of demons entered into his head. He made for the door, but an imp, twenty feet high, with fiery coals for eyes, turned him back ; then he made for the window, but there were two more there. The only passage available now was the chimney, and into that Soker thrust his head and shoulders, and began to wriggle his way up.

"There's a pretty condition for a man to get into," said Lionel, who had seemed like the twenty feet imp to Soker a few moments ago.

"Let's help him up the chimney since he seems so anxious to go," added Charlie. "Come and give a shove, Li."

"Here's a better game than that," said Tommy, coming up with a canister in his hand. "Here's some gunpowder. He thought we were devils, now he'll smell the brimstone."

And without a thought of the possible consequence of what they were about to do—boys seldom do that—Tommy made a pile of the gunpowder just below the luckless Soker, who had got half way up the chimney, and Lionel lighting a match, applied it cautiously to the train.

CHAPTER XXIII.

THE EXPLOSION, AND AN UNEXPECTED RESULT—SOKER IN DIFFICULTIES—MR. BUNGLEBOTTLE'S THEORY OF SPONTANEOUS COMBUSTION—FIRE—THE HEAD MASTER BECOMES ALARMED—TOMMY OODLINGS IN THE WAY AGAIN, AS USUAL.

IT was a moment of breathless excitement for Tommy and Drummond when at last the train of powder was ignited. It was something like hunting on a large scale, only instead of bringing their "game down," they designed to "send it up."

There was only a pound of powder, and few of our readers but are aware that such a quantity will produce a considerable effect in a small room.

In this case it blew out two windows, floored all three of the boys, especially Tommy, who was so much floored that there seemed little likelihood of his getting up again; besides both his eyebrows were neatly shaved off, and had his nose been anything but a pug of the comicallest and flattest dimensions he would have fost that as well.

But the effect produced by the powder was greatest in the perpendicular direction, that is, in the chimney, where the nether garments of Mr. Soker were so liberally displayed.

They were already a tight fit, but the explosive action of the powder concentrating itself on the seat of his pantaloons had jammed him in very firmly indeed, but that was not the full extent of his misfortune, for sundry sparks had lodged upon the cloth, and that being of a very dry and tindery nature, began to smoulder, much to the discomfort of the gentleman inside.

Lionel and Charlie scrambled to their feet, but little the worse for their fall, physically, though mentally it must be confessed that they were in no small fright at the unexpected force of the explosion.

"I say," whispered Charlie, trying to choke back a cough, for the smoke was very dense, "do you think we've killed him?"

"I don't hear any groans," replied Lionel. "But no, he can't be dead; I can see his legs kicking about."

"He must be dreadfully burnt."

"Awful. I never thought it would go off like that. It was Tommy's fault for getting too much out of the canister."

"Where is he? I'll give him a hot 'un for this," said Charlie.

"Bolted, I fancy," said Lionel, who could not see the prostrate form of the unlucky Tommy, veiled as it was by the clouds of smoke.

"That's what we'd better do then, Li. There's sure to be somebody down here directly. They must have heard the blow-up."

"How about poor Soker? Suppose he gets smothered—or something?"

"No fear of that. They'll be here in a minute. Hark—by jingo, I can hear footsteps."

Self-preservation is the first law of nature. Both Lionel and Charlie were very loath to leave the victim of their little joke to take care of himself, but they were bound to save their own tender frames from the awful infliction of the flogging-machine, and they did it.

They were only just in time, for scarcely had they hidden themselves behind a sheltering corner than the enemy came in sight, headed by Mr. Bunglebottle, with a pale and excited face, and with about a pint of water in a tin can.

He, while standing at the kitchen door envying Soker's happy lot in being intoxicated gratis for a whole week, had heard the explosion, and his mind being in a fit state for the reception of such an idea, jumped at the conclusion that it was a case of spontaneous combustion.

"He's done it," gasped Mr. Bunglebottle, turning livid with excitement. "I know'd he would at last. Here—Hi!—Mary—you Sam—run for the master, somebody—Soker's blowed hisself up with whiskey!"

"Hallo!" said Sam, emerging from the kitchen, where he had been carrying on a lively flirtation with the pretty housemaid. "Who's afire now?"

"That there Soker," replied the butler, in gasps of a syllable each, for excitement had the effect of exercise on him. "He's—com—busted hisself."

"Not spontaneyous?" said Sam, opening his eyes.

"Yes—that's it," replied Mr. Bunglebottle. "Luke, you go and fetch the gov'nor this minnit."

"I must go and hev a look at this," said Sam, brightening. "I've orfen wanted to see a cove reg ular combust hisself, but it were awful disreg

appointin', for no sooner did they get theirselves up to the rekisit pitch with gin or rum, than they was sure to die off with deridilum trimmings, or liver complaint, afore they was set alight to."

And full of a lively sort of satisfaction at the opportunity afforded him of beholding a genuine case of spontaneous combustion, Sam hurried off to the outhouse just in time to catch sight of his young master and Charlie.

"Hallo," thought Sam, "here's another disappointment, I'll wager. Master Lionel has been up to his tricks. I can smell the gunpowder from here."

And the long youth following up the track, soon came upon our hero and his chum, perched behind a corner of an outbuilding, whence they could see who approached the shed.

"Hallo, Sam. That you?"

"That's me, Master Lionel," said Sam, with a broad grin of satisfaction. "Another of your little games, eh, Master Lionel?"

"Something in that line, Sam," replied our hero, with a wink. "Is anybody else coming, Sam?"

"Anybody?" replied the long youth. "Heverybody I should say. Bunglebottle hev frightened the house with bellerin as Soker had combusted hisself spontaneyous, and he took me in till I see you boltin' round the corner, and smelt the gunpowder, then I knew what sort of a combustion it were."

"I hope they'll come soon," said our hero.

"Why so, Master Lionel?"

"Because there's a party up the chimney, who'll find it rather awkward to get out unless he's helped."

"How did he get up?"

"He climbed part of the way, and we helped him the rest with a pound or so of gunpowder."

"Rather awk'ard for his breeches, Master Lionel."

"I think it was. Anyhow, he kicked like—like —what did he kick like, Charlie?" said Lionel, hard up for a comparison.

"Like old boots," replied that youth.

"Ah, I daresay," said Sam. "A pound o' gunpowder is trying to the feelins', specially when it's let off behind a man, and he can't dodge. Here they come!"

Sam's exclamation heralded the appearance of Mr. Bunglebottle, the head master, and the professors of French and German, the latter who was scientifically disposed, carrying a note book and a case of dissecting instruments.

They were all running at the top of their speed, Mr. Stiffback being particularly active, for he feared that Soker had really fallen a victim to an excess of alcohol and knew not how far the law would implicate him.

At sight of the smoke, which still slowly rolled forth from the shattered windows, Mr. Stiffback became agonised with alarm, and illustrating the familiar proverb, "the more haste the less speed," pushed Mr. Bunglebottle down and fell over him into the shed.

Monsieur de Vinaigre and Herr Kobblersvax jammed one another in the doorway and remaining fixed there, exchanged compliments in their respective languages with a volubility that was perfectly bewildering.

"Soker—Soker," called Mr. Stiffback, in frantic tones. "Where are you?"

There was no reply, and the schoolmaster peered anxiously through the smoke, dreading to see only a heap of charred remains to tell the awful tale.

He fancied at length he saw some object moving in a corner, and rushing forward he seized it with a joyful exclamation.

"He is alive!" he cried. "Thank heaven I am not his murderer!"

Herr Kobblersvax and Monsieur de Vinaigre were still jammed tight in the doorway.

Neither would give way an inch, and the language they used was truly awful, though, fortunately for the sensitive ears of Mr. Jilk and the boys of the upper form, they jabbered so rapidly that to understand what they said would have been impossible to anyone but a native.

"Get out of the way," shouted Mr. Stiffback, struggling to the door beneath the weight of Tommy, who, although he was short, weighed an astonishing number of pounds.

But neither the German nor the French professor paid the least attention to the head master.

They were too busy quarrelling and pelting each other with words fourteen syllables or so in length.

"Will you get out of the way?" shouted Mr. Stiffback.

The professors moved not, with the exception of their tongues, which wagged away at a tremendous rate.

Mr. Stiffback was naturally angry.

Here was a man, dying perhaps, while two blockheads quarrelled in the doorway.

The schoolmaster stepped back, took a short run, and, using Tommy as a battering-ram, charged the two professors.

They went out of the doorway like a cork out of a pop-gun, and Mr. Stiffback, laying his burden gently on the ground, roared for water.

One of the elder boys ran off for some, and Mr. Jilk came forward and stared at Tommy, who was so begrimed from head to foot with powder that it was difficult to tell one end of him from the other.

"Dear me," said Mr. Jilks, "is that Soker?"

"Of course it is," replied Mr. Stiffback, sharply. "Who else should it be?"

"He's a good deal smaller," suggested Mr. Jilk.

"Well, sir, are you not aware that this is a case of spontaneous combustion? He's shrunk in the cooking."

Mr. Jilk looked at the head master as if he hardly thought this theory reconcilable with common sense; but Mr. Stiffback was his chief, and it would never have done to dispute his arguments.

By the time the water arrived, and had been emptied over Tommy, the schoolmaster's agitation had so far subsided that he was enabled to perceive that Soker had indeed "shrunk very much in the cooking."

"It's that boy again," he said, angrily. "The new boy Codlings, whom I have already punished more than once."

"No doubt of it," added Mr. Jilk, laying hold of Tommy's ear.

It may be here remarked that some curious instinct invariably led everybody to inflict personal suffering upon the plump youth in that fashion.

"Then," said Mr. Jilk, "where is Soker?"

"Good gracious me!" replied Mr. Stiffback, in a wild manner, "I don't know. I couldn't see anything but Codlings."

"Perhaps he knows. Codlings."

Tommy, just awakening to the consciousness that he was still alive and tolerably whole, except his eyebrows and a few bits of skin, sat up, and, not noticing the august company in which he was, began to sing the chorus of a recently popular and national anthem.

"'I'm out on the booze, I'm out on the booze—
What matter——'"

"That's what it matters!" exclaimed the outraged master, giving Tommy a "hot 'un" on the right ear. "Answer my question at once."

"'A frog he would a-wooing go—
Heigho! says Rowley.'"

"Comment! vat he say about a frog? Tzat mean an insult for me," said the French master, who, burning to avenge his fall upon somebody, pounced upon Tommy as a helpless victim, and, of course, began with those unlucky ears of his.

Meantime, Lionel, Charlie, and Sam were anxiously watching the proceedings from their hiding-place.

"Why the dickens don't they fetch Soker out?" said Lionel, impatiently. "What a lot of duffers they are."

"P'raps as how they didn't see him, Master Lionel?"

"Bosh! Anyone could see his legs sticking out of the chimney—they couldn't help it."

"Perhaps he's stuck in too tight," suggested Charlie.

"Oh, lor! don't say that, Charlie."

"Don't you fear, Master Lionel," said Sam. "I'll warrant there's no harm come to him. Drunkin' men can stand being chopped to pieces without hurtin' on 'em. I'll run in and see arter him."

"Do, Sam, there's a brick. We'd go too, only we're marked with the powder, and should be caught out."

"Right you are, Master Lionel; and regardin' of the cove in the chimbley. Is he to be fetched hout?"

"Of course, Sam."

"It shall be done, then, even if he have to come out in pieces."

And Sam, watching his opportunity, dived into the out-house just as Mr. Stiffback, now really alarmed at the apparently mysterious disappearance of Soker, thought of sending someone for the police.

The long youth hastened to to the chimney, and there, sure enough, were the legs of the unlucky Soker dangling over the fireplace.

His trousers were still smouldering in patches, and from time to time a convulsive jerk told that a spark of life yet lingered in his body.

"My eye," thought Sam, "he must be like a cat, blest with nine lives! and if eight and a harf of 'em ain't gone a'ready, I'm a Dutchman. Down you come."

And the long youth, as he spoke, took hold of Soker's legs just above the ankles, and gave a mighty tug.

No result, except the fall of a little soot, rewarded Sam's first effort.

"He is a tight fit, blow me," thought Sam; "but he's bound to come."

And taking a fresh hold, Sam set one foot against the back of the grate and hauled again, but Soker stirred not an inch.

"Blow it," said Sam; "he must have hooked hisself to suthin, but I think I stretched him a bit that turn."

It was just possible that Soker was aware that he was being stretched, and didn't like it, for he began to jerk his legs with renewed vigour.

"It's woke him up," said Sam, with renewed hope. "These old-fashioned chimbleys is gen'rally wide enough to give a fellow air. Dash it, I must hev him down this time though, or Master Lionel will be gettin' anxious."

Again Sam grabbed Mr. Soker by the ankles, and then, setting both his feet against the sides of the fireplace, he hauled away for dear life.

First there were two sharp cracks, proceeding from the ankles of the sufferer, then two more from his knees, then a smothered groan from that portion of Soker which was up the chimney.

"Never mind," panted Sam, "it's only like havin' a tooth out. The hagony'll be over directly."

Suddenly, and all at once, like an obstinate cork out of a bottle, Soker came out of the chimney just as Sam had put on all his strength for a final effort.

The result may be imagined.

They both rolled with a crash into the middle of the floor.

Mr. Stiffback and his assistant heard the noise, and, brightening with hope, rushed in just in time to behold the commencement of a desperate combat

Soker, frantic with pain, anger, and fear, had laid hold of Sam's hair with one hand, and with the other he essayed to cure that intellectual young gentleman of his squint for ever by the simple plan of gouging his eyes out.

"Thank heaven," exclaimed Mr. Stiffback, "it's Soker, and alive."

"I should think he wos alive!" yelled Sam. "A dashed sight too lively for me. Pull him orf!"

Mr. Jilk neatly twisted Soker away, and holding him at arm's length, propped him up against the wall.

"Now," said Mr. Stiffback, sternly, "what do you mean by it, Soker?"

Fright and pain had sobered the coachman a little, but he was still dimly conscious that he had been tortured by a legion of imps, and Sam looked almost ugly enough for one.

"What did they himps shove me up the chimbley for, then, and set alight to me?" growled Soker. "Look at my ——."

"Trousers, Soker, you should say, or pantaloons," said Mr. Stiffback, hastily. "I must have better language."

"Blow better language!" said Soker, sulkily. "Let's hev better manners fust. How would you like to be tortered like a wild Injun?"

"Nonsense, Soker," said the schoolmaster. "It is the effect of what you had to drink. Your imagination is disordered."

"Imaginashun!" said the excited Soker, turning sharply round and bringing into full view the scorched portion of his attire. "Is this here 'ole imaginashun? Is these 'ere blisters the work o' fancy or of himps? Was it fancy as shoved me up the chimbley?"

"Hush, Soker, hush!" said Mr. Stiffback, who had quite recovered his habitual coolness; "calm yourself, it is two o'clock, and the classes are about to assemble. You had better stay here to wash yourself, and put your dress in order."

"Not for me," said the coachman; "that wasn't the contrack, sir. I'm a going to get drunk, if you please."

"Wait until to-morrow morning, Soker; you have had enough to-day."

"Now that's wot I call mean," said the coachman, with strong emphasis on the adjective; "you contrack to make a man comf't'ble for a week, and cries off the first day. That won't do for Soker, Misser Stiffback."

The schoolmaster would have given a trifle to relinquish the attempt to cure Soker of drunkenness on this new principle, but to acknowledge that he had failed upon the first day, and in the presence of the boys, would never do.

"Very well, Soker," he said; "Bunglebottle and Luke will bring you to the class-room when you are in a fit condition. See that he is washed and his—er—pantaloons changed for others, Bunglebottle."

"I will, sir."

"And now, gentlemen," continued the schoolmaster, putting on his magisterial demeanour, "we will, if you please, forget this untoward accident, and proceed to the class-room."

CHAPTER XXIV.

SWIPY SOKER DEMANDS THE FULFILMENT OF THE CONTRACT, AND IS ACCOMMODATED BY MR. STIFFBACK—NEWS OF THE GRAND "MILL"— THE RENDEZVOUS IN VANSITTART'S SNUGGERY —TOMMY CODLINGS TRIES TO PLAY THE SPY, AND GETS INTO TERRIBLE TROUBLE IN CONSEQUENCE—THE NORTH-WEST PASSAGE BENEATH THE DESKS—A NEW WAY OF RUNNING THE GAUNTLET—TOMMY AVENGES HIMSELF, BUT MAKES A MISTAKE AS TO THE PERSON, AND IS SUITABLY REWARDED BY MR. STIFFBACK—A "JOLLY LARK" IN PERSPECTIVE.

IT was fortunate for Mr. Stiffback that he had secured the services of Bunglebottle and the footman to look after Soker, for that person imbibed a quantity of whiskey, in comparison with which his morning's consumption was a dose for an infant.

It had an extremely warlike effect upon him too, and there must have been some trace of Irish ancestry in his blood, for he executed part of a patthern jig in first-rate style, requested anybody present to tread on the tail of his coat, and floored Luke, the under footman, in "rale Donnybrook fashion" with an ebony ruler for a shillalagh.

Mr. Stiffback's control of his pupils was as nearly perfect as could be. They were as well drilled as a regiment of guards, but this discipline was gravely tried by Soker's exhibition.

Not to laugh, more or less audibly, was impossible. The under masters, and the professors themselves, broke down more than once in the effort to preserve their gravity; the head master alone was able to command his features.

Lionel and Charlie Drummond devoted themselves to the propulsion of peas through their shooters, and being, as our readers know, tolerably expert shots, it is possible that some of Soker's fury may have been due to the "peppering" our heroes gave him.

Lionel's interest in Soker waned a little after that day in consequence of the approaching fight between Vansittart and the town bully.

It was a proof that Vansittart had not only great onfidence, but a strong liking for our hero, that he confided to him details known only besides to a few of the upper form boys.

Some of these rather resented the introduction amongst them of a lower-class boy, but when Vansittart said that he would make it a personal quarrel if any one insulted or bullied Lionel without cause, no more was said.

"Very kind of you, Van," said Lionel. "But it wasn't worth the trouble. There's hardly a fellow in the upper form but yourself that I wouldn't mind tackling."

"Come now, young Wilful, draw that a little milder. Why there are fellows there, heavier and stronger than I am."

"There may be one or two heavier, but I'll be shot if any of 'em are stronger."

"None of your blarney now, Wilful," laughed Vansittart. "And don't forget the boxing tonight; you'll be able to put some of the bigger fellows up to a wrinkle or two."

"You're chaffing me now, Van."

"Not a bit of it. I have had a bout with them all in turn, and they're a clumsy lot."

"For all you know I may be as bad, or worse."

"Deuce a bit, you're a neat hand with 'the fives,' I know. You've had lessons, haven't you?"

"Only in an amateur way, with other fellows."

"A little polishing's all you want; but I'll see what your form is to-night, when you put the gloves on."

"There's my chum Charlie, I suppose he may come, too?"

"You haven't said anything about it, have you?"

"I only told him I thought there'd be a little sparring to-night."

"I wish you hadn't mentioned it, young Wilful," said Vansittart, in a vexed tone. "You see the big fellows made a bother about admitting you, and if I take two in in spite of its being against our own rules, it will be presuming on my being the leader, don't you see."

"You're too tender with 'em," said Lionel. "When I'm leader of a school I do as I think best, and those who don't like it can do the other thing."

"Well, perhaps I am a little too particular. I'll make it all right for you and your chum."

"Thanks, and I'll answer for Charlie that if any fellow, not quite double his size, objects to his coming in, he'll argue the point."

"That won't do either, at least not till this fight's over," said Vansittart; "for all who are in the secret are going to keep the ring."

"What, will there be a regular ring, roped and staked?" said Lionel.

"Yes. It will be all arranged prize-fight fashion. I don't like the idea I confess, but I can't draw out of it now."

"Of course not," said Lionel.

"And as there'll be a lot of shady customers there who might cut up rough, I've picked out the fellows I can best depend on to back me."

"You've paid me a high compliment," said Lionel, flushing with pleasure. "You won't regret having me and my chums with you."

"I'm sure of that. Hallo, there goes the 'study' bell. Have you got much to prepare for to-morrow?"

"Not a great deal, and what there is is easy."

"All right then, hurry over it, and meet me at the top of the dormitory stairs."

Vansittart sauntered off to the study of the upper form, and Lionel sought out Charlie and telegraphed the intelligence to him.

Tommy, who had been exiled to a distant corner by the French master, saw the signs passing, but could make nothing of them.

"There's something up," he thought, "between Li and Charlie. I wonder what it is. Blow it, now Vansittart chums with 'em they're too proud to notice me. There now, there goes Li out at the door, and he's winking to Charlie to follow. I'll go too, dashed if I don't."

And Tommy, dropping suddenly on his hands and knees, crawled under the desks and made for the door.

Unfortunately though in his progress he had to take a few turnings to avoid coming into contact with sundry obstacles, and as a matter of course he lost his way.

It was to Tommy as if he had been left amongst the pathless wilds of the South American forests. Around him was a wilderness of boots and shoes and trousers, gently agitated by the legs and feet within them.

"Here's a go," thought Tommy, "I've gone the wrong way. What form is this, I wonder. There's a pair of big check breeches, and a shoe with a crack on the side, who do they belong to? Dash it! if I could see a leg I knew I'd pinch it, and ask the way out."

Then Tommy endeavoured to peep between some of the legs, the better to trace his way, but they were oscillating at such a rate and so perpetually shifting position, that he might as well have tried to look through the proverbial mill-stone.

"Blow it," thought Tommy, "I must get out somehow," as the toe of a 'blucher' fetched him one in the jaw. "You ought to be ashamed of yourself, whoever you are, for wearing boots like this."

The passage narrowed, and the kicks were coming upon Tommy unpleasantly thick and strong. To make matters worse, he now saw that the forms and desks beneath which he was crawling were pushed close up against a wall.

"Burst a frog," thought Tommy savagely.

"Now I've got to crawl all the way back, and these fellows kicking like old boots. Dash you, will you leave off?"

An unusually smart kick, taking the skin off the bridge of his nose, caused Tommy to give vent to this adjuration, and it was hardly out of his mouth before he received another which seemed to take off the top of his right ear.

He could hardly repress a howl of agony, but he knew his especial enemy, the French master, was in the study, and he dared not avenge himself upon the leg which had kicked him.

The worst of it was that Tommy being obliged to use his hands to support himself could not ward off the blows, neither could he turn round; there wasn't room, and he had to retrace his steps backwards.

It was an awful time. Tommy thought of the passage of the Beresina, of the pass of Thermopylæ, of the charge of the Light Brigade through the Valley of Death at Balaclava, and mentally concluded that he would rather have taken apart in any one of those dangerous exploits; nay, that he would even have preferred being the Derby dog panting madly down the course before the great race, to running the gauntlet of that double line of boots and shoes.

"Dash it," muttered Tommy. "They know I'm down here and they're doing it on purpose. Oh, won't I take it out of some of those Bobbles for this."

This was a very wrong and vengeful resolution of Tommy's, for he had no knowledge that any of his ancient foes were taking part in thus torturing him, but the plump youth had got a fixed idea into his head that they were at the bottom of all his misfortunes, and that was enough for him.

Crawling backwards is at all times a slow and painful mode of exercise, except perhaps to a crab, and as Tommy could not direct his course he was perpetually cannoning against the feet and legs he hoped to avoid, and the kicking he received became more spiteful than ever.

"Blowed if I stand it any longer," muttered Tommy savagely, and halting he picked up a pin and seeing a pair of patent leather boots and neatly fitting trousers close to him he ran the instrument in up to the head.

The leg disappeared, drawn upwards with a spasmodic jerk, the pin still sticking in the wound and a shrill voice which Tommy had already learned to dread, uttered a cry of agony.

"My eye," thought Tommy, "I've done it now, It's Frenchy."

It was. The next moment the form was dragged aside, and the infuriated face of Monsieur de Vinagre appeared, then Tommy felt his ear, his tortured ear, imprisoned in his long fingers, and he was hauled out.

"Ah, c'est toi donc—petit gr—r—redin!" hissed the French master, furious with rage and pain, for the pin had gone in up to the root. "Come wiz me instantly."

Tommy would much rather have accepted an invitation to Jericho or Putney, but M. de Vinaigre had him by the ear in such a persuasive fashion that refusal was out of the question.

"Just my luck," thought Tommy. "There never was such a fellow as I am. Dash it! there's those Bobbles grinning at me. I'll warm 'em for that."

Tommy was aching all over, sore from head to foot, and yet the thought of getting one of the starchy young gentlemen into a corner, and punching his head until it was soft, was balm to his bruises.

Monsieur de Vinaigre had been in such a hurry to capture Tommy that he had not examined the wound in his leg, and he had no idea that the pin still remained in its novel pin-cushion.

It felt very sore.

He was fully aware of that, and he hopped,

rather than walked, to the head master's private study.

Arrived at the door, he "punched" it viciously, as if it had been Tommy's head, and, in obedience to Mr. Stiffback's "Come in," entered with a dramatic scowl upon his face.

"Eh? What? Dear me!" exclaimed the head master, looking up from his papers. "That boy Codlings again. Tut, tut, tut!"

"If you please, sir," began Tommy.

But M. de Vinaigre, who still had hold of his ear, gave it such a twist that the sentence concluded with a howl.

"Silence, Codlings," said Mr. Stiffback. "Do not speak until I tell you. Monsieur, let go his ear, and please to tell me why you have brought him to me."

"Monsieur," said the Frenchman, in his deepest voice, and with a melodramatic scowl, "zis boy have stab me."

"Oh! what a lie," said Tommy.

Mr. Stiffback froze him with a look.

"Another such word as that, Codlings, and I will punish you as I never punished a boy yet. Proceed, monsieur."

"Zis boy," continued the Frenchman, with the voice and gestures of a stage conspirator about to divulge an awful secret, "he have nourish up ze feelings of r-r-revenge for me because I ponish him. I do not feel safe ven I look in his eye, and I poot him in ze cornare. Ze time pass, I look round, he is go. I call, Codleens, tree time, he answer not. All of a once I feel ze blow; it is ze knife of Codleens. I turn; I see him vere he cr-r-rouch under ze desk. I gr-r-rasp ze assassin; I bring him to you. Monsieur Steefback, behold him!"

The effect produced upon Tommy was terrible.

Open-eyed and mouthed, he had watched the French master as he "denounced the assassin," and the plump youth really fancied that he had committed some deed worthy of the guillotine, so tragic were the words and attitudes of Monsieur de Vinaigre.

But the head master had seen that sort of thing before.

The romantic halo of exaggeration which the Frenchman cast about the matter did not deceive him.

"So this boy stabbed you, did he?" said Mr. Stiffback, placidly.

"He tit," replied the Frenchman, in his deepest bass voice, and frowning at Tommy so that he writhed with apprehension.

"With a knife, I think you said? Let us look at the wound."

"It is here, in my laig," replied the French master, grieved that his hurt was in so unromantic a place. "Bot it might 'ave been my 'ar-r-rt."

"No doubt," said Mr. Stiffback, drily. "I have heard of timid people feeling as if their hearts were in their boots."

Then he stooped, and, with a quiet smile, drew out the murderous pin, and held it up between his thumb and finger.

"Really, monsieur," he said, "I hardly thought you so delicate a subject that the prick of a pin would endanger your life."

The French master looked just a little ashamed of himself, and doubtless would have blushed, if he had not forgotten how.

He had no idea that the tell tale pin had been left sticking in his trousers.

"Bot 'tis no matter," he said, recovering his self-possession. "Zis boy he stab me. Ze meaning is ze same if he do it wiz a pin as wiz a dagger."

"Not exactly," replied Mr. Stiffback. "You seemed to wish me to believe that Codlings had attempted your life. A stupid practical joke is quite another thing."

Tommy gave a quiet chuckle. He thought the French master was defeated, and that he would

escape punishment, but Mr. Stiffback's next words brought all his hopes down to zero again.

"Your offence, Codlings," he said, "is quite bad enough and needed no colouring. I shall have to punish you again, for the third or fourth time since your arrival. It is really very disheartening to me to have a pupil who is so constantly offending."

"I didn't know it was his leg, sir," pleaded Tommy.

"That is not of the slightest consequence," said the schoolmaster, "you have no business to stick pins into anyone's legs, not even the legs of a table. Your tasks for to-morrow are doubled, Codlings, and you will, moreover, be flogged."

"N—not—in—the—ma—machine, sir?" faltered Tommy.

"Decidedly," said Mr. Stiffback. "Have you any objection?"

"Any ob—jection?" faltered Tommy. "Oh, lor!"

"That's not an answer to my question, Codlings," said the schoolmaster, sharply. "Remember that there are many poor boys who would highly esteem the opportunity of being chastised by such an intellectual implement."

"Are there?" muttered Tommy, in a undertone. "I wish I knew where they lived; they might have my chance, and welcome."

"What are you saying, Codlings?"

"Nothing, sir—only, if it's all the same to you, I'd rather be whacked by hand than by machinery."

This was touching Mr. Stiffback upon his tenderest point. He was fond of his invention, and was utterly unable to understand how any boy of sense should dislike the improved method.

"Codlings," he said, more in sorrow than in anger, "it is evident that your appreciation of the mechanical art is sadly deficient. Nevertheless, I hope that a closer acquaintance with my machine will enable you to appreciate the beauty of its structure, and I shall flog you with it till you do!"

*   *   *   *

While these adventures were occurring to poor Tommy, Lionel and his chum had met Vansittart, outside the study as appointed, and found that young aristocrat looking rather gloomily at a letter he had in his hand.

"What's up?" said our hero. "Anything wrong?"

"Nothing much, I suppose," replied Vansittart, holding out the letter. "Read it for yourself. It's from my man, to put the fight off again."

"He's funking it," said Lionel.

"Not a bit. I'll do him that credit; I don't believe he knows what funk is. But read away."

This was the letter—

"My Lord,
    "Hond. Sar,
    "I begs to applejize for axing yew to putt off the fit for a wheak. I want tew git sum more monney on, as I sewer to lik yew, an I no yew won't stand in the weigh of a pore man's pickin' up a sufferin or tew.

            "Yours 2 command."

"Confound it!" said Lionel, when, after some little difficulty, he made out the meaning of the original epistle. "Put off the fight for a week. Is that what he means?"

"That's it exactly."

"And what does he mean by 'getting money on' and 'picking up a few sovereigns?'"

"I told you, didn't I, that there was a great deal of betting going on over the fight. The pig-jobber and his friends are so sure that I shall lose, that they are betting ten to one against me."

"The dickens they are!" said Lionel. "I don't

know much about betting, but I think they'll lose their money."

"I'm sure they will," replied Vansittart, calmly. "Don't think I'm a boaster, young Wilful, but I've made up my mind to thrash that fellow, and I'm sure to do it."

"And so say all of us," sang Charlie. "I say, Li, shall we bet a sovereign on Vansittart?"

"You'll be able to do that easily enough in Deliverham, on Monday."

"What, are you going after all?"

"Can't afford to miss the holiday. Besides, I've got a prime piece of fun on, so that we shan't be altogether disappointed."

"What's that?"

"Come up to my snuggery, and I'll tell you. Mum's the word, though, for both of you, for I should get into a dreadful mess if I were caught out."

"Mum it is," said Lionel.

"As mice," added Charlie.

"Well, then," Vansittart continued, when they were safe in his private study, or "snuggery," "there's a girls' school in Deliverham, kept by three maiden sisters, for whom I have a special dislike."

"I dislike 'em all on principle," said Lionel. "I've got a maiden aunt who's enough to prejudice anybody against the whole sex."

"They had a very pretty little girl there," Vansittart continued, "a sort of pupil teacher, I think they called her, and these old cats used to object to my getting over the wall to meet her, or give her a serenade, and one night they took it into their heads to let two bull dogs loose in the grounds. I throttled one, but the other nearly throttled me, and so I naturally want to serve them out."

"I should think so," said Lionel.

"You'll help me, then?"

"Rather, whatever it is; eh, Charlie?"

"I'm on," replied Drummond.

"Shake hands on that. Now listen."

CHAPTER XXV.

WHAT VANSITTART SAID—THE COMPACT—THE CLUB ROOM OF THE UPPER FORM BOYS—A LITTLE DISPUTE, WHICH OUR HERO ARRANGES ENTIRELY TO HIS OWN SATISFACTION—BROWNTOP VERSUS LIONEL—"MAHOGANY" TURNS OUT TO BE A BIT OF BAD WOOD.

VANSITTART'S admonition to our hero and his chum to listen, was quite unnecessary. There was a "lark," or what grown-up persons would have called, "a piece of mischief" afloat, and that was always enough to rivet the attention of either of them.

"Fire away," said Lionel.

"It's to be kept quite dark, mind. It's more of a secret than the fight, for only we three will know anything of it."

"How about Tommy?"

"Is that the fat chap?" asked Vansittart.

"Well, yes; he is plump; but if it's all the same to you, don't mention it before him. He's touchy on that point."

"All right. I don't want to offend him, he's not a bad fellow, and I think he'll be useful in this spree."

"Will he? He's deucedly unlucky though, Van. I warn you of that."

"Unlucky. How do you mean?"

"Why he never goes in for a lark, you know, but he is certain to be caught."

"That's his affair," said Vansittart, coolly. "All we have to do is to take care that we don't get in the same scrape."

"But he might spoil your game; though I don't know what that is yet."

"No fear, I'll take care he doesn't; and now let me tell you my plan, and then we'll go and have a turn with the gloves."

Then ensued a conversation, carried on in such low tones, that the longest-eared listener could not have heard a syllable at a foot's distance, and interrupted only from time to time by a merry burst of laughter from Lionel or Charlie.

"Prime!" exclaimed our hero, when Vansittart had concluded. "It'll be a glorious spree. I won't tell Tommy a word, though, till the time comes. He's such an unlucky chap. He'd be sure to let it out in his sleep."

"I'll smother him, if he does," laughed Vansittart; "and now, you fellows, for a lesson in the noble art."

The boys in the upper form had, as we think we before mentioned, a room appropriated exclusively to their use for evening study.

It was, of course, far more often used for purposes very opposite to the acquisition of classical or mathematical knowledge, and the intrusion of boys of the lower form was resented in such a forcible manner, that the intruders seldom made the attempt twice.

So it would have gone hard with Lionel and Charlie, had not Vansittart taken them under his protection; for, plucky as our heroes were, they would have stood little chance against some twenty lads, nearly all older and bigger than themselves.

A storm, of somewhat angry expostulations, burst forth when Vansittart entered, followed by Lionel and Charlie.

"I say, now, this is too bad," said one.

"Stop, you young uns. Out you go," added another, threateningly.

"Chevy the beggars," added a third, enforcing the remark by throwing the basket-hilt of a single-stick at Lionel, and hitting an upper form boy instead.

"Stop it, now," said Vansittart, "all of you. Browntop, it won't be good for your health if you fling anything at my friends."

"What do you bring these cubs here for, then?" growled Browntop, a big, bony, dark complexioned, sulky-looking lad of seventeen. "You know it's against the rules of the club."

"Isn't it allowed that the president shall be able to set aside that rule with the consent of the other members, and didn't I ask you fellows yesterday?"

"You said you were only going to bring one."

"Well, these two are such chums that they're like one. I could no more part them than the Siamese twins. However, if all you fellows are against it I won't insist, and they shall go back."

Vansittart was very popular with the majority, and a chorus of "No, never mind—let them stay," was raised.

"Thanks," said Vansittart. "I'm going to put on the gloves with Wilful for a change. I've knocked the rest of you about so often that I'm tired of it."

"What's the use of boxing with a mopstick like that?" said Browntop, contemptuously. "Why, the wind of a blow would knock him over."

"Don't you be so sure of that, my festive chump of mahogany," said our hero, reddening a little at the complimentary allusion. "I'll bet a shilling that a dozen of your blows wouldn't do it, let alone the wind of 'em."

"Not so much of your cheek, young 'un," retorted Browntop menacingly; "you're only here because we're fools enough to let Vansittart do as he likes, so be civil."

"Set the example, then," said Lionel. "If you haven't got good looks, that's no reason why you shouldn't have good manners."

"Confound you, you young whelp!" exclaimed Browntop, crimsoning with fury. "I'll make mincemeat of you."

He advanced with his fists clenched upon our hero, who stood pale but calm, ready to receive him, but Vansittart ran in between them.

"No quarrelling now," he said in a clear, firm voice. "I won't have it, Browntop; if you come another inch this way I'll take the matter into my own hands."

"What!" said Browntop, "am I to put up with that insult and then to be bullied. D——d if I do."

"You will, though, for you began it," said Vansittart, "and, moreover, you'll pay a fine of half-a-crown for swearing. Hand over the coin."

There was a sullen gleam in the lad's small, deep-set eyes, which seemed to intimate that he would much rather have been allowed to "polish off" Lionel, who was so much younger and slighter in build; but there was an angry glitter in Vansittart's blue eyes that cowed him.

"Oh, go on," he said sullenly; "I suppose you must have your own way, Vansittart, but it won't last for ever."

"Few things will," said the young aristocrat, calmly; "and now shake hands you two, and, (here he winked at Lionel) have a friendly box with the gloves to show that there's no malice."

Browntop jumped at the notion. He was a notoriously hard and spiteful hitter, so much so that few cared to box with him except Vansittart, and he knew that by landing a blow or two with the "heel" of the hand or the side, it was easy to give an opponent as nasty a hit as if delivered with the naked fist.

But Vansittart was aware of Browntop's manœuvres, and a few rapidly whispered words to Lionel put him on his guard.

"Thanks for the tip," said our hero. "I can play that game too, as he'll find out if he tries any of his tricks with me."

"It's rather unfair," said Browntop, with a listless drawl, "to set me to box with a little chap like this, but I suppose I must oblige him."

"Very kind of you, Mahogany," replied Lionel. "I am rather small compared to you—in fact I'm afraid you'll find me too small to hit."

"I don't," said Browntop, with a savage smile.

"Perhaps not," said Lionel, calmly. "Charlie, tie this glove for me. Where do you like to be hit best, Mahogany?"

"What! Con—found your cheek. Do you think you're going to hit me?"

"I don't think so—I'm sure of it."

"Don't talk so much, you fellows, but get to work with your gloves," said Vansittart, fearing lest Lionel's cool chaff should stir up the sulky Browntop to a fresh exhibition of anger.

"All right, Vansittart, there's no hurry," said Browntop. "But this young beggar's so preciously cheeky that I'll make a bet with him."

"What is it?" said our hero.

"I'll bet you don't hit me in the face in the first six rounds."

"Done. I'll bet you five shillings I do," said Lionel, "and I'll give you the same bet that you don't touch me."

"It would be robbing you."

"Never mind, I'll chance that. Will you take the bet?"

"Of course. Five shillings each way."

"That's it; you'll see fair, Van. Here, Charlie, get a little soot out of the chimney."

"What's that for?"

"To rub on the gloves, of course. There can't be any mistake about a hit then."

Browntop could not object to so reasonable a proposition, and the soot was procured and applied to both sets of gloves, but he could not help feeling a strange sense of uneasiness at the coolness and confidence displayed by our hero. It unnerved him more than he cared to own, and he was in his heart not a little glad that the first trial was only with the padded gloves.

"It's hardly a fair bet for you, Wilful," said Vansittart. "He ought to give you odds."

"I'm satisfied," said Lionel, in the same calm, confident tone. "Will you be umpire?"

"Yes, if Browntop is willing."

"I'm willing enough," said that young gentleman, sulkily.

"All ready, then. Time!"

And the two boxers stepped out and faced one another, each looking warily into the other's eyes.

Now a great deal of what Lionel had said was "bounce," solely intended for the purpose of putting big Browntop into a state of funk, and as that young gentleman was not endowed with any great amount of pluck, our hero's dodge succeeded.

Instead of rushing at Lionel, as he first intended, trusting to his superior height and long arms to break down the other's guard, Browntop put up his hands and began to spar.

"It's all right," thought Lionel, immediately. "He no more knows how to box than a cow. I'll give him the postman's knock in a second."

And swift as light Lionel feinted and planted his gloves—one—two—on either side of Browntop's nose.

There was plenty of soot on the gloves, and two large patches encircled Browntop's peepers, making him look as if he had been engaged in a genuine mill and received very heavy punishment.

"Bravo!" exclaimed Vansittart, clapping his hands, "you put your left in beautifully, Wilful. You're done, for a dollar, Browntop."

The other boys were all laughing heartily, and applauding the big 'un's discomfiture, not so much because Lionel had made the first hit and won half the bet, but because Browntop did the most foolish thing boy or man can do under defeat—he got angry.

"What are you fellows making all that cackling about?" he growled. "The cub only hit me by accident. I slipped and lost my guard."

"That's a lie now, Browntop, they were fair hits, and you know it," said Vansittart.

"They were not," he retorted, savagely. "If he likes I'll make the bet over again. He won't have the same luck again."

"Done," said Lionel. "But wash your face first—there isn't room for another couple of patches of soot."

Browntop uttered an oath, and springing forward, he aimed a blow at our hero, thinking to take him off his guard.

But Lionel had expected something of this kind. He stepped quickly aside, and as Browntop, by the sheer force of his own blow, was carried past, let fly with full force upon his opponent's jaw, spinning him round like a top, until he was stopped by the wall, against which he sunk down in a heap.

It was a heavy blow, delivered not only with the whole strength of his arm, but also with the full weight of his body.

Browntop's teeth cracked like a walnut in the hinge of a door, and his mouth was filled with blood.

"By jove, what a hit!" said Vansittart. "Enough to knock a bull down. Some of his teeth are gone, I'll swear."

"Well done, young 'un!" cried some of the others, beginning to conceive a mighty respect for a boy who could knock another, half as big again as himself, about like a ninepin.

Browntop had turned a sickly yellow, the nearest approach to white his complexion could assume—that is, of course, only where Lionel's sooty gloves had left the skin visible—and with his features distorted by rage and pain, he did not present a very amiable spectacle.

"By George, Browntop," said one keen, bright-eyed lad, with a perpetual smile of mischief hovering

THE PIG JOBBER WAS IN "CHANCERY," AND IT WOULD HAVE PUZZLED THE LORD CHANCELLOR TO HAVE GOT HIM OUT.

No. 22.

about the corner of his mouth, "you look like a
spoilt edition of Othello. Have you eaten Desdemona
as well as smothered her, and does she disagree
with you?"

"How many teeth have you had knocked out?"
asked another tormentor. "Save 'em up, Browntop—ivory fetches a good price now, and yours 'll do
for dominoes."

"D—— you all," growled Browntop, as he
scrambled to his feet and spat out a mouthful of
blood. "Get out of my way or I shall murder some
of you."

And tearing the gloves from his hands, he flung
them across the room, and strode out, banging the
door furiously behind him.

"There's a pretty little dear with a pretty little
temper," said Lionel.

"I'm ashamed of him," said Vansittart. "I
never thought much of him, certainly, but I had no
idea that he was such a half-hearted chap as to cut
up so rough because of a friendly turn with the
gloves."

"He hadn't even the manners to stop and pay
the money he lost," added Charlie.

"Oh, I'll see that he pays that. Besides it's a
point of honour."

"I wouldn't trust much to the honour of a fellow
like that," said Lionel. "He swears like a common
blackguard."

"And he'll be fined for it, and if it occurs again,
expelled our club," said Vansittart. "I hope,
young Wilful, you don't judge me and the others
by him."

"No—no!" replied our hero, earnestly. "I
didn't mean to insinuate anything of that sort.
Besides, I was wrong, perhaps, in noticing it, for I
know some fellows consider it manly to swear."

"We don't then," said Vansittart, decisively.
"I don't pretend that we're angels, Wilful, but I
can say we're not blackguards. But, there, enough
of that, pitch those sooty gloves away, my boy,
put on these, and let you and me set to."

"With all the pleasure in life," said Lionel, with
a laugh, "only I suppose it will be my turn to get
rolled over."

"Never fear, we play light here."

"Except, of course, Browntop."

"Yes, he was a rough-and-tumble boxer, always
snarling and wrangling. I'm glad he's gone."

And then the two began to spar. Charlie had
also put on the gloves, and two or three other
couples were engaged with the single-sticks or
foils, but they soon quitted their own sport to
watch the prettiest display of boxing which any of
them had ever seen.

As we shall have presently to describe a fight of
much more serious and absorbing interest we do not
intend to waste our descriptive powers on a mere
glove fight. Let it suffice to say that a sharp twenty
minutes' work was rewarded by a hearty round of
applause from Charlie and the boys of the upper
form, and that they felt such a respect for our hero's
skill, that, suspending the rules of their club, they
at once elected him an honorary member, with all
the rights and privileges of an upper form
boy.

Charlie looked on with admiration, and some
small taste of envy, if the truth must be told, but
he was by far too generous and high spirited to
show it.

When they were together in the dormitory that
night, though, Lionel, thinking that his chum might
feel a little sore, spoke on the subject.

"I say, Charlie, old chap, you're not put out, are
you?"

Charlie knew quite well to what his chum alluded,
but of course he appeared to be ignorant.

"Put out, Li? About what?"

"Why, you know. Because these upper form
boys made me a member of their club as they call
it, and didn't ask you."

"Not I, Li. I'm not such a fool as that."

"Because, you know, I shan't go there unless
you're allowed to come as well. I don't care for the
upper form boys so much, that I'd drop an old
chum for their sakes."

"I know that, Li. Don't say any more about
it, or I shall get waxy."

"Well, then, we'll talk about the lark on Monday."

"Did Vansittart say anything fresh about it?"

"No, only that Tommy's to be regularly dressed
up like a baby. He's going to get a big basin and
a spoon."

Here Charlie instantly dived beneath the bed
clothes and for some two minutes there issued forth
muffled sounds, as of some one dying in mortal
agony, but he was only smothering his laughter so
as not to be heard by any officious master prying
in the corridor.

"My eye! It will be prime," said Charlie when
he at length emerged from beneath the sheets.
"Have you told Tommy yet."

"No, poor old chap; he's in for another dose of
the flogging-machine to-morrow morning, and I'll
tell him of the lark before we go into class; it'll
ease his pain a bit."

"Blow that flogging-machine! We'll have to
bu'st that up, Li. I've got a presentiment that if
we don't we shall get a taste of it."

"We'll talk it over, Charlie, as soon as we've got
the lark on Monday, and the fight off our
minds."

"What a fight there will be," said Charlie,
thoughtfully, "if that pig jobber is anything like
a match for Vansittart."

"You're right; it's enough to make a fellow's
mouth water to think of it; but let's go to sleep
now. I want to dream about it if I can."

And with that noble ambition present in his mind,
Lionel turned over, coiled himself comfortably
up, and in a very few minutes was in dream-
land.

CHAPTER XXVI.

MONDAY MORNING—THE DELIVERHAM CHRONICLE,
AND HOW MR. GROWLAGAIN READ IT—JOHN
MAKES INQUIRIES, AND INQUIRIES ARE MADE
FOR JOHN—THE HAYSTACK, AND WHAT OC-
CURRED BEHIND IT—TOMMY CODLINGS GOES
OUT MILKING, WITH A VERY UNUSUAL RESULT—
THE NEW FOUNDLING HOSPITAL AN IMMENSE
SUCCESS TO EVERYBODY CONCERNED, EXCEPT
THE FOUNDLINGS—TOMMY CODLINGS' SECOND
APPEARANCE IN LONG CLOTHES, AND WHAT
THE MISSES GROWLAGAIN THOUGHT OF HIM.

IN such peaceful content as age combined with
virtue, and an income sufficient to procure all
the comforts, and many of the luxuries, of this
wicked world, the three Misses Growlagain
slid in a genteel manner down the hill of life,
towards the grave, which awaits us all at the
bottom.

They followed the delightful occupation of training the youthful feminine mind in the way it
should go, including also such fashionable by-
paths as French, Italian, Music, and the use of the
globes, and they were, moreover, the sisters of that
Mr. Growlagain, whose pupils trespassed upon the
domains of Mr. Stiffback, and received, in consequence, such a warm reception at the hands
of our hero and his chums.

It was against the peace of these three
amiable ladies that, we regret to say, the "lark"
projected by Vansittart was directed, but, all unconscious of the designs of these young miscreants,
the Misses Growlagain slept peacefully that Sunday
night, and no thought of the coming trouble caused
their frilled night-caps to toss uneasily upon their
pillows.

Deliverham, in which town the Misses Grow-
lgain's collegiate establishment for young ladies
was situate, boasted the possession of a weekly
newspaper, called the " Deliverham Chronicle," but
as the editor thereof admitted into his columns
vulgar and scandalous reports of thefts, murders,
suicides and—monstrum horrendum—divorces, the
Misses Growlagain decided it was improper, and
refused to admit the contagion of its pages into
their lamb-fold.

Not so Mr. Growlagain, at his collegiate establishment for young gentlemen. He enjoyed the
robberies and suicides, devoured the murders, and
chuckled over the "spiciest" portions of the divorce
cases, and on this very Monday morning, at breakfast, prepared, as usual, to unfold his Chronicle,
when an advertisement in the most conspicuous
portion of the front page arrested his attention,
and made him gasp for breath.

This was the gasper :—

" TO ALL POOR PEOPLE WITH LARGE FAMILIES :

" The Misses Growlagain, compassionating the
destitute condition of so many unfortunate children,
have decided upon transforming their well-known
Collegiate Establishment for Young Ladies into a
branch of the Foundling Hospital, and hereby give
notice that they are now ready to receive any number of applicants.

" Babies under twelve months only admitted.

" Twins not objected to.   Triplets sixpence
each extra.

" Certificates of vaccination must be produced
with each baby.

" All babies sent by post must be pre-paid.

" Apply at 9 a.m., this day, Monday, to the Misses
Growlagain, High-street, Deliverham."

Mr. Growlagain laid down the paper, let off a
snort of astonishment, rubbed his eyes, took up the
paper, read the advertisement carefully through,
laid the paper down again, and gasped for breath
the second time.

" What on earth have the old fools been up to?"
was his unfraternal and impolite ejaculation.

Then he rang the bell for his servant, a faithful
old man, who had been with him for many years,
and who would have scorned to let anybody rob
his master but himself.

" John," said Mr. Growlagain.

" Yes, sir."

" Am I sober, this morning ?"

John cocked his head aside, and closing an eye,
surveyed his master deliberately with the other.

" Tol'able, sir, I should say, unless you've took
anything in your tea this mornin'."

" Confound you, no," said Mr. Growlagain, tes-
tily ; for he had not expected so practical an answer. " Read that—and read it aloud."

The faithful John took the newspaper, felt in his
pocket for a pair of spectacles, which weighed
about half a pound, fixed them on his nose, and
then, with much deliberation and many pauses, read
the advertisement.

" It is there, then," said Mr. Growlagain, with a
sigh of relief. " I'm not dreaming—or mad !"

" Not more'n usual, sir," said the faithful John.

" Hold your tongue ; you're an ass, John."

" You're a good judge of 'em, sir."

' Hold your tongue, I tell you," bawled Mr. Growlagain ; " and go and look at my sisters' house, and
tell me if you see anything strange about it."

John departed on his errand, and he certainly
did see something strange about the house, something that had had no place there until that morning, when, in the grey dawn, and ere the earliest
bird had sallied forth to pick up the matutinal
worm, our hero and his chums had been at work.

There, on the front of the house, in the most
conspicuous portion possible, was a huge board,
and on it, painted in large letters, a second but

shorter edition of the advertisement which had so
shocked Mr. Growlagain.

" Dash my weskit," thought John. " It is right,
then. Wot on airth put the old gals up to sich a
rummy move. But lor, there's no accountin' for
women."

Just then a feeble wail attracted John's attention, then another, and another, and looking down
the road he perceived a sort of procession of
females, each of whom carried one or more bundles
of something which kicked and emitted the cries
before mentioned.

" Here comes the fondlinks," muttered John, who
entertained the sort of affection for a baby which
most people feel for a spider or a black beetle.
" This is too good for me—I'm orf."

And off he went, but only to encounter another
procession coming up the other way, whereupon
he adopted the plan of Ulysses, and stopped his
ears to shut out the cries of the sirens.

But the reader will naturally ask where are the
conspirators, where the prime movers of this diabolical plot against the peace of mind of those
respectable and virtuous elderly maidens, the
Misses Growlagain.

Behold them, then, snugly pic-nicking in the
rear of a hay-stack, near the main road, and so
situated that they could command a view of the
doomed house.

No consciousness of guilt seemed to haunt them,
the figure of remorse had not withered them particularly on account of what they had done, or at
least it had not affected their appetites, for all four
were doing justice to a loaf of bread, cut in slices
with a clasp knife, and spread with jam, a good
fresh looking sausage, and a battered old can full
of milk.

" Those cows were jolly handy," said Charlie, as
he took another drink, and exhausted the contents
of the can. " I say, Tommy, you know how to
milk ; cut over and get some more."

" All right," replied the plump youth, who was
always ready to oblige, and, taking the can, he
ambled away across the field to where the cows
were peacefully grazing.

" This is a jolly idea," said Lionel, with his
mouth full of sausage. " I never combined a picnic with a lark before."

" The best of the fun is to come yet," replied
Vansittart. " I hope they put those advertisements
in the papers all right ?"

" Sure to. How many papers did you send it
to ?"

" All I could think of within thirty miles of this
place. I got a list of 'em out of the county
directory."

" There will be a swarm," said Charlie, with a
laugh. " A regular army, and they'll keep coming
all day, too."

" Yes, the old gals will be kept pretty lively,"
said Vansittart. " I said I'd pay them off for letting those bull dogs loose on me."

Suddenly there was a yell as of some mortal in
distress, and the three boys looked round just in
time to see Tommy and the can turning somersaults
over the hedge.

They ran and picked him up, almost before he
knew that he had fallen, and stood him on his feet
looking very pale and frightened.

" What's up, Tommy? What made you come
over the hedge in that fashion ?"

" Why, the horns of that beastly old bull," said
Tommy, ruefully.

" Didn't you get any milk ?"

" No, I didn't," replied Tommy shortly. " I went
up to him—I thought he was a cow—and when I
tried to milk him he turned round, picked me up
with those dashed horns, and pitched me over the
hedge."

" Ha, ha, ha !" roared the three boys in chorus.
" Ha, ha, ha, ha !"

"Laugh away," said Tommy, sulkily. "You don't catch me going after milk again in a hurry, unless it's to a shop."

"Oh, my eye!" said Charlie faintly, as he leaned on Vansittart for support, and wiped away his tears. "Fancy Tommy trying to milk a bull."

"Don't laugh at him too much," said Lionel, in a whisper, "or he'll get sulky and cut away."

"I can't help it," said Charlie in a faint voice. "Oh my, I shall split!"

Had not Tommy been the most good natured of boys he must certainly have taken mortal offence. To be tossed by a bull even when the horns do no more than tear your clothes is bad enough, but to be laughed at as well is enough to make the conventional saint lose his temper.

But in a little while all was peace again behind the hay-rick, the bread and jam and sausage vanished, Tommy receiving an extra share in consideration of his sufferings, and then watches were consulted.

"Half past seven," said Vansittart. "Time's getting on."

"An hour and a half to wait yet."

"Oh, some of 'em will be there long before nine,' said Vansittart. "First come, first served."

"Won't the old girls be in a stew," chuckled Lionel.

"They just will; but come, Codlings, it's time you were dressed up for your part."

"I'm ready," replied Tommy. "But I say, mind you don't drop me, for I'm precious sore, and the bull grazed me with the tip of his horn."

"Never fear, Tommy, you shan't be dropped, and mind you howl well when you're pinched."

"I'll howl without pinching. You can leave that part out."

There was a neat little bundle lying beside the hay-rick, which on being unfastened proved to contain a long night-gown, and a night-cap with a deep frill round the edge.

"I hope there's a photographer in the town," said Charlie. "Tommy ought to have his portrait taken in this costume."

"Comes so natural to him, don't it?" added Lionel. "I say, Tommy, you never ought to have been weaned."

"Unless he had a bull for a wet-nurse," said Vansittart, upon which little joke at Tommy's recent misfortune all three burst out into a fresh roar of laughter.

Codlings got very red in the face, and getting up made a run at Charlie with the amiable intention of blackening one of his eyes, but the long night-gown was in the way, and pitched him on his nose.

"There's a precocious infant for you," laughed Lionel, "trying to run before he can walk."

"Look here, you chaps," said Tommy, getting up red and indignant, "if I have much more of this chaff I shall cut it altogether. So, now then."

"All right, Codlings," replied Vansittart, soothingly. "They shan't chaff you any more. I'll take care of that."

"You? Why you're the worst."

"Never mind, I'll be the best now. Hark, Wilful, didn't you hear a baby crying, away over there?"

Lionel listened, and the cry of not one, but many babies became audible.

"Time's up," said Vansittart. "Now, Tommy, tuck up your petticoats and keep behind us till we get to the road. Have you got that basin of pap, Drummond?"

"Yes," replied Charlie, bringing out a huge yellow basin, holding about half a gallon of some thick pasty-looking substance, and a mighty wooden spoon, such as is seldom seen out of a pantomime. "Will you have a little now, Tommy, don't say no if you'd rather not."

"If you put any of that stuff near me I'll give you a domino in the eye," said Tommy, who was still rather sulky.

"You mustn't give a baby pap till it cries for it," said Lionel.

"Oh, that's the rule, is it?" Charlie said, and winked. "I'll not forget."

By that time the four boys had reached the hedge which separates the field from the main road, and they could see that women, singly and in groups of two and three, all armed with babies, were steering on in the direction of the High-street.

"Now comes the worst part of the job," said Vansittart.

"What's that?"

"Carrying the baby, of course, and that'll be no joke. How much do you weigh, Codlings?"

"I don't know—not more than I ought," replied Tommy, who as we know was rather touchy upon the subject of his plumpness.

"You do, though—you weigh eight stone if you weigh a pound. But never mind, I'll carry him first."

So the procession was formed: Vansittart in the centre, carrying the baby—a remarkably fine child he looked by-the-by; Lionel on the right, flapping his handkerchief to keep the flies away, and Charlie on the left stirring the pap, and terrifying Tommy by pretending to give him a spoonful.

"There's the board still up, just as we left it this morning," whispered Lionel, as they neared the new Foundling Hospital; "and my eye, what a lot of people!"

There were indeed a "lot of people," as our hero termed them. The whole population of Deliverham seemed to have turned out to welcome the inauguration of this refuge for destitute babies, and the air was musical with the screams and shrieks of discontented childhood.

"I wonder if they smell a rat yet," said Lionel, looking up at the house.

"Don't think so, or there'd be a row," replied Vansittart. "They won't think of looking up there at the board just yet. But look out now, you fellows, and keep steady; don't grin; and leave me to speak if anyone chaffs us."

The warning came only just in time, for, as they drew near the crowd, remarks of a very personal nature began to fly about.

"Oh lawk!" said one, "here be a whoppin' fond-link, Bill."

"That he be," replied Bill, who had an infant of the ordinary size in his arms, which was shrivelled into insignificance by comparison with Tommy.

By this time Vansittart, marching gravely on, attended as before by Lionel and Charlie, had got into the thick of the crowd of expectant matrons, and their attention was naturally directed to the phenomenon.

"Be my sowl," exclaimed one strapping Hibernian lady, with a baby strapped to her back, "did ye ever see the likes o' that. How owld may your babby be, alanna?"

"Three months," replied Vansittart, without the shadow of a smile.

"Three months! *Three!* Howly saints! Is that the thruth ye're tellin' me?"

"Perfectly true, ma'am," continued Vansittart. "But poor little chap he's very small and sickly for his age, not a bit like the rest of us."

"Millia, murther," gasped the listener. "Hwhat's that ye're sayin'. Small and sickly. Faix, what do ye be afther callin' big."

"I'm his brother," said Vansittart. "I'm six year old and I'm considered pretty tall for my age. The other two are four years old, but father don't think much of them."

The Irishwoman and half a dozen others who were within hearing stared open-mouthed and eyed at this wonderful family.

"Ye're father now," suggested the Irishwoman, "he'll be a fine man now?"

"Pretty fair, ma'am," replied Vansittart. "He ought to have been here this morning; but it takes two hours to wake him, he's so tall, and as I was afraid I should be late I came on without him."

Before the Irishwoman could express her opinion upon this final "staggerer," it became evident that the unaccustomed crowd in the High-street had attracted the attention of the inhabitants of the collegiate establishment for young ladies.

The blinds were suddenly pulled up, and behind the window panes could be seen scores of feminine faces flattening their noses against the glass and staring in evident wonder and perplexity.

"There are the old gals," said Vansittart to our hero. "There at the drawing-room window. You can't mistake 'em, they're so ferociously ugly."

Just then the lower sash was pushed up, and the eldest and ugliest of the maiden sisters poked her head out.

The baby carriers, thinking that this was the signal for them to advance pressed forward. Some of the more fervent, the Milesian ladies specially, showering blessings upon their supposed benefactress.

"May glory be your bed this blessed night," exclaimed the lady whom Vansittart had chaffed, as she held up her infant for inspection. "Look at him, my lady, as foine a che—ild—sivin months owld, and all his teeth cut."

"What do you mean?" ejaculated Miss Growlagain, from the window. "Go away, you low persons, or I'll call the police."

"Look here, mam," shouted a brawny, tramping woman, 'turning up' her baby with a most reckless disregard for the proprieties. "Here's a foine boy for yer, nine months old, and had every blessed complaint under the sun, 'cepting the geut, good as gold, and not a squeak in him."

"Go away!" shrieked Miss Growlagain. "Will you go away?"

And almost frantic with fear lest the indecent exhibition of the tramper's baby should have been seen by any of her innocent young pupils, Miss Growlagain shook her head at the intruders with such energy that her cap and false front dropped off.

Her sisters were to the full as energetic, and, aided by the cook and a couple of elderly housemaids, raised such a chorus of "Go away!" that the crowd began to see there was something wrong.

"We've come to the wrong shop," said one.

"Deuce a bit," said another. "Look at the board up there between the windys."

"Then it's shwindled we are," shouted the Irishwoman.

"Shame!" cried our hero and chums in chorus.

"Let's pelt 'em," suggested another disappointed matron with twins.

"No," said Lionel, "don't do that—let's leave the babies at the door and go away—they must take 'em in then."

This proposition was received with shouts of approval, and Vansittart approached the door, when it was thrown open and the eldest Miss Growlagain, with the aspect of a Grenadier, dashed forward.

CHAPTER XXVII.

A SHORT, AND IT IS TO BE HOPED, INTERESTING ACCOUNT OF MISS GROWLAGAIN AND HER SEMINARY FOR YOUNG LADIES—TOMMY CODLINGS IS LEFT OUT IN THE COLD—THE ARRIVAL OF THE POLICE—THE DISCOVERY—TOMMY IS FOUND OUT—THE CROSS-EXAMINATION.

FOR five-and-fifty years had the peaceful current of the eldest Miss Growlagain's life flowed serenely onwards, rippling along its calm and shady channel, as far from the noisy and disreputable haunts of busy man as was consistent with earning a respectable income as a trainer of the young of the gentler sex.

For those "dreadful males," or "odious men," as Miss Growlagain would style mankind when she condescended to mention them at all, which was seldom, were regarded with a steady animosity which no power short of death would overcome.

She would have ignored them altogether, would have blotted them out of the scheme of creation, had it been possible.

Miss Growlagain had indeed been heard to acknowledge that there were such creatures, and even owned, when pressed upon the subject, that she had once had a father; but it was done with the same sort of reluctance with which a man views a hump on his back or a boil on his nose. Denial is useless in such a case.

No creature of the male persuasion was ever allowed to enter the sacred gates of Minerva House.

The tradesmen transacted their business through the railings or left their baskets on the gravel-path, and then retired to a safe distance, when the cook or one of the satellites would advance and pick them up after the fashion of cautious mariners dealing with the natives of an unknown country.

Even the official position of the tax gatherer and collectors of rates did not exempt them from this stringent rule. They dropped their little communications into the letter-box, and received an answer by post when it suited Miss Growlagain's convenience.

Hence arose the legend that the eye of mortal man had never yet beheld the sacred mysteries of the interior of Minerva House.

It was known that the dogs, to use an Hibernianism, were not dogs at all, but females of the canine species; and it was even said that Miss Growlagain sorted the mice and blackbeetles, but this is probably an exaggeration. Over the cats, of course, she had no control; those gay and reckless libertines would make love on the very tiles of Diana's Temple without a blush.

It was hard indeed, then, after taking all these stringent measures to shut out, not only the male sex, but everything that could remind her innocent young lambs of the existence of such wretches. It was very, very hard, we repeat, that suddenly, and without warning, she should find herself invaded by a whole army of babies and their shameless mothers.

The sight was too much for the venerable spinster, and for a moment she turned faint, and reclined gracefully in the arms of her youngest sister; but a particularly shrill yell from Tommy, caused by a pin being run into him, acted like smelling-salts upon her, and she stood erect once more.

"Wretches!" she exclaimed, with a tragical air worthy of Miss Bateman. "Retire!"

"Bad luck to ye!" said the stout Irishwoman, wrathfully. "Retire is it? Faix, it's meself that will retire, immediate; but *I'll lave the baby!*"

And, bestowing on the child a parting slap as a token of affection, the Irishwoman laid the infant on the step and marched away.

The example was contagious. A youthful and blooming matron with a clothes-basket full, followed suit; and in less than a minute the space from the front door to the front gate was paved with babies.

"Let's drop Tommy, too," said Vansittart, who, although he was assisted by Lionel, had quite enough of practical nursing.

"All right," replied Lionel. "Up here, against the door-post."

"Here, I say, no larks," said Tommy, in a tone of alarm. "No cutting away and leaving me here, you know."

"All right, Tommy," whispered our hero. "We'll come back for you. You just lie there and kick and howl like old boots."

"Oh, yes, I dare say, and have that old cat down on me like bricks," growled Tommy; but it was of no use to remonstrate. In that long night-gown, which came far down over his fingers, and reached a yard below his toes, he was helpless.

Miss Growlagain was fairly drove frantic by this last "dodge." She glared at the novel kind of floor-cloth that had just been laid down for her, looked helplessly at the surging mass of infantile arms and legs, and mentally compared their wailing cries with the sweet voices of her own pupils when the singing lesson was on.

She was utterly bewildered, and was debating whether she should faint away, and be ill until the trouble was over; or whether she should order out her retinue of servants to sweep away the babies.

Before she could make up her mind, there was a commotion in the crowd near the gates, and the next moment Mr. Growlagain and a constable appeared at the entrance.

Mr. Growlagain stopped there, and lifted up his hands and eyes in speechless amazement and disgust.

The policeman looked on with a calm, contented air. Miss Growlagain had reported him twice to his inspector, on suspicion of prowling around the house in search of the cook and cold pie, and that little job was "nuts" to him.

"Well!" said Mr. Growlagain, as soon as he found the use of his voice, "confound it, they **done** it now!"

"I rayther think so too, sir," replied the constable, cheerfully; "and if they don't clear these kids away pretty soon, I'll have to take out a summons ag'in 'em, for unlorful exposure."

Just then Miss Growlagain caught sight of her brother and the policeman, and hope arose in her virgin bosom.

"Gregory!" she faintly squeaked. "Police-man!"

"Well?" bawled her brother from the gate. He couldn't get any farther without risk of tread-ing on the babies, who were rolling and crawling about as lively as worms after a shower of rain. "You've got yourself into a pretty mess this time, and no mistake."

"Oh! help me, Gregory—do," said Miss Growl-again, fairly broken down by the weight of her misfortunes. "Clear these little wretches away, for goodness sake."

"What?" ejaculated Mr. Growlagain.

"Turn these babies out,' shrieked the school-mistress. "Make the policeman do his duty. What's he standing staring there for?"

"Well, blow me! I like that," said the constable, indignantly. "Look'ee 'ere, marm. It's my dooty to inform you that if you don't take your babies in immediate, I'll have to issue a summons ag'in you."

"*My* babies," said Miss Growlagain, in an awful voice. "Man, what do you mean?"

"Just what I ses, miss," replied the policeman, slowly. "If you advertises for babbies and they comes, why you're bound to take 'em in, or take the consekences."

"*Me—advertise!*" repeated the schoolmistress; "and for *babies!* This is too much."

"Come now, Jerusha," said Mr. Growlagain; "the constable's quite correct. You did advertise—you know you did. I read it in the paper myself, this very morning."

His sister looked at him with a cold and stony glance. Somebody was mad, she had no doubt; she was only waiting to see whether it was her or her brother.

"I saw the advertisement in the 'Deliverham Chronicle,' repeated Mr. Growlagain, empathically, as he kicked a baby or two out of the way, in his endeavour to make a clear path for himself to the door.

"Advertisement!" repeated the schoolmistress, with a hysterical giggle.

"Yes. But you affect ignorance, Jerusha? Did you or did you not advertise?"

"It's in lots of other papers too," added the con-stable; "we received 'em at the station this morn-ing."

"There, you hear what the constable says, Jerusha. Hang it, if you want to turn your school into a foundling hospital, and take to nursing babies in your old age, don't be ashamed of it; you might do worse."

"Worse!" exclaimed Miss Growlagain. "What, Gregory, abandon the principles of a lifetime, and make my home the refuge for a pack of dirty, squalling little brats? No, Gregory."

"What did you advertise for then, damme?" ex-claimed Mr. Growlagain, who was rapidly working himself up to a pitch of madness.

"I did not advertise, Gregory; you know me better."

"Then," almost yelled Mr. Growlagain, "why did stick the board up?"

"What board?"

"Come out," said her brother, wrathfully, and, starting forward amongst the babies in a reckless manner that threatened a repetition of Herod's massacre of the innocents, he grasped Miss Growl-again by the arm, dragged her out, upsetting Tommy, who was on the doorstep, and pointed to fatal board.

Miss Growlagain gave one glance, and as she comprehended what she read, exhausted nature could bear no more, and she fainted in earnest.

"Damme," growled the schoolmaster, "here's a go. Help me in with her, policeman; never mind the babies."

"Oh, ah, I daresay," said the officer, who was carefully picking the babies up and piling them in a heap by the side of the path; "I don't want no werdicks of infannyside give in agin me; let her wait."

Meanwhile the crowd in the High-street had got thicker and thicker, and a great deal noiser and more demonstrative, as a rumour was spread that the Misses Growlagain had lured the babies into their school for the purpose of converting them into soup and pies for the pupils.

"I say," said Vansittart, "there'll be a jolly row over this."

"Yes," added Lionel, "I wish we hadn't left Tommy behind."

"Why?"

"Because he's sure to get into trouble; he always does."

"We'd better slip in and haul him out, then."

"I don't see how we can, now all these people are about. Besides, there's old Growlagain, he'd be sure to spot us, and that would blow the whole affair."

"So it would. Confound it, here come more of the bobbies!"

In effect three of the local constabulary came rushing through the crowd with much dignity, and taking up their station by the gate, attempted to force the populace to move on, in the performance of which feat one lost his helmet and the other two their tempers.

Meanwhile our plump friend Tommy was enjoy-ing himself very much.

He was comfortable on the doorstep, for he had one baby to sit on and another at his back by way of a pillow, while he chuckled mightily at the alarm of Miss Growlagain and the discomfiture of her brother.

"Blow it," thought Tommy, "this is prime. I wonder what they'll do with us babies. Take us in and put us to bed, perhaps. My eye, that wouldn't do for me though; I should be twigged in no time. I'd better slope."

This was excellent advice for Tommy to give himself, but unluckily he could not follow it; the

Xtra policemen were already at the gate, and, moreover, Mr. Growlagain, bearing his sister in his arms, was coming towards the steps.

The constable, with a grim, unholy satisfaction, followed closely, picking the babies off the path, stacking them in a heap near the door, for he was resolved that they should find an asylum beneath the sacred walls of Minerva House, to avenge himself on the schoolmistress for reporting him.

"There's a nice little pile of 'em," he chuckled. "I know the workus people won't take 'em orf her hands till they is obliged, and that won't be for a couple o' days. My eye, fancy the old gals tryin' to feed 'em, and bein' kept awake all night with the squallers!"

"Blow it!" thought Tommy, breaking out into a cold perspiration as the policeman came nearer and nearer, "what does he want to pick up the babies for—I'm sure to be nailed?"

But he was saved by Mr. Growlagain, who as he reached the hall, paused to call out to the constable—

"Stay there a minute, my man, will you?"

"I'm a going to stay here," replied the policeman, "until these here babies is all took in, and the sooner it's done the better."

Slight as this interruption was it saved Tommy from being discovered at that moment.

He chuckled, and thought himself lucky. Little did he think that it would have been twenty times better for him to have suffered there and then from the avenging boot of the policeman.

The crowd had, if possible, got denser, and more noisy.

A slight shower of rain came on, wetting the babies and making them sing half an octave higher.

The crowd became furious, and the windows of Minerva House were only spared out of consideration for the luckless infants, whom a stray stone might have injured.

The genuine parents, of course, took no part in this demonstration; they had, in common parlance, "made their lucky," in case they might be called upon by the police to take their babies away again, a proceeding to which they had a decided objection, as was only natural, considering how much trouble they had had to bring them there.

"Shame!" cried one half of the crowd.

"Bring 'em out and duck 'em," roared the others.

"Hark to the poor little things a crying there; it's 'art breakin'," added a gentleman, who was a professional mender of boots and shoes, and an amateur breaker of the heads of his wife and children. He had in his pocket at that very moment a summons for wearing out a two-inch strap upon his eldest daughter, and blacking his baby's eyes, so that it might match its mother when they appeared in public, and yet he had room in his manly heart to pity other people's children. Such is the power of sympathy.

Meanwhile, Miss Growlagain, in a very pale and limp condition, was in the drawing-room, attended by her sisters and as many of the pupils as were bold enough to squeeze in.

The fragrant aroma of burnt feathers, vinegar, and smelling-salts filled the air, much to the apparent discontent of Mr. Growlagain, who stood by the window grumbling and swearing at intervals.

"Fling a bucket of water over her," he growled after an uneasy ten minutes' waiting; "that'll bring her round. Make haste, confound you, or the mob will pull the house down."

"The brute," said the cook in a semi-audible voice; "poor dear. There, give her another whiff of the salts, Miss Melindy, while I sends her cat. Bucket o' water, indeed!"

Miss Growlagain now showed some symptoms of returning consciousness, but whether the happy effect was due to the mention of the bucket of water, or the extra whiff of salts, we are unable to state positively. Suffice it to say that she shivered, groaned, and opened her eyes.

Mr. Growlagain at once elbowed his way to the sofa, and unceremoniously pushing the cook out of the way, came to the front.

"Now, Jerusha," he said, "if you want to save your house from being pulled to pieces by the mob perhaps you'll explain matters."

"Explain, Gregory—explain what?" replied Miss Growlagain, faintly.

"What?" ejaculated the schoolmaster, shooting the remark out of him as if he had been a pistol. "You disgrace yourselves—disgrace me, ma'am, me, by advertising for a parcel of squalling babies, and when they come provoke a riot by turning 'em out again, and then have the impudence—yes the majestic impudence—to pretend to know nothing about it."

"But indeed, Gregory, I don't," pleaded Miss Jerusha, tearfully.

"Who advertised in the Chronicle, then," demanded Mr. Growlagain, pulling that journal out of his pocket and slapping it violently as if it had been a boy, "and a dozen other of the county papers? Tell me that, Jerusha."

"I don't know," replied the bewildered sister, giving symptoms of going off into another fainting fit.

"Then who stuck up that board in front of the house?" said Mr. Growlagain, getting more and more violent.

"I don't know, indeed, Gregory."

"Don t know," repeated Mr. Growlagain, contemptuously. "Damme, if any one had dared to stick up a board in front of my house, I'd bet a hundred pounds that I'd know who did it—ah, and let him know too."

Here Miss Growlagain, overcome with emotion and alarm, murmured something about "poor, weak, unprotected females," and began to weep bitterly.

"Blow and dash the whole lot of 'em," growled the schoolmaster (he used stronger words than blow and dash), "this will be in all the papers, and we shall be the laughing-stock of the country, to say nothing of the damage it'll do to my school."

Here the policeman, who was getting more and more cheerful as the prospects of a riot increased, put his helmet a little way into the room.

"Now, Mr. Growlagain, it's my duty to inform you that if you don't take them babies in doors the crowd'll burst the gates, and four of us won't be able to restrain their violence much."

"Bring 'em in, dash 'em," said the schoolmaster, viciously. "Damme, I wish they were all smothered."

"'Tain't no part of my duty to carry babies," replied the constable. "You'd better get some of those gals to help; there's enough of 'em."

"Go and help, some of you," said Mr. Growlagain, sharply; "and you, Melinda, and Martha, carry your sister away to her room, or she'll be screaming and squalling more than all the babies put together."

"But, Gregory," said Miss Melinda, "we can't have the babies in the house—Jerusha will go out of her mind."

"You must have 'em whether you like it or not, and as for Jerusha, she's out of her mind already."

With which complimentary remark, Mr. Growlagain kicked a wandering cat on to the top of the piano and felt better.

Half a dozen of the oldest of the young lady pupils were already at work baby gathering, and very well they did it too. It was capital fun for them; girls of their age take so naturally to babies.

Tommy Codlings, stuck up against the door-post,

felt a little uneasy at first, but when he saw how pretty most of the girls were, and how they kissed and fondled the infants as they carried them away, the young rogue began to think that he should rather like it.

"Dash it," he thought, "how they do cuddle 'em. It'll take two of 'em to carry me though. Hallo, there's a nice girl with black hair."

And Tommy set up a dismal howl in order to attract the nice girl's notice.

She turned and saw the plump youth with his countenance twisted into an expression indicative of intense suffering.

"Oh, Louise, Louise," she called to another very pretty fair-haired girl, "do come. Here's such a big baby, and it is so ugly."

Tommy turned scarlet with indignation, and thought that the young lady with black hair was not such a very nice girl after all.

Miss Louise came running up, and instantly turned up her pert little nose at Tommy.

"Well, that is a big, ugly, fat baby. Don't touch it, dear, it's sure to be some nasty German baby."

This was a dreadful insult, a slight not to be borne, and Tommy, quite forgetting his assumed character, turned redder than ever as he said angrily—

"No, I ain't German. Now then, Miss Carrots."

"Why, it's a boy," exclaimed the young lady with the black hair.

"Ugh, the odious little wretch," added the fair one, whom Tommy had wrathfully spoken of as "Carrots."

"Hil—lo—," said the constable, opening his eyes and mouth at the extraordinary six months' old baby, speaking strong and idiomatic English. "Hillo, where did you come from ?"

With that the officer stirred Tommy up a little with the toe of his boot, and of course selected a very tender part, the one on which the flogging-machine had operated.

"Here, you just leave off, will you. Oh !" and Tommy, receiving a second and similar touching up, attempted to rise, but was tugged up by the night-shirt and fell upon a pile of babies who had not yet been fetched away.

"This here is a wery nice little go o' yourn, ain't it," resumed the constable, hoisting Tommy on to his l   by means of his right ear. "You come alon   , young man. I smell a plant in this."

Nothing horticultural was elicited by this last remark. The guilty Tommy knew too well what was meant. The game was up, the plot was discovered, and he was the victim.

He made one frantic effort to escape, and aimed a kick at the policeman, which would infallibly have lamed him, but the nightgown got in the way as usual, and all that Tommy gained by his manœuvre was a twist of the ear, which seemed to turn it red hot.

"Kick, would you, my joker ? I'll teach you better than that. Come on."

And helpless Tommy was hauled along the passage and so into the drawing-room, where Mr. Growlagain stood looking out of the window and using some very bad language in a very audible voice.

"Now then," he growled, "what the dickens are you bringing 'em in here for ?"

"This ain't a baby, sir."

"What is it then," demanded the schoolmaster, looking at Tommy in a way that made him shrink.

"A plant, sir, There's always boys in these here games, as you ought to know. Miss Growlagain didn't know nothing of that there board, I believe, sir."

"She said so; but women will say anything."

"Well, I'll bet this boy does ; look here, sir."

And with one sharp pull the policeman stripped the night-gown from off Tommy's back, and with a second pulled off the cap, leaving our plump friend standing in the ordinary costume of a youth of the nineteenth century.

Mr. Growlagain stared at Tommy, and then a grim look of recognition stole over his features.

"I've seen you before, I think, my friend." he said, slowly. "You were one of the young blackguards who stole my pupils' clothes a week or so back, and insulted me into the bargain."

Now, as our readers know, poor Tommy had taken no part in that expedition. He had not even participated in the fun, but it was just his luck to be mistaken for Lionel or Charlie, neither of whom he in the least resembled.

"No, indeed, it wasn't me, sir. I was miles away at the time."

"So you do acknowledge knowing the circumstance, at least ?" said Mr. Growlagain. "Now, answer another question. Are you one of Stiffback's boys ?"

"I am, sir."

"That's quite enough." said the schoolmaster of Deliverham, getting into a towering passion at a jump. "The villain is envious of me, and this is his work. Confess at once, you young rascal, and perhaps I'll let you go."

"Confess what, sir ?"

"Don't repeat my words, you—you quintessence of all that's villanous, or I'll kick you from here to Jerusalem and back. Is not that scoundrel of a Stiffback the man who prompted you to disgrace me in this manner ?"

"I ain't acquainted with any scoundrel of the name of Stiffback, so I can't say."

Tommy saw that his case was desperate and that he would get into just as much trouble if he pleaded for mercy as if he "cheeked" Mr. Growlagain ; so he reluctantly adopted the latter course.

"None of your impudence, you hardened young b'ackguard, or I'll skin you alive."

"You can't do it," said Tommy, calmly.

"What ! can't do it."

"No," was Tommy's reply. "I was skinned yesterday, and the new skin hasn't grown yet."

The policeman laughed a short dry laugh of approbation. Mr. Growlagain was no favourite of his, and he liked chaff, when it was not addressed to himself by the rude little boys on his beat.

"What are you grinning at ?" demanded Mr. Growlagain fiercely.

"I'm not aware, sir, as larfin is against the regulations," replied the policeman ; "and not bein' unfortunate enough to be one o' your pupils, sir, I shall larf, corf, and sneeze, as natur may require."

Here Tommy thought it would only be friendly to back up the constable with a laugh, but Mr. Growlagain stopped him with a box on the ear, which made him gasp for breath.

"You want to drive me mad between you, I think," said Mr. Growlagain, casting a desperate look at Tommy. "Policeman, will you lock that boy up ?"

"Cert'ny, sir, if you'll take the 'sponsibility."

"Of course I will."

"What's the charge, sir ?"

Mr. Growlagain hesitated, and cursed the formalities of the law which required a specific charge to be brought against a prisoner.

"Felony, sir," suggested the constable. "It's a good crime, and looks well on the charge-sheet."

"But what has he stolen ?"

"I don't know," replied the constable, calmly. "You charge him—I take him up—that's division of labour. What do you say to manslaughter, or to bigamy."

"You're an idiot," exclaimed the furious Mr. Growlagain. "Get out, I'll take the boy myself."

"Very good, sir, it's all the same to me. I've seen that the babies was took in, and my mates have got the crowd away. So I'll wish you good mornin'."

And away sauntered the constable, in a calm and happy state of mind. He had saddled Miss Growl-again with a score of squalling infants, of whom the parish authorities would not relieve her for a couple of days at least, and he had driven Mr. Growlagain into a state of incipient madness.

But how about our old friend Tommy? He was in anything but a calm and happy state of mind, and the record of what Mr. Growlagain did to him and what he did to Mr. Growlagain must be told in a fresh chapter.

CHAPTER XXVIII.

OUR HERO AND HIS CHUMS HOLD A DISCUSSION RESPECTING THEIR LOST "BABY"—VANSITTART PURCHASES A LITTLE VALUABLE INFORMATION FOR THE SMALL SUM OF HALF-A-CROWN—THE AMBUSH—LIONEL'S MOTIVE FOR A READY-MADE DISGUISE—THE APPROACH OF THE CAPTOR AND HIS VICTIM—TOMMY'S "CHEEK" TAKES EFFECT UPON MR. GROWLAGAIN—A LITTLE PRELIMINARY TORTURE—THE RESCUE, AND THE SCHOOLMASTER'S COMMENTS THEREON.

WHILE the interesting events recorded in our last chapter were taking place within the boundaries of Minerva House, Lionel and his chums were waiting with no small anxiety for some sort of sign of Tommy's safety.

They had not seen how Tommy had been detected by the policeman and hauled into the presence of Mr. Growlagain; as, for considerations of safety, they had moved away from the gate at the arrival of the other constables.

"I told you," said Lionel, "that Tommy would be sure to get into trouble."

"Then we must get him out of it—that's all," replied Vansittart.

"Easier said then done, I fancy."

"We don't know that he's got into trouble at all, yet," said Charlie. "If he keeps quiet where we put him, he won't be noticed."

"Ah, but do you think they'll let him stay quietly where we put him?" added our hero. "They must move the babies away somewhere, and then Tommy will be spotted to a certainty."

"We must see how things are going on," said Vansittart. "Let us stroll quietly by, and look n as we pass."

They did, and saw to their dismay that all the babies, Tommy included, had been taken away.

"I wonder what they've done with him."

"Put him to bed, most likely, with the others," laughed Lionel. "They haven't taken the pap in, though. I can see the basin up there by the steps."

"Confound it, we're fixed," said Vansittart. "It may be hours before they find out that Tommy's not a baby after all."

"Oh! no it won't," said Drummond, who was an authority, as he had two or three near relations who were babies. "They have to feed 'em every ten minutes or so, and undress and spank 'em, and they're sure to find out Tommy then."

"He'll take to the feeding if it has to be done every ten minutes. That's just in Tommy's line."

"Not if they give him pap or gruel," said Charlie. "He won't take to that."

"Or—ha! ha!—suppose he's treated to a wet-nurse," said Vansittart, with a laugh. "I'd give something to see Tommy then."

"It would be worse than the bull."

"That's so. But hush, you fellows. Here comes the peeler out of the house. Keep quiet, as we may get something out of him."

Vansittart waited till the constable had passed out of the gates, and then accosted him with an easy, off-hand manner.

"Morning, policeman."

"Mornin' to you."

"Had a bit of a shine here, eh?"

"Well, no, not exactly; but there might ha' bin if I hadn't come hup in time and hawed the mob."

"Just so. And the babies? Did they take them in at last?"

"They couldn't help theirselves. They had to do it."

"Ah! and I suppose they're in clover now?"

"Not much o' that. The old lady's in eggstericks, and the old gent is cussin' away at a rate that 'ud ruin him if he was fined five bob a cuss."

"No, no. I meant the babies," said Vansittart. "They're being well looked after, aren't they?"

"Not bein' a family man, I can't say what is rekired for the comfort of a babby. But they're all 'owlin' away like barrel orgins, if that's a sign o' happerness."

"Are they?"

"Yes, 'cept one, and he'll do his 'owlin by-and-by."

"How's that, constable?" asked Vansittart, speaking carelessly, but feeling a good deal concerned for the fate of his plump chum.

"Why, you see," continued the policeman, eyeing our friends in a curious way, "this baby ain't a baby at all, but a boy, and he's one o' them who got up this little game. You happen to know something about it too, maybe?"

And the policeman indicated the unlucky signboard, which had not yet been taken down.

"Oh, dear no," said Vansittart, in a very hasty and decided tone. "What should we know about it?"

"All right," replied the constable. "It's no consarn o' mine. I ain't had horders to take anybody into custody *yet*."

And he laid especial emphasis on the last word, as if to imply that it would not be long before he was required to apprehend the criminals.

"And what's old Growlagain going to do with him?"

The constable winked, and went through some very expressive pantomime, suggesting a boy undergoing the torture of the cane.

"And if you'll take my hadwice, young gents," he added, "you won't be in the way when he comes out, for he's down on boys this blessed day to an orful extent."

"Thank you for your information," said Vansittart, producing a half-crown as if by accident. "You don't happen to know when he's coming out, do you, and whether he's going to bring the boy with him?"

The policeman did not know, but the sight of the half-crown stimulated him into the possession of the gift of prophecy.

"He'll be out in about 'arf a hour, and he's going to take the boy to his school and whack him until he owns who put him up to this little game."

"The dickens he is," said Vansittart, looking serious.

"That's the programmy, sir," replied the policeman, as he pocketed the half-crown, saluted, and walked away towards the Deliverham market place.

"This is bad news," said Lionel. "Poor old Tommy."

"Yes, Growlagain is sure to know that he belongs to our school, and he'd welt him for that out of pure jealousy, without any other reason," said Vansittart.

"But Growlagain has no right to keep him or whack him," added Drummond. "Can't we make him give Tommy up?"

"Stiffback could if he applied to the station; but they wouldn't take any notice of us," said Vansittart. "Stiffback's his legal protector, you know."

"Then I'll tell you what, we'll get Tommy back ourselves," said Lionel. "We three are more than a match for old Growlagain."

"Not a bad notion, young Wilful," said Vansittart. "By George! we'll do that. His school lies up the road yonder, and he has to turn down a narrow little lane—just the very place for an ambush."

"Off we go then," said Lionel, gleefully. "It'll be like a bit out of Fenimore Cooper's 'Deerslayer.'"

It was a shady little lane, bordered by trees of a very respectable size, and, selecting three of the largest, Lionel, Charlie, and Vansittart proceeded to ambush themselves.

"I say, though," said our hero, "stop a bit. Can't we disguise ourselves? He'll recollect us if we don't. Remember the trick we played him."

"Ah! ah! so he will. I didn't think of that in the hurry," said Vansittart. "But what can we do?"

"Turn your jackets inside out first, and then tie your handkerchiefs over your faces, just below your eyes. I'll bet he won't know us then if we pull our caps well down."

No sooner said than done, and a most effectual disguise it was.

It was hardly completed though, and the boys safely ensconced behind the trees, when Mr. Growlagain appeared at the top of the lane, holding Tommy fast by the arm.

He was talking, too, but he didn't seem to be very affectionate in his manner, for there were stronger expressions than are generally used in loving converse.

"Damme," they heard him say, for he was speaking very loudly, "I'll have it out of your stubborn young hide somehow. I've got canes that would tickle and sting the truth out of a marble statue."

"Then why don't you try it on the marble statue?" said Tommy, coolly. "You won't get anything out of me, and so I tell you."

Mr. Growlagain was one of the most fierce and wrathful of pedagogues.

His own boys trembled at the very sound of his voice, and yet here was an undersized young rascal, who first nearly drove him mad with a practical joke, and then, in vulgar language, "cheeked" him.

It was more than flesh and blood could stand, and Mr. Growlagain pulled Tommy up again with a jerk that half throttled him.

"Damme," he growled, giving, as usual, vent to his favourite expletive, "I must take some of this out of you, my lad, before I get you to the school. You're full of sauce, and I'm afraid that my boys will catch it like the scarlet fever."

So saying, he twisted Tommy's head under his arm with a dexterity that could only have been acquired by long practice, and lifted him up so as to tighten his trousers a little, while with his right hand he took from his pocket a short, but broad and flexible, piece of leather.

"I don't know," he said, half musingly, "that I ever flogged a boy in the open air like this before, but there's a novelty in it that gives it a relish. It would be capital exercise before breakfast. I'll pick out some of my smallest boys to practise on."

Mr. Growlagain had been so absorbed in his preparations for beating Tommy, who was kicking frantically, but uselessly, in the powerful grasp of his captor, that he had not noticed the gradual and stealthy approach of the ambushed party.

His eyes were fixed upon the plump rotund figure of his captive, his right hand was already raised to deliver the first whack, when three figures bounded out upon him, and in an instant, it seemed to him, Tommy was snatched from his grasp, and

he was rolling in the bottom of a ditch, full of fine healthy nettles, and with his hat knocked right over his eyes by one well-directed blow.

He scrambled out of the ditch, uttering anathemas which would infallibly have withered up the whole of the nettle plants on the face of the earth had curses any power in these degenerate days when witches are out of fashion, but by the time he was on his legs again and had got his hat off, skinning his nose in the process, there was not a trace of the rescued nor the rescuers in sight.

"Never mind," gasped Mr. Growlagain frantically; "that rascal Stiffback shall pay for this: and as for that—that sausage of a boy, I'll flay him when I catch him, damme, I will. It must have been some more of Stiffback's boys who got him away just now. Oh lord, oh dear me, how I do smart—but their time will come to smart too."

Whether Mr. Growlagain's prophecy was correct, this faithful history will tell in its own good time.

We have now to record the great fight between Vansittart and the young pig-jobber, which is remembered at Lake House School to this very day with no small feeling of pride.

CHAPTER XXIX.

AFTER THE LITTLE PRACTICAL JOKE AT DELIVERHAM—VANSITTART RECOUNTS THE PARTICULARS OF A LONDON ADVENTURE, AND WHAT OCCURRED TO HIM IN CONSEQUENCE—THE DAY OF THE GREAT FIGHT—THE JOURNEY TO THE BATTLE FIELD—THE FIGHT—VICTORY!

AND now the day which our hero and his friends had awaited so anxiously came at last—the day for the big fight between Vansittart and the young pig-jobber.

For the first day or so after their adventure in Deliverham with Mr. Growlagain and his sisters, our friends had felt some little anxiety for the result.

Every moment they expected to see the rival schoolmaster arrive, armed with the authority of the law, and demand the surrender of the culprits.

"That policeman may have peached, you know," said Vansittart. "I'm almost certain that he twigged us."

"What does it matter if he did?" replied our hero. "It was only a lark, after all. They can't lock up anybody for a joke."

"Can't they, though?" said Vansittart; "I know they can. Four other fellows and myself spent a night in Vine-street Police Station when we were in London last holidays; and all through a practical joke."

"What was that?"

"Why, we picked out a quiet little street where we knew that most of the people were quiet old fogies who went to bed about ten as punctual as sunset; and about eleven one night we went down and tied a dozen knockers together on one side of the street, and then carried the string over the way, and made it fast to a knocker there, then one of us gave a tremendous ring at the bell, and away we dodged round the corner.

"In a minute or two, down comes a red faced old boy in his shirt and trousers, and flings open the street-door; of course, the minute he did so, "bang-bang!—rat-tat! bang!" went all the dozen knockers on the other side.

"The old chap looked up the street and down the street, and over the way; but there wasn't a soul in sight, and we could hear him growling away like a good 'un.

"Presently he went in, but he'd hardly shut the door, when a stout party in a long dressing-gown and a nightcap, opened his door over the way, and of course the old boy's knocker was set going again.

"Out he bounced, in a tremendous rage, and seeing nobody but the old lady, who looked as much like a man as a woman in the dressing gown, he bolts over and collars her.

"'I've got you, you scoundrel, have I,' says he, 'I'll teach you to come waking decent people up at this time of night!'

"And with that he gave her a shake that shook her cap off into the middle of the street; but she, being a plucky old party, fixed her fingers in his hair, and made him howl with pain in no time.

"Then two or three more of the doors opened, and out came the neighbours to see what was up.

"We were at the corner roaring with laughter, and thinking what a prime joke it was; when, before we could move half a leg to bolt, half-a-dozen bobbies were on to us.

"The one on duty in the street had seen us before, and finding we were too many for him to tackle, had fetched his mates to help."

"Couldn't you make a fight of it?" said Charlie.

"We could, of course; but it would only have made matters worse. We couldn't all get away, and our motto was, 'One in, all in,' so we took it quietly and went to the station."

"What did they do to you there?"

"Oh, we made ourselves pretty comfortable. A few shillings tipped the policemen on duty, and they gave us something to lie on, and brought us some refreshment, and we smoked and sang songs all night; and in the morning, after a wash in the police yard, we went before the magistrate, who gave us a long lecture on the folly of practical joking, and let us off with a small fine."

"It was well worth that, to see the old ones dodging in and out of the houses, after the runaway knocks, though," said Charlie. "That's a prime lark; we must try it on in Deliverham, Li."

"You won't be able to," said Vansittart. "The benighted inhabitants don't put knockers on their doors, and the houses are too far apart; but there are plenty of other tricks, you fellows, some of which we'll try as soon as Monday's over."

For at least three days, Vansittart had attended strictly to his training. With Lionel, Charlie and Codlings, whenever that little young gentleman did not oversleep himself, he took a header in the lake, and then did half-an-hour's running before breakfast.

The sparring, too, was regularly gone through as often as opportunity would present, and when at last the day came round, he was in as good condition as if a regular trainer had prepared him; "fit as a fiddle," Vansittart called it.

To avoid suspicion, and to prevent the possibility of any who were not in the secret joining them, it was arranged that they should all be up by four in the morning, and row across the lake in the eight-oared galley, which would just accommodate the party.

"We shall get a pœna from Stiffback, for it," said Vansittart, "but that don't matter much. Pull away, boys."

And so at a quarter past four, long before any one else was stirring, Vansittart and his backers, fourteen all told, embarked in the galley and were soon safely landed on the opposite shore of the lake.

The space where the fight was to come off was a small field at some distance from the main road, and so sheltered by trees as to be liberally secure from any chance interruption.

It was about a mile and a half from Lake Island, and as the time appointed was half-past four, our heroes had plenty of time before them, and beguiled the tedium of the way by various games at "touch" and "leap frog," in which Vansittart joined as heartily as the others.

"Don't tire yourself, old fellow," said Lionel, "you've got some hard work to do."

"Never fear, Wilful; I'm only stretching my limbs a bit. I feel as if I could walk a hundred miles and then lick the pig-jobber."

It was nearly five when the field was reached, and early as were Vansittart and his party, they found some of the pig-jobber's friends there before them, measuring out the ground and driving in the stakes to form the ring.

They were a rough-looking lot, but good humoured and apparently bent upon getting as much out of the fight as possible; for as soon as they caught sight of Vansittart and his friends, they first cheered and then clapped them.

Stinger senior was there, driving in the stakes with a big mallet, and as Vansittart approached, he received him with a broad grin.

"Mornin', young gen'leman—mornin'. You be come then, arter all."

"Why, of course," replied Vansittart. "Didn't you expect me?"

"I did; for I knows a good plucked 'un when I sees 'un; but some o' they chaps said you were safe to get funky when th' toime cum."

"Much obliged to them," said Vansittart, "for their good opinion. After I've licked your son I shall be happy to oblige as many of them as dare to say that same thing again."

"Licked my son," exclaimed the old pig-jobber—"licked my—— But there, thee be a cool hand, thee be, and do carry't off uncommon well. Lick my Bill! Ha—ha—ha! that be th' best joke I ha' heard for many a day."

"Your Bill won't find it much of a joke, I can tell you," said Vansittart, in the same calm confident voice; "unless he funks the fight and stays away."

"Lookee here," said the old man, solemnly: "why when my Bill were no higher then a three-legged stool he ne'er turned his back on anything he stood up to. I'd ha' wrung his neck if he had, and well he knowed it. My feyther did the same by me, and when Bill marries and has kids he'll do the same by them."

"Well," said Vansittart, with a laugh. "That's one way of educating children."

"Ah, and a darned good way tew," retorted the pig-jobber. "Bring a lad up so's he can use his fists, and stand up square 'fore anything on two legs, and that lad won't go far wrong, I tells 'ee."

"Yours is a very simple code of morality, Mr. Stinger," said Vansittart.

"Ah, things ain't wot they was when I was a lad, and they was better still in my feyther's time. Then, if a couple o' chaps had a diff'rence 'bout anything, they'd orf wi' their coats, and turn to wi' their pistols till one on 'em was conwinced as he was wrong. Now, dang me, 'stead o' settlin' quarrels in a manly, straightforrard fashi'n, they goes to law and summonses one another."

And the hearty old pig-jobber was at least honest in his convictions, and acted up to them by always offering the ordeal of battle to anyone who chanced to differ in opinion with him.

As the time drew near, Lionel was conscious that his heart beat quicker, and his face alternately flushed and grew pale, as though he himself was about to engage in single combat with the pig-jobber in lieu of Vansittart.

Charlie too was fidgetting uneasily on the grass, and looking towards the quarter whence young Stinger would make his appearance.

Tommy was absorbed in the consumption of a gigantic sandwich, and did not seem in the least nervous.

At length the sound of many voices, singing a good deal out of tune that inspiring American anthem, "We'll all get blind drunk when Johnny comes marching home," was heard, and Mr. Stinger gave forth expressions more forcible then elegant—

"YOU BE TAM!" HOWLED THE FRENCH MASTER, "GO AWAY, OR I MAKE GERMAN-SAUSAGE OF YOU."

No. 23.

"Dash they fules! what be they bawlin' for, like that?"

"Never, mind," said Vansittart; "let 'em sing now, they'll change their tune before long."

"Will they; and what tune will they change it for?"

"'The Dead March in Saul,'" replied Vansittart, gravely.

The old man looked at him in deep disgust for a moment, and then went forth to meet "his Bill," roaring a gentle hint the while to "hold that noise."

"I say," said Charlie, filled with excitement, "here they come, Vansittart, here they come!"

"Time they did," said the young aristocrat, looking at his watch. "It's five minutes past the half-hour already."

"You take it coolly," said Lionel, looking admiringly at him.

"Best way, old fellow. I shall be warm enough presently, you may be sure."

"Bother me, if I don't think I'm more nervous about it than you are."

"Very likely, dear boy. I should be more nervous than you if you were going to fight. Seconds always are. Ah, here's the pig-jobber; give him a cheer, you fellows—they gave me one, and we won't be behind hand in politeness."

The Lake House School boys, led by Lionel, raised a hearty "Hurrah!" which was so liberally responded to by the new-comers, that old Stinger was obliged to restrain the demonstration by distributing a few open handed-smacks from a fist like a shoulder of mutton.

"Now for business," said Vansittart, getting up from the grass. "Wilful, tie my colours to the stake—the one nearest you. Have you got the bottles all right, Pryce, and the sponge?"

"Every thing's ready, old fellow," replied Pryce, a handsome Welsh lad of seventeen. "Shall I help you peel?"

"Yes; but let us get into the ring first. There goes Bill's cap. Ha! Bill, how do you feel? Ready for a little exercise?"

"Ay," replied the elated Bill, with a wide grin; "you and me'll have plenty o' that, my lad, and we'd best get to work afore the sun gets too 'igh, fur it'll be a blazin' hot day."

Both our hero and Charlie were now looking "with all their eyes" at the man of Deliverham, who, it was expected, would gain so easy a victory over the young aristocrat, and it must be confessed that Lionel and his chum felt their hopes sink a little when they got a nearer view of him.

He was quite as tall as Vansittart, but so much broader and thicker that he seemed some inches short of his real height.

The muscles of his arms and legs, shown up by his tight clothing, had attained a development seldom seen except in the limbs of a professional athlete.

It was said of him that he had once taken a bullock by the horns and threw it to the ground by sheer strength; and he certainly looked quite capable of performing the feat.

"My stars," said Lionel, in a low tone to Charlie, "what a brute! Look at his arms, Drum; they're as big as my legs."

"He is a whopper," returned Charlie, in the same tone. "He could crack a fellow's ribs like a nut. I hope Vansittart won't let him close."

"Trust him for that," replied our hero. "Van knows what he's about."

But although Lionel's words were confident enough, there was a despondency in his expression which told plainly enough that he was no longer so hopeful as he had been before he saw with his own eyes the herculean proportions of the young pig-jobber.

Meanwhile the few remaining preparations for the contest were going rapidly forward and old Stinger, still superintending them, was offering to bet any amount of money, from one pound to fifty, upon the result of the fight.

"Here you are," he roared out, "back your man, you young gen'lemen from the school. Five to one I'll bet that my boy gives him a licking. Six to one—seven to one I'll lay. Who'll make a bet?"

But there was an ominous silence amongst the boys of the upper form.

They, too, had seen the huge muscles of the young pig-jobber, and drawn an inference unfavourable to the victory of their champion.

"Wal," exclaimed old Stinger, with a hearty laugh, "funkin' a'ready, are ye? Then I'll tell 'ee wot I'll do to give ye a pluck up. Dang me if I don't lay ten to one on my boy Bill. There now, who's on?"

"Hang it," said Lionel, "we must have a shy at that. How much money have you got?"

"I've got two sovereigns and five-and-sixpence," replied Drummond.

"I've got three. That'll make five. Hand me your two, Charlie."

Charlie reluctantly pulled out the two yellow boys and passed them to his chum.

"I say, though, one'll be enough, won't it?"

"Not a bit. If I had twenty, and was certain to lose 'em all, I'd bet, if it was only to keep Van's spirits up. Here, governor, we take your bet."

"Well, I'm glad to see one of you's got pluck enough to back your friend," said the pig-jobber. "How much? a fiver? All right. If t' young lord whops my Bill, I'll have to give 'ee this back, and fifty pun beside. See?"

"Oh! I see," replied Lionel, shortly.

And turning, he went back to Charlie, with very little hope of ever seeing the money again.

Shamed by the example of the younger boys, the others now began, but in a half-hearted way, as if they had no confidence in the opinion they had "backed," and glad enough were they when old Stinger pulled out his watch and called—

"Time!"

"Now, Wilful," said Vansittart, looking at our hero with a cheerful smile, "pluck up your spirits, man."

"Your's are all right apparently," replied Lionel.

"First rate. I'm sure to win. But hang all those fellows I've brought with me, they look as if they were going to be hung."

"They're afraid of losing their money, perhaps."

"Precious little that they have put on," replied Vansittart. "You did a plucky thing when you put that price on, Wilful. But you shan't lose your money."

"I'm not afraid of that."

"I don't think you are. But they're putting the pig-jobber up, and I must step out. One last word. If he gets a fair hit at me, I shall very likely be stunned. Don't you be alarmed at that, but pick me up, and throw all the water you can get over my head and neck."

"I won't forget," said Lionel. "There's old Stinger calling 'Time!' Go in and win."

Vansittart nodded, smiled again, and then, with a light, elastic step, walked forward to the scratch.

Slogging Bill stepped out at the same time, and then, in the good old English fashion, the combatants shook hands as heartily as if they had met for the purpose of having a good breakfast instead of a "bellyful" of the hardest knocks they could deal out to one another.

For one moment each looked full into the other's eyes, and saw no signs of quailing there.

Then they stepped back a few inches and put up their hands.

The fight had begun!

Hardly daring to breathe, and with staring eyes, Lionel and Charlie now watched the combatants.

Tommy Codlings had lost his chance of a good place by taking too long a time over his sandwich, and in making a desperate endeavour to climb up a tall man who was in front, received injuries which deprived him of all interest in that fight.

It was evident stalwart Bill thought that he had a very easy job in hand, for he began the fight by dancing, in a playfully elephantine way, in front of Vansittart, pretending to hit out, feinting and dodging his head from side to side, and such small pleasantries, till suddenly Vansittart saw an opening, then, like a flash, his left fist shot out, struck the pig-jobber flush in the nose, and felled him as if he had been shot.

"First knock down, and first blood, I claim," shouted Pryce, as Vansittart turned and came calmly walking back to his corner.

"Don't make such a fuss about it," growled old Stinger savagely, as he raised the discomfited Bill from the ground. "Wot did 'ee go dancin' aboot like that 'ere fur, ye darned fule?"

"Shut up," growled Bill, in reply, as he tasted the blood that came trickling into his mouth.

"Shut up," returned the old man, angrily. "Be that t' way to talk to thy feyther? Tell 'ee wot, Bill, if ye don't polish him orf in a couple o' rounds, darn me if I don't slip into thee myself."

"Much good you'd get that way," said the undutiful Bill. "Hold your tongue, and just sponge my face, will you?"

On Vansittart's side of the ring all was joy and congratulation.

Those who had looked the most despondent a few moments ago now crowded round, and said "They were sure of it;" "Vansittart was certain to win;" "The pig-jobber would be doubled up in five minutes;" and so on.

"Stop it, you fellows," said the young champion, coolly. "You know you were all in a blue funk about your money five minutes ago. Besides, I haven't won the fight yet by a long way. There's a good hour's work before me yet."

"Time!" roared old Stinger, giving his son a shove that sent him to the scratch in a most undignified hurry.

"Ready," responded Pryce.

And Vansittart, stepping out in the same light, firm manner, again confronted his foe.

Bill's face was pale, with the exception of his ears, which had blushed a deep crimson, as if at the indignity of being punched; but there was a set look about his wide mouth, and an ominous gleam in his little eyes which told Vansittart that this time he meant mischief.

Indeed, they had scarcely got into position, when Bill, without ever feinting, delivered two heavy blows, right and left, intending to follow them up, break down Vansittart's guard, and close with him.

But the young champion was not to be "done" by such simple tactics as these.

He avoided the blows by stepping out of distance, and then, springing in before Bill recovered his guard, dealt him two tremendous "facers" in the mouth.

It seemed as if the blows would have beaten in the side of a house, so heavy were they, but the pig-jobber only reeled a little, recovered himself, and then, with a savage growl, rushed in again with the fury of a bull.

"Stop, Bill, thee fule!" cried the old man; but it was too late. The mischief was done, Vansittart's left arm coiled round Bill's neck with the grasp of a boa-constrictor. Bill was in chancery, and it would have puzzled the Lord Chancellor himself to have got him out without injury.

Now the excitement was at its height. Men and boys roared, screamed shouted, clapped their hands, danced even in a kind of frenzy as Vansittart's right fist, with the rapidity and force of a sledge-hammer, battered the features of the hapless Bill.

Vansittart seemed endowed with the strength of Hercules: his legs were, despite the frantic struggles of his foe, as rigid as a bar of steel. To and fro they staggered, their feet tearing up the fresh green turf, and still with a dull smacking sound the blows fell swiftly and heavily, until suddenly the pig-jobber ceased to struggle, his arms dropped to his side, and Vansittart, panting and almost breathless, let him fall in a huddled heap upon the ground.

The old man, with a face as white as a sheet, ran forward, and with the help of the bottle-holder carried him to his corner, while Vansittart walked over to where Lionel, pale and anxious, stood waiting for him.

"He's not dead," said our hero in a low tone. "You haven't killed him?"

"No fear of that. It would take a battering-ram or a ball from the 81-ton gun to do that. Whew, he's the strongest chap I ever had in a grip. Sponge me well, Wilful, and be quick. We shall have another round or two yet."

The sponging was indeed needed. Vansittart's right hand and arm as far as the elbow were dyed red, while his breast and face were spattered with splashes of blood. He looked as if he had been busily engaged in a slaughter-house for a day or two.

"Do you mean to say that he'll come up to time again?" asked Lionel, as he sponged away vigorously at the young champion. "I made sure you'd killed him."

"Not a bit of it. He's got strength and wind, ay and pluck enough too, to fight the rest of the day; but I've blinded him, my boy. He won't be able to see a haystack when he stands up again."

"Blinded him! I hope not."

"Not for good. I didn't mean that," said Vansittart, with a laugh. "He'll see as well as ever in a day or two. I've only put up the shutters, that's all."

"Oh, that's all, is it," replied our hero. "Then I'm precious glad of it, Van; for I now own I thought he was too much for you."

"So he would have been, if he had only kept as cool as I did, but the fellow's like a bull, or a mad dog, and rushes in anyhow. Hillo, there's old Stinger putting him up again."

In effect the veteran pig-jobber, anxious for his son's honour and for his own money, had persuaded Bill to "have one more go."

"Only get a holt of him, Bill," he whispered, "and then never mind punching him, but give him a back fall, and mind 'ee falls on top."

"I'll mind," growled Bill, feeling round with his tongue for his lost teeth; "but dash it, I can't see a bit. Ye look like the Tower o' London, feyther."

"Ne'er moind wot I looks like; do ye go in and do wot I tell 'ee."

And putting his son in a line with the scratch, the old man gave him a gentle shove and waited anxiously for the result.

It was pretty evident what that would be. Vansittart well knew in what Bill's only chance consisted, and it was not likely that he would give the opportunity that was sought.

So, as soon as Bill in a groping, uncertain way reached the scratch, Vansittart, who was waiting for him, let out his left and knocked him down.

With that dogged determination so characteristic of the Anglo-Saxon race, Bill came up again and again for six times, and six times in succession Vansittart floored him.

"Darn thee," roared the old man in an agony of rage at his son's defeat, "let 'un have a chance, let 'un close with 'ee. Try a wrastle, now do."

"No," replied Vansittart, coolly, "I want to get home with sound ribs. Put him up forty times if you like, and I'll knock him down for you."

"Darn thee," growled old Stinger despairingly. "Chuck up t'sponge, feller. Darn thee, Bill, but I'll flay thee hide for this when thee gets whoam. I'm nigh a hunderd pound out o' pocket, 'sides the shame on the fam'ly."

The sponge was thrown up, and the signal of victory was hailed by our hero and his chums with a "Harrah" of rejoicing.

A cool head and good "science" had again proved themselves better than brute strength and obstinacy, as they always have done and ever will.

Old Stinger paid his debts to Lionel with ten greasy five-pound notes, and his last words, as he led Bill off the field, were to the effect that the family was disgraced, and that he was off to Australia the very next week.

CHAPTER XXX.

AFTER THE FIGHT—THE SWEETS OF VICTORY— WHAT'S TO BE DONE WITH THE MONEY?— LIONEL'S PROPOSAL—THE BREAKFAST AT THE "GEORGE"—OUR HERO PERFORMS AN ACT WHICH OUR READERS MAY THINK FOOLISH OR NOT, ACCORDING TO THEIR DISPOSITIONS—THE PICNIC—THE RETURN—THE SPIRIT OF MISCHIEF AT WORK AGAIN.

VANSITTART, as he himself acknowledged, had had wonderful good fortune in his contest with the pig-jobber. His face was left untouched, though he had been heavily punished about the chest and arms, and spat a quantity of blood, but no material harm was done, and now the fight was over he readily acknowledged the misgivings he had had.

"I really thought, Wilful," he said, "that I should have been carried off somewhere with a face like a raw beefsteak, not a tooth left in my head, and a couple of ribs broken, and here I am, safe and sound, except these bruises, which will keep sore for a week."

"And for my part," said Lionel, laughing, "I thought I should go home with empty pockets, and here am I and Charlie with fifty pounds to share. I don't know what to do with it; I never before had anything like so much money."

"Take care of it, young Wilful; you'll find use enough for it, I dare say."

"I know how I mean to use some of it," replied our hero.

"How?"

"Why, in a little treat, to be sure. We'll all go over to the 'George,' in Deliverham, and have a royal breakfast, and then we'll take a couple of traps or a waggonette and drive somewhere to picnic for the rest of the day."

"That's a good plan," said Vansittart, "only we must keep out of the way of old Stinger. I should not like him to think that we were crowing over him."

"Never mind him; if his son Bill has been licked, why, he must take his licking in good part, as an Englishman should."

"All right," said Vansittart; "that's good sense anyhow. Hillo, you fellows, who's for a breakfast at the 'George,' and a picnic after? Wilful's going to stand treat."

Our readers may well imagine that nobody said "no" to this proposal. Even those (and there were a good many) who envied Lionel his good fortune in winning such a bet, agreed that he was a jolly fellow, and knew how to spend his money when he did get it.

It did not take long to reach Deliverham, for they were hungry, and hunger lends wings to the feet, when there is a good meal at the end of the journey.

The landlord of the "George Inn" was rather startled at such an invasion of fierce and hungry boys, and still more so at the liberal idea Lionel entertained of a breakfast, the list comprising nearly everything edible and palatable in the house and a good many things that were not.

While the breakfast was preparing, Lionel and the others contented themselves with a pint or so of milk apiece, and a little fruit by way of getting up an appetite for the more substantial repast.

The landlord himself presided, and if he had been astonished at the liberality of the orders, he was yet more at the liberality of the appetites displayed.

The hot rolls, the toast, the ham and eggs, preserves, mutton chops, game pie, and other little trifles of that sort disappeared with startling rapidity, and even then two or three, invited thereto by Tommy Codlings, called for the cold round of beef, and disposed of several pounds in a thorough business-like way.

"I've heard," the landlord afterwards said confidentially to his wife, "that the schoolmasters do cut the boys' wittles down uncommon fine, and no wonder. I wouldn't feed that little fat chap by contrack for less then two pound ten a week. Why, he eat a bottle o' pickles all to hisself, and when they was all gone he took greengage jam with his beef instead."

The "little fat chap" alluded to by the landlord, was, of course, none other than Tommy Codlings, who had found in a good breakfast a panacea for the injuries inflicted on him by the tall man.

"Now, landlord," said Lionel, when the feast was fairly over, "we want a waggonette and a pair of horses for the day."

"Can you wait a hour, sir?"

"We can, but we'd rather not."

"If you can make it convenient, I can let you have the nicest little turn-out in the town, and a couple of real good horses to pull it along. Corn-fed—none o' your starve-on-chaff skelintons."

"What do you say, Vansittart?"

"Better wait, I think. An hour isn't long, and there are the things to be packed for the picnic, and that'll take time."

"So it will, and it's early yet, too. All right, landlord, and pack up a couple of hampers with something tasty to eat and good to drink."

"I'll ... to that while you take a stroll through the town. I'm going to stay here and rub a little opodeldoc into my ribs to take the sting out."

"All right, I'll take a stroll into the town. I should like to pick up some little present for my mother, and Sam—poor Sam !—I've quite neglected him lately."

"Cut away then, young un; that money's burning a hole in your pocket already."

"It's always the way—I can't keep it," laughed Lionel. "Come on, Charlie. Will you come, Codlings?"

"No thanky. I think I'll have a nap."

"Does that beef suet lie heavy on your chest, Tommy? If he snores, shy a brick at him, Van."

"I'll pitch him out of the window if he does."

But Tommy had already curled himself up on the sofa, and was two-thirds asleep before Vansittart's amiable intention was expressed.

There was a jeweller's shop in Deliverham, and a very showy, attractive shop it was, full of glittering chains, rings, pins, studs, bracelets, and other gaudy ornaments with which the civilised savages of the nineteenth century are wont to decorate themselves.

Against the plate-glass front of this establishment Lionel and Charlie flattened their noses while they discussed the comparative value of the stock-in-trade.

"There's a pretty pair of ear-rings now," said Lionel, pointing out a pair shaped like warming-pans, with a bullion fringe depending from the lower half. "I'd like to buy those. But my mother wouldn't wear 'em, I'm afraid. They're rather showy."

"Showy? Not a bit of it," said Charlie. "You should see a pair my cousin wears; they weigh a quarter of a pound a-piece, I'm certain."

"And there's a ticker, Charlie. Look! My eye, what a beauty. What does it say on the ticket?"

"'Magnificent gold repeater,'" said Charlie, reading from the label. "'Double gold cases, plate-glass front, treble check action, jewelled in four hundred and thirty-seven holes, magneto-electric-galvanico regulator, warranted quiet in harness, self-winding action, strikes the hours, half hours, and quarters, and will also strike anybody who attempts to steal it. A bargain, forty pounds.'"

"That's something like a watch," said Lionel, thoughtfully fondling the pocket-book in which the bank notes were stowed away. "I should like to have it, Charlie."

"Too much money, old boy."

"Let's go halves in it; we've got fifty-five pounds between us."

"I should be afraid of a ticker like that, Li. There's too much of it. Why, you haven't a pocket you could get it into."

"We should have to wear it round our necks, like a medal, Charlie."

"We couldn't both wear it, you know."

"Of course not. I'd have one week and you the next. Besides, think how prime it would be to tell the time in the night. You've only got to touch that little knob there, and it strikes the hour directly."

"Oh ah, and how fine it would be if old Stiffback or any of the masters were to hear it, and come after the clock."

"I suppose you're right, Charlie; but we must buy something. There's a jolly scarf-pin—a skull and cross-bones, with diamond eyes. How much is it? Oh two pounds ten. And there's a ring that will just please Sam. Come on."

And Lionel dragged Charlie into the shop, nearly upsetting a pretty girl, shabbily dressed in black, hovering timidly near the entrance.

"Beg your pardon, miss; hope I didn't hurt you;" and the next minute Lionel and Charlie were deep in the examination of a tray full of scarf-pins, while the sharp-nosed proprietor explained the beauty of the various designs.

Lionel fixed upon the skull and cross-bones, and Charlie selected a design which appeared to represent an unfortunate worm which had lost its way in a red currant bush, but that, as the jeweller explained, was a correct likeness of the original serpent as he appeared in the Garden of Eden.

"Now for the rings," said Lionel. "Some of your full-sized ones, governor, that you can see a quarter of a mile off, you know."

The jeweller smiled, and was about to bring out the rings, when the pretty girl whom Lionel had so nearly upset at the door, came in, and stood, not speaking a word, but looking with a beseeching glance at the jeweller.

That gentleman seemed to recognize the girl, and to know her business too, without any explanation, for he immediately said—

"Now, my dear, you really must not come a botherin' me in this way. I can't help it, you know. I'm only the agent. The brokers is in, and you must go out afore twelve o'clock to-day. That's the very latest minute."

The girl's eyes—beautiful blue eyes—they were Lionel noticed—filled with tears, but she managed to say in a faltering voice—

"But mother is so much worse, Mr. Spekler. The doctor said yesterday—that—that—if she was moved—she——"

"I can't help that, you know, my dear. I'm only the agent, and obey orders from the landlord. Why don't you go to him?"

"I did—this morning—and when he heard what I had come for! he let the dog loose, and it tore my dress, and would have bitten me if the gardener hadn't beaten it off. Is it no use, sir?"

"Not a bit, my dear. Twelve o'clock sharp's the time."

The poor girl waited to hear no more, but covering her face with one pretty little hand hurried away.

"What's all that about," said Lionel, indignantly. "What a pretty little girl; and who was the brute who set the dog at her?"

"Sad case, young gentlemen—sad case," replied the jeweller, shaking his head. "Poor gentleman in very good circumstances awhile ago—father of that girl you just saw. Bank broke last year—he was ruined out and out. Tried to get a situation—then his health failed him. Now I hear his wife's dying, and as the landlord's given 'em notice to quit through me, they'll have to go to the work-house."

"What a thundering old brute the landlord must be. What's his name?"

"Growlagain," replied the jeweller, "school-master close by. Very wealthy man. Mr. Morton—that's the sick gentleman—was a good friend to him years ago, and set him up in his school, and this is all he gets for it; but of course you won't repeat what I say."

"Charlie, did you hear that," said Lionel, excitedly. "It's the old beast Growlagain who's persecuting that pretty girl."

"Let's get all the other fellows and break his windows."

"I say," added Lionel, in a whisper to Charlie and looking very red, as if he was about to propose something dishonourable, "let's pay the money for the girl."

"Eh?" said Charlie, opening his eyes widely.

"Let's pay the money, Charlie."

"You don't know how much it is."

Lionel soon settled that difficulty by asking the question of the jeweller.

"Let me see. With costs, it's exactly twenty-two pound nine and fourpence."

Our hero seldom gave a resolve time to cool.

In fewer moments than it takes to write the word, he had taken five of the greasy notes from his pocket, and pushed them towards the jeweller.

"There," he said, turning redder than ever, "there's twenty-five pounds. You just give that to the little girl, will you?"

"What!" exclaimed the tradesman, opening his eyes more widely than Charlie had done. "You don't mean to say——"

"Yes I do. Don't make a fuss. There's the money."

"You're out of your mind," said the matter-of-fact Charlie.

For all reply, Lionel began to whistle, and walked out of the shop.

"I say, Li," said Charlie, hurrying after him, "you've forgotten the pin."

"Blow the pin. There's our breakfast and the picnic to pay for."

"But you don't suppose I'm going to let you pay for everything?"

"Shall if I like."

"No you wont; for if you don't let me tip up half at least, I won't go at all. If you like to throw your coin away on strange girls——"

"Now you just shut up about that girl and the money, Charlie," said our hero, as savagely as if he had been accused of robbing someone. "If you ever say a word to anyone about it, you and I will be chums no longer."

"Have it your own way," said Charlie.

And there for the time the matter ended.

What consequences his charitable impulse had upon his future history time will reveal.

Of one thing, though, our readers may be certain—Lionel did not enjoy his holiday any the less in consequence of what he had done.

Every good or generous action is its own reward in no small degree.

By dusk they returned, hot, dusty, tired, but happy with the happiness which youth and health alone seem to possess, and although it was yet early, "bed" was the idea uppermost in the minds of the party.

The upper form boys had already retired to their own club-room, and our hero and his two chums were on their way to their dormitory, when Lionel fancied that he heard a strange noise, as of someone moaning in distress, proceeding from the partly-opened door of a room which they were passing.

To peep in was the work of a moment, and they then saw that it was Tommy's enemy, the French master, groaning on the carpet, and giving out a very strong smell of eau-de-vie.

"Here's a chance for you to have your revenge, Tommy," said Lionel. "What shall we do with him?"

"I know," replied that young gentleman; "let's put him in Kobblersvax's bed. They're bitter enemies, and the German will give him no end of a thrashing."

"Who knows where the room is?"

"It's on this floor, I know. We're sure to find it, because it smells so of tobacco."

"Lead the way then. Lift his legs gently, Charlie, he's as light as a feather."

And so, cautiously and noiselessly, Monsieur de Vinaigre was borne along the passage by the conspirators, Tommy leading the way.

CHAPTER XXXI.

A PRETTY LITTLE BIT OF DIVERSION IN THE BEDROOM OF HERR KOBBLERSVAX—ON THE SCENT—PIPING HOT—THE ALARM—AN UNEXPECTED ENTRY—TOMMY CODLINGS DISPLAYS HIS USUAL GENIUS FOR GETTING INTO DIFFICULTIES.

"HE'S as tight as a drum," said Lionel, as he and Charlie laid the tipsy little Frenchman on the bed. "It would serve him right if we fetched Stiffback to him."

"What a stupid he must have been to get tight at all in this house," added Charlie. "He must have seen, by the way the head treated Soker, that he objects to it, even in a coachman; but what would he say to one of the masters making a beast of himself?"

"I'll do it," said Tommy, suddenly. "He's sure to get the sack if he's found out."

"Of course he is. What are you going to do, Tommy?"

"Tell Stiffback, of course."

"Then you'll just do nothing of the kind."

"Why not?"

"Why not?" repeated Lionel, indignantly "The bare idea of a chum of mine turning sneak and then asking 'Why not?'"

"It isn't sneaking to round on a master, when he's served me as Frenchy has."

"Yes, it is; it's just as mean as if you were to go and tell Stiffback about the fight, or the lark we had with Miss Growlagain. Don't make any mistake about it, Tommy; there are no more degrees in sneaking than there are in stealing."

"Well, you needn't be so hard on a fellow," replied Tommy, feeling a little ashamed of himself.

"And don't make such a row, either, or we shall spoil the game. Where shall we hide to see the fun, Li?"

"Oh, under the bed would be the best place."

"Yes, for those who like to get their mouth and eyes full of flue. These curtains are good enough for me."

"Look out," said Tommy, at this juncture; "here's Pryce and some more fellows coming along the corridor."

"Are they all the right sort? Stop a bit, let me look."

Lionel peeped out at the door, and having satisfied himself that the new comers were of the right sort, called them in.

"Old Kobblersvax is sure to be here in a few minutes, for Mr. Stiffback won't let him smoke in any other part of the house," said Pryce. "But let's have a peep at Frenchy. Why he's in his night shirt. Did you undress him."

"No. We found him just as he is, in that little room, nearly opposite."

"He must have got tight in a precious hurry. It isn't long since tea time. By jove, if the head knew it, there'd be a row."

"Hide up all you who want to see the fun," said Charlie, suddenly. "I can hear old Kobblersvax coming."

In an instant, a dozen or so of the youngsters disappeared beneath the bed, or concealed themselves behind the wide curtains, and scarcely were they all hidden, when the portly figure of the German professor made its appearance.

He began to sniff the moment he entered the room, and looked all around it with a suspicious air.

"I shmell cognac," he muttered, "and 'tis as strong as der teufel. Somepoty been in de room, and go to mine cupboard."

Here Kobblersvax tried the cupboard door, but it was safely locked, and he had the key in his pocket.

"'Tis dat drunken peast, Soker," he thought; "he hafe peen passing by de door, and after what de Herr Director Steeffback gif him de oder week, he shmell tam strong of cognac. Piff! I shmoke a pipe, and drife de shtink away. But first, I take off mine close, it ish so warrum."

There was an immense German pipe suspended from hooks near the chimney piece, and taking this down, the professor crammed the large china bowl full of tobacco, lit it, and began to smoke.

And smoke away the herr certainly did. There was no taking the pipe out of his mouth after every other whiff, to throw the ashes out, or cram them further in, or any pretence of that sort—oh no! puff after puff of smoke issued from his lips, with the regularity of the steam from the waste pipe of an engine, until the whole of the tobacco was consumed, and Kobblersvax filled the bowl again.

"Dat ish better," he said to himself; "I shmell him no more now, I dink."

It would have been a wonder if the German master, or anyone else could have distinguished the odour of aught else, besides smoke. The air was thick and heavy with it, and had not Kobblersvax been rather deaf, he could not have failed to hear sundry smothered coughs and sneezes, coming from the direction of the bed.

"Here, I can't stand much more of this," whispered Charlie. "How do you feel, Li?"

"As if I've swallowed a November fog, well peppered," replied our hero; "and—here dash it, Charlie, he's going to smoke again."

"Let's cut—I shall burst if I stop here."

"We can't; he's between us and the door."

"Why don't that blessed Frenchy wake up?"

"We'll wake him, Charlie. He must be sound asleep not to be able to smell this smoke. Can you see a feather anywhere?"

"Yes, here's a little one sticking out of the mattrass."

"That'll do," said Lionel.

And taking it lightly in his right hand, he bent forward and tickled the sharp little nose of the French master.

Monsieur de Vinaigre, though he had been insensible to the effects of the smoke, could not withstand the titillating influence of the feather, and let off a sneeze of such violence that the very bed shook, and some of the china ornaments on the mantel-shelf fell down.

"Mein Gott! vot ish dat?" exclaimed Herr Kobblersvax, as the sudden explosion caused him to bite off and swallow the amber mouth-piece of his pipe.

"Sacr-r-re! mille tonnerres du diable!" ejaculated the Frenchman. "I am brok' all to leetle pieces."

"Vod!" exclaimed the German, as he recognised the voice of his foe. "It ish dat verdammte Frenchman. Vot you do in mine bet, eh?"

And the burly German, tearing away the curtain with one huge hand, rapped monsieur smartly on the head with the bowl of his pipe.

"C'est millions de baionettes!" exclaimed the Frenchman, jumping from the bed with a frog-like leap. "You strike me, eh? You wip me wiz your pipe? Alphonse de Vinaigre vill hafe your 'arrt's blood for zis; Retir-r-r-re on ze instant."

"Vot?" roared the German. "You have wot de poys call de cheek to get so drunk ash a pig, und den to come und shleep in mine bet, und den tell me to go from de room! I make you zmart for dat."

And full of wrath, the burly German took half a dozen quick whiffs of his pipe, making the bowl nearly red hot, and then flourishing it after the manner of a sabre, touched M. de Vinaigre in sundry tender places.

The Frenchman, as our readers already know, was very lightly clad, and the pipe raised blisters wherever it touched him.

He looked wildly round for some means of defence.

There was nothing available but a chair, with which he endeavoured to ward off the thrusts of the hot pipe.

"You pe tam!" howled the French master. "Go away, or I make German sausage of you!"

"Vot you call me?" bellowed the indignant German. "I gife you sausage for dat, und tam hot too!"

With these words, Herr Kobblersvax puffed at his pipe until the sparks flew out of the bowl as thickly as from the funnel of a steam fire-engine, and then aimed such a mighty blow at his opponent that the pipe broke in half.

The bowl smote M. de Vinaigre full on the nose, scattering fire all round like a gigantic rocket.

"Au feu! au feu!" he shrieked, as he danced frantically about the room, for thousands of the sparks had lodged on his night-shirt, and each was doing its little best to torture him. "I am on light. Put me out! Watere! Fire!"

The German was regarding with a rueful face the fragments of his cherished pipe, but the agonised cries of his enemy afforded him some consolation, and a placid smile of content played upon his heavy features.

"Zo I make you to dance, eh? Donnerwatter, he jump so shust like he hafe one tam big frog in him pelly."

"I say, boys," whispered Lionel, "we'd better make ourselves scarce. Frenchy's howling will bring the whole house up."

"I shan't go," said Tommy, whose little round eyes were brilliant with the light of vengeance. "I'll see this out. This is a prime revenge. I wish I had a fusee."

"What for?"

"To set light to the tail of his shirt. All the fire's in front now, and he won't be properly burned all over."

"What a malicious little wretch you are, Tommy," said Drummond. "Do you hear what he says, Li?"

"Oh, blow him! How are we to get out, that's

what I want to know? Dash that German! Why don't he get away from the door?"

But there Kobblersvax, apparently with the view of cutting off his enemy's retreat, had shut the door and now stood with his back against it, watching with a stolid smile the agonised endeavours of the Frenchman to rid himself of the sparks which were fast reducing his shirt to tinder.

Our hero's anticipations regarding the coming of the head master were soon realised, for the noise of the combat and the shouts of the combatants had penetrated into Mr. Stiffback's sanctum, where he was busy with the details of a new invention.

He went to the door and listened. The shrill yells of the Frenchman and the deeper growl of the German floated in the air, blended in one most unmusical discord.

"Those boys again," thought Mr. Stiffback. "There will be work for my flogging-machine tomorrow."

And putting on his severest and most magisterial aspect, the head master strode along the corridor and up the circular staircase until he reached Herr Kobblersvax's room.

He turned the handle of the door, but it seemed fast.

"Let me in, you boys—let me in instantly," said the master.

But the sound of his voice was drowned by the cries of the French professor, who, now in the height of his agony, began to curse all the relatives of the German from the topmost hair of their heads to the soles of their feet.

Mr. Stiffback was not a man to stand upon idle ceremony.

He retreated a few paces and then rushed at the door with all his force.

It struck poor Herr Kobblersvax on the back with a sound like that given out when a paviour's rammer smites the stubborn cobble-stone, and hurled him forward into the arms of the almost frantic Frenchman.

Mr. Stiffback followed in a much greater hurry than he intended, and catching his foot in the carpet, shot head foremost between the rival professors just as each aimed a vicious blow at the other.

Smack came the Frenchman's fist on Mr. Stiffback's jaw, while the German's heavy right hand alighted with unpleasant violence upon his nose.

When an Englishman's head is punched he generally returns the compliment first, and inquires the reason why at a later stage of the proceedings; so Mr. Stiffback, gathering himself up, let out his right and left, and "floored" the two professors in a neat and workmanlike style.

"Brayvo," shouted Tommy, unable to restrain his enthusiasm.

"You ass!" said Lionel, dragging him back. "You've let us all in for it now."

CHAPTER XXXII.

MAY DIFFERENCE OF OPINION NEVER ALTER FRIENDSHIP—TOMMY CODLINGS BECOMES THE SCAPEGOAT AGAIN, AND HIS LONG-SUFFERING EAR PARTS COMPANY FROM HIS BODY—CONSOLATION IS ADMINISTERED IN THE FORM OF SHRIMPS AND GOOD ADVICE, BOTH OF WHICH TOMMY LIKES—THE CRICKET MATCH—HERR KOBBLERSVAX MAKES A WONDERFUL HIT, AND WINS THE MATCH.

"I THOUGHT there were boys at the bottom of this riot," said Mr. Stiffback, quietly. "Codlings, that was your voice. Come out."

"Oh, blow him," muttered Tommy. "He knows my voice already. Shall I go, Li?"

"You'd better, unless you want him to come and pull you out."

"Are you coming, Codlings?" repeated the voice of the head master. "I know you're there."

"I'm coming, sir," said Tommy, dolefully.

"Make haste then," added Mr. Stiffback; "and bring me the poker out of the fireplace."

Tommy felt a cold perspiration break out all over him.

He thought that Mr. Stiffback intended to give him a preliminary half-dozen with the poker.

"You are very slow, Codlings," repeated the head master. "Will you bring the poker, or will you not?"

Mr. Stiffback was standing close by the French and German professors, who were very quietly lying where they had fallen.

"By jingo!" thought Tommy, "he's going to give Frenchy one on the nob."

With one jump he reached the poker, and with another he was by the head master's side.

"Here it is, sir. Give it to him, sir."

"Take that for being such a long time in obeying my orders," said Mr. Stiffback, rapping Tommy on the bridge of the nose, and bringing the water into his eyes in less than no time.

And then, much to Tommy's disgust, the schoolmaster, instead of applying the poker to the head of Monsieur de Vinaigre, held it to the swelling on his own face, and then addressed Herr Kobblersvax in stern tones—

"Herr professor," he said, "it is very evident that both you and Monsieur de Vinaigre have been giving way to the filthy act of intoxication."

"But, goot meinheer——" began the German.

"Not a word more," rejoined Mr. Stiffback. "This air is tainted with the vile odour of tobacco and brandy. I cannot stay in it. You, and you too, Monsieur de Vinaigre, will please to sleep off the effects of your disgraceful potations, and come to me to-morrow before breakfast."

"Mistare Steefback," said the Frenchman, in a deep, solemn voice, as he still lay upon his back, with his head under the washhand-stand.

"What do you want?" replied the head master, sharply. "You heard what I said, monsieur."

"Mistare Steefback," continued the Frenchman, in the same sepulchrally solemn tone, "you hafe ponch me in ze eye."

"And serve you right, you tipsy idiot," said Mr. Stiffback, in a rage. "Look at my own face. I shall be black and blue to-morrow."

"Mistare Steefback," repeated the Frenchman, "ze blood of my race is insolt by dat ponch in ze eye. I will batter mineself wiz you wiz ze pistol in ze morning."

"I'll batter your ugly head into a mummy if you say such things to me," said Mr. Stiffback, nearly white with anger.

"I do degrade ze blood of my noble famille when I batter myself wiz so low a man as you; but I mose hafe your life."

For a moment Mr. Stiffback looked as if he would have given the world for permission to give the Frenchman one—only one—with the poker, but he restrained himself by a mighty effort, and grabbing Tommy by one ear, picked him spasmodically off the ground as he made towards the door.

"Ow-ow-ow! Oh my! Oh don't! It's coming off. Oh my poor ear!" shrieked Tommy, in agonised accents.

But Mr. Stiffback was in such a condition of suppressed anger and shame at the scene he had just witnessed, that he was actually unaware at the moment of Tommy's presence.

He could only think of the Frenchman and his insulting words, and he punctuated his soliloquy by jerking poor Codlings into the air at every second word.

"The mean, fiddle-faced—jerk—abortion—jerk—

of humanity! To insult—jerk—a man of my standing—jerk—in such a way. But—jerk—I'll discharge him the very first thing to-morrow morning—jerk. What are you making that noise for, Codlings?"

Tommy, unable to bear the pain any longer, had given utterance to a hideous long-drawn howl, more like the wail of a Banshee than the sound of a human voice.

Mr. Stiffback let go his ear, and Tommy began the double shuffle.

"What are you making that dreadful noise for, Codlings?" he repeated.

"Oh! ah! that's good, that is. Oh! my poor ear. Oh! the agony. It's come off, I know it has. Oh! how it hurts. Oh! lor!"

And Tommy continued his dance with much vigour, though his steps were rather wanting in elegance.

Mr. Stiffback now began to have some dim perception that he had hurt Tommy, and looked at his pupil to see if an ear had come off.

"Come, come, Codlings, you must not make such a noise," he said, impatiently. "You will disturb the whole house. There are some of the servants coming up the passage now."

"Oh ah, you wouldn't like it yourself," sobbed Tommy, dropping on his knees and feeling about on the oil-cloth with one hand.

"Get up, sir; what on earth are you doing there?"

"I'm feeling for my ear, the one you pulled off," replied Tommy. "Perhaps if it's put on again quick, it'll grow."

"Of all the most exasperatingly stupid boys I ever knew you are the worst," said Mr. Stiffback. "Get out of my sight, Codlings, or I shall certainly knock your head off."

"I don't care much if you do," murmured Tommy "What's the good of a head without any ears on it. I'd just as soon have it knocked off as not."

This was too aggravating. Mr. Stiffback's profession had long since taught him how to control his temper, but Tommy was a little too much; and Tommy received a "spank" that made him see the ten thousand additional lamps at Cremorne, without paying the shilling to go in.

When Tommy recovered from a temporary obscuration of his intellects caused by the spank, he was seated in the passage, propped up against the wall, while Charlie was poking shrimps into his mouth, one at a time, by way of a restorative, and Lionel looked on directing the operation.

"That's it," said our hero, as Tommy opened an eye, and feebly winking, gulped down a shrimp. "I knew the taste of grub would bring him round quicker than anything. How do you feel, old chap?"

"Awful—my head feels like a balloon with the gas on fire inside."

"That's bad. Who's been doing it?"

"Who's been doing it," repeated Tommy pettishly. "Why, old Stiffback; didn't you see him drag me out of the room by the ear?"

"Not we. We were a dashed sight too anxious to hide ourselves. I flattened myself so close to the wall that I wonder I didn't stick there like a fly on new paint."

"And I got such a lot of that beastly flue into my throat," said Drummond, in a wheezy whisper, "that I believe I shall have a cough all the rest of my life."

"What's that, compared to having your ear pulled out by the root," said Tommy, with the air of a martyr.

"Who pulled your ear out by the root?"

"Why, Stiffback, dash him."

"If he has he put it on again. You've got the same two nice long ears you always had."

"I haven't," said Tommy, doggedly. "He pulled the right one off, I tell you."

"Then you must have had three ears, Tommy, for you've got two now."

"I haven't; he's pulled one off. I felt it go, and my aunt will make him pay for it, too."

"How much do you charge for an ear, Tommy?"

"A hundred pound, at least. The ears of our family ain't to be pulled off for nothing, I can tell you."

"Well, unless you want to have the other wrung off, I'd advise you to come along with us, for if Stiffback took a fancy to ear No. 2, a hundred pounds or so wouldn't stop him."

Upon this hint Tommy arose.

"Do you think he would, Li?"

"No doubt of it. I dare say he's sorry by this time he didn't have the other. Cut away to the dormitory; he won't like to pull your ear off before all the fellows."

And away Tommy scudded. In spite of his thoughts of vengeance upon Mr. Stiffback, and his "don't-care" theory, he would rather have walked a hundred miles than have the head master's fingers to come within pulling distance of his ears again.

In the morning the little interview between Mr. Stiffback and the professors came to a very satisfactory termination.

We cannot say whether this was in consequence of the head master having cooled down, or if he reflected that it would be difficult to get a couple of professors equally cheap, upon short notice, but there the fact was, the matter was hushed up and their explanations accepted.

"One liddel wort, meinheer," said Kobblersvax. "I find dis man in mine bet dronk as fiddler, and snoring as he vas do it by contract. Den I shter him up vid mine bibe, and he schlag me mit a shair."

"Mistare Stiffback," said the French master, in a voice trembling with the deepest emotion. "Hear me swear——"

"You do enough of dat last night," growled Kobblersvax.

"I was not tipsee. I could not be. I am of noble race, and ze Vinaigre nevare was drunk. I vas have a bat colt, and I rob my nose wid a candle, and I vash my foots in varm vatare. De varm vatare do not agree wiz me. It drive me off my vits, it make light in my head. I know not vot I do, and so de mistake hap; den I go into de honourable Mistare Kobblersvax. It all de fault of ze vatere, and I take mine oat dat I not vash my foots no more."

Mr. Stiffback seemed perfectly willing to accept this rather rambling explanation as the real cause of Monsieur de Vinaigre's aberration of mind, and after cautioning Tommy to keep what he had seen a secret, the head master dismissed the subject from his mind.

The time was now fast approaching for the annual match between the eleven of Lake House School and the picked members of the Deliverham County Cricket Club.

This match was for some inscrutable reasons always looked upon as a foregone conclusion for the Deliverham men, but this year Vansittart and our hero resolved to make a better stand.

"It's of no use," said Pryce, who was one of the old boys; "those Deliverham chaps are always practising and playing, and there's hardly two of our eleven who knows how to hold a bat, or bowl a slow twist, much less a left-handed shorter."

"Well, there's time yet; a few days' good practice will make all the difference. You're a good bat, I know."

"I don't want to brag, but I can get three figures off the Deliverham bowling generally."

"Come, that's promising anyhow; I'm a pretty good fast bowler myself, and I'll engage to take some of their middle stumps flying," said Vansittart. "Then there's young Wilful here, and his chum, Drummond, they're both good bats and first-rate fielders."

"But then, you see, you've only accounted for four out of the eleven," said Pryce, "and all the Deliverham fellows are good. They always make a point of sending in their best men, and beating us in one innings."

"They won't do it this time; all we want is to be properly organised and work hard in the practice field, before the match comes off. Here's pencil and paper; how shall we make up the eleven, Pryce?"

"There's the Frenchman and Kobblersvax, for two," said Pryce.

"What! you don't mean to say those beggars play?"

"Yes they do, and if they'd only attend to the game, they'd do well. Kobblersvax is a tremendous slogger, and the Frenchman as active as a monkey at fielding, but instead of working together they try to cut one another out and trip one another up, and all that sort of thing."

"That won't do, but I dare say we can manage to stop that. Now for the rest of the fellows, Pryce."

With a good deal of hesitation and rejection of unpromising candidates, a suitable eleven were formed, and Vansittart and our hero got to work with a will.

Mr. Stiffback readily granted extra time in which to practice as soon as he saw that the boys were in earnest, and more than that, accompanied them to the fields and gave them the benefit of his advice.

Lionel soon saw that both the German and the Frenchman would be valuable auxiliaries if they could only be persuaded to lay their jealousies aside during the match.

Kobblersvax's defence of his wicket was aggravatingly cautious, but when he did catch sight of a ball which suited him, he went at it like an avalanche, and seldom changed his wicket for less than four.

As Lionel showed himself a much better bat than Vansittart, the young aristocrat generously resolved that he should be elected captain, and by dint of coaxing some and bullying others, our hero succeeded in getting his eleven pretty well in hand by the day of the match.

The Deliverham C.C., though, were a little more anxious about the result of the match this year.

It was, of course, known that some new members were in the Lake Island School eleven; that one of them was the vanquisher of the redoubtable pig-jobber, and that there were two or three others who could have achieved the same feat if they had tried.

So this time extra care was taken in the selection of the team, and the hours of practice were nearly doubled. The members dyed themselves mahogany colour in the sun; their captain had four sun-strokes in the last week, and played on the match day with his head shaved and two pounds of ice in a bag on the nape of his neck.

Mr. Stiffback's interest in the match fell off very suddenly a week or so before the day, but this was accounted for by Vansittart, who told our hero that the head master was busy perfecting a new invention which was to be the marvel of the nineteenth century.

"What invention is it? Something in the flogging machine way?"

"Not exactly that. It's a feeding machine, I believe; you put your mouth to the spout, turn a handle, and enough condensed food is pressed into you to last for a month or more."

"That would be handy for travellers," said Lionel.

"You're right. Hasn't he shown you over his museum of curiosities yet?"

"No, I should just like to see that."

"All right; I'll get leave from him to show you over it. Ah! here he comes just in the very nick of time."

The required permission was asked for and at once granted, and our hero and Vansittart were soon in the museum, as its owner called it.

It was indeed a curious place, containing models of inventions for doing everything that was ever heard of, and a great many things that never were.

It was the Marquis of Worcester's "Century of Inventions" realised, and our hero, who took a great interest, as most boys do in things mechanical, was soon deep in the mysteries of springs, levers, and cog-wheels.

There were machines for saving life, and others for destroying it. By the side of improved life-boats and life-belts were models of self-feeding cannon and rifles, which could be discharged hundreds of times in a minute by means of electricity, the operator being meanwhile a mile or so in the rear of his weapons.

There was a patent gallows which did away with the necessity of either hangman, clergyman, or sexton being required to assist at the legal murder of a fellow creature.

The criminal had only to be put into the apparatus through a little door, and the spring set going, when the burial service was read by an automaton, a musical box played the "Dead March in Saul," the rope was adjusted, the drop fell, and after the usual interval, the fatal cord was severed by an automatic knife, and the body dropped into a neat little bed of quick lime beneath. It was beautifully simple, and Mr. Stiffback was willing to sell the patent for ten thousand pounds and a baronetcy.

Amidst all these complicated pieces of machinery was a small sphere, no larger than a cricket ball, and which from its very simplicity, attracted Lionel's attention.

He found from the label attached, that it was a model of a signal shell, so constructed as to burst only at a certain height in the air, and then throw out a series of smaller shells, which, in their turn would burst, and burn with coloured fires.

Some spirit of mischief prompted Lionel to take this shell, and substitute for it a cricket ball, which he had in his pocket. He had no idea at the moment to what use he should put it, but he felt tolerably certain that it would "come in handy."

He had nearly forgotten all about it, until the day of the match, when, as he was changing his ordinary clothes for his cricketing suit, he felt the ball in his pocket.

"It will come in useful somehow," thought Lionel. "I'll take it."

"Now then, Li, are you ready?" asked Charlie, putting in his head at the open door. "Time's up, and the boat's waiting. Old Stiffback's coming after all."

"Is he?"

"Yes. He asked Vansittart if our eleven was sure to win, and Van said we should, so he said, 'I'll come then, for I hear that ill-bred bully, Growlagain, is to be there, and it will do him good to lower his pride.'"

"So it will, the old beast. You remember that pretty little girl, and her father and mother, that he was going to turn out of doors?"

"Rather, and the twenty quid you wasted on 'em. Don't you hope that pretty girl will be there, Li."

But Master Lionel caught up his cricket bat with such a menacing gesture, that Charlie bolted, and stayed out of the way, until he was in the boat.

That day was a glorious one for Lake Island School. Lionel won the toss, and of course took first innings for his side. Then he and Charlie went in, and had scored two hundred and ten between them, before their wickets fell.

Then one by one the others were sent in, each adding a fair item to the score, until it came at last to the turns of Herr Kobblersvax and Monsieur de Vinaigre, to go to the wickets.

"I vill show dem," said the French professor, flourishing his bat like a flail, "I vill hit de ball so zat dey see him no more for veeks."

And round went his bat again, catching poor Tommy in the small of the back, and causing him to bolt a whole saveloy at one gulp.

"'Tis zat tam boy Codleens, he vos always get in de vay," said Monsieur de Vinaigre, with a glare at poor Tommy, who was black in the face, and with his eyes nearly out of his head, was trying to haul the saveloy back by means of the little bit of skin at the end.

"You not hit de ball at all," growled Kobblersvax—"you only tickle him a leedle; now when I shall hit de ball, I vack him so tam hard dat he burst in leedle bits."

"Nous verrons; ve shall see," replied the French professor, taking his stand at his wicket, as if it had been the Pass of Thermopylae, and he ready to defend it against a few millions of Persians.

Now Lionel, still animated by that same impish spirit of mischief, had contrived to substitute Mr. Stiffback's patent shell for the cricket ball, and the Deliverham bowler, pretty nearly fagged to death, observed not the difference, and sent it swift and straight at the wicket of Herr Koblersvax.

It was a beautiful ball, pitching about six feet in front of the wicket, and then rising to the bat as though asking to be hit.

The German's bat swept with a hiss through the air, caught the ball upon its top, and shot it into the air with the force of a rocket.

There was a roar from the field, "A catch, a catch!"—a rush of every one to the spot where it was expected to fall, but ere yet one-half of its graceful parobola was completed, there was a bright flash, a loud explosion—the cricket ball had burst!

CHAPTER XXXIII.

THE RESULT OF LIONEL'S LITTLE PRACTICAL JOKE—WHAT THE FRENCH PROFESSOR THOUGHT OF IT—WHAT HERR KOBBLERSVAX THOUGHT OF IT—AND MR. STIFFBACK'S OPINION OF THE SAME—THE SCENE IN THE TENT—"PLEASE, PITY A POOR FOREIGNER"—THE LEMONADE BOTTLES, AND WHAT HAPPENED TO THEM—LIONEL ACTS THE PART OF THE GOOD SAMARITAN—COMING EVENTS CAST THEIR SHADOWS BEFORE—THE NEW INVENTION—OUR HERO MANAGES AS USUAL TO HAVE A FINGER, AND SOMETHING ELSE TOO, IN THE PIE—AT THE WORKHOUSE — THE OPENING SPEECH — THE OPENING CEREMONY—AND THE OPENING MEDICINE.

THE eyes of everyone in the cricket field had been fixed on the ball when it burst in the sudden and alarming manner which we have indicated in the preceding chapter, and the effect, as may be imagined, was startling in the extreme.

The noise was terrific, for Mr. Stiffback had employed the fulminate of silver as the explosive medium, and when, in addition, the smaller shells were thrown out, and began to burst with a sharp crackling sound like the report of musketry, the more timid of the spectators began to think it high time to make tracks for a place of safety.

The German was as much, or more astonished at the result of his mighty hit. He stood with his bat still uplifted, staring unto the sky, and exclaiming at intervals—

"Ach du lieber Gott! Vot is dat for a shtroke I gif him!"

As for the French professor, he was fairly frightened. He really believed that his rival and foe was possessed of such supernatural strength that he had caused the ball to burst with the sheer force of the blow, and casting one more terrified look around him, he fled, but not in time to escape one of the smaller shells, which dropped down his neck and went off with a fizz like a damp fusee.

It was worse by far than the hot pipe from which he had recently suffered. It was in such an wkward place too, beyond the reach of aid from is fingers, and so, in an agony of torment, he rushed wards the tent, upsetting Tommy, who was st coming out with a couple of bottles of ginger beer in his pocket, and a hat full of jam tarts.

"Sac-r-r-re nom d'une pipe!" shouted Monsieur de Viniagre, "zat tam boy always get in ze way! Oh! mon Dieu, my pack—my pack! He is hot as an omelette!"

And bestowing on Tommy a kick which disturbed for evermore the symmetry of one ginger beer bottle, he rushed into the tent, there to seek relief from some charitable christian who would ease his suffering by pouring water down his back.

"What in the name of wonder is the matter?" exclaimed Mr. Stiffback, who was doing the honours of the refreshment table to some ladies, as the noise of the explosion and the shouts of the alarmed spectators reached the tent. "Do not be alarmed, I beg, ladies. It is nothing. Oh! d——"

Mr. Stiffback had just stepped out into the middle of the tent, when the French professor rushed in. They met with a crash, hugged each other with a fond embrace, performed a few steps of a wild kind of waltz, and then sat down suddenly on a lemonade basket.

They were up again rather quicker than a flash of lightning, and giving utterance to short ejaculations expressive of intense rapture.

The French professor was injured in a place that he could reach this time, but Mr. Stiffback, whose notions of propriety were more severe, only allowed himself to dance a little on one leg, while he condemned the broken lemonade bottles and the Frenchman with stern but silent blasphemy.

"Oh, dear me, Mr. Stiffback!" exclaimed the mayor's lady, "what is the matter with the poor man? Why does he dance like that?"

"You had better ask him, madam," replied Mr. Stiffback, who would gladly have paid five pounds for liberty to dance himself.

"And his back is smoking. I declare I believe he is on fire," said a second fair sympathiser.

"I hope he is," hissed Mr. Stiffback, between his clenched teeth.

"Oh, Mr. Stiffback, you can't mean that!" said the mayoress, with a little scream of horror. "Do something for him. Do, for my sake."

"I will!" exclaimed Mr. Stiffback, desperately, and unable to bear the pain any longer, he rushed across the tent, and with one well-aimed kick sent Monsieur de Vinagre flying through the entrance, and catching sight of Lionel as he passed, caught him by the arm, and hurried him to the rear of the tent.

There he laid himself gently down upon his face, and with a gesture that was full of dignity he said—

"Pick out the pieces."

Which Lionel did.

"It was worse than the flogging-machine twenty times, old fellow," said our hero, when he described this scene afterwards to his chums. "Some of the bits of glass had gone in, ah, more than an inch, and some twenty minutes passed before I got them all out."

"Serve him right," said Tommy Codlings. "As for its being worse than the flogging-machine, I don't believe it. It couldn't be; only wait till you fellows have had a taste of it, and you'll sing a different song."

"Poor Frenchy was the worst off, after all," said Charlie. "He had quite as much glass in him as Stiffback, and his back is awfully flayed. He won't be able to lie on his back for weeks."

"And serve him right too," said Tommy, again. "He knocked me down twice on the day of the match, and burst two lovely bottles of ginger beer that I'd got out of the refreshment tent."

"That was a judgment on you then, Tommy, for picking and stealing; you had no business in the refreshment tent," said Lionel.

"But after all," added Drummond, "that mystery of the cricket ball was never cleared up. There's been a lot of letters about it in the 'Deliverham Chronicle.'"

"I've seen them," said Pryce. "Scientific old fogeys, some of 'em fancy beyond all doubt that the ball took fire and burst in consequence of its rapid journey through the air; while others put it down to electricity; and a third lot maintain that the ball must have come in contact with a meteorite. What do you say, Wilful. I don't swallow all that the scientific chaps say, but I confess it's a puzzler."

Lionel modestly intimated that he fully agreed with Pryce, and changed the subject. He had not confided the secret of the shell to a soul, and he burst into a cold perspiration whenever he thought of what Mr. Stiffback's rage would be when the truth was known.

Herr Kobblersvax seemed to be the only one who got any glory out of that transaction.

He was looked upon as a mighty man indeed, after that famous hit upon the day of the cricket match. The labours of Hercules were trifles, Samson was just an ordinary kind of man, and Richard Cœur de Lion was a consumptive cockney in comparison with this new champion.

Herr Kobblersvax was indeed a proud man after this feat.

If he could have worn his muscle outside his coat he would have done it. As it was, he ordered a suit of clothes of superlative tightness and thinness, so as to exhibit the manly development of his figure to full advantage.

"Blow his conceit," thought Lionel. "I've a good mind to let out the truth, and chance what old Stiffback will do to me. Confound him, he hasn't got any more muscle than a sausage."

But time passed on. It was a week before Mr. Stiffback was able with any degree of comfort to resume his seat in the class-room, and then his new invention had such hold of his mind that the little episode of the cricket field was almost forgotten.

Not so, though, by poor Monsieur de Vinaigre, who lay face downwards groaning, and it is to be feared using no small amount of bad language, while his back smarted fiercely, despite the quantity of cooling ointment and lotion lavished on him.

That last kick of Mr. Stiffback's had driven two of the pieces of glass so far into him that they could only be extracted by a surgical operation, and the only consolation the unhappy Frenchman possessed lay in the mental picture he drew of himself and the head master engaged in mortal combat.

"I will look upon him wiz my eye, so. Den he vill tr-r-remble, and r-r-round himself turn to run avay. Zen wiz my sabre I vill steek him so, shust were de glass hafe stuck in me—and Adolphe de Vinaigre will be a-venge."

Quite ignorant of this neat little proposition for "steeking" him, the head master worked hard, both at his duties in the school and at his new invention, the pride of his heart, the patent feeding machine.

It had been a long while in course of construction, but difficulty after difficulty had been overcome, and it was at last ready for the first grand experimental trial.

Such an important occasion Mr. Stiffback thought could not fail to prove of service to his elder pupils, and some twenty of the upper form boys

AS THE BALL LEFT THE BAT IT FLEW TO PIECES, TO THE DELIGHT OF LIONEL AND HIS
FRIENDS.

No. 24.

were selected, with a few others who petitioned to witness the experiment.

We need hardly say that Lionel, Charlie, and Codlings were of these latter—the two first animated by the spirit of mischief which apparently guided them in all their doings, the latter urged by his natural interest in everything that appertained to the eating department.

All the morning Mr. Stiffback had been busily superintending the erection of the machine in the courtyard of the workhouse, and by the time the morning classes were dismissed he had returned, and was busy with some mysterious looking jars, bearing cabalistic labels on their stomachs, somewhat similar to those queer hieroglyphics which adorn the huge bottles in the chemists' shops.

"Who the dickens are they for?" whispered Lionel to Vansittart, as they entered the laboratory, "and what's in 'em? My eye, how it stinks!"

"That's the concentrated food," replied Vansittart, "that's put into the feeding machine. Stiffback calculates that a tea spoonful of it is equal to a diet of four good meals a day for a week."

"I say," said Charlie, in a tone of alarm, "he ain't going to try that game with us, is he?"

"Very likely. If the experiment succeeds with the paupers at the workhouse, he'll very likely introduce it into the school."

"That won't do for me," said Lionel. "Blow his concentrated food! I like to get a meal more than once a week."

Tommy looked on horrified, and thoughtfully passed his right hand with a slow circular motion over his waistcoat, as if he bade the digestive organs which reposed below, to be of good cheer and bear up under the affliction which threatened them.

Lionel said nothing, but his keen, quick eyes glanced along the rows of bottles and china gallipots ranged upon the shelves.

There was one labelled "*pulv. jalapa*," another "*senna comp.*," and a third, "*ex. rhub trip.*," and these Lionel cautiously took down from their places.

"What are you going to do, young Wilful," said Vansittart. "I wouldn't advise you to meddle with anything in this room, or there'll be the old gentleman to pay."

"You just watch the door for a minute, old fellow," said Lionel, coolly. "I'm going to spoil Stiffback's experiment. It'll never do for him to introduce that dashed feeding machine here."

And then removing the covers from the large jars, our hero dexterously tilted into each a liberal dose of the drugs he had taken from the shelves, and having thus flavoured the concentrated food, gave it a good stirring with a wooden spatala, or spoon.

"What a fellow you are, young Wilful," said Vansittart. "You don't seem to care a bit for the consequences of what you do."

"Oh, don't I though," replied our hero, with a laugh. "I know what the consequence of this will be."

"What's that?"

"Why, Stiffback will think that his patent feeding machine is a failure, he'll have to invent another, and so we shan't be bothered with it any more for a few months to come."

"Cave!" whispered Charlie Drummond, who was standing sentry at the door. "I hear 'em coming."

And in effect a few minutes afterwards came the great inventor, looking as proud and happy as a young hen over her first egg.

"Now, young gentlemen," he said, "I think that everything is ready. May I ask your assistance in carrying these jars down to the boat. Servants are so careless, and it is of great importance to the success of to-day's experiment that great caution should be used."

They were large double-handled jars, of a make now seldom seen, not particularly heavy, and there

was quite a scramble as to who should have the honour of carrying them.

Tommy possessed himself of one, but of course he instantly displayed his usual good fortune by letting go the handle, and dropping the jar on Mr. Stiffback's tenderest bunion.

A sharp smacking sound was instantly heard, caused by the application of the head master's open hand to Tommy's ear.

"You careless mass of imbecility," said Mr. Stiffback, trying hard to get Tommy within range again. "Go upstairs to the dormitory, and stay there till we return. Soker, you will lock this boy in, and give him nothing but bread and water, and not too much of that."

"I will, sir," said Soker, with great readiness, for since his conversion to teetotalism he had become the strictest and most vicious of disciplinarians, executing all Mr. Stiffback's orders relative to punishment with a gloomy kind of joy, and turning the handle of the flogging machine with twice as much rapidity.

"Poor old chap, nothing goes the right way with him," said Lionel. "If he was a king, his subjects would be always having revolutions or some little game of that sort."

"What a spank Stiffback fetched him."

"And no wonder. That jar weighs twenty pounds, and it fell plump on the old boy's bunion. See how he limps now."

Mr. Stiffback did indeed limp, for a bunion (may our readers never gain the knowledge by experience!) is peculiarly sensitive to pain, but the thought of his invention, and of the glory that would cover him with never-fading lustre, drove such a trifle out of his mind, and he was beaming and happy once again, by the time that the workhouse was reached.

That important edifice was not, architecturally considered, very well worth the trouble of a visit from the lover of the picturesque. In fact, to tell the truth, the bricks had looked much prettier when they were piled in unstudied confusion in their native brick-fields.

But this was as it should be.

Paupers have no right to expect the genius of an architect to waste its sweetness upon them, and if they did, it would most probably be all the same.

But to-day the grim and gloomy goal-like structure bore an aspect of unwonted gaiety.

Some of the windows had actually been cleaned, and, more wonderful still, so had a few of the paupers who had been selected as the subjects of Mr. Stiffback's experiment.

They looked very unhappy, though, poor creatures, and they were sniffing suspiciously at one another, for they hadn't been used to the smell of soap and water for a long time.

They might have had, too, some idea that all these unusual preparations were only the prelude to their execution, even as the sheep and oxen, when led to the sacrifice by the Pagans of old were decorated with garlands of flowers.

But now there issues forth from the principal portal of the workhouse a group of personages, much more important than the paupers.

They are the guardians of the parish, the solicitor to the board, the rector, and Sharpem Tuckemup, Esquire, one of the magistrates for the county.

All hats were raised at the approach of the great inventor.

Mr. Stiffback returns the salutation, hands are shaken all round, introductions are made, and then Mr. Tuckemup leads the way to the board room, where tasty biscuits and wine of a vintage which never finds its way into the pauper infirmary, awaits the visitors.

"Now, gentlemen," said Mr. Tuckemup, "before we proceed to the yard, perhaps Mr. Stiffback will favour us with a few words as to the nature of his great invention, which, I feel sure, will cause his name to be ranked in after years with the Stephensons, the Brunels, and the Wheatstones of this great country."

"Hear, he-ar," and a great rapping of the table and stamping of feet followed this introductory speech, and then Mr. Stiffback, the light of genius beaming from behind his spectacles, arose.

"Gentlemen," he began, "it has never been my presumption to even rank my own unworthy name with those great ones which the honourable and worthy magistrate has just mentioned. My ambition is content with more modest aims, though in their way, I trust, not less useful."

"Hear, hear," and cheers by the peck followed this remark.

"I say, gentlemen, that my native modesty has ever endeavoured to curb that noble ambition, to get ahead of his fellow men, which is one of the proudest birthrights of a Briton ;—(more cheers)—and the object for which we are met this day, gentlemen, is to witness the trial—the successful trial, I hope—(immense cheering)—of a machine, the main object of which is the saving of Time."

"Hear, hear," cheers and a glass of wine all round.

"The philosopher has remarked, gentlemen, that time is money——"

More cheering here interrupted the speaker, for every gentleman was individually reminded of the truth of the aphorism by recollecting the fact that each received a couple of guineas and a good lunch for an hour's attendance every board day, and there was a proposal to raise the fee to three guineas instead of two.

"*That* time is money, gentlemen," repeated Mr. Stiffback, emphatically. "I have long seen and regretted with heartfelt emotion the enormous amount of time wasted by the working population of this country in the consumption of food."

Murmurs of indignant assent from the assembled gentlemen, who none of them could possibly have thought of dining in less time than two hour

"Taking the working population, gentlemen, in round numbers as 15,000,000, and the number of working days in the year as three hundred and seven and a quarter, I find the average waste per day, per man, woman, and child, to be two hours and a half, giving a total for the year of——"*

"Shameful !" "Horrible !" "Put it down !" were some of the murmured sentiments of the shocked gentlemen of the board.

"What man could view with an unmoved eye such a record as I have ventured to give you, gentlemen ?" said Mr. Stiffback. "Who would not be filled with a burning desire to reclaim those wasted hours, and enable the working man to toil cheerfully on from dawn to dark without allowing his mind to be disturbed by those coarse appetites which demand to be satisfied with breakfasts, dinners, teas, and even suppers ?"

"Truly noble ; I've felt it for years," murmured the rector, as he wondered whether the salmon packed in ice would arrive from London in time for his dinner-party at the rectory.

"Blow old Stiffback and his speeches !" interposed Charlie. "Now he's wound up he'll go on for a year."

"Oh, no, he won't be long. He's eager to get his machine at work," replied Lionel. "Cheer away like anything whenever the others start ; he'll finish then."

"For a long time, gentlemen," resumed the inventor, "for years, I may say, I sought in vain for the means, but at length the idea dawned upon me —the light, I will not say of genius, gentlemen."

"Yes, yes ! genius, genius !" from all parts of the room.

"You are too complimentary, gentlemen," said Mr. Stiffback, with a grateful smile—"we will say genius, since you insist upon it. The light of genius smiled upon my labours, and its genial warmth has—if I may be allowed the expression—hatched the patent feeding machine, which I shall have the honour to exhibit to you this day."

"Hear, hear," again, and very loudly from the bottom of the room, where the boys were.

"It was my intention, gentlemen, to have made the first experiment on some of my own pupils—(a very audible groan from the boys)—but our respected and reverend friend, the rector, was good enough to suggest that the inmates of the workhouse, the paupers in short, afforded a more extended field for the trial."

"Fiat experimentum in corpore vili," murmured the rector, with a smile, as if conscious of having made a neat little joke.

"Ha, ha ! very neat—very neat, indeed," said Mr. Stiffback, approvingly. "Corpore vili—ha, ha ! just so. But to resume. As I was saying, gentlemen, our reverend and facetious friend, if he will allow me to call him so, suggested the paupers. Well, gentlemen, the paupers are ready—the machine is ready—I am ready—and if you gentlemen are in a similar condition, we will proceed to the trial."

More cheers and more port wine followed the conclusion of Mr. Stiffback's address, and then Mr. Tuckemup, who was winking a good deal under the influence of the wine, led the way to the exercise yard of the workhouse.

"I say," said Lionel, as they came in sight of the wonderful machine, "what a queer looking affair, it's a cross between a coffee pot and a mangle."

"And just look at the paupers. Did you ever see such a shadowy lot ?" replied Charlie. "Anyone would think that they had dressed up a lot of skeletons out of the anatomical museum."

"They are thin," said Lionel, thoughtfully. "I'm glad Tommy Codlings didn't come."

"Why ?"

"Why ! Just fancy how the sight of a plump, well-fed boy like Tommy would aggravate these poor chaps. I wonder if any of 'em ever had a real good tuck out ?"

"Precious difficult to say, Li ; if they did it must have been a long while ago."

"I'm deuced sorry I put that rhubarb and jalap in the jars now," said our hero. "I didn't know the poor devils were as thin as this. My eye, Charlie, won't it make 'em ill ?"

"Never mind, Stiffback and the others will taste it first."

"Not they."

"They will though. It's the rule, you know, whenever the swells visit an infirmary, or a hospital, or a prison, they're always expected to taste the regulation grub, and then you read in newspapers how good it was, and how grateful the poor ought to be for being fed like that."

"It can't be the same sort of grub, Charlie. The swells wouldn't be fools enough to touch that."

"Perhaps you're right, Li. Hallo, look out! Now they're going to begin."

CHAPTER XXXIV.

IN THE INTEREST OF SCIENCE MR. STIFFBACK MEETS WITH A LITTLE ACCIDENT, AND HAS THE FIRST TASTE OF THE CONCENTRATED FOOD—HOW THEY FED THE PAUPERS—A FAILURE—THE LETTER FROM THE ANALYST—A LIGHT DAWNS UPON MR. STIFFBACK.

THEY was indeed about to begin, and the beginning was apparently anything but satisfactory to the paupers, upon whose bodies the experiment was about to be made.

---

* We regret we cannot give the figures quoted by Mr. Stiffback, but the number of cyphers required was far too great for the resources of the printer.—ED.

First the jars were brought forward, the covers lifted off, and Mr. Stiffback, armed with a long wooden spoon, stirred the contents of one with the air of a professed cook about to decide upon the merits of a new sauce.

"This, gentlemen," he said, tapping the jar, "is the sublimated essence of that compound vulgarly known as 'skilly,' condensed by a secret process which I alone possess. One teaspoonful of this contains sufficient nourishment to support a full-grown man for a week. Taste it for yourselves,"

Mr. Stiffback held out his ladle full, which contained about half an imperial pint, but no one offered to touch it.

"My eye, I hope they do!" said Lionel; "that's the jar I put the rhubarb in."

"Catch them doing that, when they've all got a good dinner of three or four courses waiting for 'em at home."

Charlie was right: the benevolent guardians smelt it, stirred it with the tips of their fingers even, but they could not think of depriving the poor paupers of the food prepared for them.

"Try a little of this then," said Mr. Stiffback, opening the second jar. "It contains the concentrated essence of beef, and one teaspoonful is equal in point of nourishment to ten pounds of steak. A man can live well for a fortnight upon that quantity."

"I put the jalap in that jar," whispered Lionel. "I don't think a man would feel very comfortable if he had nothing for a fortnight but a teaspoonful of that."

But the guardians were equally obstinate both with regard to that jar and the next, which Mr. Stiffback said contained essence of potatoes, equalling in nutritive power a five-acre field of that valuable vegetable.

"Now, gentlemen," said the schoolmaster, "we will proceed to place the contents of these jars in my machine. By turning the handle the skilly, the meat essence, and the vegetable, become thoroughly incorporated. We will then proceed to administer the proper quantity to the patients."

"Poor chaps," said Lionel. "It's an awful shame. I wish I hadn't done it now. Jalap, rhubarb, and senna, all at once. They'll be dreadfully ill, I'm afraid."

"I'm afraid so too," laughed Charlie. "There goes the stuff into the machine."

A short ladder had beeen placed against the side of the machine, the top lifted off, and the thick, gluey looking essences tilted in.

"Think, my friends," said the rector, addressing the lean, hungry-looking paupers, who were looking anything but happy, "think what a blessing the invention of this estimable gentleman will be to you. Laborare est ovare, which signifies that work is prayer, or in effect, that a good day's work is equal to going to church three times on Sunday and a prayer meeting in the evening. Now, instead of wasting so many hours in gormandising and guzzling, you will be fed by this wonderful machine once a month or so, and all the rest of your time from early morn till dewy eve, will be spent in the useful and beautiful processes of stone-breaking and oakum picking. Oh, my friends, do you not feel truly grateful to the genius of this gentleman, which has worked out such a blessing for you?"

"I doan't," said one obstinate-looking, grey-headed old pauper.

"And why not, my friend?" said the rector, with a sweet benevolence touching to behold.

"I likes to chaw my wittles, I does," growled the old pauper.

"My friend," said the rector, who became more and more touching and impressive as he went on, "do you not see in this the finger of providence?"

"I sees the finger o' meanness, that's wot I sees," growled the pauper. "Feed a man once a month! Wot next? As if we wos over fed now."

"My venerable friend," continued the rector, "age has not taught you its most precious lesson, that of patience ; you are old, your teeth must soon fail you, if indeed they are not already gone, and what then becomes of your power to 'chaw your wittles?' You can't do it, you bolt your food, and what follows? indigestion, and a train of other ills. My friend, be wise, and see in this, as I do, the finger of a bounteous and all-merciful providence."

The obstinate old pauper was heard to mutter something very irreverent concerning providence, and the rector in particular, and the reverend gentleman, greatly shocked, was feeling for some good little tracts peculiarly suited to the occasion, when his attention was distracted by a cry of alarm from the spectators, and looking up, he was just in time to see Mr. Stiffback tilt over into the concentrated food.

For a few moments the horrified spectators stood gazing at the intellectual legs of the schoolmaster, which were jerking convulsively to and fro; then Vansittart, who was the first able to control himself, ran forward, and hauled Mr. Stiffback out, gasping and sputtering for breath.

"Oh, oh, ugh! oh, dear me!" he murmured, faintly. "Oh, Lord, I'm choked. Oh, how nasty it is—ugh!"

"Did you swallow any of it, sir?"

"Did I swallow any of it? I should think I did. I've swallowed it all, I believe. Get me some brandy. Get me some water."

And Mr. Stiffback, who had been propped up against the apparatus, shuddered so violently that the machinery inside rattled loudly, and the ladder was shaken down.

"He's tasted it," said Lionel, with a chuckle.

"Tasted it!" repeated Charlie; "he must have swallowed enough to keep him going for a year. I heard him go 'Guggle-guggle,' before Vansittart fished him out."

"He'll let the paupers off, I should think."

"Dickens a bit of it. I shouldn't wonder if he made us taste it all round now, just to square accounts. Did you hear him say how nasty it was?"

"Yes, and he's about right. It couldn't have been a very festive compound before, but now it's flavoured with Rhubarb, Jalap, and Co., it must be truly exquisite."

"Just so. Hullo! there go the paupers for the first dose."

In effect, Mr. Stiffback, after retiring into the workhouse for ten minutes, and coming back with an exceedingly pale visage, and his handkerchief pressed tightly to his lips, as if to keep down the emotion that was struggling to arise within him, asked the master of the workhouse if all was ready

"Quite ready, sir."

"Very good, then, we'll begin at once. Soker, go to the handle, and turn it every time I raise my hand."

Soker obeyed with a smile of gloomy content upon his face.

Deprived of whiskey, he had now become a misanthrope, whose chief delight was to work evil to his fellow man.

"Now then, up with you, Gorgles—you're first," shouted the master.

"No I bean't," returned Gorgles, who was the obstinate old pauper before mentioned. "I don't want none o' that there kind o' grub."

"Stand back," said the tyrant of the workhouse, "You'll have bread and water for a week, and hextry stone work for this, my man."

"I ain't pertikler," rejoined the surly pauper. "I ain't agoin' to hev my wittles pumped into me if I knows it."

"Be off. Next one there. Make haste."

And the master, anxious to show off his importance before the guardians, hustled up a poor, long, lank, old man, and bumped his head against the spout.

"Ready, sir," he said, as soon as he had got the old pauper to open his mouth.

Mr. Stiffback raised his hand.

Round went the wheel, and the poor old man writhed and wriggled as about half a pint of liquid stomach-ache was pumped into him.

Another and another followed in rapid succession, until all the paupers were satisfied.

More than satisfied, indeed, if one might judge from the hideous contortions of their features.

"Well, my man," said Mr. Stiffback, addressing the first pauper, "and how do you feel? Is it soothing? Is it balmy? Does it seem to penetrate the whole of your inner man with a sort of delicious satisfaction?"

"No, IT DON'T!" was the reply, delivered with such emphasis that Mr. Stiffback retired a few paces, and demolished a corn or two that didn't belong to him.

"It's very strange," said Mr. Stiffback. "They ought not to feel like that."

"It's tolerably certain that the effect is not—er—altogether—er—soothing and balmy and—er—so on," said Mr. Tuckemup. "Depend upon it, my dear sir, you made the compound too rich."

"Do you think so?" said Mr. Stiffback, doubtfully.

"Beyond a doubt. Their stomachs, inured to a course of—er—plain, but perfectly wholesome and —er—and nourishing food, are unable to digest all at once such a mass of nutriment as they have just received."

"Quite so, quite so," added the rector. "Fancy, Mr. Stiffback, what the effect upon any of us would be, say, of taking a week's dinners—only a week's —at one meal."

"They ought to have had a little practice first," rejoined Mr. Tuckemup. "Dear me, how they are groaning."

"And—and I really fear," said the rector, whose stomach was delicate, "that some of them are going to be ill. Oh!"

Almost before the words had left the clergymen, one of the paupers was ill—very ill—with that peculiar complaint known to the vulgar as "shooting the cat," and over the clergyman's coat, too.

That was enough.

In less than a minute the yard was cleared of all save the paupers, and Mr. Stiffback, declining the invitation to luncheon, mustered his pupils, and returned to Lake Island School, a sadder, if not a wiser man.

He couldn't make it out at all.

He had fancied or hoped, beyond a doubt, that his invention must succeed, and yet the first trial absolutely declared the contrary.

For two whole days he pondered the matter, but it was still a mystery.

On the third, he received a short note from the parish doctor, which somewhat enlightened him.

This is the note:—

"Sir,—I have submitted to analysis the concentrated food you purposed to administer to our paupers, and I find that it contains considerable quantities of jalap, rhubarb, and senna. As these drugs are not usually considered nourishing, and the effect upon the men has been serious, the board desire me to make this communication, to which you may reply as you think fit."

"Jalap! Rhubarb! Senna!" exclaimed Mr. Stiffback, as, filled with emotion, he kicked his footstool through the front window. "I see it all now. Oh! those boys, those boys! Soker! So-ker, oil the flogging machine, put fresh canes in, and send Codlings, Wilful, and Drummond to me instantly."

CHAPTER XXXV.

SOKER'S ERRAND—ITS EFFECT ON TOMMY CODLINGS—THE HEAD MASTER SHOWS HIMSELF SKILLED IN THE CURE OF CASES OF TEMPORARY INSANITY—A LITTLE REFRESHMENT AND THE RESULTS THEREOF.

BUT Mr. Stiffback was a just man, and even in the very height of his resentment determined to have full proof before he either accused or punished the suspected ones.

"Let me see," he said, thoughtfully; "the doctor mentions jalap, rhubarb, and senna, and they must have been of full strength, too. Now where could the boys have got the drugs"

Mr. Stiffback reflected for a few moments, and then it occurred to him that some of the boys had been left in the laboratory for a while, where there were drugs enough to stock Apothecaries' Hall; and sure enough, when he examined the jars, the three which had contained the proportions of jalap, senna, and rhubarb were empty.

"The case is clear," thought Mr. Stiffback; "now, the difficulty is to find out the guilty one. It will not do to break my rule, and put the question direct to the boys—that would be tempting them to tell a lie in order to escape the consequences, and it would be worse than foolish to flog them all for the sake of one; and yet I am resolved that this trick shall not pass unpunished."

Mr. Stiffback had given himself a puzzling riddle to solve; indeed, he saw no way of getting the answer, unless the culprit chose to confess, which was extremely unlikely, and as we said before, it was against the schoolmaster's principle to force a boy to convict himself.

"I must suspend that rule, though," he thought, "if this sort of thing goes on. Never before, during the whole course of my life, was I so worried as I have been since these new boys came. If I could find out who is the ringleader I would expel him. I strongly suspect Codlings; he pretends to be stupid, but that is only his cunning."

While Mr. Stiffback was thus deliberating upon the course he should pursue, Soker, the converted one, had reached the schoolroom, and with a ghastly grin of pleasure, singled out his victims with his eye, and glared at them one by one in a manner that was extremely discomforting.

"What on earth is that chap staring at us for?" said Lionel, indignantly. "Blow him! if he don't leave off, I'll send my Latin grammar at his head."

"I know," said Tommy, who had become remarkably pale. "Stiffback's found out something, and we're going to be in for it."

"Shut up, Tommy; you're always in a funk, you are."

"And good reason too," said Tommy the unlucky. "Isn't it always me that gets whacked and knocked about, when I've done nothing?"

"Never mind; you have your share of the fun."

"*Do* I? p'r'aps I don't then—there now. Did I see the fun at the workhouse?"

"S-s-s-h, you donkey; what do you want to talk about that for? That's the very way to get caught."

"As if we weren't caught already," retorted Tommy. "I know it, by the way Soker looked at us."

"You be blowed," said Charlie, impatiently. "What do you want to be always giving a fellow the cold creeps in his back? I'll give you a domino on the nose after school's over."

"No quarrelling amongst chums," said Lionel; "and 'pon my word, I believe Tommy's right. There goes Soker to the machine."

In effect, that misanthropic gentleman had unlocked the cupboard, and drawn out that instrument, the very sight of which was enough to strike terror to the hearts of evil doers.

"What are you doing with that, Soker?" asked the second master. "I have none of the boys' names down here for punishment."

"Mr. Stiffback have," replied Soker, with a grave and solemn emphasis. "I've got horders to hile the machine and put fresh canes in, and to send Masters Codlins, Wilful, and Drummond to the libery immediate."

Every eye was turned upon the three unfortunates.

Tommy turned as white as ashes, and fainted in the arms of Bobbles junior; and even our hero and Charlie looked more than a little uncomfortable.

"We're in for it," whispered Lionel. "Who could have peached?"

"Can't say. Stiffback's found it out, most likely."

"Dash that flogging machine. Do you think he'd let us off if we made a clean breast of it?"

"Hardly likely; especially if he's found out all he wants to know already."

"Hang it, that's a confounded nuisance. I say, Charlie?"

"Well, old boy."

"Suppose we keep steady after this. No more larks or anything of that kind, eh?"

"Suppose we try, Li. I don't think it will be of much use, though."

Just as they reached the door, on their way to the library and the dread presence of the headmaster, Vansittart passed a piece of paper into Lionel's hand.

Our hero opened it, and read these words hastily scribbled with a pencil:—

"Keep cool. It's about the lark in the workhouse. Listen to all he has to say, but own to nothing, and you're safe.—V."

"That's easier said than done," muttered Lionel, as he passed the paper to Charlie. "Read that, Charlie; and you, Codlings, mind you keep your mouth shut, and if you're asked any questions you don't know anything about it. D'you hear?"

But Tommy was looking straight before him with a wild and ghastly stare, and muttering to himself in short and broken sentences the form of approaching punishment; and a bump on the head, caused by Bobbles junior letting him fall on the floor, had deranged his wits a little.

"Tommy," said Lionel, shaking him by the arm; "don't you hear me?"

"Hear," murmured Tommy—"noun substantive, the organ of hearing, conveniently situated on the side of the head, for the purpose of being pulled or boxed. Box, verb active, to strike, to smite at, as Mars, Bacchus, Apollo—virorum. Please, sir, I don't know any more."

"Here I say, Tommy, wake up," exclaimed Lionel, becoming alarmed. "He's gone out of his mind, Charlie."

"He'll soon come back then, for he can't have gone far," said Charlie, with a laugh.

"There's nothing to laugh about. What a fellow you are, Charlie," replied our hero, sharply. "Don't you hear what nonsense he's talking?"

"That's nothing new," said Charlie. "When did you ever hear him talk anything else. Come on, let's see old Stiffback and have it over."

They were now at the door of the library, and as the best thing seemed to be to follow Charlie's advice and have it over at once, Lionel knocked viciously at the door, and marched in with the air of one who was going to execution, but was determined to face the matter out bravely.

"Aha, Wilful, is that you?" said Mr. Stiffback, sweetly. "Come in, come in, and you too, Codlings, and you, Drummond. Are there any more?"

"No, sir," replied Lionel.

"Never mind, take a seat each of you; make yourselves comfortable," said the head master, smiling still more sweetly. "Will you have a little refreshment?"

The boys naturally enough were puzzled, and looked with a puzzled and suspicious eye upon their preceptor. It was not natural for him to be so civil when he had brought them there for the express purpose of punishing them, unless the offer of refreshment was satirically intended to apply to the flogging machine.

"Come, young gentlemen," said Mr. Stiffback, "you do not even reply to my invitation, and that is hardly polite, you know."

Lionel and Charlie shifted a little uneasily in their seats. Tommy smiled a wan and ghastly smile, and then, without any previous warning, began to sing his favourite melody of, "Tommy, make Room for your Uncle."

Mr. Stiffback let him go through the first verse without interruption, but when it came to the chorus, into which Tommy infused a tremendous amount of uproar, the schoolmaster struck in, and beat time on his head with a ruler.

It hadn't the least effect. Tommy smiled away like a well-regulated piece of machinery, and sung on to the end, when he suddenly stopped, looked Mr. Stiffback full in the face, and put to him the following astounding question:—

"Why is a wild rhinoceros, fed upon tea-leaves, and wound up once a year, like the Monument when it's Susan's Sunday out?"

"Bless my soul!" said Mr. Stiffback, starting back and turning very pale. "What's the matter with the boy?"

"I think he's a little out of his mind, sir," said our hero.

"Ah!" said Mr. Stiffback; "and what do you say, Drummond?"

"I think so too, sir."

"When did he begin acting in this strange manner?"

"In the corridor, sir; just before we reached the door."

"Oh, indeed! It seemed to come on suddenly, did it?"

"Very, sir."

"Oh, just so," said Mr. Stiffback, with a frown. "Then it had better be driven out of him in the same way. The artful young rascal, I'll teach him that these tricks, cunning as they are, will not impose on me."

And twisting Tommy's head under his left arm with great dexterity, he played upon the seat of the unhappy one's breeches with a stinging rapidity, which could alone have been rivalled by the flogging machine itself.

"There, Codlings," said the master, when at last, panting for breath, he set that young gentleman on his legs; "are you better now?"

But Tommy was too busy dancing his favourite hornpipe and howling an accompaniment, to heed Mr. Stiffback's question. One thing, however, was certain—the glare of insanity was gone from his eye, the "spanking" had effectually banished his temporary aberration of intellect.

"I don't think, my boy, that you will try that trick again with me. Don't you feel a little warm, though, after the exercise?"

"I do indeed, sir," replied Tommy, tearfully.

"Thirsty, perhaps."

"Very, sir."

"Then you would like a little refreshment?"

"I should indeed, sir," said Tommy, wiping off half-a-pint or so of tears which were trickling down his plump countenance. "A bottle of ginger-beer, if you please—or lemonade, sir, if it's handy."

"I will give you something better than that, my young friend," said Mr. Stiffback, as he fetched out of a cupboard a bottle of wine and a glass. "Will you also like a little, Wilful?"

"If you please, sir," replied our hero, incautiously, for of course he thought that Mr. Stiffback alluded to the wine.

"And you too, Drummond?"

"Thank you, sir, I will," said Charlie, following his leader, as usual.

Mr. Stiffback smiled, poured out a glass of wine, drank it himself, and then fetched from the cupboard a stone jar, and a wine glass without a foot.

It was one of the jars which had played so conspicuous a part in Lionel's last little joke. The doctor had sent it back with the remainder of the consolidated food in it, and this was the refreshment Mr. Stiffback meant to give them.

Lionel's mind was made up in a moment.

"I'll take it," he said to himself; "better a stomach ache than a turn in that dashed flogging machine. If we refuse to take it he'll know we're guilty."

"This," said Mr. Stiffback, filling the wine glass as he spoke, "is the patent concentrated food, an experiment with which you witnessed the other day. Do you know why that experiment failed?"

"I heard the rector say," replied Lionel, with an unmoved countenance, "that the food was a little too rich for the paupers."

"Just so," said Mr. Stiffback. "Now that remark will not apply to you boys, for you are all remarkably fond of, and used to, rich and nourishing food, especially Codlings."

Tommy groaned.

"Have you been taking anything which disagrees with you, Codlings?"

"Yes, sir."

"When was that?"

"Just now, sir," replied Tommy, tearfully, as he tenderly stroked the injured part of his anatomy.

"Pooh—nonsense. I was not speaking of that. You know what I meant, sir. Don't play the fool with me."

"Never had the chance, sir."

"I'll take care you never have again," said Mr. Stiffback sharply. "Come here, Codlings. Take that."

And he held out the wine glass full of concentrated food, and it was out of that particular jar in which our hero had stirred the rhubarb, and smelt anything but like eau de cologne.

"What am I to do with it, sir?" said Tommy, sniffing suspiciously at the brim.

"Drink it, of course, you—you—booby," retorted the head master; "and mind, you shall take a fresh glassful for every drop you spill."

Tommy cast a despairing glance round at his chums. Lionel signed to him to drink it; and Codlings, with a face expressive of the most intense disgust, gulped it down.

"Does it refresh you, Codlings? Don't you think it's more invigorating and reviving than wine—or ginger-beer?"

"It's ever s'mush—nastier, sir," gasped Tommy. "Oh, dear! if you please, sir, I think I'm going to be ill."

"If you are ill before I give you permission, Codlings," said the master, sternly, "I shall make you take a fresh dose. If you are ill, it will be only out of sheer ingratitude."

Tommy moaned, and ramming half-a-yard of cotton pocket handkerchief into his mouth, turned black in the face by slow degrees, and wondered if he should be able to hold out till the head master gave him permission to depart.

"Now, Wilful," said Mr. Stiffback, holding out the wine glass to our hero.

Lionel took it.

He had at first some idea of doing a little piece of conjuring, by passing it down his neck or into his wristband, much as Jack the Giant Killer did with his hasty pudding; but Mr. Stiffback was not so easily fooled as the Welsh giant—his eyes

watched every motion—and our hero was compelled to swallow the dose.

"How do *you* like it, Wilful?"

"It's not at all bad, sir," replied Lionel, trying hard to repress a convulsive shudder. "I really wonder at Codlings making such a fuss about it."

"Perhaps you'd like another, then, Wilful."

"No, thank you, sir," said our hero, with great readiness. "One is quite enough at a time."

Then Charlie was compelled to undergo the ordeal, which he did with so much spluttering that he barely escaped having to swallow a second dose.

"Now," said Mr. Stiffback, "you can return to your duties. I hope you feel perfectly comfortable."

"The people at the workhouse," continued Mr. Stiffback, sternly, "circulated a ridiculous report that the concentrated food was drugged, and that that was the reason of the illness of the paupers. Now, if that food had been mixed with any deleterious substances, I was well aware that one of you three boys must be the guilty party, but from the readiness with which you have swallowed it, and the agreeable effect it has upon your systems, convinces me that you are innocent. Will you have any more?"

"No, thank you, sir," mumbled Lionel, with his mouth shut.

Tommy was standing on one leg, with the other tightly drawn up, after the manner of a fowl roosting, while both his hands were pressed over his stomach, and short moans of agony escaped him at intervals.

"Did you say you would like a little more, Codlings?" said Mr. Stiffback, sweetly.

Tommy's only answer was a convulsive hop, and a louder moan.

"Speak a little more plainly, Codlings," said Mr. Stiffback. "Will you have another glassful?"

But Tommy dared not open his mouth.

To do that would bring on the crisis which he felt was fast approaching.

"Well, then, if you are quite sure that you will not take any more," said Mr. Stiffback, who saw that it would not be safe to detain the boys any longer if he had any regard for his carpet, "you may go."

Before the last word had left his lips the three chums had left the room.

Then there was a mad rush into the play-ground, a short period of convulsive agony, during which were exhibited the symptoms usually attendant upon a bad attack of sea-sickness.

"Oh, my!" gasped Lionel, as he leaned his head against the pump for coolness, "I didn't think it was as bad as that. Ugh!"

"It was awful. Those poor paupers, Li. How they must have suffered."

"Don't mention it. They must have had a pint each. Poor chaps! This is a just judgment on us, Charlie."

"It is, Li."

"Let's give up larking, then, shall we?"

"Yes; let's make a solemn vow, Li."

"All right. Where's Tommy. He'll be in it too."

But not a sign of Tommy was anywhere visible. That young gentleman had mysteriously disappeared.

CHAPTER XXXVI.

TOMMY'S WONDERFUL DIGESTION—HE RUNS AWAY—HIS THOUGHTS ON SUICIDE—ADVENTURES AFLOAT AND ASHORE.—A "FOWL" DEED.

AS they had no time to lose, and were, moreover, not much disposed to take more exercise than was absolutely necessary, Lionel and Charlie returned to the class-room looking decidedly pale and woe-begone, in spite of an attempt they made to get some colour into their cheeks by holding their breath until they were nearly suffocated.

"It'll never do to let the other fellows know what has happened," said our hero, "or we shall be laughed at for a month to come.'

"Let any of the fellows try it on," said Charlie, grimly. "Oh! Li, I should like to have a little turn-up with somebody just now."

"Pick out the eldest Bobbles, and have a 'go at him after school."

"I think I will. He's a capital chap to practise on. It's like punching indiarubber, only he hollers, which is more satisfying to the feelings."

"Don't talk like that, Charlie, or you'll make me savage, and then I shall have to fight somebody. By-the-by, I wonder where Tommy is. He hasn't come back yet, has he? I don't see him anywhere."

"He's a good deal worse than we are, Li," said Charlie. "He had his dose first, and his stomach is more delicate than ours."

"Is it? I like that, now. Tommy's stomach delicate! Why, that chap can eat anything. I remember once he swallowed a quarter of a pound of indiarubber that he was chewing to get soft, and it never hurt him a bit."

"Draw it mild, Li."

"It's a fact. I believe that chap would fatten, like an ostrich, on cast-iron nails."

"Silence there," said the second master, sternly. "Wilful and Drummond, you have just returned from punishment, and you are talking in class, and incurring the risk again."

"Beg your pardon, sir," said Lionel, coolly, "but we have not returned from being punished."

"Did not Mr. Stiffback send for you?"

"He did, sir, but it was only to offer us a little refreshment."

"Indeed," said the second master, looking doubtfully at the boys. "Well, you must be quiet now, if you please."

"Codleens," said the sharp voice of the French master. "Vere is dat boy Codleens? Wilful, he did go out wiz you."

"He did, monsieur," replied our hero.

"Zen why is he not come back also?"

"I'm sure I can't tell you, monsieur," replied Lionel. "Perhaps he liked the refreshment so much that he's gone back for a little more."

"I gif him some ven he shall come back," said the ill-tempered French professor. "He is ze baddest boy as ever vas in dis vorld."

Let us now follow the footsteps of poor Tommy, when, maddened by the pain which the triple extract of rhubarb inflicted upon his unfortunate interior, he rushed from the library.

Borne onwards by the impetuosity of his feelings, Tommy raced across the play-ground, and stayed not his course until he reached the edge of the water, where he tripped over the root of a tree just in time to save him from rushing headlong into the lake.

The shock of the fall completed the work.

Lying face downwards on the ground, Tommy heaved and retched, and was as ill as any mortal man or boy could wish not to be.

For full half an hour his pangs endured, and by the time he had given his last gasp and heave, Tommy was as empty of everything but wind as a new drum.

He really thought for awhile that, in the graphic phrase of the American humourist, he had "brought up his immortal soul."

"I won't stand it," he said, looking wildly around him. "What right has he got to dose a chap with—— Ugh! Oh, lor! Oh, dear me!"

And Tommy gave another ineffectual heave.

A groan of mingled agony and despair, and then sitting up, he cast a wild and frenzied glance around him.

"I'll put a stop to this," said Tommy, desperately. "I'll jump into the lake, and write a letter first to the Lord Mayor to say old Stiffback drove me to it."

Tommy arose and looked at the water.

It had a very cool and tempting appearance on that hot summer day.

But then Tommy thought of the mud at the bottom, and then of the eels, and, somehow, drowning was a very unpleasant kind of death, and ungraceful, too, there was so much kicking and splashing and gurgling.

"Besides," thought Tommy, "I should be a stupid to go and drown myself on his account. But I know what I'll do. I'll leave my clothes on the bank here, and stick a note in my cap to say that Stiffback's cruelty drove me to the deed."

Tommy had already taken his jacket off, and was unlacing his boots, when it occurred to him that it was a long way across the lake, and that he might be attacked with cramp, in which case the note in his cap would have a great deal more truth in it than would be at all pleasant.

"Blow it," thought Tommy, "that will never do. Fancy committing suicide by accident. They'd think I did it on purpose, and I should be buried in a cross road, with a stake through my body, or something dreadful like that. Oh, I know; I'll have a boat."

Tommy knew the way to the boat-house, but unfortunately for his plan, it was locked, and the only vessel at his disposal was the eight-oared galley.

"That's a whopper for one chap to manage," said Tommy to himself, "but I'll have a go at it."

Luckily for Tommy it was already in the water, for his unaided strength would never have been able to land it, and after scribbling a short despairing note on the back of an old exercise, and tucking it into the lining of his cap, Tommy left them on the bank, seized an oar and pushed off.

His adventures were very nearly terminating at this point, for not being well skilled in the management of a boat he thrust the blade of the oar so deep into the bank, that endeavouring to pull it out the boat shot away from under him, and had not one of his feet caught against a thwart he must have been soused into the river.

As it was he gave himself a beautiful black eye against one of the thole-pins, and "barked" his right shin from the knee to the instep.

But his real troubles began, when, with an oar in each hand, he tried to pull the boat across the lake.

Tommy was unaware of the difference between oars and sculls. He had often seen his chums rowing, but it was not in his nature to acquire any kind of knowledge, except at the cost of ten times as much trouble and labour as any other boy would expend.

"Dash it," growled Tommy, as he made a desperate endeavour to pull his right hand over home, and missing his water knocked himself backwards with the butt. "Dash the things, they can't be right. How precious long they seem to be, they reach right across the boat."

But the plump youth was not easily daunted; he scrambled up and tried again, but only with the effect of grinding all the skin off his knuckles, as the oars somehow mixed themselves up.

"Ow-ow! oh my!" yelled Tommy, letting go the oars, and performing that peculiar dance which seems to afford so much relief to juvenile humanity when in physical suffering. "Oh, what an unlucky chap I am! Every blessed bit of skin off."

But the torture he underwent only served to influence his mind with a more intense desire to get farther away from Mr. Stiffback, whom he regarded as the more or less remote cause of all his trouble.

"Only wait till I get on shore," muttered Tommy, as he enshrouded his bleeding knuckles in strips torn from his pocket handkerchief. "I'll join the gipsies. The kind of life they lead, always wandering about in the open air, is just the very thing to make a fellow strong and active, and in a year or so I'll come and wait round the corner for Stiffback, and when he ain't looking I'll let him have one, such a beauty, and knock his ugly old head off."

But as a preliminary to the due execution of this scheme of vengeance, it was necessary that Tommy should get the boat ashore, but how could he do it.

"I've seen chaps," mused Tommy, "stand in the stern of a boat and waggle one oar about. I should think that was easy."

As this seemed to involve no further sacrifice of the epidermis of his knuckles, and as the standing position was decidedly more comfortable than sitting after the spanking Mr. Stiffback had given him that morning, Tommy resolved to try the "waggling dodge," as he called it.

It was easy to drop the oar over the stern of the boat. Tommy managed this part of it beautifully, but as there was no groove for the oar to work in, and our plump friend had not the least idea how to give the blade the peculiar screw-like motion necessary to propel the boat forward, he made rather less progress than before.

"Dash it!" growled Tommy; "I never saw such luck as I've got; other fellows can row, or skate, or swim the first time they try, and I never get any further than knowing how to hurt myself."

Suddenly a brilliant thought struck Tommy—if he could not row the boat, he might be able to propel her after the fashion of a punt, but what was he to do for a pole?

Tommy tried to sound the water with one of the oars, and, of course, in so doing very nearly plumbed the depth with his own plump little body.

"It's too deep again; just my luck. But stop, though; I can tie two together, they will be long enough for anything."

It took him about ten minutes to lash the blades of the oars firmly together, and, to his delight, Tommy found that his pole answered the purpose admirably—he could touch the bottom and leave plenty of hand room to spare.

Now a fresh difficulty presented itself: Tommy could move the boat, and a very pleasant gliding sort of motion it was, but so eccentric, that the plump youth seemed further off than ever from any chance of landing.

When he plunged the pole into the mud on the larboard side, Tommy was not at all certain whether the boat would go forward, backward, or sidelong, like a crab. Sometimes it would do all that at once, and spin round with a teetotum like motion that made him giddy.

Then, too, when he did succeed in giving his obstinate craft a propulsion in the desired direction, the pole obstinately stuck in the mud, and refused to come out until, with a sudden wrench, Tommy would succeed in freeing it and fall on his back with a crash.

At last Tommy dropped the oar, and sitting down, lifted up his voice and howled with rage and despair.

He stamped on the thwarts until he broke them, and run no end of splinters into his legs; he kicked the sides of the boat until he hurt his toes; and finally he hurled every moveable object on which he could lay his hands into the lake, and if he had only known how—which we are glad to say he did not—he would probably have used some very bad language.

But coming at last to the very sensible conclusion

that, if he wished to land, sitting down and crying would not help him much, Tommy got up again and called necessity, the mother of invention, to his aid.

He was somewhere near the middle of the lake by this time, and an average swimmer would have thought nothing of the distance to be covered.

But Tommy's powers of natation were not to be relied on. If our hero had been there to keep him company, the plump youth would have struggled gamely over twice the distance.

"I'm blessed if I know what to do," muttered Tommy. "It's like being ship-wrecked. Let me see, what do chaps do when they're cast away at sea. I know, they draw lots about eating one another, but I can't do that, for there's nobody to eat, even if I felt inclined that way, which I don't. Then I know they hoist signals of distress, by tying a shirt to the top of an oar, and then they holler, but that won't do either, for they'd hear me at the school, and I should be fetched back and whacked again."

The very thought of such a catastrophe put Tommy into a cold perspiration, and when he noted the damage he had done to the boat, and made a mental estimate of Mr. Stiffback's rage thereat, he resolved to take any means, however desperate, that presented themselves for his acceptance.

"I know," said Tommy, resolutely. "I'll get out behind, and shove the boat along. I can't get drowned that way, and I'm sure to get to shore some time. What an ass I was not to think of it before."

No sooner said than done. In two minutes Tommy's clothes were deposited in the stern of the boat, and the plump one lowered himself over the side, and, striking out vigorously with his legs, pushed the boat towards the shore.

It was dreadfully slow work though, for Tommy was a weak swimmer, and the boat was heavy, but at last he had the satisfaction of feeling the keel grate on the ground, and wading to the shore he sat down, and gasped out his gratitude.

"That's over, thank goodness," panted Tommy. "I wonder if all chaps who run away are as unluckly as me; I shouldn't think so, or they wouldn't do it twice. I wish I'd waited now, and asked Wilful to come. What a fellow that is now; he can do anything, and nothing ever seems to go wrong with him; but there, it's my luck, and it's no use grumbling—a chap can't be a gipsy without a little trouble."

With which piece of philosophy Tommy consoled himself while he dressed, and then struck into the by-path which led to the main road.

As if fortune, satisfied with the troubles Tommy had already experienced, determined to smooth matters for a while, the plump youth met with no further mishap for the space of an hour or more, when his empty condition, aggravated by the bath and the walk, began to impress itself fearfully upon his notice.

"My eye!" said Tommy, stopping in sudden alarm; "what am I to do for grub—I never thought of that."

The idea of starving was far worse than that of being drowned, and Tommy hastily felt in all his pockets, producing therefrom a medley of bits of string, odd marbles, a few buttons, a half-sucked bull's-eye, some crumbs of biscuit, a French sou, and a battered farthing.

"Here's a go," said Tommy, pallid with consternation. "I shan't be able to buy anything to eat with this. There's the bull's-eye and the biscuit crumbs; but they won't keep a chap alive for long, and I don't know what you can buy for three-farthings, except apples and seedy biscuits."

Tommy put his treasures ruefully back into his jacket pocket, and mused upon the important subject of ways and means, the while he grew more and more ravenous each moment.

"I'm going to be a gipsy," said Tommy, with sudden desperation, "and I'll do as the gipsies do. I'll have a rabbit, or a hare, or a fowl, I don't much care which, and cook it in the woods. That's the way they live, I know, because I've read about it in books. Here goes."

Having thus made up his mind to do this evil deed, Tommy cast about him for some available hen-roost in which he might exercise his felonious intent.

Some good man somewhere, says the spirit of evil soon finds an opportunity for those whose hearts and hands are disposed to wickedness; and so Tommy found it, for scarcely had the resolve entered into his head, than there was a sudden clucking and chirruping, and a hen accompanied by about a dozen little chickens broke through the hedge, scarce a yard in front of him.

The temptation was irresistible.

Tommy darted forward, there was a loud outcry from the hen, a fluttering of wings, a spasmodic croak, and the guilty Tommy had made orphans of some fourteen bereaved chickens.

The deed was scarcely done, and the pallor of conscious guilt yet whitened Tommy's cheek, when a broad red face arose on the other side of the hedge, and the body belonging to it made frantic efforts to break through into the road.

"Hoy! Bill! Tummas! Ge-arge!" roared the lout. "Here be tramp priggin' the chickerns. Com' on. Mak' ha-aste, wi' 'ee!"

Tommy stared for one moment aghast and petrified with fear, and then dropping the murdered fowl, fled for his life down the road, hotly pursued by a crowd of lumbering louts and cow-boys.

CHAPTER XXXVII.

THE CHASE—TOMMY DISTANCES HIS PURSUERS— EXHAUSTION—BALM IN GILEAD—A LITTLE MISUNDERSTANDING BETWEEN TOMMY AND THE MAID OF THE INN—A FREE LUNCH—TOMMY TAKES REFUGE IN A NOVEL KIND OF SANCTUARY —THE RESCUE.

IF we were to say that Tommy Codlings was never before or since so frightened in his life as he was at the moment of which we write, it would hardly be an exaggeration.

As the fearful cry, "Stop thief!" was yelled after him by that fast increasing crowd of rustics, his youthful soul was chilled with the awful thought that he was a criminal fleeing from justice, and subject to the direst pains and penalties of the law.

Even as he tore along, his mouth wide open, his breath coming thick and short—for Tommy was like Falstaff, fat and scant of breath—his eyes almost forced out of his head, like hat-pegs; visions of Newgate—of the scaffold—of the exe-cutioner and the fatal noose—of himself in an hideous suit of drab, with a number on his back, and huge, heavy manacles fettering his limbs, flitted before him, and enabled him to run at a rate which soon left his pursuers far behind.

But it is "the pace that kills," as Tommy found out, for by the time his little fat legs had covered a mile he was exhausted, and dropped panting by the roadside, in a condition as insensible as that of a Hampstead donkey on the evening of a Bank Holiday.

Tommy was dry—dreadfully dry—but so was the ditch, and though the plump youth thought he would have perilled his very life for a draught of the dirtiest water that ever required a Parliamen-tary Commission, there was none to be had.

"Oh, dear me," gasped Tommy, "how dry I do feel to be sure. I should like to see the man that could squeeze a tear out of me now. I believe that if anyone put a lighted match to me, I should flare up like gunpowder. Never mind, though,

I've got rid of those dashed louts. My eye! how I did run."

And Tommy, with a great effort, managed to get into a sitting position, and tried to moisten his lips with a tongue that was like the sole an old boot in point of flexibility.

"Blow it!" said Tommy, continuing his soliloquy. "What an ass I was to run away. If I'd thought a gipsy life was anything like this, I'd rather have had a double dose, every week, of the flogging-machine. I can't have gone the right way to work either; real gipsies don't make fowls squeak as I did, and when they're found out poaching, they slip into the keepers, and welt 'em over the head with sticks. But there, it's just my luck; nothing ever goes right that I do, and nothing ever will."

But this meditation did little towards allaying the pangs of thirst and hunger, which was gnawing Tommy's vitals.

A little while since, while flying from his pursuers, he had felt how extremely wrong it was to steal; now we regret to say, he was eagerly longing for an opportunity to grab "what wasn't hisn," regardless of the warning of the poet who tells all such evil-doers that when "they're cotched they're sent to pris'n."

A little further up the road there stood, prin-cipally for the benefit of all weary travellers, a sign-post, whereon was depicted a scarlet lion in a blue forest, benevolently beckoning to the general public with his right fore-leg.

"There's a sign-post," gasped Tommy, "and where there's a sign-post there's sure to an inn, and where there's an inn there's sure to be some-thing good to eat and drink."

Tommy might have added that payment was sure to be expected for the good things to eat and drink; but, as the old proverb saith, "A hungry belly hath no conscience," so the plump one arose, brushed his jacket and trousers as well as he could, smoothed his hair, and with a mind sternly re-solved to get something to eat and drink, or perish in the attempt, marched to the inn.

Now it so happened that a few days before, a party of juvenile picnickers had halted at that same inn, and defrauded the landlady by consuming sundry bottles of lemonade and ginger beer, and then departing in a hurry, without making due payment therefor.

This wrong still rankled in the mind of the hostess, and as from her position in the bar she beheld the advent of one who looked like another fraudulent picknicker, she sallied forth ready, in her own forcible language, to be "down on 'im like a 'ammer."

"Now then, young gen'leman," she said, "you've come arter some more o' that there ginger beer, I reckon."

"Yes, ma'am," said Tommy politely, and with much delight at his request being anticipated, he supposed in consequence of some mistake on the part of the landlady.

"So I thort," she said with a grim smile; "and how much do 'ee want to-day—will 'arf-a-dozen bottles soot 'ee?"

"Nearly, ma'am," gasped Tommy, his face beaming with delight and perspiration.

"And you bean't a goin' to pay for 'em, I 'spose," said the landlady again; "you wants 'em on trust, like the last?"

"If you please, ma'am," said the unsuspecting Tommy.

"Oh! certingly, and ain't there anything else you'd like on the same terms?"

"Well, ma'am," replied Tommy, "since you are so kind, I think if you can cut a few sandwiches, and——"

"A few sandwiches!" said the landlady, with a burst of overwhelming generosity. "Take the 'am—do have a 'ole 'am; and there's a fresh-baked quartern loaf, and a new cheese, and sum sassingers. Don't say no—now don't 'ee."

"I won't," said Tommy, whose mouth would have watered, had he not been so totally devoid of all internal moisture; "I'd take 'em, ma'am, but I haven't got anything to put 'em all in."

"No more you hev," said the landlady, affecting surprise; "'spose I lends you a box—a nice large box—one as yer wouldn't bring back, yer know."

"Thank you, ma'am," said the unsuspecting Tommy, with fervent gratitude; "I'll take great care of it, ma'am."

"Will ye? There it is then."

And she gave poor Tommy the "box," not the one he had expected, but a tremendous "box" on the ear, which spun him round like a teetotum, and finally deposited him on the sanded floor, amidst a heap of spittoons.

"There, how d'ye like that?" said the enraged hostess; "the cheek o' you young warmints bangs everythink. Only to fancy a boy havin' the inpidence to rob a poor lone woman one day, and then to come back the very next, as bold as brass, to do it again."

"I didn't," roared Tommy, as he picked himself up out of the spittoons. "Don't you go hitting me, or I'll fetch the police."

"Wa'at!" said the landlady in a vindictive shriek, as she glared around her for a broom. "Here, Jem, come and turn this young rascal into the road, or I shall bang the life out him."

Jem was a lumbering, red-headed lout, who did all the dirty work of the inn, and lived upon stale beer and sawdust, if one might judge from the smell of those delicacies which hung about him, and flavoured the atmosphere for an area of a dozen yards around him.

"Here I be, mum."

"Turn that boy out," said the landlady, "neck and crop, Jem, and gi' him a lug o' the year afore you lets him go."

"You come near me, and I'll shy this at you," said Tommy desperately, as he picked up one of the earthenware spittoons.

But Jem was apparently used to such delicate attentions, for, taking no notice to Tommy's threat, he lumbered up, dodged the missile, which the plump youth hurled with ineffectual aim, and grabbed his victim by the hair.

"Out ye goo," grunted Jem, giving Tommy a shake, which nearly deprived him of breath; "kick away?—ye won't hurt my shins. Be I to pull both his years, missus."

"Yes, you gaby, pull three if you can find 'em. Let me have one more bang at 'un afore he goes. Dang the lad, I'll teach 'un to come swindlin' people out o' their prop'ty. See if he's got any brass, Jem, I'll make 'un pay for what he and his mates stole t'other day."

"I never stole nothing," yelled Tommy, in complete defiance of the rules of grammar, and determined to fight for his only half-penny to the very last gasp. "Murder—police—stop thieves!"

At that moment, the last words uttered by Tommy were taken up as if by some faithful echo, and the cry of "Stop thief!" was borne upon the breeze.

"Hullo," said the landlady, "wa'at be that, Jem?"

"Chaps a hollerin'," replied Jem, shortly.

Nearer and nearer came the voices, still huskily vociferating, "Stop thief!" and the terror-stricken Tommy almost sank into his boots with fear, for he knew that his pursuers, instead of giving up the chase, had continued it, and were now coming to avenge the murder of the fowl.

As they came lumbering heavily round the corner, and caught sight of Tommy, they uttered a roar of laughter, and the plump one, endowed with supernatural strength by reason of his fear, broke away from Jem and began to run.

But unluckily for him, his retreat was cut off—behind him were Jem and the landlady, in front the louts. It is instinct, we believe, which teaches cats to climb a tree, when a dog is after them. Something of that nature, then, now inspired Tommy, for, as a last desperate resource, he seized the sign-post and clambered up it with wonderful agility.

Tommy would have been better off had he dodged the louts, and cut his way through them. They were slow and heavy, and he would probably have got clean off at the cost of a few smart punches; but it was too late to think of that now—he was "treed."

"Here be the warmint," roared one huge cowboy, who still grasped by the neck the slaughtered fowl. "Where be Tummas?"

"Gone to fetch t' coonstable," was the reply, and Tommy, who heard the dreadful words, nearly fell from his perch.

"What ha' the young vagabone done?" demanded the landlady.

"Been priggin' the chicking, marm."

"Ah! he's a bad 'un, a right down bad 'un, I were goin' to let 'un off too easy, but now I'll goo up afore th' madgistrit again 'un."

"Oh, my eye!" roared Tommy, "what an unlucky chap I am—I shall be locked up, and what will my aunt say. I'm disgraced for ever."

"Come down, will 'ee," bawled the cowboy. "Come down and be locked up."

"I won't, I'll die first," said Tommy, clinging to the portrait of the scarlet lion, as if that noble animal was the dearest friend he had.

"Fetch 'un down, if 'un won't coom," suggested another. "Here be Billie Beer—he can climb, he can. Up 'ee goes, Billie."

Billy, the acknowledged champion of the greasy pole at all the fairs for miles around, spat liberally on his hands, tucked up his smock frock, and swarmed up the pole.

Tommy, with one eye cocked downwards, like that of a raven examining a mutton-bone, waited for him, and when his red head was within convenient distance, Codlings let go his right leg, and hit the lout with the force of a paviour's rammer.

The lout slid down as if he and the pole too had been both well greased, and two of his mates, who were standing at the foot looking up at him, were prostrated on the ground.

"Hoy, dang thee, whear be 'ee coming tew, Billie—my nose be flatted."

"And I ha' lost two o' moy front teeth," mumbled lout number two. "I'll punch thy head, Billie."

But Billie sat on the ground, staring before him in a bewildered fashion. He was slow of comprehension, and it took him a long time to understand the position.

"Ge-arge," be said at length, and in a thoughtful manner.

"Well, Billie."

"Who hit oi in the yed, Ge-arge?"

"Schule-boy kicked thee, Billie."

Thus informed of the circumstance attending his downfall, Billie arose, rubbed his head, then picked up a nice hard lump of clay, about the size of his fist, and hurled it at his foe.

The missile whistled past Tommy's right ear, smashed itself against the sign-board, and filled Tommy's eyes, nose, and mouth with dust.

"Hooray," shouted the louts, "that be good idee, Billie; we'll pelt 'un till he comes down."

And the next moment a shower of clay, turf, and stones darkened the air, and smote the unprotected youth upon divers tender parts of the body.

It was an awful time, and he almost longed for the arrival of the constable, that he might escape these merciless foes.

But help of a more satisfactory kind was at hand, though the plump youth little expected it.

THE UNHAPPY PAUPERS GROANED AND WRIGGLED, AS EACH HAD A PINT OF COMPOUND ESSENCE OF STOMACH-ACHE PUMPED INTO HIM.

No. 25.

After an hour had passed, and Tommy remained still absent from the school, Lionel and Charlie grew a little anxious, and when the classes dispersed, both hurried out into the grounds in search of him.

Searching every yard as they advanced, the chums soon reached the water's edge, and there Lionel, espying some dark object in the long grass, picked it up, and found it was Tommy's cap with the letter tucked into the lining.

"Oh, Charlie, look here!" exclaimed our hero, turning pallid as death. "Poor Tommy's drowned himself."

"What!"

Lionel held out the note, Charlie took it, read it, and turned as pale as his chum. Then without another word, they exchanged a look and set off running to the house as fast as they could, and never stopped until they reached the library, into which they burst without the ceremony of first knocking at the door.

"Now what do you mean by this?" exclaimed Mr. Stiffback, angrily.

"Oh, if you please, sir," they replied, both speaking at once, "Codlings has drowned himself."

The schoolmaster changed colour, but only for a moment.

"Nonsense," he said, sharply.

"Here's the letter, sir. We found his cap on the bank, with this tucked into the lining."

This was the note which Tommy had scribbled :—

"I've drownded miself. I couldn't stand any more wackins, and the fizzic was more than any boy could put up with. Whoever finds this, tell old Stiffback, and say I'll 'aunt him with my gost. My love to Li and Charlie. Tell 'em not to fret; but if old Stiffback won't let 'em alone, to drownd theirselves too, and then our gostes will 'aunt him in company. T.C."

"Nonsense," said Mr. Stiffback, looking very red and angry, as he threw the paper into the fireplace. "He's hiding somewhere, and when I do catch him, I'll—I'll flay him alive."

And then, without waiting to put on his hat, Mr. Stiffback strode away down to the lake, and following up Tommy's trail with the sagacity of a Red Indian, traced him to the boat-house, and at once noted the absence of the galley.

"And," continued Mr. Stiffback, after he had pointed out this fact to our hero and Charlie, "if further proof were wanting, there is the boat itself grounded on the opposite side."

"He changed his mind, I suppose, sir," suggested Charlie.

"I shall not change mine then," replied Mr. Stiffback, quietly. "Wilful, go back to the school and ask Vansittart and half-a-dozen of the upper form boys to come to me."

Wilful ran off with the rapidity of a bullet from a Snider rifle, and soon came back, bringing Vansittart, Pryce, and three or four more.

"Codlings," said Mr. Stiffback, "has run away, and he must be found, and at once, before he has time to degrade himself and me by any fresh eccentricities. Take the boats, and when you reach the other side, divide yourselves into twos, and hunt him down. He cannot have gone very far, for he has little more than an hour's start."

"He may have gone to the railway station and taken the train, sir," said Vansittart. "I daresay he had some idea of going back to his home."

"I know that he had no money," said Lionel, "for I had promised to lend him some this evening."

"Then he could not have taken a train," said Mr. Stiffback, "but for all that, two of you had better go there and inquire."

"May we go too, sir?" asked Lionel.

"Well, yes," said Mr. Stiffback, after a doubtful pause. "He knows you better than the others, and would be less likely to hide if he saw you in pursuit. But no tricks, mind. I warn you that I have had enough of them for the present."

"We will be careful, sir."

"Mind that you are," retorted Mr. Stiffback, meaningly. "Now, out with the boats, and off with you."

This was just the sort of fun the boys liked.

The love of the chase is an instinct especially strong in our nation, and the idea of hunting down a runaway was truly delightful.

None of them, we regret to say, thought much of what would happen to Tommy when he was brought back.

"That was his look out," as Pryce observed.

There were eight of them, and obeying Mr. Stiffback's directions, they separated into parties of two, and choosing the four most likely paths, started on this novel kind of boy-hunt.

Lionel and Charlie, more by instinct than choice, had hit upon the very road which the unlucky Tommy had taken when he went gipsying, but they found no trace of him until they came to that part where he had turned out his pockets to see if he had any money.

Then Lionel's quick eye detected a scrap of paper, in which was a flattened-out old brace button, which Tommy highly prized, insisting that it was a coin of immense antiquity, probably worth an immense amount of money.

"Hush!" exclaimed Lionel, "we are on the right track, old boy. Here's that blessed old button which Tommy used to say was a coin of the time of the reign of Adam the First."

"Is it? Oh, ah! I recollect it now. He wanted me to lend him half-a-crown once, and offered it to me for security. Hurry along, Li; we shall soon come up with him now."

The two chums broke into a run, both looking and listening carefully for the least sign or sound of their runaway chum, until at length the sound of distant shouting, mingled with laughter, and the cries of someone in pain fell on their ears.

"Hark!" said Lionel, "I do believe that's Tommy's voice."

"Too far off yet to be certain," said Charlie. "Put on a spurt, Li."

They did, and another five minutes' sharp trot brought them in view of what they sought.

And only just in time, for the unfortunate Tommy was on the point of "falling" into the hands of his enemies, when Lionel and his chum arrived, and sent forth the welcome cry of—

"Rescue!"

CHAPTER XXXVIII.

THE BATTLE WITH THE LOUTS—TOMMY'S ARTILLERY COMES INTO PLAY, AND DOES IMMENSE EXECUTION—THE DEFEAT—SIGNING THE ARTICLES OF PEACE—TOMMY DECLARES HIS RESOLVE TO BECOME A GIPSY—HOW LIONEL PERSUADED HIM TO CHANGE HIS MIND—THE PIC-NIC—UNDER THE SHADOW OF THE WINDMILL.

"COME on, Charlie, be quick," said Lionel. "Down with the louts. Hold on Tommy, we're coming."

"Stop a bit, Li; I must have a laugh," said Drummond. "Look at Tommy, perched up there, for all the world like a organ grinder's monkey. Ha! ha! ha!"

"Drive those beggars away and laugh afterwards," said our hero. "How would you like it yourself."

"All right, only I say, Li, look out, there's more than a dozen of 'em, and some are big chaps too."

"Bother that—we've to get Tommy out of his fix, and think of how many louts there are after."

"Let's give 'em a volley first, and I say, Li, here are some hedge-stakes—we can charge into 'em with these after."

"Not a bad notion, Charlie, and it won't be cowardly, for they're six to one. Give us hold."

"Here's a beauty, with a knob at the end, Li."

"That'll do. I'll raise a knob or two in a lout's skull with this. Ready?"

"All right, Li."

"Fire then."

And in quick succession, half-a-dozen good sized stones flew into the midst of the louts, sending three of them yelping away, while the rest, at the well-known cry of "Chevvy the louts!" "School to rescue!" turned and ran.

"Hurrah!" shouted Charlie. "Victory! Down you come, Tommy."

And down Tommy did come, in a much greater hurry than Drummond either wished or expected, for the plump one, quite exhausted, let go all at once, and fell upon Charlie's upturned countenance.

"It's lucky your nose was flat already, Charlie," said Lionel, "or I'm blessed if Tommy wouldn't have spoiled its shape for you."

"That's all the sympathy a fellow gets for helping a friend," growled Charlie. "The next time you want to fall on me, Tommy, just let me know and I'll keep out of the way."

"A lot you've got to growl about," retorted Tommy. "I wish you'd been at the top of that dashed post for half-an-hour, instead of me."

"Thank you for nothing," said Charlie, who was in a very unsaintly temper, for his nose was bleeding freely, and refused to be coaxed into stopping.

"Look out," said our hero, suddenly, "there's the louts coming back."

"Shall we cut and run?" said Charlie. "Tommy can't fight. He's not much good at the best of times, but now he'd be useless."

"Shall I," retorted Tommy, with a savage glare in his eye. "Let us have a go at 'em and you'll see. I've marked that big chap with the cock-eye—that's the one who kept on hitting me with hard bits of clay, and always in the same place."

"What place was it, Tommy?"

"Never you mind," said Tommy, sulkily.

"Old Stiffback knows where it is, don't he, Tommy?"

"I'll give you one in the eye, if you don't leave off."

"Stop that wrangling now," said our hero. "The louts will give you quite as much pinking as you want, and more too. They're making up their minds to rush at us now. Come over here, and get your backs to the hedge, we mustn't let 'em get behind us."

They had scarcely time to execute this piece of strategy, when, with a hideous howl which the war cry of a Chippewa Indian could hardly have surpassed, the louts came lumbering at them.

Tommy's particular enemy, the cock-eyed lout, was in front of the plump youth. He'd prepared a mass of tough clay, about as large as his own head, and taking careful aim, he let him have it with full force upon the very top of a particularly big nose.

It spread the lout's nose all over his face, so completely was it flattened, and with a yell the wounded one fell on his back and jerked his legs in convulsive agony.

The fall of the leader checked the others for a moment, and Tommy had time to get another lump ready.

"Bravo, Tommy!" said Lionel; "aim at the front one, then the fellow behind is sure to tumble over him."

Tommy let it go, and so effective was his aim that the missile glanced from the head of the first lout and chipped off the gristly part of the ear of a second, who flinging out his arms in his agony

floored a third, so that out of a dozen foes only about half were left to encounter.

"Hurrah!" shouted Lionel; "give it to 'em, Charlie—strike with both hands, and aim at their shins."

The value of this advice was soon evident, for the heavy hedge-stakes, wielded by their strong arms, took three of the louts off their legs at the first blow, and of the five who were left two turned tail and bolted, while the others sued for quarter.

"We ain't done nawthan to 'un," said one. "What do 'ee want to be punchin' o' us fower?"

"Because you were pelting my chum," said Lionel. "What business had you to be doing that?"

"That be good 'un, that be," retorted the lout. "He stole my feyther's chickens, that's whoy we chased 'un."

"I say, Tommy, is that true?" said Lionel.

"Well," said Tommy, hesitating a little, "I was going to be a gipsy, you know, and they do it."

"Yes, and get locked up for it. What a one you are, Tommy."

"Same to you," growled Tommy, in a subdued voice.

"Now how much will you have the cheek to charge for that fowl?"

"She wur worth two shillun', I know, 'cos I heerd my feyther say so t'other day, and she did lay 'nation foine eggs. I used fur to zuck 'em!"

"Look here, then," said Lionel, "here's a shilling, and you've got the fowl. Will you take that, and say no more about it?"

"'Ees," said the lout, with a grin. "Gie us holt."

"There you are then," said Lionel, tossing him the coin, "and mind you keep your word, or I'll find you out and give you the neatest tanning you ever had in your life."

But the lout, with his wounded companions, was already half way across the road to the inn, the landlady of which, relying on the ability of the boys to keep Tommy safe, had gone a little way up the road to hasten the coming of the constable.

"Now come on," said Lionel, "and thank your lucky stars that we came up when we did, Tommy, or you'd have been locked up by this time."

"I'm not going back to school," retorted Tommy Codlings, obstinately.

"Ain't you? I think you are, though," said Lionel. "Why where, in the name of goodness, do you want to go?"

"I'm going to lead a free and roving life, I am," replied Codlings. "I'll join the gipsies, and perhaps they'll make a king of me in time. No more beastly school, or lessons, or whackings then."

"A pretty gipsy you'd make. Why you can't even prig a fowl without being chased half over the county, and getting pelted like a mad dog. No, Tommy, you come back with us."

"I won't."

"You will, though. If you won't walk, we'll carry you, and get you back that way. We promised Stiffback, didn't we, Charlie?"

"We did. We said that if we had to cut him up and bring him back a piece at a time that we'd do it."

"None of that, you know—no larks," said Tommy, a little alarmed at the serious way in which Charlie spoke.

"Make up your mind, and come quietly then. Why, where would you expect to get your grub, and where would you sleep?"

"Well, I am precious thirsty and hungry too, I own," said Tommy. "I didn't think it was so difficult to get anything to eat."

"Didn't you, though? Well, I tell you what,

Tommy. If you'll promise to go back quietly, I'll stand a good tuck out."

"I'm on!" cried Tommy. "Lemonade or ginger-beer, Li?"

"Both, if you like."

"I consent to go back and be hung for two bottles of lemonade," said Tommy, who, now that the excitement of the fight was over, felt the pangs of hunger and thirst return with redoubled violence.

As, after his late adventure in the inn, Tommy was too modest to wish to intrude again, Lionel volunteered to go, and soon returned, his pockets full of gingerbeer and lemonade bottles, two more under each arm, his cap full of sandwiches, and a goodly supply of bread-and-cheese in his hands.

"Let's make a picnic of it?" suggested Charlie.

"Ah, and here come Pryce and Barnes to make up the party," added our hero. "Yo-oicks, Pryce what cheer?"

"Hullo! you've found him, then?" said the Welsh boy, as he came up in a canter.

"Yes, and now we're going to feed him. We'll have a snug little picnic in that field yonder, by the windmill. You two run to the inn, and bring some more gingerbeer and prog with you."

And in the course of another quarter of an hour they were seated beneath the shadow of the sails of the old windmill, as cosy a little party as ever attempted to ruin their digestions by mixing up new bread, strong cheese, fat bacon, and ginger-beer in their stomachs.

But as Tommy sat there, happy once again in the possession of an efficient substitute for a good meal, he little thought in what dreadful peril one short quarter of an hour would place him and his companions.

CHAPTER XXXIX.

TOMMY CLAIMS HIS REWARD, AND GETS IT—VISIONS OF APOPLEXY, AND OTHER ILLS WHICH FLESH IS HEIR TO, HAVE NO TERRORS FOR THE PLUMP YOUTH—A SHORT SLEEP AND A SPEEDY AWAKENING—TOMMY FINDS HIMSELF ELEVATED INTO A HIGHER SPHERE, BUT DECLINES PROMOTION SOLUS—UN MAUVAIS QUART D'HEURE—MOTHER EARTH ONCE MORE.

HERE, beneath the rich refreshing shade of the windmill, the party encamped, to refresh themselves after the toil of battle.

Tommy's first proceeding was to seize upon half a dozen bottles of lemonade and ginger-beer, and sitting upon five to secure them from pilfering hands, opened the sixth, and put the neck to his mouth.

For a minute or so there was a gurgling sound, intermingled with Tommy's gasps of enjoyment, and when he set the bottle down it was empty, and his plump features were radiant with happiness.

"Was it good, Tommy?" said Lionel, who was busily engaged with Charlie, Pryce, and Barnes, in demolishing the sandwiches.

But Tommy was in too blissfully thirsty a state to talk. He swallowed the contents of a second bottle of lemonade, then a third, and was twisting the wire of number four, when our hero spoke again—

"Take care what you're about, Tommy. That's awfully gassy stuff, and if you drink so much you'll burst."

"I don't care," replied Coddlings. "Oh, ain't it lovely."

As he spoke, the cork, released from the restraint of the wire, flew out with a loud "pop," and smote Drummond sharply on the bridge of the nose.

"Look at that," exclaimed Charlie, as both his eyes filled with tears, and half a sandwich pre-maturely bolted went the wrong way and nearly choked him. "Dash it, Tommy, why don't you mind what you're at?"

But Tommy was blissfully unconscious of everything in the world but lemonade, and before Charlie had wiped the water from his eyes, and taken the sting of the pain from the bridge of his nose, the plump one had emptied his fourth bottle, and unwired the fifth.

"Stop it, Tommy," said our hero. "Do you think you're made of cast iron or india rubber? You'll burst, as sure as little pigs wear curly tails."

"A promise is a promise, Li," replied Tommy, "and I did think you were a chap to keep your word. You said I should have as much ginger beer and lemonade as I could drink, and I haven't half done yet."

"All right," said our hero; "if you put it in that way, of course I'm bound to keep my promise, but let's tie you down first."

"Tie me down. What for?"

"Do you want to go to the moon?"

"No, I don't think I do."

"Well, then, let us make you fast to something, for if you fill yourself full of gas out of the leme-nade you'll float away presently, as sure as your name's Codlings."

"Let it," said Tommy. "How many bottles do you think will do it, Li?"

"How many have you had?"

"This is the fifth."

"Well, two more, or say three at the outside, and then up you go."

"Do you mean it, Li; you're such a chap for a joke."

"You won't find it a joke, Tommy, I can tell you," replied our hero. "The going up will be all very well, but you won't find the coming down so very pleasant."

"Take a few sandwiches, Tommy," said Drummond, "they'll act as ballast."

As this suggestion agreed with the plump one's views, he got to work upon a goodly heap of sandwiches and bread and cheese, but first he drank his fifth bottle of lemonade; no persuasions of our hero could induce him to relinquish that.

"Well," said Lionel, as he watched the rapid disappearance of the eatables, "I promised you a good tuck out, Tommy, and you must own that I've been as good as my word."

"I haven't had enough yet," replied Codlings; "hand over some of those seed cakes, Charlie, and I think I'll take another bottle of gingerbeer."

"Give 'em to him," said Lionel. "He shan't say that he was stinted, only who knows where the nearest doctor lives?"

"We passed a doctor's house on our way," said Pryce. "It's only a little way up the road."

"Then perhaps you won't mind going there and asking him to come in half an hour or so, and tell him to bring his stomach-pump and lancets."

"What for," demanded Tommy, looking a little alarmed. "I don't want any doctors; I'm well enough."

"If you eat another sandwich or drink another bottle of beer," replied our hero, solemnly, "you'll burst, or have a fit of apoplexy, and when the coroner's inquest is held, I don't want to be blamed for not sending for the doctor."

"What a fellow you are, Li," said Tommy Codlings. "What do you want to go frightening a chap for."

"I don't want to frighten you, only if the doctor comes in time he may be able to save your life by bleeding you and using the stomach-pump."

"You be blowed," said the incredulous Tommy. "I've eaten twice as much as this before, and never felt ill."

And without paying any further attention to our hero's remonstrances, he devoured all the available sandwiches, took a quarter of a pound of cheese or so, to aid digestion, and then "topped up" with a seventh bottle of lemonade.

"How do you feel now, Tommy?" said Lionel.

"Beautiful!" replied Tommy, as he licked his lips and looked eagerly around him. "I think I'll have a nap now."

"That's the first symptom," said Lionel.

"The first what?"

"The first sign of the apoplexy coming on," said our hero. "People always feel sleepy just before a fit. Cut off for the doctor, Pryce."

"If you bring any doctors here I shall kick 'em."

"If you do you'll have to be bled to weaken you, Tommy."

But the plump one was in such a luxurious state of drowsiness that he paid no further heed to Lionel, but curling himself up snugly on a soft piece of turf, was asleep in that impossibly short period popularly known as "less than no time."

"I say," said Charlie, "what a game it would be to give him a lift, and make him believe that the gas of the lemonade had made him into a sort of balloon."

"How could we do that?"

"Fasten him to one of the sails of the windmill, and then set it going."

"That wouldn't be a bad lark; but we mustn't let it go too far or he'll get hurt."

"We'll take care of that. There is no one about, is there?"

"I don't see anyone. It's an old affair, and looks as if it was deserted."

"Let's see, how do you set a mill going?"

"There's some kind of affair inside by which you turn the sails so as to catch the wind," said Barnes.

"There's precious little wind."

"All the better," replied our hero; "we don't want to carry Tommy too high. Come on, you fellows."

The mill was, as Lionel had said, a very old one, and had evidently not been used for a long time. Close by the spot where they had held their picnic was a mound, just beneath one of the sails, and lifting Tommy, whose slumbers were not easily disturbed, Lionel and Charlie after two or three ineffectual attempts, succeeded in hooking their victim by the slack of his breeches to a strong nail which projected from the lower portion of the sail.

"Look out," said Charlie; "he'll wake up now, and then he'll kick."

"Deuce a bit," replied our hero, with a laugh. "I think he's snoring now."

And in fact, Tommy, not in the least discomposed by the change of position, was sending forth most terrific snores from his little pug nose, the while he was suspended almost upside down.

"There never was such a chap for eating and sleeping," laughed Lionel. "Hullo, here come Barnes and Pryce out of the mill. All right?"

"Yes, we found the lever; but it's all precious dusty and rusty. I don't think the machinery will move."

"I think the wind will get up presently; those clouds out yonder seem to be scudding along pretty fast."

"It'll have to be a gale to move this rusty old affair," said Pryce. "Hullo, you've hung Tommy up."

"Yes. Hush, don't shout, he's asleep!"

"Asleep! why so he is," and Pryce burst into a fit of laughter.

"I say, he's getting red in the face too," added Barnes; "and ain't he snoring, just."

"Yes, the little beggar; that's the tune he keeps me awake with often in our dormitory, until I've shied about a peck of boots at him."

"Look out," said Lionel, suddenly. "I think I saw the sail move then."

Just at that moment there came a gust of wind full upon the sails of the mill, and yielding a little to its influence, they moved round a yard or so with a harsh creaking sound.

Either that noise or the sudden jerk awoke Tommy, his little round eyes opened with amazement and terror, and uttering a yell, he made a grab at Pryce, and seized him with both hands by the hair.

"Oh, my!" shrieked the unfortunate Welsh boy. "Let go o' me, will you? Oh, lor, he's pulling my hair out by the roots!"

Lionel and Charlie ran to his assistance, but before they could reach him, a second gust of wind more violent than the first whirled the sails still further round, and Tommy clinging with all his might to the unlucky Pryce's hair, dragged him quite off the ground.

Charlie, springing up, was just in time to catch Pryce by the legs, and the weight so added checked the upward motion of the sail.

But only for a moment. The wind was rising rapidly, and Charlie, clinging tightly to Pryce's legs, was also lifted from the ground, when Barnes caught the tails of his jacket, and held on with the tenacity popularly attributed to Death when in possession of a dead "nigger."

The agony which Pryce now suffered was of the most excruciating character.

By the hair of his head alone—a double-handful of which Tommy still clung to with a tenacious grip—he was supporting the full weight of himself Charlie, and Barnes.

Every nerve in his body seemed in process of being pulled out by the roots with his hair, and the skin of his face was stretched so tightly that it seemed ready to crack.

"Ow-ow-ow!" he shrieked. "Let go, Tommy, you brute! why don't you let go of my hair? Oh, my! Pull him off somebody. Mur-der!"

Lionel could hardly repress a laugh, for the sight was a comical one enough, but threatened to have a serious termination if Tommy's breeches did not give way before the wind had power enough to carry the sails round.

"I'm bothered if I know what to do," thought our hero. "If I hook on to the others, my weight will only drag poor Pryce's hair right out. Oh, I know, I'll get a rope and fling it over the end of the sail."

Fortunately for Lionel's purpose, there was a coil of rope close by where some workmen were repairing a small foot bridge; and seeing this, he hurried back to the mill, tying a running noose in the rope as he ran.

"Make haste—oh, make haste!" yelled poor Pryce, whose face was stretched to twice its natural length. "Oh, I can't bear it any longer: cut my head off, and let me go."

"Hold on, all of you," shouted Lionel. "We'll soon have you down. Here come some men from the other side with a ladder."

In fact, a couple of the workmen, disturbed by Pryce's yells, imbued with a fine sense of honour, ended their dinner hour by running up the slope, and displaying far more agility than when engaged in their legitimate occupation—as is the custom of wayward human nature.

Lionel arrived only just in time, for the wind was getting up—and so was the string of boys who hung suspended from the sail of the mill.

He hurled the rope lasso-wise, and at the first attempt caught the end of the sail just in the noose; then hauling with all his strength at the rope, he made it fast with what sailor's call a clove-hitch to one of the mill posts.

"Now for the ladder," said Lionel. "Make haste, my men; plant it against the sail—that's it."

"I suppose you'll stand a drop o' beer, young mister," said one of the men.

"As much as you like, only make haste, or my

'hum's hair will be pulled clean out by the roots."

That promise was all the labourers wanted. In an instant the ladder was placed in position, and one man was half way up, when suddenly Tommy's breeches, which had hitherto held out with such wonderful tenacity, gave way, and with a crash, boys, ladder, man, and all, came headlong to the ground.

Tommy gave a howl of terror, but he stuck fast to Pryce's hair, and when our hero, who had just managed to escape this human avalanche by jumping aside, returned to the rescue, Pryce had freed himself from Tommy's hold, but only at the sacrifice of a double handful of what looked like tow, but was in reality the best part of his hair.

"I shall be bald for life," moaned Pryce. "Fancy being scalped by a fat-headed duffer like Codlings. And ain't it sore! Oh my, it feels red hot."

"Never mind, Pryce," said our hero, soothingly. "If it won't grow again, you can wear a wig."

"Blow the wigs. I'd rather have my own hair."

"And think what a lot of money you'll save by not having to go to the barber's."

"Don't chaff, there's a good fellow. Does it look very bad, Wilful."

"Not at all. It's rather pretty than otherwise— and then think how cool it will be in summer time."

"I'll warm that Codlings for this," continued Pryce, with a savage air of resolution. "I can't make him fight me; but I'll pay him in another way before the week's out."

"Don't be spiteful, Pryce. Remember it was our fault; we put him up there, and it was only natural when he felt himself going up, that he should grab the first thing that came in his way."

"Oh, ah, I daresay. It's all precious fine to talk; but if he'd snatched you bald-headed, you wouldn't take it so easy."

Meanwhile, Charlie, Barnes, and the others had disentangled themselves from one another, and from the ladder, and proceeded to examine each into the nature of the injuries he had received, and also to pass, with wonderful unanimity, a vote of censure upon Tommy.

"This," said one of the labourers, who had a very bad black eye, caused by Tommy's head coming into contact with it, "is gratitood. A cove leaves his pipe, and his beer, and all his little well-arned comforts, to help a feller creetur in distress, and no sooner have he come, than that feller creetur falls right atop of him, and does his best to make a crooked cripple on him for life."

"I didn't do it on purpose," said the goaded Tommy. "What are you all pitching into me for, like this? I didn't want to fall down."

"If there's one thing I 'ates more nor an-other," said the labourer with the black eye, "it's a mean excuse. If you'd owned up to wot you did like a man, I'd have took a shillin' and a drop of beer; but now nothing less than arf-a-crownd will square me."

"And I wants eighteen-pence," added the other labourer, who had been trying very hard to find out some place where he was hurt. "I ain't a goin' to see my mate put upon for nothink."

"There's the ladder, too," continued he with the black eye, "is shook fearful, and it was almost a new 'un, barrin' a few rounds as were gone, and a splice or two in the sides. That'll hev to be paid for, say three bob, and my arf-a-crownd, makes it five and a tanner."

"And my eighteen-pence brings it up to a clean seven shillins," said labourer number two, "and say a tanner extry for beer,"

"No, we'll let him orf the beer. I was never hard on a gent—a real gent, mind you—who cashed up sharp, and didn't offer to git out of payin' wot was doo."

"But I haven't got any money," said Tommy,

beginning to feel alarmed at the resolute manner of the labourers.

"If I don't hev that thar coin in five minutes," said the one with the black eye, "I'll have you instead. Me and my mate wants a boy to mix mortar and chip bricks, and you'll just do. You're a trifle fat at present, but I'll lay as we don't over feed you."

Tommy turned cold all over, and looked appealingly at Lionel and the others, who had drawn away from him, and appeared inclined to leave him to his fate.

"I say, Li," said Tommy, "don't desert me."

"What can we do?" replied our hero. "I've spent all my money; besides, you want to go gipsying, and this is next door to it."

"Is it?" replied Tommy, "I don't think so. I'm not going about the country in a dirty smock, carrying bricks up a ladder, so there now."

"What will you do, then, Tommy? Those men who came so kindly to help you must be paid for their trouble and damage."

"Why don't Barnes, or Pryce, or Drummond pay them?—they were in the same fix. That'll be two shillings each. I'm sure to have some tin from my aunt before long."

"Pay be bothered," growled Pryce. "Who's going to pay me for my hair? I'm not going to be made bald before my time for nothing."

"It was the only thing that there was to lay hold of," said Tommy. "You'd have done the same if you'd been in my place."

"Should I? No, I shouldn't, now then. Who could lay hold of such a set of half-inch bristles as you call hair?"

"It's better than yours, anyway," retorted Tommy, reddening under the insult, and holding up the handful which he had plucked from Pryce's head. "The stuffing out of a chair would make better hair than this. It ain't fit to put on a Injun. It's oakum, that's what your hair is."

"If you say that again, Codlings, I'll give you a prop in the eye," exclaimed Pryce, smarting under the double injury of first having had his hair pulled up by the roots, and then of its being held up and reviled.

"None o' that, my young master," said the labourer with the black eye. "He belong to me, he do, and I ain't goin' to have him spiled, urless you pays the seven shillins he owes; then you an do wot you likes—eat 'un for all I cares."

"You won't catch me paying anything for him," replied Pryce; "and as for eating him, why he'd turn the stomach of a cannibal. He's all blubber!"

"I'll blubber you," exclaimed the wrathful Tommy.

And scrambling up, he literally fell upon Pryce, and commenced pummelling away with such energy that the Welsh boy had a black eye and three of his front teeth loosened before he well knew what had happened.

It would have gone hard with Tommy then had not our hero and Drummond interfered, for Pryce was much bigger and stronger, but their timely intervention saved him for awhile.

"Let me go," roared Pryce. "Let me get at him, and I'll punch him into a jelly. Dash him, look at my eye!"

"Never mind, Pryce," said Lionel, trying to soothe him.

"Oh, ah! never mind! I like that. I'm to be knocked about and have my hair pulled out, and then told to 'never mind.' Let me go, Wilful, or I'll slip into you."

"You can do that if you like," said our hero, "but don't touch Tommy. Think how he's suffered, poor chap."

Pryce was about to explode into a fresh burst of wrath at the idea of pity being wasted on Tommy, when the labourer interrupted him—

"Lookee here, young masters, how much longer are we to wait for that seven bob? Our time's wallyable—ninepence a hour's the figger, and beer and wittles extry."

"You won't get any money out of me," said Tommy. "I haven't got any."

"Then come on," said the labourer. "There's a lot o' mortar wants mixin, and you may as well work it out, while me and my mate finishes our beer and has a pipe or so."

And the man caught Tommy by the arm and jerked him a yard or two into the air.

"I won't go," roared Tommy. "Let me go. Wilful—Drummond—help!"

"You'd better go," said our hero. "Think what a healthy life it is—always in the open air, no books, no lessons, no whackings."

"Except wot I give him," growled the labourer. "I must hev a boy to whack when I ain't got my missis 'andy."

"I won't go, I tell you," yelled the unhappy Codlings, almost frantic with desperation. "You're a nice set of chums, you are, to let a bricklayer take me away and murder me perhaps."

"You must pay your debts, you know, Tommy. That's only just."

"Debts be blowed! I don't owe him anything, or if I do, I'll pay him the very next time my aunt sends me some money."

"I ain't agoin' to wait for no aunts," growled the bricklayer. "Come on."

And he began to drag Tommy away in spite of a few vigorous kicks which that young gentleman dealt him, when our hero thought it time to strike in and effect a compromise.

"Look here," he said, "if I get you off you'll have to pay me back."

"All right," replied the tearful Tommy, eagerly.

A few minutes' private and confidential conversation then passed between Lionel and the bricklayer, which resulted in the departure of that gentleman and his mate, much to the relief of Master Codlings, who owned emphatically that Lionel was a "brick."

But all was not over yet.

He had forgotten that little interview with Mr. Stiffback, which could neither be delayed nor averted, and which of a surety would result in a performance on the dreaded flogging-machine.

CHAPTER XL.

THE RETURN TO THE SCHOOL—TOMMY'S SENTENCE —PLAYING AT GIPSIES—LIONEL AND CHARLIE HOLD A CONSULTATION—SOKER IS BRIBED—THE INTERVIEW IN THE PADDOCK—TOMMY LIGHTS HIS LAMP—AND SOMETHING ELSE WHICH IS NOT SO EASILY PUT OUT.

TOMMY'S interview with Mr. Stiffback was short, but the reverse of sweet, for the worthy schoolmaster was particularly enraged by the bare idea of any boy having the audacity to run away from such an earthly Paradise as Lake House School.

"So, Codlings," he said to the unhappy culprit, "you thought you would like to be a gipsy, eh? Well, you shall have a taste of it for a week, and then, if you are still in the same mind, I'll write and ask the consent of your aunt to your joining a tribe. Soker, put a kettle and a supply of firewood and a flint and steel in the paddock. Master Codlings is going to turn gipsy. You can also give him a few yards of old tarpauling, which you will find in the lumber-room; then he can make himself a tent if it should rain."

"Am I to stay out there all night, sir," said Tommy, aghast.

"Yes, Codlings," replied Mr. Stiffback, sweetly; "and every night for a week. I have no doubt you will be charmed with the experiment."

"I'll be dashed if I shall," thought Tommy. "Oh, lor, every night for a week; and it's quite a lonely place!"

"You will also provide Master Codlings with a loaf of stale bread; there is plenty of water in the lake."

"Is that all I am to have to eat, sir?" faltered Tommy.

"That depends upon yourself, Codlings," replied Mr. Stiffback. "Gipsies generally forage for themselves, you know. I believe that they occasionally plunder hen-roosts, or steal ducks, or poach a little."

"But if you please, sir, you wouldn't like me to steal your hens?"

"If I caught you doing such a thing, Codlings," said the schoolmaster, amiably, "I would give you the choice of being prosecuted at the sessions, or of taking six dozen in the flogging-machine; but gipsies disregard the law, I am informed, and risk the chances of punishment. You can do the same, if you like."

"Likely that," thought Tommy, in a cold perspiration at the bare idea of making a foray upon Mr. Stiffback's preserves. "I would as soon try to break into the Tower and steal the Crown jewels. Dash it, what an unlucky chap I am!"

Such were also the opinions of our hero and Charlie, and they tried hard to think of some plan whereby a mitigation of Tommy's hardships might be effected.

"How the dickens will he get on at night?" said Lionel. "He don't know how to rig up a tent."

"No, especially with such bits of tarpauling as old Soker will give him," added Charlie. "Suppose we give him a lift."

"Stiffback won't let us."

"We needn't ask his leave."

"But how are we to get out? It's a deuce of a place for bolts and bars."

"We'll ask Vansittart. He's up to all the dodges of the place."

Vansittart was accordingly consulted, but he shook his head at the proposal.

"If you take my advice, young Wilful,' he said, "you'll leave Codlings alone. Stiffback is dreadfully riled on account of the tricks that have been played him lately, and he's sure to be down heavily on you fellows, if you come between him and Codlings."

"I'll chance that," said Lionel. "I don't like leaving a chum in the lurch."

"And I wouldn't advise you to do it either; but it's next to impossible to get out of the house after it's locked up for the night; and, besides, I don't see how you could help Codlings if you did go to him."

"We could take him some grub, and a candle and some matches, to make things a little more cheerful."

"Better let it alone, I tell you. If there was a reasonable chance of your being able to get to him without being dropped on, I'd help you myself, but there isn't, unless you can get Soker on your side."

"That'll be the plan," said Lionel. "We'll bribe him. I've got a little money left."

"If you haven't enough, ask me, and I'll lend it you."

"Thanks, no; I never borrow if I can help it."

"And I never lend if I can help it, especially to a fellow I like, for it's pretty sure to lead to unpleasantness in the end," said Vansittart, with a laugh.

Soker was then sought out, and caught just as he was on his way to the paddock with a bundle of dusty rags and bits of tarpauling, and after extorting a bribe, which nearly exhausted the contents of Lionel's pocket, he consented to add to Tommy's comforts to the extent of furnishing him with a light and something better to eat and drink than dry bread and water.

"It's quite a load off my mind, now that's done,"

said our hero. "As long as Tommy has something good to eat he's happy—that's one consolation."

"He's an awfully nervous chap, though," said Charlie. "He'll be in a blue funk all night about ghosts, or something of that sort."

"He'll keep his light burning," added Lionel. "I hope Soker will give him a whole candle."

"He ought to. How much coin did you give him?"

"Five shillings, pretty nearly all I've got."

"Well, you can soon get some more, for I've quite a little bank left, and so would you if you hadn't been so liberal. By-the-by, have you seen anything of that girl since—the one you gave your money to?"

"Shut up about that girl," said Lionel, turning red at the recollection, "and if you're wise you'll get your Euclid prepared, and won't bother about what don't concern you."

Charlie winked, but said no more.

He knew his chum too well to venture to urge a subject which was distasteful to him.

Meanwhile Soker had marched off with his bed to the paddock, where, seated in the centre, the monarch of all he surveyed, Tommy was looking the very picture of misery.

"Never, in all my born days," said Soker, as he paused at the gate, "did I come acrost a young gent as took things so contrairy as you do, Master Codlings."

"And enough to make me, ain't it?" said Tommy. "If you'd gone through what I have to-day you'd feel miserable too. See how sore I am; there isn't a place as big as a pin's head about me that hasn't a bruise on it."

"Wot's bruises to freedom?" said Soker, carrying his head aloft with the air of an Arab of the desert. "Here's a tent, lots o' 'olesome grub, the blue sky above (leastways, when it ain't cloudy); and no-think to do but to—to think."

"Blow thinking!" retorted Tommy, savagely. "Who wants to think? I've got nothing to think about."

"And wot a blessin' that be," said Soker, con-templatively. "No rates, no taxes, no butcher's and baker's bills—not even the landlord to think on. Ah! it's a blessed thing to be a boy."

"Is it?" replied Tommy, bitterly. "I'd rather be a winkle, or an oyster, lying quietly in a shell right away under the sea."

"Now there's taste," said Soker, as he flung down the bundle of tarpauling with an air of dis-gust. "Here's a boy—a live boy—who may yet grow up to be a blessin' to his parients—a boy with a undeweloped relish for skittles and whisky—and he acterally wants to be a winkle, a thing as is picked out with a pin, and swallered. If I'd hev knowed as your tastes was so low," continued Soker, with emphasis, "blow me if I'd a brought yer these here hextry luxuries."

And untying the bundle, Soker produced from the interior a small lamp, a tin can, which gave forth the peculiar odour of paraffin, a loaf, part of a German sausage, a piece of something that looked like cat's-meat, but which Soker declared to be the "best cold round," a slice of cheese, a box of matches, and a stone jug of beer.

"Now," said Soker, as he pointed to these deli-cacies, "now do you wish you wos a winkle?"

"You're a brick," said Tommy, reaching after the sausage. "I'll give you a handsome tip at the end of the 'half.'"

"I'd rayther hev it now," replied Soker. "You young gents gen'rally gets to the end o' your money by the time you gets to the end o' the half."

"I won't forget you, Soker—I won't indeed," said Tommy, already half-way through the sausage, and glancing with a speculative eye upon the cheese and beef.

"I hopes you won't, Master Codlins," said

Soker. "The price o' pervishons is rose fearful; that meat costes thruppence a pound and find your own sticks, and the ile is of the first quality, so be careful o' the lamp."

"So this is gipsying, is it? thought Tommy when Soker had departed and allowed him to conclude his meal in peace. "Well, it isn't half so bad if Soker only brings me grub all the week. I wish I'd asked him to put up the tent for me, and I could have had a nap in it."

Tommy looked helplessly at the tarpauling and the sticks which Soker had brought, but as he had not the faintest idea of how to rig a tent, he let the materials lay where Soker had dragged them, and used them as a pillow.

After a refreshing nap of an hour or so, Tommy awoke and had some more bread and beef, then another nap, and so on alternately, until it grew dark.

Then came the question of lighting the lamp. Tommy knew as much about lamps, paraffin or otherwise, as a First Lord of the Admiralty knows of the art of navigation; but he tried even as the First Lord tries, and with the same result—disastrous failure.

Firstly, he screwed the top of the lamp off after a desperate effort to unscrew it the wrong way, and when he had done that, he sat down on the glass chimney, and ruined that for ever.

"Bust it!" exclaimed Tommy, as he arose with a short howl, and felt tenderly for the pieces of glass. "There's the lamp done for now; how the dickens am I to get a light."

CHAPTER XLI.

THE FIRE, AND HOW IT WAS PUT OUT—AND SEVERAL OTHER PEOPLE BESIDES—THE COURSE OF THIS VERACIOUS HISTORY IS DIVERTED TO-WARDS SAM SCARECROW—TREATS OF THAT YOUTH'S FIRST LOVE ADVENTURE, AND THE ARTFUL MEANS WHEREBY HE OBTAINED AN INTERVIEW WITH THE FAIR LADY OF HIS AFFECTIONS.

NECESSITY, says the proverb, is the mother of invention, but in Codlings' case she could at best have been only a step-mother, and a bad one at that—the inventions she sug-gested to him were such poor and meagre things.

In the present instance Necessity prompted Tommy to use the tin can which held the paraffin itself for a lamp, and accordingly he transferred the neck from the lamp to the can, fastened it in with a wedge of wood, and got the matches ready.

"It'll make a prime lamp," he thought. "There's no chimney to it, but it'll burn well enough if I keep it sheltered behind the tar-pauling."

But Tommy had reckoned without taking into account his usual ill-fortune. Just as he struck the match and applied it to the wick, the wind which had been seemingly lying in wait round a corner, caught the end of the tarpauling, flopped it against the can and upset it.

In an instant a stream of blazing paraffin ran along the ground, and catching the dry canvas and tar-pauling, set them on fire.

Tommy had only just time to gasp "Oh, lor!" when a long tongue of flame, urged by the wind, curled itself around his legs, and made him jump with a liveliness that a kangaroo might have envied.

He had some faint idea for a moment of putting the fire out, and to that end took the cork out of the stone jar and sacrificed what was left of his beer.

But beyond a faint hiss and splutter the sacrifice produced no effect at all, and the flames leaped high into the air, as if dancing with glee at Tommy's dismay.

"They'll see it up at the school," thought the unlucky Tommy, "and then shan't I catch it. Oh, dash this wind, it's flaring the fire into the wood stack."

In fact the wind had suddenly increased to a little gale, and showers of sparks were now being driven in the direction of a large stack of brushwood, which the heat of the sun had made as inflammable as tinder.

Tommy ran frantically in that direction, but before he could reach it, long jets of flame had broken out in a dozen places, and in another five minutes the whole Metropolitan Fire Brigade could not have saved it, while from the school-house there now arose the alarm cry—

"Fire! Fire!"

Our readers will readily believe that a gentle man of Mr. Stiffback's inventive capacity had not suffered the claims of so important a machine as the fire-engine to escape his notice.

In fact there were no less than three of Mr. Stiffback's invention; but the first was of so powerful a nature that the jet of water it threw knocked down and utterly demolished everything with which it came in contact, and was in fact rather more dangerous and destructive than the fire itself.

Number two was ingeniously constructed to throw sixteen jets in every direction at once, but unless it was possible to plant the engine in the very middle of the fire, ten out of the sixteen jets inundated the bystanders, and put them out a great deal more effectually than the fire.

Number three was of the ordinary kind, to which the schoolmaster had only added as yet a few extra valves, which rendered it a matter of pleasing uncertainty for the first quarter of an hour whether the engine would work or burst.

The boys were regularly exercised in the fire-engine drill, and fine fun they thought it, but never before within the recollection of any of them had a case of genuine conflagration occurred, so that when the red glare of the flames in the direction of the paddock and the alarm cry of "Fire! Fire!" was raised, the excitement was immense, and just fourteen times as many volunteers as were necessary rushed to the shed where the engines were kept, while Vansittart, our hero, and the other leaders of the school tried in vain to establish order amongst them.

Mr. Stiffback was almost paralytic with rage and indignation, and when Soker rushed into him with the alarming intelligence, he seized him by the collar and shook him until he had a bad toothache.

"Wot's that for?" growled Soker. "Wot do you want to go shakin' a man's ed orf like that for, sir?"

"What do you mean by coming to me with such a cock and bull story?"

"I never said nothing about no cocks, nor yet about no bulls," retorted Soker. "I sed the paddock was a fire—and so it is. Look out o' windy, sir, if you don't believe me."

One glance was enough—the red glare above the tree tops, and the shouts of the boys, told the tale only too well.

"It's that—that Codlings again," groaned Mr. Stiffback.

"That's about it, sir," said Soker. "Reg'lar bad boy that, sir."

"He is," replied Mr. Stiffback, mournfully. "My hair is turning grey before its time because of him, Soker."

"Yes, sir."

"Do you think that there is any chance of Codlings—you know," and Mr. Stiffback winked a wink of awful meaning.

"Of his havin' caught afire you mean, sir," said Soker. "Well, it ain't unlikely. He was werry fat, and would catch alight as easy as drippin'."

"We must go and see," continued the schoolmaster. "I should be dreadfully sorry you know, Soker, if anything happened to the boy, but if he *will* set himself on fire it's not my fault."

"Nor mine, sir."

"Certainly not, Soker. There is no one to blame but himself," added Mr. Stiffback, almost cheerfully; "but really, it will be a happy release. Only think of such a boy growing up. What mischief would he not work on the world."

By the time this brief colloquy was at an end, the schoolmaster and his aide-de-camp had reached the fire-engine shed, whence all the engines had already been dragged by the enthusiastic scholars, and were now in process of being shoved and dragged towards the fire.

"Come on, Soker," said Mr. Stiffback, who was in a state of feverish excitement. "Run, man—faster—a little exercise will do you good."

"Oh, ah; so would a little summat else as I knows on," growled Soker, in an undertone; "but I ain't likely to get it."

"What do you say, Soker?" asked Mr. Stiffback, suspiciously.

"Only that I ain't quite ekal to wot I wos, sir. When you cuts orf a man's whiskey, you cuts orf his wital powers."

"Nonsense—nonsense."

"Oh, ah, it's all wery well to say 'nonsense', retorted Soker; "but I knows as my 'staminerer' is reduced, and I must take my hexercise accordin'."

With which remark he slackened his pace to a walk, leaving Mr. Stiffback to canter onto the scene of the fire, where, of course, the very first figure he encountered was that of Tommy himself.

"What!" exclaimed Stiffback. "Is that you, Codlings?"

"Yes, sir," replied Tommy slowly, as he looked at the schoolmaster with a doubtful eye.

"You are not burnt then, Codlings?" he continued in a tone of sorrowful anxiety.

"No, sir; that is, not much, sir—only just a little on my—just here, sir."

"You're not hurt internally, are you, Codlings? Not at all likely to be laid up in bed for a month or so?"

"Oh, dear no, sir," replied Tommy, cheerfully, and wondering why on earth the master did not tackle him about the fire.

"Only burnt a little behind, eh?" said Mr. Stiffback, in a tone of bitter resignation. "Show me the place, Codlings."

Tommy unsuspiciously turned and stooped. On the instant Mr. Stiffback moistened the palm of his hand, and brought it down with a tremendous smack, that was heard above the crackling of the flames and the clank of the engines.

"Take that for disappointing me," said Mr. Stiffback. "Now, Soker, take him back to the school and lock him up; he shall have two dozen on the flogging machine to-morrow."

"Oh, mercy!" gasped Tommy, faintly. "Two dozen, oh, it's awful, and you've just broken the blister."

"There'll be another one to break by to-morrow," said Mr. Stiffback. "Take him away, Soker. Don't let him have a light on any account."

"He shan't have so much as a used up lucifer."

And gripping the unlucky Tommy by the nape of the neck, Soker hurried him away, fearful lest the culprit should let out something respecting the can of paraffin and the matches—while the schoolmaster devoted his energies to extinguishing the blazing remnant of the wood pile; but by the time the engine was got into working order, the flames had exhausted themselves, and there was no longer anything but smouldering ashes on which to pump.

Then, in a temper the reverse of angelic, Mr. Stiffback ordered the boys back to the school, and instead of some reward for their exertions, they, to their intense surprise, received what they termed a "jolly rowing," for having come out at all without authority.

"There's gratitude," said Charlie Drummond. "I thought, at the very least, he would have let us stop up an hour later, and given us something extra for supper. I've been working like a nigger."

"So have I, and I am just thirsty too," said Lionel.

"And so you'll have to stop," added Charlie. "He might have served us out an extra glass of beer apiece—they always do in London when the fellows work at a fire. I've seen it."

But grumbling was of little use. Mr. Stiffback was out of temper, and they had to bear the brunt of it. The water jugs suffered severely though, and there was a scant supply of the pure element the next morning for the necessary ablutions of the boys.

But here we must pause, and turn our attention from the doings of our hero and his chums, to those of an individual, whom for some time we have sadly neglected—meaning our, and we trust our readers' old friend, Sam Scarecrow.

During the past few weeks a great change had come over that young gentleman, and a keen observer, if he had been so minded, would have remarked that the change took place simultaneously with the departure of Mary, the pretty housemaid, from Lake Island.

She had left in consequence of a disagreement with the cook, relative to the attentions paid by the butler to her superior charms, and no sooner was she gone than Sam discovered that he was hopelessly in love.

Our readers, remembering the little peculiarities of Sam's face and figure, may perhaps wonder at the audacity of the long youth indulging in the tender passion, and above all, that any fair one should return his affection. But love is proverbially blind. Titania, the beautiful Queen of the Fairies, fell madly in love with Bottom when decorated with an ass's head, and Venus herself, the Goddess of Love and Beauty, married lame, sooty, horny-handed Vulcan.

Sam knew that he squinted as it is given to very few mortals here below to squint; he knew that his hair was of the "fiery and untamed" species, and that not one of his limbs matched its fellow; but in course of time he had come to regard himself as a rather choice rarity—good-looking men were comparatively common—but where was it possible to find another so wonderfully ugly as himself?

"Besides," said Sam, as he busily employed himself in the vain endeavour to smooth his obdurate locks with a warm flat iron—"besides, 'tain't always the looks as a gal cares about, it's manners wot does it."

And before the broken looking-glass, Sam rehearsed a particularly killing kind of strut, accompanied by a leer which he hoped would do immense execution.

"I wonder, now," continued Sam, caressing gently the one solitary hair which was the representative of the moustache which he hoped one day would adorn his upper lip—"I wonder, now, wot Mister Lionel would think of this here little game? I orter tell him, I know, but I dursent. No, fust I'll win her, and then I'll come like the coves I've seen in the pictur, and harm in harm with Mary, we'll kneel afore him and ax his blessin'."

Touched by the affecting scene thus conjured up by his imagination, Sam grinned harder than ever, and leered and squinted so frightfully, that the very looking-glass tumbled off its nail, and shivered into a dozen fragments on the ground.

"Blow it! and I hadn't practised that last fancy smile yet," said Sam, disconsolately. "But, lor, it don't matter; I think she loves me. When she woz larst in the kitching, she chucked the lid of a biler at me, and whacked me on the 'ed with a broom handle, and a gal don't do that unless she means somethink."

Perfectly convinced of the affection of his lady love, Sam picked up the broken looking-glass as well as he could, and proceeded with the adornment of his person, for that night he was bound upon an expedition to the house of Mr. Growlagain, in whose service Mary now was.

Sam had donned the smartest suit of demi-livery that he possessed; but, alas, the tailor's art was hopelessly employed in the effort to conceal the angularity of Sam's figure. He was flat where he should have been round, and round where he should have been flat, and such an extensive assortment of knobs no mortal youth probably ever before possessed.

But happily unconscious of this, the lanky youth completed his toilette, provided himself with a couple of aprons, to prevent his clothes from being soiled by contact with the boat, sprinkled himself liberally with a sixpenny bottle of scent, and so departed.

The youthful galley slaves who ferried him over the lake were plentiful with the chaff they bestowed upon Sam, but the lanky youth, happy in the prospect of the bliss which awaited him, cared not, and smiled away, as Sam Weller says, like clockwork.

Owing to the suspicious nature of Mr. Growlagain, Sam had to make his entrance in an uncomfortable manner, climbing over two fences, then a row of spikes, and finally through a back window, all of which processes had a more or less damaging effect upon his gorgeous attire.

After the usual manner of the coquettish portion of the fair sex, Mary affected to be anything but delighted at the appearance of her lover, and gave him what may be termed a reception of thirty-two degrees Fahrenheit—that is, freezing.

"Now, wot's the matter?" said the injured Sam, as he tried to rub out the smart of a slap which he had received in lieu of a kiss. "Ain't I dressed well enough?"

"No, you ain't, now then. You look all hind side before, and how you do smell. Why, you've been upsetting the paraffin over you!"

"Paraffin!" exclaimed Sam, "and I paid sixpence for a bottle on it, at the 'air-dresser's—hextrack of millyflowers, he said it was."

"Then Milly Flowers must be a nice creetur, that's all I can say," retorted Mary; "p'r'aps you'll tell me what you've come botherin' here for."

Here was a facer for Sam! He had been thinking of nothing else, dreaming of nothing else, ever since the appointment was made, and now he was coolly asked why he had "come bothering!" Oh, woman, woman, verily thy name is vanity and vexation of spirit.

"Eh?" said Sam; "what—me. Mary, don't you recollect?"

"Recollect what?" retorted Mary, pettishly.

"Why, this is Toosday, ain't it?"

"Well, what if it is."

"Oh, blow me!" ejaculated Sam, clutching at his hair, and spoiling the symmetry of a parting which it had taken half an hour and a flat-iron to accomplish. "Oh, Mary, you'll drive me to construction. Where's the pison?"

And Sam rushed towards the scullery, and madly seizing a blacking bottle, prepared to imbibe the deadly contents, when Mary, with one well directed blow, knocked the bottle out of his hand, with a second gave Sam a sound box on the ear, and then sinking back into a chair began to cry.

As soon as Sam recovered from the dizziness produced by the blow he had received, he fell upon his knees at Mary's feet, and calling himself all the hard names he could think of, offered to jump out of a fourth story window, or commit suicide in the back yard with a carving knife.

Finding that these liberal promises produced no effect, Sam did what he ought to have done at first, and drew from his pocket a brooch he had bought for a present.

Mary's sobs instantly became less violent, and after looking at the ornament a little while out of the corners of her eyes, and finding it satisfactory, she let fall her apron, snatched the brooch away, and gave Sam a conciliatory slap, which made his eyes water with mingled pain and satisfaction.

For nearly two hours this blissful state of things continued, and Sam was nearly red-hot with slaps and happiness, when Mary happened to glance at the clock, and started up with a little scream.

"Wot is it?" said Sam—"a black-beadle. Where is it? I'll settle him!"

"No, stupid! Look at the time—it's nigh on nine o'clock, and master 'll be home directly."

"And wot o' that? He don't make love to you, do he, Mary?"

"He, indeed! I should like to catch him at it," said Mary, with a great show of indignation.

"So should I," added Sam, as he doubled up one bony fist in a highly suggestive manner.

"You'd better go now, Sam," continued Mary, "for when master comes home from the club, he's always tipsy and afeard of burglars, and he marches all over the house with a cutlash in one hand and a pistol in the other, and if he saw you he might——"

"No fear," said Sam; "I'd take two like him. But can't you hide me up somewheres, Mary? It's too early to go yet."

"No, Sam, there's no telling into what place he might poke his nose. Most likely he'd pitch on the very one where you was hid."

"I'm not agoin' yet," said Sam, "that's flat, Mary."

"Oh! do, Sam. I should lose my place, and—and my character too, if you was found here by master."

"I say, Mary," said Sam, "didn't you say as he wos timid like, and afeard o' burglars and sich, when he wos tipsy?"

"Dreadful timid," said Mary in assent. "Worse than any of us girls."

"Then I'll tell you wot—we'll give him a start that'll keep him outside the door for a hour or two."

"What do you mean, Sam?"

"You'll see," replied the lanky youth.

CHAPTER XLII.

IN WHICH SAM SCARECROW'S LITTLE JOKE IS BROUGHT TO A TERMINATION, TO THE SATISFACTION OF EVERY ONE BUT MR. GROWLAGAIN.

MR. GROWLAGAIN, wending his way homeward from the snug club-room of the Black Bull and Periwinkle, about half an hour after the conversation recorded in our last chapter had taken place, seemed said to be in that stage of inebriety which is popularly known as the "cantankerous."

Wine, which according to Iago is "a good familiar creature," or its equivalent brandy and water, never had the effect of making Mr. Growlagain's heart merry; on the contrary, the more he drank the harder, instead of softer, he became, the louder in his arguments, the more combative in his gestures; so that the timid members stole away when Mr. Growlagain had reached his sixth tumbler, and the boldest dared not call his soul his own after the tenth had been called for, and brought pallid waiter with shaky knees.

Mr. Growlagain had been in particularly good form that evening—he had even demolished the chairman, a stolid old farmer, who was so deaf that it was popularly believed to be beyond the power of mortal man to make him hear.

Mr. Growlagain had done it, though, that evening. After victoriously crushing all the members, he procured an old speaking-trumpet, which had been hanging up for years in the bar-parlour, and placing the tube close against the chairman's ear, he roared out such a volley of abusive epithets that the poor old man turned pale, bit off and swallowed about a foot of his "churchwarden," and finally backed out of the room, at least six tumblers short of his usual allowance.

"I made him hear," murmured Mr. Growlagain, pausing a moment to pick up his hat, which had in some unaccountable way transferred itself from his head into the middle of the road. "Request me to resign, will they? I don't think they'll try to do that again. 'Gentlemen,' says I, 'what mean and paltry hound has dared to move such a resolution? I acknowledge, gentlemen,' I went on, 'that you have a right, by the rules of the club, to make the request, but by the lord Harry, gentlemen,' says I, 'banging my fist down in a way that made 'em all jump, 'I here solemnly swear to skin alive the proposer and seconder of the resolution, and every rascally blackguard who dares to vote for it. That settled 'em. They know I'm a man of my word, and what I say I'll do. Con—found it, what'sh matter with lamp-post."

For about the fourteenth time, Mr. Growlagain came into violent collision with one of those blessings of modern civilization, and, losing his balance, he sat down with considerable emphasis on the paving-stones.

There was a policeman on the other side of the way, and he, not recognising the person of the redoubtable Mr. Growlagain, smelt out a case, and pounced upon him and dragged him up.

"Now then, none o' this. You get along home sharp, or I'll run you in."

Just then the light of the lamp shone full upon the schoolmaster's features.

The policeman recognised him, and trembled in his bluchers.

"Beg your pardon, sir," he said, humbly. "Didn't know it was you, sir. Little accident, sir."

"And thish," said Mr. Growlagain, swaying unsteadily to and fro, "thish is fame. For forty yearsh have I toil for feller man, and hersh a bobby—a low bluebottle—a peeler—who don't know me. It'sh heart-breakin'."

"Beg your pardon, sir, know you quite well—Mr. Growlagain."

"It'sh my 'pinion," returned the schoolmaster, slowly, "that you're drunk."

"Oh! no, sir, I ain't, indeed," said the constable, in no small terror, for he knew that a word from Mr. Growlagain would cause him to be dismissed the force.

"I can shmell," said the schoolmaster, thickly, "I can shmell branny-an'-warrer quite shtrong."

Which was very likely, for Mr. Growlagain himself was as nearly saturated with that cheerful beverage as anything out of an anatomical museum could well be.

"I haven't had a blessed drop of anything all day, sir," said the man, fervently.

"I inshish 'pon your walking to my 'oushe. Cashe hold my arm, and I see if you walksh straight."

So, leaning heavily upon the policeman, whose whole strength was needed to support the weight, Mr. Growlagain lurched along, delivering meanwhile a fervent, but rather rambling address upon the evils of intoxication.

HE FELT THAT IT WAS DECIDEDLY UNCOMFORTABLE TO PLAY BLIND MAN'S BUFF AMONG A CROWD OF HALF-MADDENED CURS.

No. 26.

The distance was not great, but by the time the house was reached, the unlucky policeman was wet through with perspiration, and trembling from head to foot with exertion.

"Pleeshman," said Mr. Growlagain, propping himself up against one of the pillars, "I come to 'clusion that you're not so very drunk after all, and so I'll let you off thish time, but don't do it again. Whatsh marrer with th' man?"

Mr. Growlagain might well ask what was the matter, for the constable, his knees knocking together, his face ashy pale, and his eyes standing out like hat-pegs, was staring horror-stricken at the door.

"Oh! oh!" he gasped. "Look at the knocker."

And turning, he fled away down the street at the top of his speed, in company with a couple of cats, whose amatory proceedings in the area had been disturbed.

Mr. Growlagain, still holding on by the pillar, slowly turned, and then almost fell backwards with sheer fright.

He felt a cold chill pass suddenly throughout his frame, as if he had been an ornament iced for an evening party, while the hair of his head slowly erected itself and stiffened until the "quills of the fretful porcupine" would have seemed thistle down by comparison.

And no wonder, for in place of the lion's head which for so many years had assaulted the door, obedient to the fingers of the knockers, there now glared at him a horrible, fiendish face, full three sizes larger than his own, which is saying a great deal—a face with huge fiery eyes, a set of teeth that would have done credit to the wildest lion of the most desolate desert, and a pair of jaws that snapped and smiled at him in a dreadfully suggestive manner.

What with fear and brandy-and-water, Mr. Growlagain was much too far gone to attempt flight.

He could only stare, and shiver, and gasp, wondering whether it was not a dreadful dream, or a still more dreadful reality.

Oh!" he murmured at last, "what that confounded doctor said has come true at last, and I've got an attack of delirium tremens. Oh! it's awful. If anyone would only take me away, I'd pay him five pounds."

Here the jaws of the fiendish face were moved again, and a deep, sepulchral voice seemed to issue from between them.

"Growlagain."

"Oh! lord, yes—that's me."

"How much money have you got?"

"I—I don't know," moaned the schoolmaster.

"Turn your pockets out," said the voice of the demon, which, by the way, was remarkably like that of Sam Scarecrow. "Every copper, mind; no larks with me, or you're done for."

Mr. Growlagain, far too tipsy and frightened to reason upon the improbability of a demon requiring its victim to part with current coin of the realm, fumbled in his pockets, and finally produced two bank-notes, a respectable little heap of gold, and a handful of silver and copper.

"Put it down on the doorstep," said the demon-voice.

Mr. Growlagain obeyed, and put himself down on the doorstep as well, and so effectually that he did not seem very likely to get up again for a while.

"Now," continued the demon, "take a walk, and mind you don't come back this way till midnight; if you do, there's forty more, all uglier than me, waiting to frighten you into fits."

"Oh, lord!" gasped Mr. Growlagain.

And without attempting to get upon his feet, he scrambled off on all fours, and never stopped until he ran his head against a dead wall, and sank flat down, exhausted from the combined effects of brandy and water, fear, and fatigue.

No sooner was he at a safe distance, than the door gently opened, and the well-known face and figure of Sam Scarecrow emerged and gave a low whistle, first, though, carefully picking up the money, and transferring it to his pocket.

At the signal, there descended from the lamp-post a small, sharp-featured boy, who held a string, the other end of which was attached to the lower jaws of the mask which Sam had ingeniously affixed to the knocker.

"You did that werry well, Tony," said the lanky youth, approvingly, "only you might ha' worked the string a bit sharper, Tony."

"I was afraid of somethin' givin' way and spilin' the lark," replied Tony. "But, my eye! weren't he in a stew!"

"Just," chuckled Sam. "There's the bob I promised you, and mind you keep your mouth shut, and Mary and me'll be friends o' yourn."

"I'm fly," replied Tony, who filled the post of odd-boy at Mr. Growlagain's establishment. "Thankee for the bob, but I would have helped for nothink to serve him out. He's allus a luggin' my years and kickin' me for nothink."

"Right you are, Tony," said Sam. "Now mind you keep watch outside, and give me the orfice if you see him coming back."

And Sam, more ardently in love than ever, because of the forced delay he had experienced, returned to bliss and Mary.

CHAPTER XLIII.

SAM'S RETURN—THE CONFESSION—BATHING DAY.
—TOMMY GETS A SITUATION AS WET NURSE,
AND GOES IN FOR THE SCRUBBING-BRUSH LINE
OF BUSINESS—A CATASTROPHE—"I'M AFLOAT,
I'M AFLOAT!"

THE money with which Mr. Growlagain, under the influence of his fears, had presented the demon, amounted to a little more than twenty pounds; and that sum, neatly wrapped in paper, Sam forwarded to a local charity which the schoolmaster particularly abominated, with the compliments of F. Growlagain, Esq.

His wrath at this may be imagined, for he had caught one of the largest-sized colds through going to sleep up against the wall, a bran-new suit of clothes was spoiled for ever, and now he had the mortification of seeing his name printed in "large caps" in the Deliverham Chronicle, as the generous donor of twenty pounds to the "Asylum for the Widows and Orphans of Indigent Cats'-meat Men."

Of course, when he became sober, Mr. Growlagain was perfectly certain that some one had played a trick upon him, but then who could it have been?

"It was too late," he thought, "for any of Stiffback's boys to be in the town, and I'll swear that none of mine would so much as dare to think of playing a practical joke on me. Could that policeman have been in it?"

To settle the doubt, Mr. Growlagain sent for the man; but he was still almost as much terrified as he had been the previous night, and his alarm was so evidently genuine, that even Mr. Growlagain, suspicious as he was, could not think him guilty.

But what riled him more than anything was the silence he himself was obliged to keep respecting the matter.

To make public inquiry would be infallibly to expose his own little weaknesses, and that was not to be thought of.

So Sam returned to Lake House School doubly victorious, for he had gained an avowal of love from Mary, and he had achieved a victory over the rival schoolmaster, the latter of which achievements he was not long in communicating to his young master.

"Bravo, Sam," said our hero, giving him a

friendly tap on the shoulder which made him reel again. "I owe that old Growlagain a tremendous grudge, and you've helped to pay it off. But how did you happen to be in the house?"

"Well, you see, Master Lionel," said Sam, turning scarlet until his complexion well nigh matched his hair, and squinting horribly in his endeavours to look unconcerned. "I—that is—me—and—and another party as lives close by—so you see, Master Lionel, that's how it was."

"I'm bothered if I do," laughed Lionel. "But how's this, Sam?—why, you're blushing! Oh! Sam, Sam, don't tell me that you're spooney!"

"Me, Master Lionel?" stammered Sam, turning redder than ever.

"Yes, you. I see it all now. I know why you've been buying those new neckties, and why you've smelt like a hairdresser's shop with all the bottles broken, for the last fortnight. Oh, Sam! I did'nt think it was in you."

"I'm wery sorry, Master Lionel," faltered Sam.

"Whose the girl, Sam? Which is the happy maiden?"

"You remembers Mary, as was parl'ur-maid here awhile ago?"

"I remember her. A pretty girl with black eyes and hair, and a nice little mouth that seemed made for kissing."

"That's her!" said Sam, licking his lips with a rapturous remembrance of having tasted Mary's the previous evening.

"And when are you going to be married, Sam?"

"Oh, we haven't got as far as that yet, Master Lionel.

"All right, Sam; when you do let me know, and send me some cake. But you're wanted down at the boat house. This is bathing-day."

And away Sam went, chuckling, while our hero returned to the class-room to get up his lessons for the next day, and pass his exam., before getting permission to bathe.

On taking his place in the class-room, Lionel, as usual, cast his eyes round to see who was there, and, to use somewhat of a bull, who was not.

His eyes fell upon Tommy Codlings first, and then went no further in their search.

Edging his way up behind the unfortunate one, he said—

"What on earth is the matter, Tommy? Look out, or you'll have Stiffback on to you directly."

Tommy replied, if reply it could be called, with a wriggle and something very like a snort.

Our hero, feeling that he could not wait for the answer to his question, passed on to his seat, but turned his eyes back again in the direction of Tommy Codlings, and saw that that worthy was in the same state of agonised suspense that had first attracted his attention.

Feeling certain that it would be useless to attempt to save Tommy from the consequences of whatever scrape he had now got into, Lionel bent all his attention onto the tasks of the day.

Mr. Stiffback had already enthroned himself, and was smiling benignantly at his assembled pupils.

He was just making up his mind as to whom he should pounce on first, and was merely hesitating between Lionel and Vansittart, when a sharp crack was heard, and Mr. Stiffback, in a most undignified manner, clapped his hand to his nose and gave vent to something which can hardly be called by any other name than a howl.

Turning alternately white and purple with wrath, the irate schoolmaster almost shrieked out—

"Who did that? Who was it that dared to strike me on the nose?"

There was no answer—but none was needed.

Poor Tommy Codlings stood self-convicted.

The beads of perspiration stood on his brow like the dewdrops which Dr. Kenealy shook from his lion brow in the face of the Commons of England.

Mr. Stiffback's keen eye signalled out the delinquent in a twinkling.

"Codlings, come here."

Poor Tommy, with a peculiar sidelong shuffle, made his way up to the rostrum.

"What in the world is the matter with him?" said Lionel to his next neighbour. "I never saw Tommy walk like that before."

"Hanged if I know," was the reply. "He looks as if he'd got a red-hot poker in his breeches pocket."

"By jove! so he does," replied Lionel.

But all further talking was stopped by the excitement of the scene now being enacted.

Tommy, having edged his way up to Mr. Stiffback's throne, now stood there the cynosure of all the eyes in the class-room.

And a pitiable object he looked.

Mr. Stiffback, in a voice of thunderous depth, said—

"Pick up the pellet which you aimed at my nose, Codlings."

"Please, sir, it isn't a pellet; it was only one of my blessed buttons, which took it into its head to bust itself off into your face," replied Tommy, in a voice in which indignation struggled for the mastery with the apprehension of punishment to follow.

"Then pick up the button, Codlings, and do not answer me in that tone of levity," said Mr. Stiffback, who was gradually recovering his dignity as his nose ceased to smart.

Rolling his eyes round until they seemed on the point of starting from his fat cheeks, poor Tommy at last espied the offending button lying on the floor beneath Mr. Stiffback's seat.

With a venomous grin he lurched forward to pick it up.

As he did so a stream of water, not of the cleanest description, appeared to arise from the ground, which said stream of water seemed to have no other purpose than to lodge itself on the schoolmaster's broad white-bosomed shirt; and it must be said that it succeeded most perfectly in its object, for every drop that did not fall on the shirt, found its way into Mr. Stiffback's eyes and mouth.

The whole school stood literally aghast at this unexpected interlude.

Lionel and the rest of Tommy's friends looked at one another in speechless, but inquiring wonderment.

Each fancied that the other was in the "joke," if joke there was.

But each met nothing but blank amazement wherever he looked.

The suspense was soon broken by Mr. Stiffback.

With an unearthly snort or growl he spluttered the water out of his nose and mouth, then he brought his left hand with full force against Tommy's right ear, and catching him on the rebound, repeated the performance with his right hand on the unfortunate youth's left ear.

This exhilarating exercise he kept up for the space of two minutes and an half, then pausing to gain renewed strength and breath, he said fiercely—

"What does this disgraceful conduct mean, Codlings?"

Tommy, with something very like a whimper, albeit 'twas a defiant one, replied—

"'Twasn't my fault that the button bust itself off; and how was I to know that that squirt would go and let itself off—right in your face too?"

This speech was the signal for a roar of laughter from the assembled boys.

"Squirt!" almost shrieked the schoolmaster, "what business had you to bring a squirt into the class-room?"

'Please, sir, I—I—I—I brought it in to wash my slate."

This was too much, even for Mr. Stiffback's equanimity, and breathing vows of "flogging machine, &c., &c.," between his clenched teeth, the schoolmaster gave orders that the studies, so disgracefully interrupted, should be continued.

Luckily for the peace of the school, every one was, if possible, more than letter perfect in his allotted task, and Mr. Stiffback's ruffled temper soon regained its equanimity as he reflected that, with such pupils, he could not fail to gain considerable honour and eclat for his school and system at the approaching "local."

Everything having now settled down into its normal state, Lionel ventured to ask the usual permission to bathe.

This was granted as far as Lionel and some of the others were concerned.

"But as for Codlings," said Mr. Stiffback, "he shall not bathe with the rest, but will be in charge of the tub. Vansittart, I expect you particularly to notice Codlings' conduct."

"I will, sir," said Vansittart. "Come on, young Codlings."

"What's up now," growled Tommy. "I can't even be allowed to wash myself like anybody else. What's the tub, and what have I got to do with it?"

"Never mind about the tub," said Lionel, as they had now got clear of the class-room. "Tell us, what was the meaning of the little comedy which you have just entertained us with?"

"Comedy, do you call it?" said Tommy, tenderly feeling his ears, which looked more like a couple of kidneys ready for the gridiron than anything else in nature. "Comedy—ugh; but it didn't mean anything—only one of my blessed buttons busted itself off as usual."

"But how about the water—the squirt, or whatever it was?"

"Well, how was I to know the dashed thing was going off like that?"

"Well, but how did it come to be in a position to go off, eh, Tommy?"

"'Twas just my luck. I'd been trying how many flies I could squash with my squirt, and had knocked over a proper lot; then I had just filled it again out of the basin, so that I could knock over a few more as I came along to the class-room; when I'd no sooner left my room than who should clap his hand on my shoulder but old Stiffback—bust him."

"Never mind, Tommy, don't give vent to your feelings; finish your story first."

"Well, the long and the short of it is that I shoved the squirt into my pocket handle downwards—and you know the rest."

"And quite enough too," said Lionel; "now come on."

"But what about that tub," asked Tommy, with a curious gleam of apprehension in his eyes.

"You've got to wash the little boys in it," said Lionel, with a wink aside to Vansittart; "it's the large washing-tub that's down by the bank where the slaveys go for the water."

"Here, dash it," said Tommy, "no larks; he don't expect me to do that, does he?"

"He does, though, and I'd advise you to do it. Have you got the soap?"

"No," growled Tommy, sulkily.

"Then go to the kitchen and ask for the tub of soft soap and the scrubbing-brush—some of those little chaps are precious dirty."

"Oh!" moaned Tommy, "this is too bad. How many of 'em are there?"

"Only a dozen, I think. Cut away now after the soap."

"All right," said Tommy, desperately, "if I've got to do it, I have; but won't I scrub the little beggars—and if the soap gets in their eyes, that will be their look out."

And away Tommy sallied for the soap and scrubbing-brush; while our hero and his chums made for the water-side and spread the news of the coming fun amongst their friends.

Tommy, quite unsuspicious of the neat little joke prepared for him, marched off to the kitchen, and there readily found a small tub of soft soap and a huge scrubbing-brush, which would have polished the hide of an elephant.

Armed with these implements, Tommy reached the bathing place, where the boys were already stripped, such of them of them as could swim disporting themselves in the water, while the more timid stood hesitating on the bank, watching with envious glances the evolutions of their more skilful chums.

Among these latter were the Bobbles brothers, not one of whom could swim, and who never, by any chance, entrusted their precious carcases in more than a foot depth of water.

There they were, a blissful sight to Tommy, standing all five in a row, and witnessing with a spiteful relish the swimmers whom they had not pluck enough to emulate.

"This is prime," muttered Tommy. "There they are. I'll wash 'em! If I don't wear out this scrubbing-brush, it won't be for want of trying."

And quickening his pace, Tommy hurried to the bank, and as a polite preliminary, sat down the tub of soft soap on the toes of the elder Bobbles, and gave another a sounding "spank" with the back of the scrubbing-brush.

"What are you doing that for, you Codlings?" demanded Bobbles senior, as he limped painfully about on one leg.

"I'll soon show you," retorted Tommy, as he watched the agony of his victim with a sort of savage joy. "You come and be washed."

"What?"

"Come and be washed and scrubbed," repeated Tommy, with a flourish of the brush; "and if that won't make you clean enough, we'll try sandpaper."

"None of that now," said Bobbles junior, backing almost into the lake in his alarm. "No larks, Codlings."

"You won't find it a lark. Come now; who's first?"

"Make haste there, Tommy," called Lionel, who was playing touch with Vansittart, Charlie, and a few others of the best swimmers. "Hurry up and wash those youngsters, or you won't have a swim yourself."

"Oh, ah, I daresay," said the elder Bobbles. "Come now, Codlings, you just let me alone."

"I'll let you alone when I've washed you, not before," replied Tommy. "It's Mr. Stiffback's orders, so you'd better take it quietly."

And by way of assuring his prey that his intentions were serious, Tommy scraped up a handful of soft soap, and planted a dab in his victim's eye.

"Oh my! oh lor! oh dear!" howled Bobbles, as he spun round like a teetotum, with excess of agony. "Oh, how it hurts!"

"Does it?" retorted Tommy, raking up a fresh dab of soap, "I meant it to. Now will you come to be washed?"

And the unlucky victim, unable to dodge, by reason of the soap, which blinded him, was seized by the neck, and in a twinkling tumbled over into the big washing tub.

Once there, he was at the mercy of Tommy the merciless; and the tortures he suffered would have shamed those of the inquisition.

Eyes, nose, and mouth were all filled with the soft soap. He smelt nothing else, tasted nothing else, and if the expression may be allowed, heard nothing else, for his very ears were crammed full with it.

In vain he coughed, gasped, and spluttered, in

an attempt to appeal for help, and equally useless were his struggles, for Tommy had adopted a process familiar to those who deal with restive horses, and sat upon his head.

There was quite an audience now gathered round the "wet-nurse" and his victim; and as a matter of course roars of laughter greeted each fresh attempt on the part of Bobbles to escape.

Tommy having, as he thought, sufficiently well soaped his patient, now brought the scrubbing-brush into play, and the very touch of the bristles brought forth such a long-drawn hideous howl of agony, that fairly set everyone's teeth on edge.

"Oh my, there's music!" said Charlie Drummond.

"Put some more soap in his mouth, Tommy," suggested our hero, "if he makes that row again, all the pigs for a couple of miles round will think their relatives are being murdered, and fly to the rescue."

"I say, you let my brother alone," said the boldest of the family. "I'll go and fetch the governor if you don't."

"Fetch away," said Tommy, cheerfully, as he soaped four square inches of skin off the small of his victim's back; "but wait till I've washed you; it's your turn next."

"Is it? Oh, no, it ain't, now then."

"You'll see. Stiffback said I was to wash you all, and I'm going to do it, for I like the job."

And with a dexterity that was really wonderful, Tommy reached out, and catching him by the waist-band of his drawers, jerked him head-first into the tub.

Another stepped forth tremblingly to rescue his fallen brother; but it was an unlucky move, for Tommy grabbed him too, and now the tub was filled with three helpless, sprawling victims, who, in their struggles to get free, soaped themselves far more effectually than their tormentors had done.

The tub was standing, when the same spirit of mischief which has so often prompted our hero in his pranks, urged him to pull the tub a little further in.

It was already half afloat, and before the unlucky Bobbles had time to realise their position, it was whirling round and round a dozen feet or more away.

"I say, no larks," shouted Tommy. "They're not half washed yet."

"Come out here and finish your job, Tommy," said Lionel. "Don't forget the scrubbing-brush."

This just suited Tommy's views, and with a sweet smile lighting up his expressive countenance, he waded out and grasped the edge of the tub.

"Oh!" shrieked the terrified Bobbles brothers in chorus. "Take us back; we shall be drowned. Help, he—lp!"

"Hold that row," growled Tommy, giving his edge of the tub a pull which nearly upset it, and enforcing his commands by rapping the nearest over the head with the brush. "Wait till you're asked before you sing like that."

The three unlucky youths were now holding on like grim death to the tub, while their pallid faces and stony eyes testified to the reality of their fright.

"Oh, do let us go, Codlings," pleaded one; "I'll promise not to say a word to Stiffback if you'll take us back to the shore."

"When you're washed I will," replied the plump youth, "not before."

"You're not going the right way to work, Tommy," said our hero. "You ought to be in the tub, and they ought to stand in the water while you wash 'em."

"Well, that would be more convenient," said Tommy. "Get out, will you?"

And leaning on the edge of the tub, he tilted it in a most alarming manner.

"Oh—oh! Don't!"

"What funky beggars you are," said Tommy. "I'm quite ashamed of you. Out you go now—come."

And exerting all his strength, Tommy succeeded in turning the tub quite over, shooting the three victims head over heels into the lake.

Then they verily thought that their last hour was come—the water rushed into their mouths and up their nostrils, choking back their cries for help. They closed together, and though they were in shallow water, kicked and struggled as if they were in the middle of the Atlantic Ocean.

Tommy was installed in the tub, and, armed with a long stick which he used after the manner of a shepherd's crook, leaned over, and grasping the nearest one by the hair of his head, touched him up smartly with the scrubbing-brush.

To capture one was to secure all three, for they clung fondly to each other, exhibiting quite a touching affection in the hour of peril, in appreciation of which Tommy bumped their heads together until they ached.

But now that he was afloat, the plump youth found that it was particularly difficult to pursue his cleansing avocation.

The tub wobbled about in such an unsteady manner that he found it as much as he could do to preserve his balance.

Seeing his difficulty, Lionel swam to the tub and caught hold of the edge, but somehow, and, of course, purely by accident, our hero jerked the tub about worse than ever, and more than that, pushed it into deep water.

"I say, Li, mind what you're after. You'll have me over, and, dash it, you've let them Bobbles chaps get away. Hi! come back and be washed."

But the youthful victims did not seem to see the necessity for obeying this request, and still clinging fondly to each other, made for the shore, where their two remaining relatives were waiting to cheer them with their sympathy,

"You leave off, Li," bawled Tommy. "You're doing it on purpose, I know you are. 'Pon my word, I'll drop you one with this stick if you—oh!"

Before Tommy could complete the sentence or execute the threat, a more violent jerk than the others tossed him out of the tub.

He went down like a plummet, and was such a long time before he rose to the surface, that Lionel, a little alarmed, was going to dive after him, when his plump head bobbed up like a cork.

"Hullo, Tommy," said Lionel. "What have the fish got for dinner?"

"Why, they—very—nearly—had—me," gasped Tommy. "Dash it, Li, what did you want to upset me for? I got stuck in the weeds down there, and—ugh!—a beastly long eel came clinging round me."

"Why didn't you catch it?"

"Catch it!" growled Tommy, who was holding on to his tub, which was now bottom upwards. "The weeds had caught me, I tell you, and that was all I could think about just then."

"I was just going down to look after you, Tommy."

"Very kind of you," said Tommy, in a sort of growl. "If it hadn't been for you, I shouldn't have gone down at all. Shove us on to the shore, Li; those wretched Bobbles are dressing, and they'll get away if I don't make haste."

"Oh, let 'em alone now, Tommy."

"But they're not half washed. What will Stiffback say?"

"Oh, he won't mind. It's only a matter of form. Let go the tub, and have a game at touch."

"You don't catch me letting go this tub yet awhile," said Tommy. "I haven't got my breath yet."

"Hold on tight, then, and come out in the middle to see fair. Wait a minute, and I'll right the tub."

And before Tommy could remonstrate or offer any opposition, Lionel had turned the tub over, and Tommy himself went for the second time down among the little fishes.

When he came up again, he glared at Lionel with a vengeful and watery eye, and as he grasped the edge of the tub and returned to the lake the few quarts of water he had swallowed, he spluttered forth a defiance to mortal combat.

"I'll warm you for this, Wilful," he said, with a red and wrathful countenance. "I ain't afraid of you; only let me get ashore, and I'll have a turn up with you."

"What a bloodthirsty character you are developing into, Tommy," said Lionel, with a laugh. "Wanting to punch the head of his best friend."

"What's the matter, Li?" demanded Charlie.

"Tommy wants to have a round with me, that's all. There's ingratitude; and I've just saved his life."

"You be blowed, you and your saving," growled Tommy. "You've upset me into deep water twice, and let those Bobbles go before they were half washed."

"And here comes Stiffback to see whether you have done your work properly," added Charlie. "Look out, Tommy."

"Then I'll just tell him who's been hindering me," replied Tommy. "You may call me a sneak if you like—I don't care."

And still holding on to the tub, Tommy kicked out with his short, fat legs, and reached the shore just as the Bobbles' family had concluded the tale of the wrongs they had endured at the plump youth's hands.

"Codlings, come here," said Mr. Stiffback.

Tommy pulled up the tub after him, and advanced with a cheerful smile.

"Yes, sir."

"Is this true, Codlings?"

"What sir?"

"Is it true what these boys tell me? Did you force them violently into that tub?"

"I did, sir; they wouldn't go quietly, sir."

"And why should they have gone in quietly, Codlings?"

"They had to be washed, you know, sir," replied Tommy, not quite understanding the drift of the head master's questions.

"I admire your zeal in the cause of personal cleanliness, Codlings," said Mr. Stiffback, sweetly; "but you should have exhibited it at the proper time and place. Bobbles senior says that you have abraded a considerable portion of the epidermis of his dorsal region, or, in plainer words, that you have scrubbed a large piece of skin off his back."

"He wouldn't keep still while I washed him, sir."

"But why did you wash him at all, Codlings?"

That question was a staggerer for Tommy, but he replied in all innocence—

"Why, you told me to, sir."

He was just within range, and Mr. Stiffback gave him a spank on the side of his head, which rolled him back into the tub, and caused him to set up a most dismal howl.

"Hold that noise, sir, and come here," said Mr. Stiffback, sternly. "Now, what do you mean by such a barefaced accusation?"

Tommy saw at once that he had been the victim to a hoax, and for a moment malice prompted him to split, and let the wrath of Mr. Stiffback fall upon Lionel; but he was far too good-hearted a fellow to let such a mean motive sway him for long, and he faltered an excuse which only made matters ten times worse.

"Will you have the kindness to repeat your impudent falsehood, Codlings," said the schoolmaster, in a tone of voice which made Tommy shiver with apprehension.

"I—I—I didn't mean actually—that is to say, sir, I didn't mean what you mean; only it must have been a—a—sort of a dream, sir."

"Indeed," said Mr. Stiffback, who thought that Tommy was chaffing him, and got dreadfully angry in consequence. "Take that, you insolent young scoundrel. I'll give you something to dream about. Go up to the school at once."

"Let me dress myself first, sir," sobbed Tommy.

"You can dress yourself after I have done with you," said Mr. Stiffback, meaningly. "Soker, carry Master Codlings' clothes into the schoolroom, and get the flogging-machine ready."

Poor Tommy nearly fainted.

That dreaded machine was bad enough at the best—what would be its effect when only a pair of thin, wet cotton drawers interposed between his skin and the stinging, blistering, whalebone rods!

CHAPTER XLIV.

TOMMY'S WOES—SWEET OIL AND SYMPATHY—THE HOLIDAY, AND WHAT OUR HERO AND HIS CHUMS DID WITH IT—THE MEETING AT THE TOWN HALL OF DELIVERHAM—OUR HERO AND A SELECT PARTY INVITE THEMSELVES—A NEW USE FOR STRAY DOGS—WHO ARE YOUR HATTERS?—THE BEADLE IN DIFFICULTIES.

IT was soon over—the whalebone had done its fell work, and poor Tommy, laying the dust with his tears, crawled away on all fours to the dormitory, where Lionel and Charlie soothed him with sympathy, lard, and sweet-oil.

"Feel any better, Tommy?"

"Yes, a little," moaned the unfortunate Codlings. "But I say, Li, you shouldn't have sold me like that."

"I didn't think Stiffback would be down so heavy upon you, Tommy—on my word I didn't; and then you cheeked him, and he can't bear that."

"I never meant to cheek him when I said I dreamt that he told me. It was the only excuse I could think of for the time."

"Never mind, Tommy; make haste and get well, for we have another holiday the day after to-morrow."

"He won't let me go, you see if he does," said Tommy. "Something's sure to happen to prevent my going."

"Not it. We'll get you away somehow, even if he locks you up in Newgate. So cheer up, old chap."

And Lionel, forgetting for the moment Tommy's half-flayed condition, gave him a friendly slap which made him howl dreadfully; but he took it in good part, as indeed he did most things, for he was a firm believer in the folly of "crying over spilt milk."

The day of the holiday arrived at last, and Tommy's doleful prophecy as to his being kept in proved false, for he was not only allowed to go but was even given the choice of selecting the party he preferred to join, instead of being kept beside one of the masters as a dangerous character it was imprudent to let loose upon society.

"It won't last, you see," said Tommy, not much elated by the good news. "Something 'll happen to spoil the fun, or at least my part of it."

But as it so chanced that Tommy got safely across the water and even into the town, without any accident occurring, his spirits revived, and he was the cheerful, happy Tommy Codlings of old, ready to take his share in anything—be it fun, fighting, or frolic.

"I say," said Lionel, halting near the town hall, where on a hoarding a monster bill was displayed. "There's something going on. Stop a bit."

And our hero glanced hastily on the poster, which announced that a meeting was to be held that day to denounce the atrocities committed by the Russians and Austrians upon the Poles in the course of a certain nice little war then being carried on, and in which a certain General Haynau figured rather prominently.

"'Indignation—Public sympathy—People of England—Flogging of Polish women!" murmured Lionel. "'Chairman, Mr. Growlagain.' I say, you fellows, let's go in, and hear what old Growly has to say on the flogging question. He ought to be good on that."

"Oh, there's no fun to be got out of these meetings," said Pryce. "Let's go on."

"Yes, let's go on," added Tommy, "It must be near lunch time, and I'm getting precious hungry."

"You won't get anything to eat for an hour to come yet," said Lionel. "Come along in, you fellows; we're sure to get some fun out of it. We can spoil old Growly's speech, anyhow."

And taking the lead, Lionel walked boldly up the steps, where at the top stood a pompous beadle, dressed in a gorgeous hat and cloak, and armed with a staff of portentous size.

"Good morning, sir," said Lionel, saluting him with sweet politeness. "Is the meeting over?"

The beadle, during a long and arduous term of office, had learned to regard boys as his natural enemies; but our hero's courteous address overpowered his antipathy, and he replied, civilly enough—

"Jest in full swing, young genelman. Be you a goin' in?"

"If you please," said Lionel. "We're come to cheer Mr. Growlagain. Has he begun yet?"

"He's done one a'ready, and he's just agoing to begin another. This way."

"Don't trouble yourself," said Lionel. "We know the way, thank you."

And in a body, but walking as demurely as if they were entering church, the youngsters passed into the vestibule and halted opposite a door, even through the double green-baize covered thickness of which the deep, hoarse voice of Mr. Growlagain could be distinctly heard.

"I say, Li," whispered Charlie, looking cautiously round. "See what I found in the beadle's pocket while you were talking to him."

And Charlie produced a huge red cotton handkerchief, which, on being opened, proved to contain a half-quartern loaf made into sandwiches with some very underdone beef.

"It's the beadle's dinner," chuckled Charlie. "My stars, won't he be wild when he finds it's gone. What shall we do with it, Li?"

"Hush!" said Lionel. "There are dogs about somewhere. Listen!"

After a moment's silence, the boys distinctly heard a short yelp or two, followed by a few smothered barks, and proceeding apparently from a little door at the further end of the vestibule.

"Come along," whispered Lionel. "That's where the dogs are put till the meeting's over. They'll take care of the beadle's dinner."

"Take care, young Wilful," said Vansittart. "They may bolt out when you open the door, and then we should be neatly dropped on by the beadle."

"No fear—they'll be tied up. That's why they're yelping."

And opening the door, cautiously though, Lionel peeped in, and then opening it widely, beckoned to his companions.

The dogs instantly set up a joyous howl in concert, for they thought possibly that they were about to be released from an unwelcome confinement.

"Shut the door, Charlie—quick," said Lionel,

"and give me the grub. Here, good dogs—good fellows, there!"

A few of the sandwiches, judiciously distributed, quieted the clamour, and our boys had time to look about them, and note that the little ante-chamber was also used as a cloak-room, for hung on pegs about the walls were great-coats and hats, while in one corner stood quite a collection of sticks, whips and riding-canes.

"They've put the dogs in here to ta e care of their masters' property, I suppose," said Charlie. "By Jove, Li, what a lot of shiney tiles."

"Yes, they do look pretty," said our hero, taking one with a ferociously curled brim from its peg. "This is old Growlagain's, I'll bet."

"I wonder if his dog's here."

"He's too mean to keep one," said Lionel. "We'll see if any of 'em know it."

And the mischievous youth presented the hat in turn to each of the dogs, some of whom only smelt it, while others tested it by licking, while a few bit an inch or so out of the brim, and worried it like a rat.

"You've done it now, Li," laughed Charlie. "That was a new tile, and won't he be down on somebody when he finds it spoilt."

"They shouldn't have tied the poor beasts up then—that makes 'em savage. I've a good mind to let 'em all loose."

"And give 'em the hats to play with, and keep 'em quiet," added Charlie.

"I'll tell you a better dodge: tie the best hats to the dog's tails," said Vansittart; "then when the beadle comes to let 'em out, there'll be some rare fun."

No idea could have chimed in better with the mischievous spirits of our hero and his chums. All hands went immediately to work, the shiniest and most expensive hats were selected, and in five minutes the caudal appendages of some twelve or fourteen dogs were decorated with the hats.

"Now," said Lionel, "give 'em the rest of the grub to keep 'em quiet, and then the word is 'slope'."

The rest of the sandwiches was thrown amongst the dogs, and while they were growling and scrambling, the boys took advantage of the opportunity and got out into the vestibule.

It was fortunate that they did so in time, for from the great hall came sounds indicative of the breaking up of the meeting long before the appointed hour.

But one or two of the gentlemen on the platform, not knowing the sort of man they had to deal with, ventured to disagree with Mr. Growlagain, whereupon he emptied the vials of his wrath upon them in something like the following words, prefacing them by folding his arms, directing a withering scowl at the delinquents, and uttering a short laugh of the double-knock description:—

"And this, gentlemen, is poor England, and these miserable dastards, who have just had the audacity to move that amendment, do not tremble from fear lest the ground should open and bury their slimy villany for ever. ("Order!") No, gentlemen, do not think that I am to be frowned down, or bawled down, or hissed down, by any quantity of geese. ("Order!") I move again, that this meeting do unanimously call upon the Government to declare instant war with Russia and Austria, and that every Englishman under the age of forty-five (Mr. Growlagain was forty-six) be called upon to take up arms, and never to lay them down again, until the enemy have been annihilated; and furthermore, that every one who does not vote with me for this resolution is an ass—("Order!")—a coward, a liar—("Order, order!" "Chair!")—a nincompoop, a blackguard—("Order!" "Pitch him over!")—a thief, and, in short, gentlemen, a most unmitigated——"

Mr. Growlagain got no further with his list of

epithets, for one of his opponents, a stout man, who had been getting rapidly purple in the face with indignation, raised a very dropsical umbrella, and floored the ferocious schoolmaster.

"Order, order!" "Chair!" "Serve him right!" "Police!" were the various cries which now sounded from all parts of the hall, while showers of apples, plums, nuts, and other light refreshments were shied upon the platform.

In the midst of all this hubbub, the chairman (who was well used to this sort of thing, having been an electioneering agent for forty years) put the amendment to the vote, rejected it by a show of hands, declared the original resolution carried unanimously, passed a vote of thanks to himself for his able conduct in the chair, adjourned the meeting, and then adjourned himself by a back way, and left the meeting to fight it out if they thought proper.

"It's unconstitutional," said one hoarse defender of Mr. Growlagain. "You had a right to wote, Parsons, but it was wrong to wote with a umbrella, 'specially when a man's bald on the top of his head."

During the progress of this argument, Mr. Growlagain was being restored by the application of cold water without and brandy-and-water within, and when he had taken about a quart of the latter mixture he declared himself better, and demanded that the gentleman who had argued with the umbrella should be immediately produced in order that he might demolish him.

"I will so damage that fellow's countenance," said Mr. Growlagain, bringing his right fist down with a tremendous thump upon the table, "I will so maul that ass's head, that his own tailor won't know him, even if he owes a two years' bill, which is more than likely."

But the friends of order had already removed the obnoxious individual with the umbrella, and Mr. Growlagain's acquaintances proposed an adjournment to the club-room of the Black Bull and Periwinkle, where all might once again be peace and happiness.

"Very well," said Mr. Growlagain, in a resigned tone. "Have your own way for this time; but let me tell you this, the next time I meet that Parsons, I'll—I'll flay him, and make his skin into parchment to write my will upon."

And as he gave utterance to this awful threat, the irate schoolmaster marched out into the lobby, and there shouted for the beadle, in a voice which made that functionary run trembling to the spot.

"Why ain't you in your place when you're wanted?" growled the schoolmaster, in a way that turned the beadle white. "Go and get the hats, you insolent scoundrel, or I'll report you."

The beadle was off in a minute, turned the handle of the door, and threw it wide open, but before he could set foot over the threshold, the dogs, wearied by their long imprisonment and by the efforts they had already made to rid themselves of their new burdens, rushed out, yelping and barking, and fled madly along the vestibule towards the entrance.

"What in the name of ——" began Mr. Growlagain, but before he could finish, a terrier, with a hat behind him big enough for its kennel, bolted between his legs, and shot him on to his nose.

"Hoi!" roared a huge farmer. "Hoi, Jobley, there goes thy dog wi' my hat tied to's tail. Stop 'un, will 'ee."

But Jobley was too busily employed in trying to stop his own hat, which was running away with a dog three sizes smaller than itself, and paid no attention to the farmer, who lumbered ineffectually after his own property.

Our hero and his chums, after getting up that nice little piece of mischief in the cloak-room, had returned to the market-place, and giving the unsus-

pecting beadle an affectionate farewell as they passed, waited quietly, if not patiently, round the corner for the result.

It was not long in coming, for scarcely had they posted themselves, than a hideous uproar, compounded of yelping, barking, shouting and swearing was heard, mingled with short howls of agony from those human sufferers who had been either bitten by the dogs or upset in the general rush.

"Here they come," said Lionel, in an excited whisper. "Put a mark on old Growlagain, Vansittart. Chevy the dogs well, you other fellows."

First came the dogs, snapping, snarling, howling, raising such a clamour, that no pack of foxhounds in full cry could have equalled its music.

Then followed the beadle. He came down the steps head first, and got his cape so entangled with his cocked hat, and his head so mixed up in both, that he was temporarily blinded, and he found it decidedly uncomfortable to play blind man's buff among a crowd of half-maddened curs, and lively youngsters, who relieved the monotony of their existence by running pins into his legs.

Last of all came the crowds infuriated of gentlemen who had lost their hats, using a most extraordinary quantity of bad language in an incredibly short space of time. Indeed, Vansittart, who was fond of mathematics, calculated that each man swore an average of fifty-nine oaths and a quarter per minute, which is really approaching the verge of profanity.

Mr. Growlagain, as our readers will easily imagine, was far beyond the others in the violence of his actions and his language, and chancing to espy the hapless beadle, he kicked him twice round the market-place, and invented no less then thirty-seven entirely new and original oaths to suit the occasion.

And now the fun (for our boys) began in real earnest. Half of their number devoted themselves to hunting the dogs and preventing them from running out of the market-place, while the balance devoted themselves to the beadle and Mr. Growlagain, and the other hatless members of the meeting.

In vain did the farmers run themselves into a red heat, and shout themselves breathless in their endeavours to stop the dogs or chase them into a corner.

In vain too, did they throw stones, for with those missiles they only succeeded in damaging windows, and inoffensive passengers who were not slow in returning the compliment, and demanding compensation in language more remarkable for profanity than politeness.

It was not, indeed, until our boys thought that they had had enough of the fun, that the dogs were captured and the hats were recovered.

Hats! Shades of Christy and André forgive us for bestowing such a name upon the battered, ragged remnants of felt which Lionel and the others now bore with as much care and tenderness as if they had been brand-new.

"Here you are, sir," said Lionel, politely offering the brim, and part of the lining, of his hat to Mr. Growlagain. "This is yours, I think, sir."

"That mine!" said the rival schoolmaster, looking suspiciously at our hero. "You don't call that a hat; why there's no top to it."

"Just the thing for a bald-headed man, sir. Let the hair in," said Lionel, attempting for the first, and let us hope, last time in his life, to make a pun.

But Mr. Growlagain did not appreciate wit, good, bad, or indifferent, and Lionel's only reward was a frown of the same pattern as that with which he had annihilated his opponents in the town hall.

"My eye, what a mug!" exclaimed our hero, pretending to be terribly frightened at Mr. Growlagain's expression. "What do charge per hour for frightening naughty babies, sir ?"

This was too much—the schoolmaster rather prided himself upon his dignity of expression, and here was a rude boy, who not only refused to be affected by it, but replied that he, Mr. Growlagain, was only fit to frighten badies.

Mr. Growlagain used the only argument left to him—he boxed Lionel's ears, or rather he would have boxed them, but when his hand arrived, the ear had moved, and the smiter smote one of his best friends below the belt, and doubled him up upon the kidney-stones, gasping—

"I'm verry sory, Jobling, but double dash that boy, he got out of the way just as I was going to hit him."

But Mr. Jobling was too much damaged to listen to excuses—he pressed one hand to his injured stomach, and stretching out the other, caught Mr. Growlagain by the ankle, and with one tug brought him to the ground.

"Dang thee," growled Mr. Jobling, "I'll knock thee two eyes into one."

"Don't," pleaded Mr. Growlagain, for his foe had the grip of a giant. "Let go, Jobling."

Mr. Jobling's only reply was to tuck his enemy's head in a convenient position under his left arm, and to begin punching with his right.

"Hurrah!" shouted Lionel. "Here's a fight! Come on—make a ring."

It was a false move on our hero's part, for the beadle, who by this time had released his head from the cloak, began to suspect that those remarkably polite young gentlemen had more to do with the matter than at first appeared.

In this suspicion he was more than confirmed by discovering Tommy Codlings, seated on one of the steps of the town hall, munching a sandwich which bore a suspicious resemblance to those which had been stolen from the bundle.

Tommy had, in fact, been guilty of appropriating one to his own use, and feeling as he generally did, more inclined for eating than exercise, the beadle found him an easy prey.

"Now youngster, wot's that you're eating of?" demanded the beadle.

"Sandwich," muttered Tommy.

"Where did 'ee get it from ?"

Tommy looked up from his occupation, recognised the beadle, and turned faint with apprehension.

All was discovered, and flight was the only remedy; but behind him was the town hall, and in front was the beadle, armed with a staff big enough to fell a bullock.

"I'll tell 'ee whar 'ee got it from," said the beadle, sternly; "that was my dinner, that was, and it's you and your mates wot let them there dogs loose."

"Oh no, indeed, sir," said Tommy, looking round in an agonised way for some loophole of escape, but there was none—the beadle's hand had grasped his collar, and the beadle's staff beckoned the constable.

"Hullo, have ye got one ?" said that official.

"Yes, off wi' 'un, and come back quick, and we'll cop the rest."

"What's the charge?"

"Priggin' my sangwitches. Petty blasphemy," replied the beadle.

And away went the constable to enter this novel crime against Tommy, who kicked and protested vainly, while the beadle enlisted a dozen or so of amateur constables, and advanced towards our hero and his chums, who were intent upon the progress of the fight between Mr. Growlagain and his friend Jobling.

CHAPTER XLV.

THE CAPTURE—MR. GROWLAGAIN TRIUMPHANT—THE CHARGE AT THE POLICE STATION—IN THE CELLS—PLANS OF ESCAPE—SAM SCARECROW TO THE RESCUE.

"NOW be mighty careful wot you're doin' ou wi' these boys," said the beadle to his assistants. "They be as difficult to lay hold on as a hornet, and sting nigh as sharp, some on 'em dew."

"Wa'at had we best do then ?"

"Knock 'em down, and then sit on 'em," replied the beadle, complacently. "That's your only chance, and doan't let 'em git up till they be well nigh smothered, or they'll slip off easy as a eel."

Fortified by these beautifully simple instructions and a promise of floods of beer if they captured the comrades, the beadle and his "specials" advanced upon the youthful culprits.

Mr. Growlagain and Jobling were still hard at it, and the efforts of their friends to part them were as yet unavailing, for the latter was tremendously strong, and held on to his foe with the hug of a grizzly bear.

Our hero and his chums, thoroughly absorbed in the interesting spectacle, were cheering the combatants with might and main, when suddenly and without an instant's warning, each one felt himself encircled by a pair of huge arms, which gripped him as in a vice.

Vansittart's great strength enabled him to wrench himself free, but an unlucky stumble spoilt his chance of escape, and before he could recover himself two more of the specials were upon him, and he was a prisoner.

In the course of the capture Mr. Jobling had been more trodden upon than he at all liked, and, having by this time knocked most of the skin off the knuckles of his right hand, and distributed a little strong language for the benefit of the company generally, he made all sail for the Black Bull and Periwinkle, there to lay up in fort, and repair damages, external and internal.

The beadle's plan had been so far successful, for the superior might of their captors, and the way in which they were pinioned from behind, rendered escape for the present almost impossible.

"Confound it," thought Lionel, "it's all my fault. I ought to have kept a better look out. Dash the beadle, I thought he was too thick-headed to suspect us. Hullo, Charlie, how do you feel ?"

"All right," replied Drummond, "only this chap stinks so confoundly of stale tobacco and onions."

"So does this one," said Lionel. "I don't think the soap manufacturers make a fortune out of him either."

"Soap wouldn't be of any use to these chaps," said Drummond; "they have to be scraped down like the front of a house, and then painted flesh colour."

"I should like to know what business they have to touch us at all," said Vansittart, "I hear there's a low fellow named Growlagain, who is going to make some kind of charge against us."

"You can make a solemn affidavit of that, young man," mumbled Mr. Growlagain, who had been informed of the capture by the beadle, and was now busily enaged in binding up his wounded jaw with a pocket handkerchief. "If you get off with less than six months' labour each, call me a fool."

"I'll call you a fool without that," retorted Vansittart. "You're a nice article, aren't you, to bring charges against us—a fellow who gets drunk and fights in the open street in the middle of the day."

"That's libel," gasped Mr. Growlagain. "I'll make you pay for that."

"And I'll make you pay for arresting me on a false charge, old fellow, or rather no charge at all.

But here we are at the station—let us see what you will say here."

They entered in a body, Mr. Growlagain a little less confident, but still too much annoyed to perceive that he was playing a tick'ish game; besides, he was a great man in Deliverham, and was accustomed to do pretty well as he liked.

The inspector gave him a sweet smile, and then scowled with awful severity upon the culprits.

"What, more of these mischievous young rascals! Tapper has brought one in already. What's the charge—drunk and disorderly?"

"No, sir," said the beadle; "not drunk, I think."

"I shouldn't wonder if they were," said the inspector, sniffing as if there was a whole rum cask somewhere about. "Do you think they're intoxicated, Mr. Growlagain?"

"I couldn't undertake to say," replied that gentleman; "they're quite capable of it, I believe. They had better be seen by the divisional surgeon, perhaps."

"Certainly, sir. Now, beadle, what's the charge?"

"Petty blasphemy," said the beadle, conscious of having got hold of a good sounding legal phrase, and determined to make the best of it.

"Eh?" said the inspector.

"They stole my sangwitches," said the beadle. "That's blasphemy."

"Larceny, my good man, larceny," corrected the inspector. "Very well, go on."

And down went the crime in the charge-sheet to Tommy's account.

"Furdermore, likewise," continued the beadle. "I charges him with having perspired with the other pris'ners——"

"Conspired, you mean, I suppose."

"I means, Mr. Inspector," said the offended beadle, "exackly what I ses."

"You can't charge a man with perspiring," said Mr. Growlagain. "Go on, and don't meddle with words you don't understand."

The beadle sniffed in an exasperated manner, and muttered something about everybody not being schoolmasters; but he took Mr. Growlagain's hint, and in pretty plain language accused our hero and his chums, jointly and severally, with being directly engaged in stealing his sandwiches, and causing wilful damage to divers valuable articles of property—to wit, fourteen hats; the said hats being at the time in charge of the said beadle.

"This isn't felony, you know," said the inspector, looking doubtfully at Mr. Growlagain, and scratching his head thoughtfully with his pen. "I shall be exceeding my duty if I lock 'em up on such a charge."

"Haven't they stolen the beadle's dinner?" retorted Mr. Growlagain, "and burglariously entered a room in the town hall; and isn't that felony?"

"Is the beadle sure about the identity of those sandwiches?"

"Sartin," replied that official, holding up a fragment which Tommy had left undevoured. "I captured him a-eatin' of it; and I can swear to the beef as they was made on."

"That settles him," said the inspector, pointing his pen at Tommy; "but how about the others?"

"I'll take the responsibility," retorted Mr. Growlagain, who was rapidly working himself into a fresh passion. "Charge 'em with felony—arson—burglary—anything, only lock 'em up."

"If you make the charge I'm bound to take it, of course," said the inspector, coolly. "Now, you young shavers, what are your names?"

The boys answered gravely enough, for matters were beginning to look serious, and the inspector wrote them down without the least emotion, until it came to Vansittart's turn.

The announcement of Vansittart's title, and the fact that he was heir to an earldom, produced a wonderful effect. The inspector hesitated, the

beadle looked ready to sink into his official shoes and even Mr. Growlagain was moved by something of that reverential feeling with which most Englishmen are apt to regard a title.

"Beg his lordship's pardon humbly, I'm sure," faltered the beadle. "I'm sure if I'd ha' knowed his lordship was a lord, his noble lordship—oh, Lord!"

This last ejaculation was caused by young Lord Vansittart digging his lordly elbow, with some violence, into the beadle's waistcoat.

"Enough of that," he said; "my rank has nothing to do with the affair. If one is charged so must all."

"Away with 'em, then," said Mr. Growlagain, with the air of a stage baron ordering a few dozen of his retainers to be executed. "Lord or no lord, he goes to prison."

"You distinctly charge his lordship with felony, then?" said the inspector. "Be cool, Mr. Growlagain, recollect yourself, sir."

"I recollect myself, sir, and you too," thundered Mr. Growlagain. "Do your duty, sir!"

There was nothing left for it now but to put the boys in the cells, and after promising to communicate the intelligence with all speed to Mr. Stiffback, our hero and his chums were placed in durance vile—charged with an offence which, little more than half a century ago was punished with death by the hands of the hangman.

The inspector was in what is popularly called "no end of a stew" at the proceedings of Mr. Growlagain, and he tried as far as possible to mitigate the rigour of confinement.

The instant the wrathful schoolmaster had departed for his own house, there to repair the damage inflicted by the venomous Jobling, the inspector hurried to the cells, laden with cushions and rugs, and followed by one of his men carrying the private store of chairs.

"I don't know who the others are," he thought to himself, "but it's as well to be civil to the lot, as they is chums of this young lord, and go to the same school. Growlagain will get into trouble over this, for the earl owns nearly all the county, and a good half of the next, and has no end of influence."

"Beg your pardon, my lord," he said, aloud, as he entered the cell; "hope you won't bear me no malice for doing my duty, but I'll try and make you as comfortable as I can. Is there anything your lordship or the other young gentlemen would like?"

"I should like——" began Tommy, when the inspector cut him short.

"It's no use you asking for anything," he said. "You're in for felony, and after eating the beadle's dinner I shouldn't think you'd much of an appetite."

"I only had one," said Tommy, "and the beef was beastly, and there was enough mustard on it to make a plaister of."

"You're very good," said Vansittart, carelessly. "As we're to be done out of our picnic we may as well have something to eat here. What do you say, boys?"

There was an unanimous chorus of assent to this, for the prospect of imprisonment on a charge of felony had by no means spoiled their appetites.

Vansittart took a pencil and paper, and wrote down the names of such a list of good things that the inspector opened his eyes thereat.

"You can get them at the hotel, you know," added the young lord. "There's the money, and you can give the change to your men for beer."

"That's jolly enough," said Lionel. "But I say, Mr. Inspector, how long shall we have to stay here?"

"Until you go before the magistrate. You see, I can't take bail at once, as if you was only locked up for being disorderly. The magistrate will have to see to that."

And when will he see to it?"

"To-morrow, most likely."

"That's comfortable; and shall we have to sleep here?"

"I'm afraid you will. But I'll let you have some mattresses and so on, so that you'll be well off."

"And our holiday lost," growled Charlie. "I say, Mr. Inspector, can't you let us go, and we'll promise to come back when you want us?"

The ghost of a wink quivered in the inspector's left eye—a wink of incredulity—but he only said—

"Really couldn't do it, gentlemen. I should be dismissed the force, lose my pension, and everything."

"Take it quietly, Drummond," said Vansittart. "We can pay old Growlagain out for this afterwards. 'Begone, dull care,' and make yourself as jolly as you can."

But it so happened that someone was already "serving out" Mr. Growlagain—and no less a personage than our old friend Sam was engaged in the process.

Sam had of course, like a true and ardent lover, devoted his holiday to the fair Mary, and crossing by the first boat reached the house just as Mr. Growlagain was preparing to go to the meeting.

Of how that meeting was prematurely broken up our readers are already aware, and in consequence Mr. Growlagain's return was hastened by several hours, much to the disgust of Sam and Mary, who had anticipated a blissful evening.

"Drat the man!" exclaimed the lovely but impatient Mary; "I never see such an aggravating creature. But lor! there, it's your fault."

"Oh, Mary!" expostulated Sam, almost tearfully, "don't say that."

"So it is. You're the unluckiest sweetheart I ever had. Why, when young Barlow used to keep company with me we'd be together for hours, and nobody would ever come anigh us."

"Mary," said Sam, in a voice husky with suppressed emotion, "you don't mean to say as you ever had any other sweetheart but *me*?"

"Oh, dozens!" replied the pretty housemaid, with a toss of her head and an emphasis which implied that she might have said "hundreds," and yet have kept within the bounds of truth.

"And—and—did you *love* 'em, Mary?" faltered Sam, half distracted at the idea that others besides himself had entwined that taper waist and printed kisses on those rosy lips. "Don't say you were fond of 'em, or I shall go wild."

Mary saw that she had gone a little too far.

"I'm not fond of 'em *now*, Sam; that ought to be enough for you, anyhow. But there's master's bell. Let me go—see how you're tumbling my hair—do ha' done now!"

And breaking away from Sam's embrace, Mary ran out of the kitchen, and so upstairs to her master's "snuggery."

Mr. Growlagain, as our readers may suppose, was not in the most amiable of tempers, for he was dreadfully sore, and every tooth in his head was aching with the violence of Mr. Jobling's blows.

"Hot water," he growled, "and look sharp about it."

"In a basin, sir?"

"Ah, and in a jug too—and the sugar and a lemon."

The schoolmaster had a tolerable notion of comfort, and so, seated in his easy-chair, he sipped a glass of stiff grog, while Mary bathed his wounds with the warm water.

There was something very nice and soothing about this dual performance. Mary was such a pretty girl, too, and did her office so gently, that Mr Growlagain began to feel quite comfortable, and mixed his second tumbler.

"Do you feel better, sir?"

"Much better," replied Mr. Growlagain, actually smiling.

"Shall I leave off, sir?"

"No, Mary, not yet; it's very soothing, really," and the grim schoolmaster not only smiled, but with his disengaged hand tickled Mary under the chin.

"Lor', sir!" exclaimed Mary, drawing back and blushing.

"You're a very pretty girl, Mary, do you know?" said Mr. Growlagain, who not only smiled this time, but actually winked.

Mary looked down, and the water in the basin she held reflected the rosy tinge of a full-sized blush. Mr. Growlagain was elderly, and fat, and ugly withal—but the ugliest man in the world appears passable to the woman he flatters.

"I think," continued the schoolmaster, upon whom the grog seemed to have produced a very rapid and peaceful effect, "that I'll raise your wages, Mary."

"Thank you, sir."

"How much do you get now, Mary?" continued Mr. Growlagain, while his left arm vaguely wandered about in search of the housemaid's waist.

"Ten pounds a year, and all found except beer."

"Except beer," murmured Mr. Growlagain, fondly. "What does 'beer' rhyme with, Mary? 'Dear,' doesn't it? Come a little closer, Mary. Mix me a lil more grog, and have a lil drop—'self—hic!"

Mary looked doubtfully at her master. She had seen him in most of the phases of intoxication before, but this was the first time that he had passed through the amorous stage.

"Mix lil more grog, and let's be jolly. Sing's song, Mary."

"I can't sing, sir."

"Nonshensh! Give's kish, then."

And Mr. Growlagain, getting suddenly up from his chair, gripped Mary before she had any idea of his purpose, and with elephantine playfulness tried to snatch a kiss from her fair lips.

Matters had just reached this interesting stage when Sam, who was of a tremendously jealous disposition, began to feel alarmed at Mary's prolonged stay, the more especially as he entertained a mortal distrust and hatred for Mr. Growlagain.

"I'll just take a peep, and see wot he's arter," thought Sam. "He's a reg'lar bad 'un; but if he tries on any larks with Mary, I'll be down upon him."

Acting upon this resolution, Sam crept upstairs, and arrived in the passage just in time to hear Mr. Growlagain's outrageous demand for a kiss.

Sam was in the room in an instant, and taking aim at the schoolmaster, he butted just in the middle button of his waistcoat, and sent him doubled up and gasping back into the arm-chair.

There was a length of cord lying on a case of books which had arrived the day before, and this Sam seized; and before Mr. Growlagain had recovered sufficiently to offer any resistance he was fast bound to the back and legs of his chair.

"There, you hoary old sinner," said Sam, shaking his fist so close to Mr. Growlagain's nose as to tickle it. "How d'yer like that? Yer'll go a kissin' other people's prop'rty agen, will yer? You're a nice old man to be a eddicator of youth, ain't you?"

"Hush! Be quiet, Sam," said Mary, in a terrified whisper; "go away, do, or you'll be locked up."

"Locked hup," replied the lanky youth, with tremendous but unnecessary emphasis. "I should like to see him do it. A pretty hobject I'd make of him afore the madgistreet. Raise your wages, will he? I'll raise something upon him, and that's bumps."

And here Sam, unable to restrain his feelings any longer, smote Mr. Growlagain with considerable violence in the eye, and made him roar again.

"Oh, don't Sam—don't, for my sake!" pleaded Mary.

"Mary," said Sam, melted in a moment, "you know I'd do anythink for you; and precious lucky he may think hisself, for if it hadn't been for you he'd a been at this werry moment a gory corpse a weltering in his gore."

MR. STRRIT ASSUMED AN ATTITUDE OF INDIGNATION AS THE NEW PUPIL WAS INTRODUCED.

Or, Young Wilful's Schooldays.

LONDON: HOGARTH HOUSE. BOUVERIE STREET. FLEET STREET. E.C.

WHILE OLD GROWLAGAIN VAINLY ENDEAVOURED TO BURST HIS BONDS, SAM KISSED THE BLUSHING MARY AGAIN AND YET AGAIN.

With which bloodthirsty words Sam concluded his speech, and then, folding Mary in his arms, he kissed her blushing face once again and yet again, whilst old Growlagain, writhing with fury, vainly strove to burst his bonds.

"There," said Sam, finishing up with a "smack," which might have been heard a quarter of a mile off—"there, yer were talkin' about kissin'. Wot d'yer think of that one? *You* kiss my sweetheart. Why, you—you bloated old conkybine! You hoary-'eaded, treacherous receiver, you!"

Sam had now raised his voice to such a pitch that the other servants, and even some of the boys in the distant schoolroom, heard the tumult, and now hurried to the scene.

It would have been an awkward time for Sam then if Mr. Growlagain had been popular, for the lanky youth could hardly have hoped to gain the victory over a score or two of foes.

"Come away, Sam," said Mary, when she heard the arrival of the reinforcements. "Some of the masters will be here directly, and the police, too, perhaps."

"Let 'em," retorted Sam; "but if the ole bilin' was a listenin' I wouldn't care. I'd say just the same as wot I have said. And afore I go I means to let him have another topper—one as he'll reklect for a week; and if he's man enough to want to give it me back he knows where I'm to be found."

So saying, and before Mary could interpose, Sam let out his long right arm and smote Mr. Growlagain on the top of his nose, which, from mingled excitement and grog, had become extremely red.

"Help! Oh, murder!—Police!" yelled Mr. Growlagain.

"Come away!" shrieked Mary.

"Let me give him another—only one.

But Mary was a young lady of decision. She took Sam by the collar, and before he could offer any resistance ran him out of the room into the passage, where quite a crowd was already gathered.

"What has he been doin' of, now?" asked the cook, in a whisper.

"Kissin' Mary, or leastways wantin' to, afore my werry eyes," replied Sam.

"The old beast! A man of his hage!" said the indignant cook.

"Ah, but he won't try it on again in a hurry," added Sam. "I've give him one or two for hisself, and now he's tied in his harm-cheer, where he may stop and bust hisself with hollering afore I let him go."

"Bravo!" said one of Mr. Growlagain's pupils, but in a very low tone of voice. "You're a rum 'un to look at, but you must be a good plucked one to tackle our governor. Are you sure he can't get loose?"

"Sartin," replied Sam.

"Then I'll have a peep," said the boy, and, followed by three or four of the boldest of his companions, they ventured to look round the corner of the door upon their imprisoned master.

To them it was a joyful sight to see the tyrant with the tables so fairly turned upon him.

There he was, pinioned hand and foot, the crimson fluid trickling from his nose all down his shirt-front and immaculate white waistcoat, while his mouth gave utterance to language to which that of a tipsy costermonger would have been mildness itself.

Meanwhile Sam had taken an affectionate farewell of Mary, and after exacting a promise that she would let him know if ever Mr. Growlagain renewed his familiarities, darted away in search of his young master.

CHAPTER XLVI.

OUT OF THE FRYING PAN INTO THE FIRE—THE END OF HOLIDAY AND THE BEGINNING OF FRESH TROUBLES—TOMMY GOES TO ROOST ON A STRANGE PERCH, AND IS CAUGHT NAPPING—A NICE LITTLE GAME OF SKITTLES.

OF course, our hero and his chums did not remain long in durance vile after Mr. Stiffback had received the inspector's message. He went at once to the magistrate, Mr. Tuckemup, and explained the facts of the case.

Mr. Tuckemup went with him at once to the station, saw the boys, heard the evidence of the beadle, a good deal softened down, and in conclusion took Mr. Stiffback's bail for them all.

"Growlagain, of course, won't press the charge," said the magistrate; "and if you pay the damage you'll hear no more of the matter? But really, Stiffback, you must keep these youngsters of yours in better order. Fun is fun, and no one liked it better than I did when I was a boy, but when it comes to breaking the law, you know why really—"

"I never had any of this trouble with my boys, during all the many years I have been in the profession," said Mr. Stiffback, fixing his eye slowly on Tommy, "until *that* one came. It is he, I firmly believe, who has sown the seeds of discord, rebellion, and mischief in my school, but I will drive it out of him or know the reason why."

A dreadful creepy feeling poured all down Tommy's back, and he began appealingly—

"Oh! if you please, sir."

"Silence!" continued Mr. Stiffback, in an awful voice. "Hardly a day passes, Tuckemup, but I have to punish that boy for some flagrant act of disobedience, and now he is endeavouring to qualify himself from the interior of Newgate. Only a few days since he set on fire a stack of brushwood."

"It was quite an accident, please sir."

"*Will* you hold your tongue?" said Mr. Stiffback, giving Tommy a chuck under the chin, which nearly caused him to bite off an inch of his tongue.

"Indeed, sir," said Vansittart, who saw that Mr. Stiffback really believed Tommy to be the prime mover in the mischief, "I am much more to blame than Codlings."

"Your motive, Vansittart, in endeavouring to shield your companion may be praiseworthy from your point of view, but nothing which you can say will cause me to alter my opinion. Good morning, Tuckemup; thanks for your kindness in taking so much trouble. Come, young gentlemen, you will accompany me back to school."

"Here's a sell," whispered Lionel to Charlie—"we shan't get another holiday yet awhile. Ain't old Stiffback in a way?"

"Awful. It's all your fault though, Li. If you hadn't gone into that confounded town hall, we might have had a jolly day."

"Well, we had a good lark while it lasted. It's no use crying over spilt milk."

"I shall have something to cry about, presently," moaned Tommy. "Flogging machine unlimited for me, I know. I'm a regular rainbow now."

"We're all in for it, for the matter of that," said Lionel.

"Ah! but I'm sure to get it hotter than you. See how Stiffback looked at me while he was talking to the magistrate. It made me crawl all over."

"Silence there," said Mr. Stiffback, sternly. "If I catch you talking again, Codlings, until I give you leave, I'll make you wear a muzzle for a month."

"Oh, lor!" groaned Tommy. "Down on me again."

And so, with nothing but mournful anticipations before them, the little party returned to Lake Island, where, in accordance with Mr. Stiffback's promise, they were very soon provided with something to talk about and cry about too.

Over their sufferings we will draw a veil, for it is—especially as far as Tommy is concerned—too harrowing a picture to dwell upon. Suffice it that our hero and Charlie made a solemn vow to compass the destruction of the terrible instrument of torture by which they had suffered. Whether they were successful or not will be developed in the course of this faithful and veracious narrative.

Tommy was too sore for sympathy. His pangs were so acute that he sought out a quiet spot, where he could bewail his fate, and plot vengeance upon Mr. Stiffback in solitude; and, of course, with his usual luck and discrimination, he selected the dormitory of the boys of the upper form, thinking that they would not return until late.

So far Tommy was right, but when he threw himself down upon the most comfortable-looking bed and went to sleep, he committed an error of judgment for which he was doomed to suffer severely.

Instead of the quiet half-hour's nap which he intended to take, Tommy slept calmly on until not only was supper-time past but bed time arrived, and with the hour of nine the boys of the upper form came into the dormitory.

The bed Tommy had appropriated belonged to a big bony lad of seventeen, who with a tremendous yawn approached it, and not noticing the intruder, flung himself at full length upon him.

He was up again, though, rather quicker than a flash of lightning, for the howl of anguish which Tommy uttered was truly appalling, and no wonder, for one long elbow of the big boy had very nearly impaled him.

"What's that?" exclaimed Wilson, turning pale with affright; "who made that row?"

"There's something in your bed," said another, pointing to the counterpane, which was being violently agitated, as if by the convulsions of some creature in its death-throes.

"It's a mad dog, I believe," added Wilson, getting farther away; "they yelp just like that—I've heard 'em before."

At this there was a general movement of the boys in the direction of the door, but just then Tommy, with a kick of extra violence, cast off the counterpane, and disclosed his well-known features, which now bore an expression of doleful anguish.

"Dash it, it's that young whelp, Codlings," said the exasperated Wilson, coming forward and collaring the unhappy Tommy, who was still gasping with pain, and letting off fresh howls whenever he found wind enough for the exercise.

The momentary alarm of the upper form boys was now changed into wrath against Tommy, for having been the cause of it.

"Wring his young neck?" growled one.

"Pitch him out o' window," was the mild suggestion of a second, while the others were all ready enough with proposals as to the disposal of the intruder.

"You let me go," gasped Tommy. "What have I done?"

"There's cheek," growled Wilson; the beggar comes here, sticks his dirty little carcase in my bed, and spoils it, and then wants to know what he's done? You'll find out what I've done, my beauty, before I let you go."

"What shall we do with him, then?"

"I know," said a third. "These little beggars have been getting a deal too cocky since Wilful and Drummond came to the school. We'll teach some of 'em a lesson. Who'll volunteer to go into No. 3 dormitory and capture a few?"

"I will"—"and I"—"and I"—and so on until there were half a dozen volunteers ready for the service.

"But what are you going to do with them?" asked Wilson. "I don't care much for meddling with the little beggars; they squeak like a lot of young pigs when the butcher's come, and then old Stiffback will drop down on us."

"Don't funk, Wilson, why there'd be no fun at all if we always thought of Stiffback. Come on, you volunteers."

And swooping down upon the unsuspecting youngsters, even as the kite pounces upon a bevy of innocent chickens, the big fellows captured ten of the smallest and most timid, and returned to their own room in triumph.

"Don't kick up that row," said Barkum; "we're not going to kill and eat you."

"What are you going to do then?" snivelled one of the Bobbles family, for all five of that helpless body of relations had been captured.

"We're going to have a nice little game of skittles!" replied Barkum.

"Skittles!" cried Wilson. "How in earth can you manage that?"

"Easily enough. Don't you remember what a game we had at that little roadside inn a month ago?"

"Oh, ah! where we quarrelled with the louts over who should pay for the beer, and we gave 'em a licking. I remember. But you can't play 'em. Where are the pins?"

"Here," replied Barkum, tapping one little boy on the head with his knuckles. "They'll make first-rate skittles. The big fellows at a school where I was four years ago used to play. I've been a skittle-pin myself often."

The others saw the plan now, and entered into the joke with a readiness which was not surprising when it is considered that they were only players and spectators.

The human skittles howled dismally when Barkum and two or three others began to bind their arms to their sides and fasten their ankles together.

It was so uncommonly like that piece of pinioning performed by Calcraft and his brother executioners upon the candidates for the gallows.

The preparations were soon effected, and the skittles ranged in order at the further end of the dormitory, where, especially the front "pin," they looked as miserable and unhappy as boys could well look.

"Now for the ball," said Wilson. "Come on, young Codlings."

"Here, I say, none of that, you know," remonstrated Tommy, who, while chuckling over the discomfiture of the Bobbles family, had forgotten that he too was a victim. "Help!"

"Hullo!" said the voice of Vansittart at the door. "What's up? Here Li; here's your chum, Tommy, in trouble again."

"Now, Vansittart," said Barkum, "we don't want young Wilful in here. You know it's against the rules for lower form boys to come into our dormitory."

"You're keeping the rules perfectly well, yourself," replied Vansittart, pointing to the human skittles. "Who brought those in?"

"We did, of course."

"Well, then, I've a right to bring Wilful and Drummond in. If it's only a bit of fun you're having we won't interfere."

"Not we," added our hero. "But what has Tommy done?"

"Went to sleep in my bed, the young beggar," growled Wilson. "It's as hard as a deal board now. No chance of getting it made again."

"Then he must suffer for trespassing," said Lionel; "only don't be too hard on him, for he must be precious sore."

"We won't hurt him," said Barkum, cheerfully, now that he saw his game was not likely to be interfered with. "Now, Codlings, take it quietly."

"You're a nice sort of chum, you are," growled Tommy, "to let a chap be made a skittle ball of and not help him."

"You shouldn't have spoiled Barkum's bed, Tommy. If you break the rules you must take the consequences. Charlie or I would have to besides it won't hurt you, so take it quietly."

Barkum and Wilson had by this time tied Tommy up, as nearly in the shape of a ball as his figure would allow, and, taking him between them, they began to swing him to and fro.

"Play!" shouted our hero, while the unfortunate skittles nerved themselves for the coming shock.

At the word Tommy was launched through the air, the front "pin" received the "ball" full in his middle, and, doubling up with a groan and a gasp, he fell, flooring four others, while Tommy, cannoning to the right, sent down two more with a crash upon the flanks.

"Seven pins down," said Lionel, who acted as "sticker up."

"Put 'em up again," said Vansittart. "Drummond and I will play you."

"Oh, don't!" sobbed the unlucky Bobbles, who had done duty as a front pin. "It hurts so, it does indeed."

"Nonsense, you don't know what's good for you," replied Lionel, putting him in the front place again. "You'll begin to like it by-and-bye."

"Oh, shall I? I'll tell Mr. Stiffback; you see if I don't."

"It doesn't matter if you do. You know he won't listen to sneaks. How are you, Tommy?"

"Prime," replied that young gentleman, who would have endured any amount of torment if his pet foes the Bobbles only suffered as well. "Give us a good swing this time, Li. Let the front pin have it on the nose."

They did swing him well, and again the skittles were floored, the front pin suffering dreadfully, for Tommy's knee had smitten him on the extremity of his little sharp nose, causing it to bleed with a profuseness almost alarming.

"Oh, you've killed me!" he bawled. "I'm dying. Oh lor—oh lor! Fetch a doctor."

"Stick him up again," said Tommy, with a grim smile of satisfaction. "Never mind his crying—that's only pretence; he can cry whenever he wants to."

"Stop his noise, anyhow," said Vansittart, "or we shall have some of the masters down upon us Pass the water-jug, Drummond."

Drummond ran for it, and Vansittart, with very little ceremony, emptied the contents down the back of the howling Bobbles, who, thus suddenly deprived of breath, gasped and snorted worse than ever.

Seeing, as they thought, their dear brother at the point of death, the four junior Bobbles began to bewail his fate at the top of their voices, and, ere our hero and his chums could stop them, a heavy tread was heard in the corridor without, and the tall figure of Mr. Stiffback entered the dormitory.

CHAPTER XLVII.

SAM HAS THOUGHTS OF TURNING SHEEPSTEALER— THE APPEARANCE OF THE BEADLE—AND THE LOSS OF THAT WORTHY'S SECOND SUPPLY OF PROVISIONS.

SAM had no sooner left the domicile of Mr. Growlagain than the mutterings of his interior system reminded him that the premature return of Mary's master had, as he put it, "choused him out of his grub."

He knew that it was useless waiting till he got back to Lake Island, as it was one of the rules of that methodical establishment that any one who had a holiday was supposed to provide himself with sufficient provender for the day.

As Sam thought of this he groaned audibly, and said—

"Bust it, if I has to wait till to-morrow morning I shan't be able to find myself when I wakes, I shall be so blessed thin."

So, still keeping a keen look out for his young master, he cast his eyes about with a view to finding something wherewith to satisfy the demands of his stomach.

Never at the best of times flush of money, owing to his inordinate love for hardbake, pastry, figs, candied peel, and all that sort of thing, Sam had of late found an extra demand on his purse in the shape of ribbons, trinkets, &c., wherewith to captivate the capricious heart of Mary.

He found himself, therefore, at this present moment without a copper in his pocket, and his credit was worse than his hunger.

However, he was gradually growing desperate, and cast wolfish eyes on a flock of young muttons which a drover was convoying through the town.

"Blest if I couldn't eat one of yer ror," said Sam to himself, and then as a brilliant thought struck him, he added. "and I'll have one of yer, too. I've heard as how the Mexicans cut ror steaks off their 'osses and eats 'em, and they can't hang a fellow for sheepstealin' now, I've heard."

And Sam would doubtless have carried his ideas into effect, for the drover had entered a public-house with the intention of obtaining his evening pint.

But his felonious intentions were frustrated by the appearance of the beadle, who was still bewailing the loss of his sandwiches.

Sam, who possessed all the London street boy's antipathy to the constitutional authorities, especially as represented by Bumbledom, no sooner saw the beadle than he prepared to run.

To his surprise, however, the pompous functionary drew a shilling out of his pocket, and beckoned mysteriously to Sam.

Sam eyed the shilling with wondering looks, and, as if fascinated, slowly moved towards the beadle, muttering to himself as he did so—

"Blest if he ain't a-going to give me a bob—well this 'ere is a rum go."

But no such generous thought pervaded the breast of the hungry official.

He, like Sam, was on the look-out for something to replace his lost banquet, and feeling that it was beneath his dignity to "run his own errands," he spotted Sam as a likely substitute.

"Come here, my boy," he said, as Sam approached. "Go and get me a nice knuckle of pork at Mr. Giles's. Ere's a shilling. and mind yer brings me back the right change, or I'll run yer in. Bring 'em into the parlour of the 'Lion.'"

"All right, sir," responded Sam, as he seized the proffered coin and departed on his mission.

The pork butcher's reached, Sam entered, and with the air of a millionaire demanded a nice knuckle of pork and a piece of bread.

His order supplied he coolly asked if he might be allowed to eat it there.

"No, my lad, I ain't licensed as a refreshment-house keeper, and I should be fined if I allowed you to eat anything in my shop."

"Wot a blessed shame!" said Sam, as taking up his purchases he walked out into the street.

Then looking about he spied a convenient recess, into which he dived, and in two minutes the beadle's anticipated feast had disappeared within the cavernous recesses of Sam's jaws.

No thought of the dishonesty of the act he had just committed entered the lean one's mind.

But his inner consciousness told him that he must draw the line somewhere—and that somewhere was at the fourpence he had received out of the shilling.

So carefully wiping away all traces of his feed, Sam sauntered into the presence of the hungry official, and tendering his change said—

"The knuckle of pork ain't quite done yet, sir," which, considering all things, was hardly the truth.

"Oh!" growled the beadle. "I suppose Mr. Giles 'll send it in here to me."

And he went on smoking his pipe as if he had a perfect right to send Sam where he liked.

"Well, yer are a mean 'un," said Sam, in disgust, "yer might give a feller a drop of beer for going of an errand for yer."

The beadle turned up his eyes till only the whites were visible, and groaned out—

"What is the world coming to?" I sends a boy out for me—*for me*—and he expects to be paid for it. My boy, you should consider that the honour and privilege of serving me has brought its own reward."

Sam, with a chuckle, said—

"Yes, sir."

"And for a lad like you are to expect a glass o' beer or anything else for doing of such a thing for me is out of all sense."

"Yes, sir," again responded Sam, this time compelled to vent his overcharged feelings in a loud guffaw.

"What be ye a laughing at?" asked the beadle.

But Sam, feeling sure that he could not better his position, was already half way out of the door.

So the irate official resumed his seat and his pipe, anxiously awaiting the arrival of the knuckle of pork.

Half an hour passed after Sam's departure, but there was no sign of the arrival of the provender.

After Sam had left the inn the beadle waited for the arrival of his knuckle of pork with patience worthy of Penelope.

But no pork made its appearance.

At last a substitute in the shape of Mr. Giles entered the parlour, and that worthy calmly seated himself in his accustomed corner.

Our friend the beadle sniffed vigorously three or four times, then hemmed then hawed, and at last said—

"Giles, where's my knuckle of pork?" the last few words being given with an extra amount of emphasis.

"Knuckle of pork! What dost mean?" answered the irate pork-butcher.

"Mean! what do I mean? I call thee mean, man. Here's I paid for a knuckle of pork 'arf an hour agone, and 'tain't arrived yet. Gie us my knuckle of pork or my money, or I will run you in."

"You're mad!" responded Mr. Giles, with an utter contempt for Lindley Murray. "I knows nothink about no knuckle of pork. What do yer mean by such langwidge to me?"

"I means to say as I sent to thee shop for a knuckle of pork, and I means to say as I ain't 'a had it yet."

"And I means to say as how you ain't ordered any knuckle of pork from me, and what's more you don't get it till I've seen the colour of your money—and that's more."

The appearance of the beadle at this moment as the horrible thought flashed across his mind that Sam had served him with the knuckle of pork in the same way that Tommy Codlings had with the sandwiches, would have furnished a study for some modern Hogarth.

But, all the same, he felt himself compelled to stand upon his dignity, and the consequence was that a very pretty scene ensued between the aggrieved pork-butcher and our friend, the beadle.

Both feeling that they were in the right the argument waxed stronger and stronger, until fisticuffs were resorted to as an ultimate arbiter.

Over the closing portion of this evening's entertainment we must draw the curtain; meanwhile, Sam, with the comfortable feeling that is born of a full stomach, was again wandering in search of his young master—and mischief.

CHAPTER XLVIII.

MR. STIFFBACK PICKS UP THE BALL AND MAKES A BAT OF HIS SLIPPER—TOMMY VOWS VENGEANCE—SOKER IN DIFFICULTIES—TOMMY HAS IT OUT WITH THE BOBBLESES.

THE boys were fairly caught. Their little game of skittles had made such a noise that Mr. Stiffback was in the dormitory before they had time to even attempt to conceal themselves or their proceedings.

There was for a moment a deep hush—a profound silence, resembling the lull before the outbreak of a thunderstorm; then the lightning of wrath and indignation flashed from Mr. Stiffback's eyes, and the deep diapason of his voice was heard in awful tones.

"So, young gentlemen of the upper form, this is the example you set to your younger schoolfellows, is it? Vansittart, you are the head boy of this room, perhaps you will be kind enough to favour me with an explanation of this uproar."

To attempt to excuse himself would only make matters ten times worse, so Vansittart took the most sensible course, and pleaded guilty.

"We were winding up our holiday with a little game, sir," he said; "but we did not intend to make so much noise."

"Indeed," said Mr. Stiffback; "and pray what is the nature of the little game in which you seemed so pleasantly engaged?"

"It was a—a—sort of game—at skittles, sir," replied Vansittart.

"Oh!" said Mr. Stiffback, looking curiously at the pile of damaged boys at the further end of the dormitory. "Those were the pins, I presume?"

"Yes, if you please, sir, and I'm the ball," said a voice, so close to Mr. Stiffback's feet that he jumped as if a dog had suddenly barked at his heels.

The schoolmaster looked down, and there was Tommy, still curled up like a ball, but with innocent enjoyment beaming from every feature of his plump countenance.

But at the sight of Tommy Mr. Stiffback's countenance darkened ominously, and he glared at Tommy in a way that iced that young gentleman's spine.

"So that is you again, Codlings, is it? But I might have foreseen this, for as surely as there is a piece of mischief or insubordination in the school, so surely are you the prime mover and instigator of it."

"Yes, sir, whined that member of the Bobbles family who had been the front pin, "he's knocked me down twice, sir. Look at my nose, if you please, sir."

Mr. Stiffback glared at Tommy in a hopeless manner, as if his many delinquencies were really too much for him; then he lifted Tommy up by the nape of his neck, and flung him on one of the beds.

Then he stooped down and pulled off one of his slippers, and gave it a flourish or two to try its flexibility.

"I am very sorry, Codlings, that your obstinacy compels me to chastise you so often; but I am obstinate, too, in my way—I am resolved to cure you, and we shall see who first gets tired."

Here our hero, Charlie, and Vansittart made an appeal to Mr. Stiffback to spare Tommy, alleging, what was perfectly true, that Tommy was not in fault at all, and that he had been made a skittle-ball of against his will.

"Silence," said Mr. Stiffback, sternly. "Don't let me hear another word. I will not allow you to perjure yourselves to save Codlings from a well-merited punishment."

Poor Tommy was in a beautifully favourable position for the administration of corporeal chastisement—for he was still tied neck and heel, so that he could not move an inch of his own accord. He knew this, and when Mr. Stiffback turned him over so as to get the wrong end of him into the right position, he uttered a dismal howl for mercy.

"Too late, Codlings," said the schoolmaster; "you should have thought of that before."

And then with a beautiful precision he brought down the slipper, and a smack and a howl were heard simultaneously, proceeding from opposite ends of Tommy's rotund person.

"Poor old chap," whispered Lionel; "it must be awful. Were you ever hided with a slipper, Charlie?"

"Yes, my governor does it often; but I am never tied up like that, though."

"That makes it ten times worse, and he can't wriggle, either—all the whacks come in the same place."

"Yes. My eye! how he is laying it on. That makes two dozen, Li."

But Mr. Stiffback ceased not until for exactly eight-and-forty times the slipper had descended upon Tommy's tightly-stretched skin; and then, with the same calmness and deliberation which characterised his general movements he put on his slipper, and after taking down the names of all those who were parties to the little game of skittles, he ordered them to bed, and made sure that his commands were obeyed by waiting till all were snugly tucked up.

The next day was a day of whaling (if we may be forgiven the pun) and lamentation throughout the school. Soker was in a state of gloomy joy and profuse perspiration, for he had to work the flogging-machine the better part of the day, and wore out three sets of canes.

Poor Tommy was, as usual, by far the greatest sufferer, but he comforted himself with the prospect of a speedy vengeance.

"I'll serve 'em out," he said to Lionel, as they sat together at tea-time. "I'll make 'em pay for this, Li; you see if I don't."

"Who? Stiffback and old Soker, I suppose you mean?"

"No, I don't. I mean those sneaks of Bobbleses."

"But what have they got to do with it, Tommy? They were served out very nearly as bad as you were."

"Oh, were they though? I know better—it was all owing to them that I got into the mess. Didn't you hear that beast tell old Stiffback that I'd knocked him down twice? Just as if I could help it."

"Let 'em alone, Tommy—you'll only get into more trouble."

"I don't care," replied the plump one, recklessly. "I can't be sorer than I am now, that's one comfort; but I'll take it out of these Bobbleses the very first chance I get."

"The fact is," replied Lionel, "we had better devote our attention to the flogging machine. If we can only manage to smash that up old Stiffback will be so occupied in making a new one, altering and improving as he goes on, that he won't have time to flog you."

"That's all very well, Li," said Tommy, "but I must have vengeance on those beastly Bobbleses. I can't rest till I've had it."

"Well, have your own way, Tommy, only don't get into any scrape."

"All right, Li. What shall we do now?"

"Why, my idea is to have a lark with Soker—he's pretty sure to be half fuddled by this time, and I know he always lies down in the loft to sleep off the fumes of the day's potations about this time, so as to pull round in time for prayers."

"Well I'm on." What shall we do with him?"

"I hardly know yet, Tommy, but depend upon it we shall think of something by the time we reach the loft."

"Shall we take any one else?"

"No, Tommy, we'll do the deed ourselves."

Having made their way to the loft they carefully reconnoitred, the result being that they found Soker as Lionel had predicted, in a very uncomfortable attitude, enjoying a drunken snooze.

"What shall we do to him, Li?" said Tommy, as soon as they had effected an entrance.

"I've got it," replied Lionel; and he took a small phial from his pocket.

"Lor! you don't mean to poison him, do you?" gasped the affrighted Codlings.

"Poison him, no—he's poisoned enough now. Faugh! How he smells of drink."

"Well—sniff—yes—sniff—he does," answered Tommy, with his little snub nose tilted a little more heavenward than usual.

Lionel, in the meantime, had withdrawn the stopper from the phial, which Tommy eyed with wondering suspicion.

He saw Lionel carefully take a little brown stick, not much thicker than a piece of slate pencil, from out of the phial, and then a light dawned on his bewildered mind.

"Phosphorus!" he exclaimed.

"Yes," answered Lionel. "And if we rub it well over his hands and then wake him up, he'll think, in the half-darkness, that he has spontaneously combusted himself."

"But, I say, Li, suppose he has got so much rum, gin, and brandy inside him that the phosphorus ignites him. Shouldn't we be hung for murder?" And Tommy's knees quivered visibly.

"Don't be afraid, young Codlings, I know how to use it—and I'll take every precaution."

Five minutes later Soker presented a sufficiently diabolical aspect to satisfy Lionel's fastidious taste, and, half closing the shutter which formed the door behind them, they left the loft.

"How are we to wake him?—that's the next question," said Lionel.

"Shy a brick at him—the beast!" replied Tommy, as he affectionately rubbed the part most affected by contact with the canes of the flogging machine.

"No, we won't do that; but this old potato basket will do him no harm, and if we pitch it judiciously it's sure to wake him."

No sooner said than done. Lionel pitched the basket carefully through the aperture, and it landed neatly across Soker's nose.

Poor Tommy quivered again; he thought that the friction caused by the blow with the basket would turn Soker into a lucifer match, and ignite the phosphorus.

But nothing so untoward occurred.

Thoroughly roused by the knock, Soker, with drunken gravity, half raised his head, and was about to lie down again, after giving vent to an unintelligible snort that might have meant anything, but which was probably the reverse of a blessing on the article which had so unceremoniously tumbled on to his nose.

Suddenly, however, he caught sight of his hands, emitting a pale, unearthly light.

With a bound that would have done credit to a professional acrobat he was on his legs in an instant.

Staggering wildly round the loft for a minute or two he sat down on the basket which had been his rest, and began mourning miserably.

"What is the matter with me? What can it be?" and then he passed his coat-sleeve over his forehead with an idea of collecting his thoughts.

This was the finishing stroke. To his horror he found that his very clothes were on fire.

"Lor'-a-mussy on me! I've eerd of people set fire to thesselves 'cos they took too much drink," and straightway he dashed at the shutter.

Luckily for Lionel and Tommy it gave way outwardly, or Soker must have knocked them down with the violence of the shock.

As it was, they took the hint and made themselves scarce until Soker had opened the latch and was seen frantically making off to the horse-pond.

"Now he'll drown himself," said Tommy, in an agony of fear.

"Not he. There's not two inches of water in the pond; it was drained off the other day. But what a nervous fellow you are, Tommy—like a young kitten."

"Er-r! It's all very well for you to talk, but you'd be nervous if you had my beastly bad luck."

"Well, never mind, old fellow. Your bad luck has evidently deserted you this time. See, Soker has emerged from his bath, looking like goodness knows what. Come along, Tommy, we must cut off. If he sees us he'll smell a rat, and then there'll be another dose of the flogging-machine."

"Well, I've had it out with Soker—and dashed if I don't have it out still more with those beastly Bobbleses," said Tommy, as he and Lionel sauntered into the dormitory, as calmly and quietly as if they had neither of them ever played a practical joke in their lives.

In a general way Tommy was as forgetful of injury as the most right-minded and rigid Christian could have wished a boy to be, but in this particular instance the idea of revenge was fixed in him, and he watched and waited for an opportunity with all the patience of a red Indian.

It came at last, and this was it.

A letter from the parental Bobbles announced that gentleman's intention to pay his offspring a visit on a certain day, and it so chanced that the day selected was also a general holiday.

Behold, then, the five Bobbles, arranged in the shiniest of tiles, the shortest of jackets, and the broadest and whitest of lay-down collars, sallying forth to meet their revered parent at the Deliverham Station.

No vulgar holiday games for them, no rough rude bawling and scrambling, and "touch," "fly the garter," "follow my leader"—they knew better. Aristocratic repose and gentlemanly deportment were the characteristics of the Bobbles family.

Little recked they of the lion in the path, as they gently ferried over the lake, and landing on the opposite shore, marched with stately gravity along the path.

They dreamt not that the vengeful Tommy lay in wait to spoil them—even as Samson spoiled the Philistines—until at a corner of the lane he stepped forth and confronted them.

There was a glare in Tommy's usually benevolent eye that told the Bobbles far more expressively than words that he meant mischief. They were five to one it is true; but, as our readers know, they were not remarkable for pluck.

"Good morning," said Tommy, with sarcastic politeness. "Fine morning, ain't it?"

"Yes, Master Codlings," replied the senior Bobbles, timidly. "Are you going for a little walk?"

"No," said Tommy, grimly. "I've been for a little walk, and now I'm going to have a little fight."

Each one of the five Bobbles burst out into a cold perspiration.

It was awful thus to be beset by a rude dreadful boy who always wanted to fight.

"Exercise is a good thing, ain't it," continued Tommy, as he leisurely took off his jacket and cap, rolled up his shirt-sleeves, and made the se other little preparations incumbent on gentlemen who are about to indulge in pugilism.

"No—no doubt," faltered the eldest Bobbles; "but—but will you have the goodness to allow us to pass, Master Codlings? We have to meet our papa at the railway station, and we don't want to walk fast, as that would put us in a perspiration, and pa says it's vulgar."

"Oh! your pa says it's vulgar—does he?" said Tommy. Then your pa's a precious old humbug, that's all; and just to prove that he's wrong I'm going to make you perspire till you haven't got a dry rag on you."

So saying, Tommy began dancing about in the middle of the road in a buoyant and cork-like manner, and then, with marvellous dexterity, he knocked off the hats of all five of the brothers, and began distributing a pleasing variety of punches amongst them, which, as they were all huddled together in a heap against the hedge, they could not avoid.

Tommy worked away with a will, for he felt that he had never enjoyed himself so much in his life before, and in something less than a quarter of an hour had given the whole five as complete a little "licking" apiece, as any boy of moderate capacity could desire.

"There," gasped Tommy, when at length he was compelled to desist, from sheer inability to punch any longer. "Now go to that precious pa of yours and ask him if he thinks it vulgar to perspire now. If he says it is, and his fighting weight ain't more than eleven stone, I'll serve him as I've done you. I should like to lick the family all round."

And so, tearful, bruised, and bleeding, their pretty clothes begrimed with dust and gore, the five Bobbles limped painfully along the road to meet their revered parent, while Tommy, chuckling with delight, resumed his jacket and cap, and prepared to go in search of his chums, little thinking that they had been highly-amused spectators of the fight.

But in the meantime, events of such importance had occurred to our hero as demand, in simple justice, a new chapter.

CHAPTER XLIX.

SOKER AND SAM HAVE A LITTLE PRIVATE AND CONFIDENTIAL CHAT UPON A PECULIARLY CHEERFUL AND ENTERTAINING SUBJECT—THE "ODD MAN" RESOLVES TO QUIT THIS WORLD OF TROUBLE—SAM'S LITTLE STORY—PREPARATIONS FOR THE DREADFUL DEED—SOKER'S CONFESSION—THE DENOUEMENT.

UPON the afternoon of a certain day Soker and Sam Scarecrow sat together in the snuggery of the factotum of Lake Island School, enjoying a little of that social converse which is one of the privileges of the lords of creation.

It was a miserable day. The sky was of one uniform dull grey tint, across which, urged by a strong south-east wind, there swept sheets of filmy black cloud, discharging with a steady downpour torrents of the very wettest kind of rain.

The grim custodian of the flogging-machine was seated at one end of the table, looking at least one hundred per cent. more miserable than any of the unhappy culprits whom it had been his duty to submit to the torture.

Opposite him sat our old friend Sam, presenting a direct and forcible contrast to the melancholy Soker as he leaned back in his chair, with his long legs stretched out at full length, his eyes squinting amiably at the ceiling, and his lips emitting huge puffs of smoke which they had previously inhaled from the stem of a clay pipe.

"I wish I was reg-lar dead," said Soker, in the most melancholy and desponding tone of which the human voice is capable.

"Then why *don't* you die?" replied Sam, refreshing himself with a heavy "pull" at the contents of a "Toby Philpot" jug which stood on the table before him.

"Mister Sammle," continued Soker, casting a look of the deepest hatred and disgust at the pot of cold tea which faced him, "life's a burden to me since I've been deprived of my whisky, for how can a man keep his spirits up when they're being continually drownded in water?"

"Then take to it again" suggested Sam. "but more moderate like. It can't be a werry luxshoorius game to have deriddledum trimmings hevery week."

"It ain't; but there's compensashings, Mister Sammle," replied the melancholy Soker. "Was you ever thirsty, now?"

"Well, I have bin took that way once or twice."

"Ah, but I mean reg'lar right down thirsty," explained Soker. "When your inuards feel like a gunpowder mill after an exploshing, and your mouth like a copper boiler on washing day."

"I can't say as I ever felt so bad as that," rejoined Sam.

"Well, then, Master Sammle, you never know'd wot it was to feel thirsty, and likewise you never know'd the 'evenly bliss of the first drink in the morning, when you can hear the licker reg'lar fizz as it goes down your throat."

"That must be nice, I should think," said Sam' reflectively; "licks the nectar an' Lambrooseyer the old kind o' gods used to tipple, into fits."

"Not a patch on it," replied Soker, with a heavy sigh. "Well, Mr. Sammle, all that's past and gone. I shall never know them joys no more."

"Why not? There's plenty of whisky left in this world."

"Not for me, Mister Sammle, not for me," said the odd man, mournfully. "Do you recklect when the guv'ner said he'd cure me o' drinking?"

"Very well indeed," replied Sam. "And a queer way o' doin' it it was."

"So I thought," rejoined Soker; "but it did the job, Master Sammle. I hankers arter licker more'n ever, but I dursn't touch a drop, and my life's a burden to me in consekence, and I wish I was reg'lar dead."

And having thus concluded his observations on temperance with the self-same remark with which he had commenced, Soker pulled a little hair out of of his head, and knocked the teapot into the fireplace.

"'Tain't no use goin' on in that sort o' way," said Sam, refilling his pipe. "If you're in such a werry desprit condition spile yourself, but don't spile the propitty.'

"I will," said Soker, recklessly, as he got up and glared around him for some implement of destruction.

"Fire away!" added Sam, cheerfully. "I'll see fair; only don't overdo it, like the chap as I once heard on."

"Who was he, Master Sammle?" asked the odd man, for whom the subject had naturally an attraction at this moment.

"He was a feller who must ha' bin in much the same state o' mind as your'n," replied Sam, "for he came to the conclusion as this world warn't good enough for him, and thought he'd try another for a change."

"Did he?"

"I'm a coming to that presently. Don't you interrupt," said Sam. "Well, being a man of business, he meant to do the thing slap-up, so he buys 'arf a gallon o' the werry best pison, a double-barrelled pistol, and six yards o' new rope, and away he goes to where there was a tree a-growing on the werry hedge of a 'igh cliff."

"At the sea-side, were it?" asked Soker.

"It were," replied Sam; "but I shan't mention the name of the place on account o' the feelings of his fam'ly. Well, this chap swallers the pison, ties the rope to a branch of a tree, puts t'other end round his neck, swings hisself orf, and fires the pistol at his 'ed at the same time."

"And killed hisse f werry dead, in course?"

"No, he didn't," said Sam. "For the bullet missed his 'ed, and cut the rope, so that he fell into the sea, then the salt water he swallered made him womit the pison, and the coastguard boat as were passin' picked him up and give him in charge—and the next day he got six months for attemptin' to commit suicide."

"That was hard lines," said Soker.

"It were disappointin'," replied Sam; "specially arter takin' all that trouble."

"Then it ain't much good my tryin'," continued Soker, in a melancholy voice. "If a man tries pisoning, hangin', shootin', and drowndin' all at once, and that won't settle him, why nothink will."

"Try 'em one at a time," suggested Sam. "I've got some pison I'll lend you. Werry strong it is too—a smell o' the cork is enough for a weak man."

"Thankee," said Soker, but there was not much gratitude in his tone.

"Don't mention it," replied Sam, and putting down his pipe he went out and returned in a few minutes, with a huge bottle on which was a label with the word "Poison" in very conspicuous characters.

"That's it, is it?" said Soker, dubiously.

"That's it," said Sam, "and prime stuff too—a teaspoonful will curl you right up like a watch-spring, so fire away."

"I think," said Soker, in a hesitating way, "that shootin's a more genteel way."

"Makes such a mess," said Sam.

"That's troo," Soker added. "There's hangin', though. That don't make no mess."

"But it's werry degrading," suggested Sam. "You wouldn't like to be reckoned along o' those manufactors as Madame Toosaws puts in the Chamber o' Orrors."

"Ill try 'em all," said Soker, desperately; "like the chap as you were a telling me about, Mister Sammle. I've got a pistol as 'll send a bullet through a brick wall a quarter of a mile off, and there's lots o' rope."

"All right," said Sam. "'Tain't for me to interfere in such a private and confidential matter; but I'll look on, if you ain't got no injection."

"Not the least," replied Soker, "It'll be a comfort to me in my larst moments."

"Cut away and get the pistol then, old feller," said Sam, "and I'll rig up the gallows for yer while yer gone."

Now, although Soker was convinced that he was the most miserable man on earth, and had fully made up his mind to quit this vale of tears, he did not in the least expect that Sam would have looked upon the affair with so much cold-blooded indifference.

He thought that the bony youth would at least have endeavoured to dissuade him from his suicidal purpose, but instead of that here was Sam as ready to help him shuffle off his mortal coil as if it had only been an old coat or a pair of boots.

He felt sorry now that he had been so rash, but it would never do to retract, and so, with a somewhat reluctant step he went after the pistol.

By the time he got back Sam had fastened a rope to the cross beam of the ceiling, and placed a tub just underneath the ominous-looking noose.

"There you are, now—all compact and comfortable," said Sam, reseating himself, and puffing away at his pipe. "Have you got the pistol?"

Soker held it out. It was an old-fashioned cavalry pistol, with a flint lock. One that required a pretty strong man, in good training, to fire, and which kicked like a mule when it did go off.

"Why, you ain't loaded it," said Sam, as he felt about in the barrel with the ramrod. "You're a nice chap to go committin' suicide, you air. Where's the ammynishun?"

Soker produced a tin can, which held about a pound of powder, and several good-sized bullets, and handed them over to Sam, who filled the barrel two thirds full of powder, and then rammed home three of the bullets—the last of which was plainly perceptible at the mouth.

"Don't you go a overdoin' of it," said Soker, anxiously. "That pistol 'll bust, and it costed four-and-nine, second-hand."

"Did yer ever come nigh sich a hold himage?" ejaculated Sam. "You don't 'spose as less than three bullets will make any impression on that head o'yourn—do you?—and you ain't likely to want it after it *do* bust."

"There's somethink in that, Master Sammle," said Soker, gloomily; but it'll go t'wards the hexpenses of my funeral."

"You needn't trouble yourself about that," replied Sam. "The coroner'll see to that."

"Will he, though?"

"Aye. You'll be took down to the cross-roads out by the town at midnight, and they'll dig a hole, and shove you in, and then run a hedge-stake through you to keep you from gettin' up agin and frightnin' people, and that's about all the funeral *you'll* get."

"That ain't a werry respectful way o' gettin' buried," growled Soker, with a sour expression of countenance.

"What do it matter?" retorted Sam. "You won't know anythink about it."

"Well, I s'pose I'd better make a hend on it."

"In course you had," said Sam, cheerfully. "When yer makes up yer mind to do a thing, do it, and hev it over."

"Think so?" said Soker, with the tone of a man who wants to be contradicted, but as Sam only the more energetically repeated his previous statement, the odd man got on the tub and fitted the rope about his neck with that curious deliberation with which a man ties his new cravat on his wedding morning.

"Shove the knot well under the left year," said Sam, handing Soker a fine old razor that was lying on a shelf. "That's the fashionable way. You can blow your brains out fust, then cut your throat, and arter that you can kick the bucket. How do the programmy soot yer?"

"Ah, Master Sammle," said Soker, becoming more and more vacillating in his manner. "I've bin a dreadful bad chap in my time."

"Lor, now! yer needn't trouble to tell me that," rejoined Sam. "Do yer think I've bin in the same 'ouse with yer all these weeks and not found out that you're the meanest kind o' man that's made? There, make haste and git it over."

"I've done a lot o' things as I hadn't orter do, Master Sammle," continued Soker. "There's a unpaid score o' nineteen and thrippence due to the Black Bull and Winkle, and I don't mind ownin' now that the whisky as Joe the potman was took up for stealin' was prigged by me."

"Well," began Sam, "of all the mean—"

But Soker interrupted him.

"Stop a bit, Master Sammle. I wouldn't ha' let the poor chap suffer for me, but I got so blazin' drunk on the whisky the werry night I stole it that I were laid up unconscious for three mortal weeks, and never know'd nothin' about it till it were all over."

Sam looked relieved, and said as much.

"But that ain't the worst," continued Soker, penitently. "Did I ever tell you as I'd bin married, Master Sammle?"

"No," replied Sam; "not as I remembers."

"Well, I was. It's sixteen years ago, and she was a woman as kept a tramp's lodgin' house in Lambeth Marsh. She was a big, tall strapper, as could thrash a navvy, for I've seen her do it. She took a sort o' fancy to me, and let me stop for a month on tick. At the hend o' the time she comes hup with a bit o' chalk in her fist, and figerin' a lot of oughts and crosses on the door. 'There,' she says, 'Swipy, that's your account—are you going to pay it?' 'Sartinly,' says I. 'When?' says she. 'The minit I gets the money, mum,' I says. 'That won't do,' says she, puttin' away the chalk and tuckin' back 'er sleeves. 'Now, Soker, I give you your choice—pay the money on the nail or marry me.' I was took aback like, but I soon made hup my mind, and I marries her."

"And a werry happy time you must ha' had on it, said Sam, with a grim chuckle. "A lady as can whip a navvy is jest the percise party to promote domestic peace and quiet."

"We had one babby," continued Soker, "and I thought as how the young 'un would put her right, but she no sooner was up than she took to lush agin, and I got so sick on it that I cut away with the babby one day, and struck out north'erd, for I had some friends at Hendon then which give me a lift.

"It was terrible cold winter weather, and I'd forgot to take any money when I started so I had to pad the hoof, and by the time I got to 'Amstead it was nigh eleven, pitch dark, and snowin' into the bargain.

"We'd got 'arf way acrost the 'eath, and I were ready to drop with the cold, when I sees a light a way ahead like the light of a pipe or a cigar, and I thought I'd run and ask whoever it were for a copper or two.

"I were afraid to run with the child, for the ground were werry uneven, so I puts it down in a holler place, out o' the wind and snow, and bolts like mad arter the light, but just as I comes up to him he turns round, and thinkin', no doubt, I were a garotter, he fetches me a wipe over the 'ed with his stick that knocked nearly all the life out of me, and when I come to it were mornin', and I were covered from head to foot with snow."

"And the babby?" said Sam, whose face had become quite flushed with excitement. "Wot became o' that?"

"Poor little thing!" said Soker, plaintively. "I thought on it the minit I come to, and I ran to the place where I'd left it, expectin' to find it stiff and cold."

"And it were, eh?" said Sam, in a trembling voice.

"No, it were gone," replied Soker. "Some one must have parst that way, and picked it up, for I never see it since."

"Then, see it now!" exclaimed Sam, jumping up, and striking an expressive attitude. "Fifteen years ago I was picked up on 'Ampstead 'Eath, in the snow. Father, behold your long-lost orphan-spring!"

CHAPTER L.

SAM SCARECROW FINDS THAT HE HAS BEEN A LITTLE TOO HASTY, AND IS ONCE MORE AN ORPHAN—THE BOBBLES FAMILY IN A STATE OF DISCORD—WHO DID IT?—A NARROW ESCAPE FOR TOMMY—THE PICNIC, AND WHAT HAPPENED THERE—BICYCLE RIDING EXTRAORDINARY.

SO startled was Soker by the extraordinary nature of Sam's statement that he slipped off the bucket, and was kicking about in all the agonies of suffocation before the lanky youth had presence of mind to pick up the razor and saw the fatal rope.

A few glasses of cold water poured into and upon the melancholy Soker brought him to in the course of a little while, and he sat up, still rather blue in the face, and with his eyes a good deal further out of his head than they had been for many years.

"Oh, Lor'!" he gasped, as he tenderly felt round his neck to make sure that the rope had not severed it. "Oh, my! Don't it hurt?"

"Never mind," said Sam, soothingly. "That'll soon pass orf, and if the mark shows why you can say it wos the ringworm. Think wot a blessed day this is for both on us. I've found a parient, and you've diskivered your long-lost cheild."

"Eh?" said Soker, looking vaguely up at Sam.

"You lost the babby on 'Ampstead 'Eath, didn't you, fifteen years ago come this winter?" replied Sam, a little nettled at Soker's apparent indifference.

"I did."

"Well, just at that werry time I wos found there, wosn't I?" returned Sam. "Wot an aggrawating old chap you are for a father! Ain't it as p ain as —as you are, that I must be the babby—grow'd up, in course?"

"It do seem probable," said Soker, musingly. "Only there's one little injection, Master Sammle, wh ch ain't easy got over."

"Wot is it?"

"The babby I lost were a gal!" said Soker.

That was a settler. For years Sam had yearned for a parent's love, and even Soker the disreputable, Soker the "swipy," would have been welcomed with the dammed-up affection of fifteen years. But that was all over now, and Sam felt unutterably disgusted at the overthrow of his fondest hopes.

His disappointment was too great for words. Full of silent sorrow he walked up to the tub whereon Soker sat, took him by the ears, knocked his head a few times against the wall, and then, bursting into tears, quitted the place, a defrauded orphan.

Let us drop a veil upon his sacred grief.

* * * * * * *

Those five elegant productions of humanity, the Bobbles, had made their way sorrowfully to the station, bent upon urging their respectable progenitor to vengeance by the pitiful spectacle they presented.

Nor were they wrong in their calculation of the effect their condition would produce upon their parent, for he was a man who made "appearances" his everyday divinity. The Almighty he only worshipped once a week, as quite a secondary Power.

Arm-in-arm with Mrs. Bobbles, and attended by the whole available staff of porters, overawed by the majesty of his appearance, the great man emerged from the station, and then beheld, drawn up in line, not five well-fed young gentlemen, habited in gorgeous raiment, but five dilapidated scarecrows—muddy, battered, and bleeding.

Mrs. Bobbles gave one look and fainted on the top of three porters, who went down like ninepins, for Mrs. B. was a woman of substance, and turned the scale at fourteen stone.

Mr. Bobbles did not faint—that was alike unbecoming his sex and his dignity. He caught the station-master by the collar, and asked him what he meant by it.

"What, sir?" gasped the station-master, whose utterance was materially impeded by Mr. Bobbles' knuckles. "I ain't got nothing to do with it."

"Tell me, man—tell me instantly," said Mr. Bobbles, in a sepulchral voice, "who are those—those low vagabonds in the garb of boys?"

"Oh, Pa!" exclaimed the eldest Bobbles, in a tearful voice. "We couldn't help it."

"And one of them," continued Mr. B., in an awful tone, "dares to address me as 'Pa.' I do not know them—I cannot. My children would perish rather than expose themselves to the public gaze in such a base condition."

Here all five of the Bobbles murmured in plaintive chorus that they couldn't help it—indeed they couldn't.

"I had intended," continued Mr. B., "to walk through the town, and with that pride a parent only can feel, say with mute eloquence to the public, 'I am a father. Behold and admire my offspring!'—but now—"

Mr B. paused—words failed him—his feelings were too overpowering, and, with slow but severe emphasis, he drew his five boys to him one by one, and smacked their heads.

"It is a fearful duty," he said (and so it was—to the boys), "but from my duty I never shrink. Porter, fetch me a fly."

The porter who had been the least damaged by the fall of Mr. Bobbles limped off to obey the order. The other two were flattened out, and were trying to squeeze themselves into shape by the aid of the waiting-room door.

The fly came—a roomy one. fortunately—and into it the five unlucky ones were packed. Then Mr. and Mrs. Bobbles got in, and the pressure was awful. Indeed, when the banks of the lake were reached they had to be forcibly pulled apart, like jujubes in hot weather.

The only thing that sustained them was the thought of the vengeance they would take on Tommy by denouncing him to Mr. Stiffback, but even this gratification was to be denied them, for one of the young galley slaves who ferried them across the lake handed to Bobbles senior a small scrap of paper, on which was scribbled, in Tommy's tipsy caligraphy—

"If you sneek on me I'll come into your room to-night and SETTLE YOU. I've got a sharp knife with twelf blades to it.—TOMMY CODLINGS."

The eldest Bobbles turned pale and shuddered; then he passed it on to his brothers, and they turned pale and shuddered as well.

They had not the least doubt but that the sanguinary Tommy would carry out his threat, and so, through very fear, they abandoned the notion of denouncing him as the culprit, and laid the blame on some imaginary louts.

But the parental Bobbles was by no means appeased when Mr. Stiffback promised to set the police on the track of the agricultural vagabonds.

"And pray, sir," said Mr. B., pompously, "what satisfaction will that be to my outraged feelings? I have seen my children torn and muddy; and, worse than all, they have had their heads vulgarly punched just as if they were common boys."

"My dear sir," said Mr. Stiffback, mildly, "accidents WILL happen."

"Nonsense, sir. In a well-regulated school, such as I thought this to be when I entrusted my sons to your care, such a thing as accidents ought never to occur."

Mr. Stiffback felt his wrath rising, and he would dearly have liked to give Mr. B. a piece of his mind, but he could ill afford to lose five pupils at once, and so he made the soft answer which turneth away wrath.

It took a whole waggon-load of them, though, there or thereabouts, to pacify the indignant parent; and, indeed, it was not until he had made a very good dinner, washed down by a couple of bottles of Mr. Stiffback's choice old port, that he became at all peaceable.

The next day he was treated to an exhibition of the attainments of his precious offspring; and as Mr. Stiffback had taken care to give them all the answers to study beforehand, they passed through the ordeal with immense credit to themselves and satisfaction to their parents.

Mr. Bobbles evinced his gratification by accepting the schoolmaster's invitation to stay for a few days, on the last of which a nice little picnic was organised, and at Mr. Bobbles' request (as it cost him nothing) a holiday was granted to the whole school.

Of course, though, the boys were not intended to mingle with the sacred festivities of their elders.

They were left to their own devices, under the guardianship of the boys of the upper forms, with strict injunctions not to get into mischief, which command was of course disregarded with the customary punctuality and despatch.

"I don't mean to get into any trouble to-day," said Tommy, who of course had joined our hero's party. "I've brought out my 'Telemachus' and 'Cæsar's Commentaries,' and I'm going to have a quiet read—a sort of intellectual afternoon, you know."

"Oh, Tommy, Tommy!" said our hero. "What do you think will become of you? A boy who'll study when he isn't obliged to deserves to be pelted to death with Greek lexicons."

"I don't care," replied Tommy. "I tell you I'm

too sore to get into any fresh trouble. Wait till my new skin has grown, and then I don't mind."

"That won't be till you've got your whiskers, and cut your wisdom teeth, Tommy," said Lionel. "But do as you like. Charlie and the rest of us are going for a bicycle ride."

"Are you, though?" said Tommy, thoughtfully. "You're not going in for any larks?"

"Not unless one falls in our way, and we can't help tumbling over it."

"I should like to know how to ride on a bicycle," continued Tommy. "Is it very difficult?"

"Easy as nothing at all," rejoined Lionel. "All you've got to do is to lean it against a wall, get into the saddle, get someone to give you a shove, and away you go—ten miles an hour easy."

"That must be prime," said Tommy. "I think I'll go."

"How about Telemachus and Cæsar?"

"Oh, they'll keep. The weather isn't very warm," said Tommy. "Blow the books! I wish I hadn't brought 'em now."

"Never mind, Tommy. You can leave them with the bicycle-man as security for the machine. Here's the shop."

"Is that a bicycle?" said Tommy, staring hard at one of the latest developments of that queer apparatus. "Why, it looks more like a magnified cobweb than anything else."

"They're the articles, Tommy. Here's one that will do beautifully for you." And Lionel pointed to one with a 56-inch driving-wheel, a bicycle which Stanton himself could hardly have managed.

But the proprietor of the establishment, having some regard for the safety of his property, if not for that of Tommy's limbs, found him one more suited to the capacity of his little plump legs, and a boy being hired to hold him on until they got clear of the town, a procession of some dozen more or less skilled bicyclists proceeded on their way.

Tommy was in a state of ecstacy at this novel method of progression—but his troubles were yet to come. He was proud of a skill he did not possess, and remembered not that pride goeth before destruction, and a haughty spirit before a fall.

CHAPTER LI.

SOKER RESOLVES TO HAVE REVENGE ON SAM—MR. STIFFBACK TO THE RESCUE—THE TABLES TURNED.

WHEN Sam left Soker in a completely muddled and bewildered condition from the violent attack made upon him by the disconsolate orphan, that worthy sat on the floor where he had fallen for fully half-an-hour.

At the expiration of that time he began to gather sufficient of his scattered faculties together to come to the conclusion that there were no bones broke, and that, after all, perhaps, he should not better himself by making his exit from this miserable world.

"No, drat un! I'll be even with the squinting toad afore I does that," and Soker looked with an air of disgust at the rope, razor, pistol, and overturned tub, which were lying in the most artistic confusion about the room.

A happy thought flashed through his brain.

"I've got it," he chuckled to himself as, with the gravity of a drunken man, he prepared to fill the tub with water.

"If I fires this 'ere wepping orf, that owdacious young wretch 'ull 'ere it, and he'll think as 'ow I've blowed my busted brains out! [chuckle.] Then he'll come rushing in in a flurry, and wollop he'll go inter the pail [chuckle]; and, darn un, that 'll about sarve the scamp out!"

Soker's preparations were very soon made.

The tub was dragged over to the door, and filled with water, into which the irate Soker had poured the contents of two jars of Day and Martin's best.

Chuckling audibly, he carefully mixed the contents of the tub, occasionally dipping a finger in to see whether the colour was all right, with quite the air of an experienced dyer.

As soon as the required consistency and colour were obtained the would-be suicide retreated to the chimney, and holding the pistol as far up it as he could, plucked up courage enough to pull the trigger.

Crash—rumble.

The immediate result did not quite come up to Soker's expectations, for the concussion caused an immense quantity of soot to dislodge itself, and as his face happened to be in convenient proximity a considerable proportion found its way into his mouth, nose, and eyes.

This, perhaps, rather heightened the effect, for the smothered yell that followed would certainly have led any listener to believe that Soker had really settled his own hash.

Sam heard the report—and so did Mr. Stiffback.

Sam's feelings are easy to imagine.

But Mr. Stiffback's defy the combined effects of imagination and description.

"Lor! bust it, but that blessed old fool's a been and gone and done it. And blow me if they won't say as how I've a-aided and abetted him in doing of it."

And literally quaking with fear Sam rushed towards the trap that Soker had so cunningly baited for him.

But Soker had reckoned without his host, or rather master.

Mr. Stiffback—who at the time he heard the report and subsequent yell was taking his constitutional walk before dinner—hastened as fast as his bewildered faculties would allow him in the direction of Soker's sanctum.

That worthy's good angel having apparently deserted him, the schoolmaster contrived to reach the door just two seconds before Sam came running breathlessly up.

"Good lor!" cried Sam, as he saw Mr. Stiffback put his hand on the handle of the door. "I'm in for it. Blest if I ain't as unfortynite as young Codlings. They're sure to hang me as a hacksessary."

But he had no time for further remark or reflection.

Mr. Stiffback, rendered impetuous by the terrible dread that had taken possession of him when he heard the report of the pistol, and Soker's groan, rushed blindly on his fate.

The door yielded to his pull. There was a stumble, a half-muttered blessing, a splash, and all that Sam could see of the schoolmaster was his feet, as they wriggled about in agony, half-way out of the door.

At any other time Sam would have been too frightened to laugh at the accident that had befallen Mr. Stiffback; but the revulsion of feeling caused by the fact that he saw Soker alive and kicking in the centre of the room, was so great, that he burst into a hysterical fit of laughter.

As Mr. Stiffback managed to extricate himself from his awkward position, and to clear his eyes of the blacking that impaired his vision, he, too, saw Soker indulging in a fanciful war-dance, indicative of his delight in having had it out with Sam.

But when the supposed Sam emerged from the tub, he said, in accents that, half-choked as they were, Soker recognised at once as Mr. Stiffback's.

"Soker—(pouf)—what—(sneeze)—do—(cough)—you mean by—(faugh)—this?"

Sam started off laughing again, and thinking discretion to be the better part of valour, stole away unobserved.

Soker stopped in the middle of his dance of delight, and, in horror-stricken tones, gulped out—

"Mr. Stiffback!"

"Yes, sir; Mr. Stiffback, and what does this disgraceful conduct mean, sir—answer me at once, or I'll kick you through the streets of Deliverham?"

"It wor that young willin, Scarecrow, wot done it, sir!"

"Don't add lying to your shameful conduct, Soker! How can you say that it was Scarecrow:

"PLAY!" SHOUTED OUR HERO, WHILE THE UNFORTUNATE "SKITTLES" NERVED THEMSELVES FOR THE COMING SHOCK.

when I saw him myself, not a minute ago, hastening, like myself, to ascertain the cause of the explosion that was heard just now!"

"I was only a-washing of myself," wheedled poor Soker, who was in such an agony of terror at the result of his little joke, that he hardly knew what he was saying.

"Washing yourself!" cried the schoolmaster; then, for the first time, he noticed Soker's soot-covered face and hands, and, he added, almost involuntarily—

"And, by Jove, you want it!"

Soker stood twiddling his thumbs, and gradually lapsing into a state of hopeless idiotcy.

"Can't you speak, sir? Can't you say something in explanation of this scandalous outrage?"

Then, as a thought flashed through his mind, he said—

"Codlings is at the bottom of this I'll be bound. Where is he?"

Hardly knowing what he was about Soker pointed to the chimney.

"Ah!" snorted Mr. Stiffback, like a bird of prey scenting its quarry.

And to push his head half way up the chimney was the work of a second.

His curiosity was rewarded by the fall of a second batch of soot, which had been some time making up its mind whether it should descend into the room or remain half way up the chimney.

Half maddened at this Mr. Stiffback knocked Soker backwards, bade him pack up his boxes and come to his study, to receive what wages were due to him.

Soker merely sat where he had fallen, and endeavoured to recollect what it was all about.

Then the schoolmaster, vowing vengeance against Codlings, started off to find that unlucky wight.

But for once Tommy's lucky star was in the ascendant.

Mr. Stiffback's search was rewarded by the discovery that Codlings had not left the refectory since tea.

So the puzzled and ill-used schoolmaster concluded that it was wisest to say nothing about the affair, and to wait and watch the progress of events, in the hope that the mystery might be cleared up.

CHAPTER LII.

A BICYCLE RACE, AND A LUCKY FINISH.

"I ALWAYS heard," said Tommy, "that riding on a bicycle was difficult, but it ain't!"

"No; it isn't very difficult—as long as there's somebody to hold you on."

"I don't want anybody to hold me on," replied Tommy, confidently.

"Don't be rash, now," said Lionel. "You'd better keep the boy a while longer."

"Not me. He can go as soon as he likes."

"You're sure you feel safe and comfortable, Tommy?"

"Lovely," replied Tommy.

"All right, then," said our hero. "There's the sixpence, young 'un. Now you can let go, and cut away."

The youth caught the sixpence Lionel tossed towards him, and letting go the bicycle, ran off to the town, to invest the coin in those cornered jam puffs, or hardbake, or some other species of those cloying comestibles in which the soul of youth delighteth.

It so happened that the front wheel of Tommy's bicycle was just then turned at right angles with the other, so that for a few moments he was able to balance himself unassisted.

"There, you chaps," he said, proudly. "Look here! I don't want anybody to hold me on!"

"Bravo!" said Charlie. "You're a genius, Tommy. But start on—let's see you move! We'll have a race!"

Tommy pressed his right foot heavily on the treadle, the wheel moved round, and Tommy took a temporary lodging in the ditch. It had a lot of nice soft mud in it though, so he wasn't hurt.

"What a splendid style you have, Tommy!" said Lionel. "Only you shouldn't try to go faster than the bicycle!"

"It's the man's fault," added Charlie. "Tommy ought to have had the machine with the 56-inch wheel. That's his size."

"You be jiggered!" growled Tommy "Come and give me a rub down, instead of standing there grinning at me. You'll fall off yourself, by and bye, I dare say. Dash it! it's as bad as trying to balance one's self on the blade of a knife!"

Tommy was soon rubbed down, and dried as well as circumstances permitted, and after a quarter of an hour's practice, and a quarter of a hundred tumbles, he managed to tack, in an unsteady way, from one side of the road to the other. But it was fearfully dangerous work, especially for the snails and worms and other insects who happened to be out for a walk that day. Tommy made jam of them by the score.

Vansittart and some of the upper form boys who were skilful riders started off as soon as they cleared Deliverham for a village a dozen miles away; but our hero was too good-natured to desert Tommy, and with Charlie and one or two others who did not feel competent to undertake a ride of five and twenty miles, stayed behind to keep him company.

Riding a bicycle is much harder work than it looks, especially for beginners, and before Tommy had covered half a mile, he was steaming with perspiration and gasping for breath.

"Oh Lor!" he panted, "let me get off and rest a bit."

"Don't do that, Tommy," said Lionel. "Here, Charlie, take the other side of him, and we'll give him a lift."

There was a slight ascent in the road, a mild kind of hill indeed, and up this they toiled, Tommy working his short plump legs as if he had been born and brought up to the treadmill business.

"Only a little farther, Tommy," said Lionel; "we're nearly at the top, and then you can go down the slope at forty miles an hour."

So absorbed were they all in the by no means easy task of getting Tommy safely to the top, that none of them heard the sound of voices, the clatter of knives, forks, and spoons, and the musical gurgle of liquor flowing out of bottles, which proceeded from the other side of the slope, and seemed to indicate the presence of a festive picnic party.

They reached the top, and thinking only to give Tommy a gentle roll to the bottom, they let him go, and almost at the same time they caught sight of an assemblage of some dozen or two of merrymakers, in the very height of the enjoyment of a feast.

Instinctively Lionel and Charlie started to stop Tommy, but he was already half a dozen yards away, shooting down the hill at a tremendous pace, and before they fully recognised their own danger they were in full swing.

The distance was about fifty yards, and in three seconds from the time Tommy gave utterance to his first agonised yelp he ran over an old lady, and plashed head first into a huge bowl of salad, which an elderly gentleman was in the very act of serving.

There was a splash, a crash, and a howl of anguish from the old gentleman, for he had been very liberal with the mustard and vinegar in the dressing, and his mouth was full of it, and so were his ears and eyes, and it trickled down his neck and tickled him there, and he was exceedingly uncomfortable.

As for Tommy, his head was right through the bottom, and when he got up he had the bowl round his neck like a sort of ruff, and a head-dress of chopped lettuces, tastefully mingled with slices of hard boiled eggs, adorned his intellectual head.

Our hero, Charlie, and the others who had started

down the hill too late to avoid the party at the bottom, made the best of matters for themselves by driving on at full speed, and trusting to luck to escape.

Lionel's bicycle ran over and demolished a small array of wine bottles that were put in the shade to cool, Charlie demolished the pastry, but Pryce came to grief over a game pie, and was taken into custody by a fierce-looking gentleman with huge red whiskers, who, in a voice which had the "laste taste in loife" of a rich Hibernian brogue, threatened to blow out his brains with an umbrella if he dared to move a step.

Of course the ladies of the party—as was right and proper under the circumstances—fainted, or pretended to faint—the latter course is quite as effectual, and not nearly so unpleasant; and a good deal of time and sympathy was wasted before they were brought round, and coupled with the assurance that it was neither fire nor thieves, nor an earthquake, nor an invasion of Fenians, nor mad bulls, nor any dangerous episode of this nature, but only the work of some bad, evil-minded boys, whereupon the ladies, deeming it anything but romantic to be alarmed at such an occurrence, expressed a burning anxiety to slap the said boys, and otherwise inflict painful corporeal chastisement upon them.

"It shall be done, ma'am," said the Milesian gentleman with the red whiskers, "but not by yer fair hands. It's meself that will take the skin off the backs of the young blaggards."

"And I'll help you," growled the old gentleman, whom Tommy had besprinkled with the salad dressing. "Stop till I cut a couple of hazel switches."

And seizing the carving knife Mr. Simpson soon trimmed a couple of young saplings, which would have suited admirably for fishing rods, and handing one to his ally, grabbed Tommy by the nape of the neck.

"Bring um round here out of sight of the ladies," said the Irish gentleman. "It's not fit that their delicate faylings should be lacerated by the spectacle of the execution of the culprits. Bring um along, Simpson, me bhoy."

Now Lionel and the others who had escaped had pulled up as soon as they were at a little distance from the party whose enjoyment they had so suddenly and violently interrupted, and on calling the roll it was soon discovered that Tommy and Pryce were absent.

"Who'll volunteer to go back?" asked Lionel. "We must rescue 'em if we can, for I expect they'll get it hot from the picnickers if we don't get 'em away."

Every one volunteered of course: not one was mean enough to leave a chum in the lurch, and so the whole five, leaving their bicycles stacked in a convenient hiding place, stole back in Indian file to the picnic.

Just as they arrived Mr. Simpson and his friend with the whiskers were proceeding to drag their victims away, but they did not believe in silent suffering, any more than a pig does; indeed we doubt who is capable of making the most hideous noise—a boy who is about to be thrashed, or a pig whose weazen the butcher is about to slit.

"Bring um along, Simpson," bawled the Irish gentleman, who found Pryce a pretty tough handful. "Faix ye young blaggard, I'll tache ye to kick a gintleman on the shins; I'll bate ye into powdher, I will."

"Look out, boys," whispered Lionel. "Pick up some turf, quick, with plenty of dirt at the roots, and when I give the word shy at their faces. I can hear them coming. Aim true and all together."

Little expecting that anything in the shape of a rescue was at hand, the gentleman with the whiskers and Mr. Simpson came out into the rear of the coppice, and each holding out his prisoner at arm's length, flourished his hazel switch to give extra vigour to the first blow.

But as it descended Lionel raised his hand, and at the signal five large lumps of turf, which might have weighed a couple of pounds apiece, whirled through the air with unerring aim.

The Irish gentleman received one full between the eyes and a second in the mouth, and gasping out "Howly saints, I'm kilt!" he dropped his switch and performed a wild kind of jig around a neighbouring tree.

Mr. Simpson, who was short and fat, received the mass of the turf just on the second button of his waistcoat, and with a sound resembling that produced by the bursting of a bladder, he sat down, gasping out "Oh, my!" at intervals of two seconds.

"Run now, for your lives!" said Lionel; and, mindful of Tommy's propensity to bolt straight into danger, instead of away from it, he took him by the arm and set off at full speed in the direction of the spot where they had left the bicycles.

They were barely in time, for some of the other picnickers, anxious to have a share in the cheap and harmless luxury of thrashing a boy or two, arrived just as our hero and his party departed; but as it was a long time before they could extract any information beyond "Oh, my!" from the Irish gentleman or Mr. Simpson, the boys had mounted their bicycles, and put a good half-mile between them and the scene of their little adventure, before pursuit was possible.

CHAPTER LIII.

MONSIEUR DE VINAIGRE AND HERR VON KOBBLERS-VAX HOLD A LITTLE ARGUMENT UPON THE INTERESTING SUBJECT OF MANLY BEAUTY, WHICH NEARLY RESULTS IN AN APPEAL TO ARMS—THE END OF A FRAY AND THE BEGINNING OF A FEAST—OUR HERO AND HIS CHUMS PLOT AGAIN—WITH WHAT RESULT OUR READERS WILL SEE FOR THEMSELVES.

THE old enmity between M. de Vinaigre and Herr von Kobblersvax had by no means diminished with the progress of time—on the contrary, it had increased, as such animosities arising out of rivalry have a way of doing.

But these rivals for the favour and caprice of Mr. Stiffback seldom allowed their jealousy of each other to be exhibited in public, for the head master insisted on harmony reigning in the school, and if he discovered that any serious enmity existed between any of the ushers, he would recommend those ushers to move.

In this peaceful state of things, however, Lionel and his chums by no means acquiesced, and since the day of the famous cricket match it had been the delight of these young gentlemen to allude, whenever it was possible, to the wonderful hit of the German professor, and to praise to the skies the marvellous strength which had enabled him to send a cricket ball through the air with such velocity that it caught fire.

"I say, Herr Professor," said Lionel, "that a picture ought to be painted of that feat, such as they do of the gallant actions of the Victoria Cross men. What do you say, Charlie?"

"I think so too," added Charlie. "Herr Kobblersvax must be tremendously strong."

"And heavy, too," said Lionel. "How much do you weigh, sir—more than Monsieur de Vinaigre?"

"More as heem!" repeated the German, with a laugh. "Mine goot poy, he weigh not so much as one of my foots!"

"C'est bien possible!" retorted the French master, shrugging his shoulders, and glancing from the German's ponderous beetle-crusher to his own elegant little boots. "It is ver' likelee, but it is not de size, it is not de vait, as make ze beautiful man. Dere is ze elephant, ze hippopotamus. Zey are bote larger and vay more as you, but nopoty call zem loavely! It is ze elegance of ze human form, de graceful shape of de limbs—dem is ze tings!"

"Vot ish dat for a dummerkopf?" growled the

Herr. "Ven a man is so tin (he meant 'thin') as his close must be stuck on to him mit paste to keep dem from tumble off, and it take two of dat size to make von shadow, I do not see much of de grace and booty dat you shpeak apout!"

"Sacr-r-r-re nom d'une pipe!" (This sounds like a very dreadful oath, but we assure the reader that it is quite harmless.) "Vat you say?"

"I shpeak de troote!" replied the German, calmly. "I see you ven you vos in de sun de oder day, and I shwear dat you hafe no more shadow as Peter Schlemil."

"Who was that chap?" said Charlie to our hero.

"A German who sold his shadow to the devil in exchange for an inexhaustible purse," replied Lionel. "I'll lend you the story to read. I've got it in my box. Hark, now! Listen!"

"Mistare Kobblersvax," said the French master, his voice trembling with passion, "you say dat I hafe no shadow. I show you now as I hafe a leetle substance. I vill fight myself wid you."

"Make a ring," cried Tommy, dancing a jig for glee. "Here's a fight."

But Tommy, as usual, put his oar in the wrong water, for his shout reminded the professors of the danger they ran in quarrelling before the boys. So as the victim happened to be conveniently near them both, each presented him with a good signal box on the ear, ordered the rest of the boys to the evening class-room and separated, glaring whole armouries of daggers at each other.

Dearly would the excitable Frenchman have liked to challenge the German to a duel; but the certain loss of his situation stared him in the face, and they were by far too scarce for him to run the risk.

"Nevare mind," he said to himself. "I vill serve him a nice leetle trick. I vill do so as ze boys to one anozare. I put somezing in his boots, or gunpowder in his snuffares. Ha! Ha! Alphonse du Vinaigre vill be a-venge!"

The old proverb says that at the end of a feast comes a fight, but it often happens that an intended fight is turned into a feast, and it so happened on this occasion that Herr von Kobblersvax received an unexpected consignment of hams, preserved meats, sausages, kirschwasser, and other things good to eat and drink from his friends in Saxony.

Now he was not a hard-hearted man, on the whole, and the sight of the tempting delicacies softened him still further, and he offered the hand of friendship to Monsieur du Vinaigre.

The Frenchman was peppery when he thought his dignity assailed, but he too was warm-hearted, and he accepted the German's invitation to a feast of erbswurst and kirschwasser.

Lionel was an unseen witness to the reconciliation and the invitation. Quite by accident, of course, for he would—as a hero should—have scorned to listen to a conversation not intended for his ears. The author of this paragraph is named "Walker" —Christian name, "Hookey."

"I can smell a lark at the bottom of this," said Lionel, when he had told in confidence the abstract of what he had heard. "They both are sure to get pretty jolly, and then they'll begin arguing again."

"And after that, fighting," added Charlie. "Bravo, Li! we'll be there."

"What did you say they were going to have for supper?" said Tommy. "Hot German sausage, eh?"

"Yes, Tommy. Real German, too. I saw one pretty near as big as you."

"Oh, my!" exclaimed the plump youth, in a species of ecstacy; "and then, perhaps, Li, while they're fighting we'll be able to get a bit."

"Always thinking of a new lining to the coats of your stomach, Tommy."

"Why not?" retorted the plump one. "It's the only one I've got, and I ought to take care of it."

"True for you, Tommy," said Charlie Drummond. "And now, Li, you're commander-in-chief—what's the programme?"

"The usual one," replied our hero. "We'll wait till the other chaps are asleep, and then crawl down and have a peep at the fun."

"Wouldn't it be better to hide ourselves in the room?"

"No; it couldn't be done, I'm afraid, because old Stiffback has taken it into his head to examine the dormitories himself, and if we were missed there'd be a row."

"If they're going to get 'jolly,' as they call it," added Charlie, "we might do something with my magic-lantern—eh?"

"That's a good notion, Charlie. Have you got any slides?"

"Some fine ones. 'Johnny Gilpin's Ride,' and—"

"Have you got any moveable ones?"

"Yes; there's a head of Mephistopheles—moves its eyes, and opens its mouth."

"That's prime, for if any of the other fellows get about, we can give them a fine fright."

Then ensued a long discussion as to the further proceedings of the evening, which resulted in a visit to the German master's bedroom, and sundry cabalistic performances with string and wire, the effects of which will be seen presently.

At the usual hour of nine the boys trooped off to their respective dormitories. At half-past, Mr. Stiffback made his rounds, and found them all apparently fast asleep; but he had scarcely quitted No. 3, when one white-robed form stole softly out of bed, and whispered—

"Hist! Charlie!" Charlie was wide awake and ready, and so was Tommy, for visions of German sausage had had the extraordinary effect of keeping the young gentleman awake.

"All ready? Where's the lantern and the slides, Charlie?"

"Here they are—under the bed."

And as Charlie stooped to fish them out he cannoned against somebody, and banged his head against the bedstead.

"Dash you, Tommy! That's you, I know. Always getting in the way."

"Quiet, Charlie. No row, or you'll wake some of the fellows."

"It's that Codlings. He's always spoiling fun somehow," growled Charlie.

Softly, stealthily, they crept out of the dormitory into the corridor, and then, lighting the lantern and carefully covering the lens, they proceeded in the direction of the German professor's bedroom, from which faint sounds of "revelry by night" proved that the "rivalry by day" had—at least temporarily—been forgotten.

The revelry was at its height when our hero and his chums reached the door, and both of the gentlemen were making much more noise than is consistent with that sobriety which the teachers of youth especially ought to practise.

As a matter of fact both the masters were a good deal more sober by necessity than by inclination. Each dearly loved to "go in a buster" now and then, but the fact had to be carefully concealed from Mr. Stiffback, or instant dismissal would have been the consequence.

Sometimes, however, inclination would conquer prudence, and they ran the risk. It was so on this occasion, evidently, for as the boys drew near they could plainly hear the spirit-stirring strains of the "Marseillaise" and the "Wacht am Rhein," mingling as disorderly and unpleasantly as did ever the Teutonic and Gallic soldiers at Wagram or Austerlitz, Reichshofen or Gravelotte.

The notes of the two war hymns, closed with each other, wrestled fearfully—now the German would seem to get the best of it, and the sonorous roll of the "Wacht" soared aloft triumphant; but then the Frenchman would arrive at the refrain, and with a tremendous "Marchons—marchons, qu'un sang impur!" knocked the "Wacht am Rhein" on the head, and concluded with a triumphant crow.

"They're going it," said Lionel. "My eye! they'll soon get to fighting if they sing those hymns against one another."

"Let's see if we can't get a peep, said Charlie. "Open the door, there's no fear of their hearing the handle turn—they're making too much row."

It was true. The professors could have hardly heard the creaking of the noisiest hinges that ever squeaked aloud for oil. The door was opened a couple of inches, and the three boys, looking through the crevice, had a satisfactory view of the two gentlemen worshippers of Bacchus.

They were seated comfortably on the ground opposite each other, while between them, spread out upon the doubled counterpane, were the sausage, the hams, and some comfortable-looking, short-necked, big-bellied black bottles, from which, despising the effeminate conventionality of glasses, the two professors drank their liquor.

"You see vot it ish, my friend," said Herr Kobblersvax, with a tipsy wink, "ven I gets tronk I likes to do de ting mit gomfort. Vot ish de use of shairs ven ve knows as ve tombles off mit de tird bottle? and vot ish de use of glasses ven ve know tree bottles go to do pellyfull."

"Vrai, mon ami," answered Monsieur du Vinaigre. "But I tink dat I holt more dan tree bottel. I tink four, par tous les dieux, or I perish in the attempt."

"Nein, nein," growled the German. "You do drink zwei, dat is two, den you zee double, and dink dat you do zwallow de odders."

At any other time the Frenchman would have resented this imputation as a deadly insult, but the fiery Hamburg sherry and the dulcet kirschwasser had taken all the fight out of him for the present, and left nothing but amiability.

After a while the Frenchman proposed a little dance, and gave the German an elegant specimen of the national *cancan*, as danced at the *al fresco* ball-rooms of Mabille and Asnières.

Herr von Kobblersvax knew as much about dancing as an elephant, and was about as well qualified in the way of "build," but the sight of the dance inspired him, and he arose and proceeded to join in.

Monsieur du Vinaigre was delighted.

"Ve vill haf such a dance as you haf nevare see," he said; "but it make too warm."

This was easily remedied by removing some of their garments, and being rendered in a measure oblivious of decency by the liquors they had drunk, they stripped to their shirts, and then began to dance with a vigour and energy which communicated themselves to the ornaments on the shelf, which danced one by one into the fender, and there terminated their career in pieces, but not in peace.

Lionel and his chums, in the absorbing interest of the scene, had opened the door by degrees until they were fully exposed to view, but luckily our hero had presence of mind to draw back just as the dance terminated, and the two professors sank exhausted on the floor.

"They'll go to sleep now, if we don't look out," said Lionel. "Where's your squirt, Charlie?"

"In the dormitory, in my jacket pocket. I—no, I've got it here, in my trousers."

"Hand it over, and we'll tickle 'em up a little."

"What are you going to do for water?"

"Oh, dash it! I forgot that. Who'll go to the dormitory and get a water-bottle?"

"I will," said Tommy. "Let me go, Li."

"Not so. You'd be tumbling over something, and waking half the school."

"The wash-hand stand is just round here by the door, Li," said Charlie. "You've got a long arm. I think you might manage to slip round and get it if they're not looking."

"They don't seem to be," said our hero. "They're both lying down and panting like young hippopotami. I'll chance it."

And as noiselessly as a serpent, and as dexterously

as a conjuror, Lionel crept into the room, and in a moment was back with the captured jug.

Most boys know how to handle a squirt with tolerable effect. Lionel was a capital marksman, and could irrigate a fly fifteen feet off, with the healthiest results to the fly, no doubt.

Herr von Kobblersvax was the first to be operated on. Lionel filled the squirt, and fired—or I should say "watered" into the air, in such a manner that a gentle dew fell upon the upturned countenance of the German.

An Englishman would not have noticed it, but the Herr did. He shuddered and groaned a little, as if it hurt him. Probably it did, for he wasn't used to it.

Then Lionel sent a thimbleful or so down his neck, and it acted upon him like a galvanic shock.

"Gott in Himmel!" he ejaculated, and sat up, looking wildly around him. "Vot ish dat?"

You see it was necessary for him to ask the question, for after he had felt on his neck with his fingers, and smelt it and tasted it, he could make nothing of it. He knew what water was by sight, for the housemaid put some in his ewer once a month or so, but it was long since he had been practically acquainted with the article.

Then Lionel aroused Monsieur du Vinaigre by sending a gentle stream into one of his ears. Its stimulating effect was such that he bounded to his feet, and, overbalancing himself with the effort, fell upon and affectionately embraced the German.

His remark was also of an interrogative character. He wanted to know "Vat it vas?"

A long discussion failed, however, to decide the matter, so they had another bottle of kirschwasser apiece, which made them decidedly drunk, and even insensible to the effects of water, for Lionel and his chums, taking it turn and turn about, emptied the contents of the ewer upon them."

"Liebe Himmel," growled Herr Kobblersvax, "It mosh pe very warrum. I am vet troo wit de perspiration."

"Moi aussi—me too," added the Frenchman, with a shiver; "but it seem to me diablement cold. I feel like frozen."

"Dry a leedle drob more kirschwasser," said Herr Kobblersvax.

"I tink I go to *mon lit*—to my leetle bet," murmured the Frenchman, who certainly looked as if his "little bed" was the best place for him.

"Fly nod yet," said Herr Kobblersvax, pathetically. "Shtay a leedle longer. Dere is noch ein flasche kirschwasser."

"Mon ami," replied Monsieur du Vinaigre, tearfully, "I regret mosh dat it ish impossible; but I not capable of hold any more. I go to my leetle bet."

"Ich hört ein Bächlein rauschen," sang the Herr, just as a fresh stream of water trickled down his neck. "Heilige Jude, vot a lot I do pershpire dish night."

The Frenchman began to perspire too, but in a fresh place—that is, having arrived at the tearful stage of intoxication, he suddenly recollected a relative who had been shot at the storming of the Bastille a couple of generations or so before Monsieur du Vinaigre was born, and began to weep over him.

"Ah, he vas so beautifool, so loafely, and to die so young! He have only seventy-one year when *ces sac-r-ré grédins* do make a hole in him wiz a bullet. But he die vile he do his dutee, and aftare ze bataille zey find him on ze floor wiz his favourite stewpan clasped tight to his breast."

"He was de cook?"

"Jais, and vat a cook, mon ami!" said Monsieur du Vinaigre, pathetically. "Ze King, only von leetle veek before de Revolution make him a connt. Only ze ozare night I see him in ze eye of my mind, and—oh, mon Dieu!"

"Ach, heilige Himmel!" gasped Herr Kobblersvax.

And both started back and clung with despairing grip to each other, for there, on the blank wall before them—there flamed out in bright and glaring colours the head of a hideous demon, whose eyes were fixed on them, and seemed to freeze their very marrow.

CHAPTER LIV.

THE TERRIBLE HOBGOBLIN, AND WHAT HERR KOB-
BLERSVAX THOUGHT OF IT—MR. STIFFBACK HAS
HIS MIDNIGHT STUDIES INTERRUPTED—THE
SEARCH FOR THE BURGLAR—AND HOW THE HEAD
MASTER FOUND HIM.

THE imaginations of both the French and German professors had been a little prepared for the ghostly apparition by Monsieur du Vinaigre's story of his dead ancestor, the cook who was also a count; and as they were by far too fuddled to reason on the subject, they took the horrible apparition on the wall for a genuine *bona fide* ghost, and quaked accordingly.

It would be an insult to the intelligence of our readers to explain to them that the magic lantern was the originator of the ghost.

"We'll scare them," Lionel had said as the two professors, happy with liquor, prepared to leave the scene of their debauch. "Give us a slide."

"Which one?"

"The ugliest, of course," replied our hero, and picking out one haphazard he placed it in the lantern; and just as the two friends rolled into the corridor, drew the cap, and, as if by magic, the painted image of the fiend flashed out upon the wall.

The only effectual way to shut out an unpleasant sight is to shut one's eyes, and this Kobblersvax and Vinaigre did, squeezing their eyelids so closely together that it is a wonder they ever got them apart.

"Ach, der lieber Gott!" moaned the German, groping about in front of him with his hands. "Ish de horrible ting—go away!"

"I do not zee him," said M. du Vinaigre, with a great deal more truth than he usually put in so short a sentence, for his eyes, like the German's, were tightly closed.

Herr Kobblersvax wonderingly opened one eye a little way, and just then Lionel moved the lantern so that the horrible hobgoblin seemed to be making a rush at him along the wall.

It was quite enough for the German: he uttered a howl which might have set the teeth of a saw on edge, and bolted, flying headlong down a flight of stairs, picking himself up at the bottom, and darting along in the first direction that presented itself.

Now, Mr. Stiffback, the great head of Lake House School, had made up his mind to pass a quiet and studious evening over the solution of some knotty problems in mathematics essential to the completion of a new invention he had in embryo.

To this end he had locked himself in his study, and seated himself at the wide table, whereon were, besides his books and writing materials, a kettle and spirit lamp, a tumbler, and a comfortable-looking black bottle; and to crown all a huge meerschaum pipe and a tobacco jar, for Mr. Stiffback was a firm believer in Bulwer's dictum that "a pipe is a great comforter, a pleasant soother; the man who smokes thinks like a sage and acts like a Samaritan."

He had already undergone the dual soothing operations of the pipe and the black bottle, and was just getting into the "sage and Samaritan" way of thinking, and the knotty point of the problem began to appear less complicated, when distant sounds—suggestive of the operation the man underwent before the Samaritan found him—fell upon his ears.

"I could almost have made an affidavit," said Mr. Stiffback to himself (he was too genteel to say "swear" even in thought), "that I heard somebody calling 'Thieves!' and 'murder!'"

Not being quite certain, he soothed himself with the balance of what the tumbler had in it; he listened again, and once more the cry "Thieves—murder!" feel upon his ears in a faint and frenzied squeak.

"I was not mistaken, then," thought Mr. Stiffback, turning rather pale, and in his agitation drinking a quarter of a pint of tobacco ash from the bowl of his pipe, which he mistook for the tumbler of soothing mixture.

As soon as he had recovered from the attack of coughing and sneezing produced by the involuntary draught, Mr. Stiffback unlocked and opened the door, and grasping an old cavalry sabre which had done duty in the Civil War, and a candle, he hurried along the passage.

"It came from the servants' rooms," he muttered. "Confound those women! I daresay it's only a stray cat or a mouse. They start and scream at anything."

Reassured by this reflection, Mr. Stiffback's courage returned, and as he felt pretty capable of coming off victor in a single combat with a rat or a cat, he flourished his sabre, and as he arrived at the end of the passage where the cook, the kitchenmaid, the scullery-maid, and three attendant housemaids were huddled together in airy attire and picturesque confusion, he demanded, in a fierce tone—

"What's all this noise about?"

Again the startling tones of the whole half-dozen replied—

"Thieves—murder!" and one of the housemaids volunteered the information that the wretch hadn't even got his tut—tut—trousers on."

"Posh—nonsense! No more have you for the matter of that," retorted Mr. Stiffback. "Stop that noise, now, and show me where he is. I'll soon make short work of *him*. Murder! I dare say it was only a cat."

"It wasn't," said the housemaid, positively. "I saw his shirt and his horrid legs, and he's in there now!"

And she pointed to the open door of a bedroom, whence there issued at intervals of a few minutes a smothered noise like groaning.

Mr. Stiffback wished heartily now that his ears had not been so keen, or that he had stayed to imbibe another half-pint of courage from the black bottle; but to draw back and leave six helpless females in tears, night-gowns and distress, would never do—and so, executing the handsomest cuts and guards, with a vigour and rapidity which would have done credit to a sergeant-instructor of a crack cavalry corps, he advanced.

He chopped a chair in half, and mowed off the top of a bed-post just by way of letting the burglar know that he had a skilful and muscular man to deal with, and then, in his very fiercest voice, he said—

"Come out, my man—come out, now! It's of no use. I see you."

But he didn't. He was looking for him all the while, and when at last a choking kind of groan sounded just at his feet, he gave a little howl and jumped.

There was a large cylindrical upright basket against the wall, such as is used for storing dirty linen, and from the upper portion of this projected two legs, which certainly belonged to a man and not a cat; and the same legs were from time to time agitated in a convulsive manner, while a groan, probably proceeding from the head which belonged to the legs, came from the bottom of the basket.

Mr. Stiffback did not recognise the legs. He might have done so had they been clad, but it is only the gifted savage who is able to recognise his friends in their native "buff," or mahogany, as the case may be.

He was a little startled, perhaps, at finding that he had really a man and not a cat to deal with, and but for the presence of the females outside, would, perhaps, have gone back to his study to think over the thing a little; but as he reflected that a man with no other armour than a shirt—and that a short one—and who, moreover, laboured under the disadvantage of being upside down, was not very likely to prove dangerous, he advanced again.

"Come out!" he said again, in his very loudest voice.

But the legs did not obey, and Mr. Stiffback advanced a little closer.

"Dear me," he thought, "there's something familiar about those legs," and he held the candle close to them.

Perhaps he singed one a little, for the legs gave a more convulsive kick than ever, the basket overturned, and there, amidst a pile of underclothing ready for the wash—and looking as if they needed it—lay the portly form of Herr von Kobblersvax!

CHAPTER LV.

THE FURTHER ADVENTURES OF MR. STIFFBACK AND HERR VON KOBBLERSVAX—THE MELEE AND HOW IT ENDED—ALSO THE END OF THE FLOGGING MACHINE—HOW IT WAS DONE, AND WHO DID IT.

MR. STIFFBACK gazed in wonder at the figure of the German Professor, who, like a fallen Laocoon, lay struggling with entwining coils—not of serpents though—but the stockings, petticoats, &c., held him nearly as fast.

The schoolmaster could hardly persuade himself that it was a reality, and to make sure he touched Herr Kobblersvax up with the point of the sabre, and the howl which followed was too unmistakeably genuine to leave room for doubt.

"Come out," said Mr. Stiffback, in his sternest voice.

"Ach, Gott!" groaned the Herr. "It ish kilt dat I vos."

"Get up!" commanded the head master again. "Keep outside the room, you girls—this is no proper sight for you."

And to make sure that he was obeyed Mr. Stiffback closed the door, and returned to the unhappy German, who now sat up, looking around him with an expression of vacant terror.

"Vere, oh, vere ish de ghost?" he moaned, faintly.

"Where, oh where is your sense of decency and propriety, Herr Kobblersvax?" said Mr. Stiffback, sternly. "How is it I found you in this shameless state of nudity, and in the bedroom of one of my servants, at this hour of the night."

"Oh, it vas hawriple!" murmured Herr Kobblersvax, thinking of the apparition.

"Horrible, indeed!" repeated Mr. Stiffback. "But you will have to give some better reason than that for your conduct. Ah! I see it all now—Herr Professor, you are intoxicated."

"No, it vash de shpirit, meinherr."

"Yes, the spirit of wine," retorted Mr. Stiffback, "that is the spirit which has degraded you below the level of the beasts. Get up, sir, and put on your clothes—I will talk to you in the morning."

Still bewildered, but sufficiently sobered by the shock of his fall to comprehend the drift of the head-master's words, Herr Kobblersvax slowly arose, but he could not don his clothes, for the simple reason that he hadn't got them with him.

But Mr. Stiffback was an inventor, by nature and habit. He selected a huge flannel petticoat from the heap on the ground, and held it out.

"Put that on," he said, sternly. "Even by night and in darkness I will have the morals of my establishment respected."

There was no escape. Mr. Stiffback's commands were not to be disputed, so the Herr took the petticoat reluctantly.

"Make haste, sir!" said the head-master, sternly. "If you have the least sense of propriety, you will recollect that you are keeping those poor women out in the cold, and in—er—and in a state of undress hardly less complete than your own."

Herr Kobblersvax looked rebelliously at the petticoat.

"Sare," he said, "I vas a man, and dish is de beddicoat vot a voman vear. I vil not mine sex disgrace by put him on mine legs."

"And I say that you shall," said Mr. Stiffback.

"And I say dat I will not!" retorted the professor, who had still enough of the kirschwasser left in him to render him defiant. "I will tie first."

"Put it on!" thundered Mr. Stiffback, flashing the sabre above his head.

"Put him on yourself!" retorted Herr Kobblersvax, and rolling the petticoat up into a ball he launched it full at his employer.

Even as the circling folds of the net cast by the retiarius enmesh the hapless secutor in their embrace, so did the flannel petticoat wind itself round and about the head, neck, and arms of Mr. Stiffback.

Now the first instinct of an Englishman when he is attacked in this or any other manner is to "punch" his adversary's head, and Mr. Stiffback, acting on this impulse, no sooner freed himself from the embarrassment of the petticoat than he darted forward and "landed" the Herr what is technically known to the Fancy as a "hot 'un on the smeller."

The blow staggered the professor, but he was a heavy man, and it did not quite upset him.

"Mistare Steefback," he said, in a voice trembling with mingled agony and emotion, "vat for dit you shmite me on de nose?"

"And why did you dare to throw that—that filthy petticoat at me?" roared Mr. Stiffback.

"Because I will him not on mine legs to put," retorted the Herr.

"You shall!" insisted Mr. Stiffback, in a voice of thunder.

"I will not, Mistare Steefback!" replied Kobblersvax, defiantly. "And I do dell you dat if you shmite me on de nose again I will fight mineself mit you."

While this bloodthirsty and exciting scene was progressing in the room the ladies outside had kept up a series of brilliant screams, which, of course, had the effect of alarming the whole house; and in a very little while all the inmates—except the cats, who had taken refuge in the kitchen chimney—were assembled in the corridor.

"Now wot's all this 'ere?" said Soker, who was the first to arrive. "Ain't a man to be allowed to take his noctoreal rest in peace and quietness? I never heerd such woices as you've got. Jackasses and dying pigs is nothing to 'em."

"Well, I'm sure!" said the cook, naturally offended at having her dulcet voice so aspersed. "Us poor women is to be murdered in our beds, then, and no notice took."

"Who's a murdering of you?" demanded Soker, sulkily. "I don't see no weppins, nor yet no gore."

"Look in that room, then, and you'll find plenty," said the cook, sharply. "But lor! here's Mister Sammle a coming. He knows how to sympathise with the fair sect."

And, in fact, just then our old friend Sam, who was devoted to the whole sex more than he was attached to one, came up in company with our hero and his chums, who looked so charmingly innocent that the most casual observer could not have failed to set them down as guilty.

"What's the row?" said Lionel.

"Who's being murdered?" asked Charlie.

"Somebody's seen a ghost—that's what's the matter," added our old friend Tommy. "I know, because I've seen ghosts myself, and I always shriek like that."

But before Tommy had time to explain his ghostly

theory Sam had opened the door and rushed in just in time to get in the way of the clothes-basket, which Herr Kobblersvax had hurled at the head of his respected principal.

Not being particularly robust the lanky youth rolled over like a ninepin, and, falling just upon the threshold of the door, he managed successfully to trip up Tommy and Charlie, who followed closely on his heels.

A drowning man, says the proverb, will clutch at a straw—if there happens to be one to clutch at; but in our opinion, a man, when he is falling, in water or anything else, will grasp at anything, whether it be a straw or a scaffold-pole; and so it chanced that Tommy, having no regard to the sanctity of Mr. Stiffback's person, grabbed him by the leg, and mixed him up in the general ruin.

Charlie did the same kind office for the German professor, and we regret to record that several paragraphs of fluent blasphemy escaped the lips of the sufferers.

Mr. Stiffback was a prompt man, and taking "Lex talionis" for his motto he doubled his fists and let fly at the body that was nearest to him.

In the natural course of things that body belonged to Tommy, and equally as a matter of course his nose, which he had already flayed by falling on, suffered the most.

There is something very tempting in a free fight. To see one man punching the head of another almost inevitably compels the spectator to double his fists, and look around for a foe.

It happened so on this occasion, for as the boys, excited by the sound of strife, crowded the doorway all at once, they intentionally jostled and bumped one another, and from jostling and bumping to pushing and wrestling is an easy and natural transition; and in less than five minutes no less than six couples were merrily milling away in the corridor, while the less warlike looked on and applauded.

Soker was not a brilliant genius in a general way, but when prompted by necessity he was occasionally delivered of an idea which had some claim to be considered original.

"Now," he muttered to himself, "I wonders how long this 'ere little game is a-goin' to last? Here's the ole blessed school a-wollopin' one another, and unless I puts a stop to it, I shan't get a blessed wink o' sleep!"

A moment's reflection, and then Soker tottered off, returning promptly with a couple of the largest-sized pails of water, which, with the utmost impartiality and accuracy of aim, he distributed amongst the combatants.

As most of the boys were very lightly clad indeed—having nothing on but their nightshirts—the cold water did immense execution.

The fighting was immediately stopped, and almost at the same moment Mr. Stiffback and Sam emerged from the room, leading Herr Kobblersvax a prisoner between them.

Sam had ingeniously effected his capture by throwing the obnoxious petticoat over his head and shoulders from behind, thus effectively pinioning him, and as he was pretty well exhausted by his previous struggles, he yielded himself unresistingly.

To say that Mr. Stiffback was angry would be to make a very mild statement. Not only had his studies been disturbed, but the peace of the whole school besides, added to which was the outrage upon morality and decency—before all the boys, too.

It would have gone hard with Herr Kobblersvax had the head-master been absolute monarch of a kingdom, with power of life and death over his subjects.

Hanging, drawing, and quartering, with a previous taste of the rack and thumbscrews, was the mildest punishment to which he would have been subjected.

"Oh," thought Mr. Stiffback, vengefully, "how I wish he was a boy—wouldn't I give him forty dozen in the flogging-machine! I have a great mind to run the risk! I wonder what fine I should have to pay for the assault?"

The next morning, though, the German professor was missing, and Mr. Stiffback was robbed of the luxury of reprimanding and dismissing him with public disgrace.

He knew that he had no hope of being forgiven, and wisely fled, leaving a short note requesting that the salary due to him might be sent to the Black Bull and Periwinkle, at Deliverham.

Mr. Stiffback's reply was short, and to the purpose. He wrote—

"Come and fetch it."

And having dispatched this laconic epistle by the hands of Soker, Mr. Stiffback proceeded to deal out punishment to as many of the boys as he could convict of having left their dormitories on the previous night.

Had he been less angry he would probably have taken no notice of the breach of discipline, or had the German been there to bear the burden of his displeasure, the youthful culprits might have escaped at a cheaper rate; but, some one had to suffer, and, of course, Tommy was the principal scapegoat.

"The time has come," said Lionel, in tragic tones. "We must carry out our plan, Charlie, and bust up the machine, before the flogging comes off to-morrow."

"It's all very easy to say we must—but how is it to be done?"

"List, and I will a tale unfold," replied our hero, taking his chair aside, after the manner of the stage conspirator, when he whispers a secret which can be heard half a mile away.

"Capital!" replied Charlie, with a chuckle, when Lionel had told his plan. "My eye! that will wake the old man up. But I say, Li; suppose we get found out."

"No danger of that. You leave it to me."

"No, no. I'll be in it, Li, if I share the fun I'll share the danger."

"All right, then; but mum's the word. Not a whisper, then."

"Not a wink, even."

And the two friends parted, fully bent upon the destruction of the feared and detested flogging machine. How they succeeded in their attempt the reader will presently learn.

Pending the completion of the scheme for the destruction of the flogging machine, Lionel resolved that Mr. Stiffback should have a dose of ghost, just to see whether his nerves were stronger than those of the ex-German master.

He carefully avoided saying anything to his chums, as he felt convinced that, were Mr. Stiffback to discover the perpetrator of the outrage, nothing short of expulsion would be the fate of the practical jokers.

So he carefully waited his opportunity, and at last it came.

One evening M. du Vinaigre and Mr. Stiffback had had a long consultation about supplying the place of Herr von Kobblersvax.

To Lionel, who was anxiously awaiting the breaking up of the conference, with the magic lantern carefully tucked under his arm, and the ugliest slide he possessed adjusted in position, it seemed as if the two would never separate.

And no wonder they were so long, for Mr. Stiffback had been using his most persuasive powers, in the shape of threats of a reduction of salary, and all its concomitant evils, if M. du Vinaigre did not at once take up the professorial chair left vacant by the abrupt departure of the German master.

All the Frenchman's natural antipathies were aroused. He teach the rising generation to speak the hated Teutonic language! No! sooner would he starve than pollute his tongue with such an office.

Mr. Stiffback tried cajolery, threats, sneers, and innuendoes.

"I believe, sir, it is thorough incompetence. You *cannot* teach the language, and so pretend that you won't."

M. du Vinaigre drew himself up to his fullest height (something under five feet), and with comical majesty repudiated the imputation with scorn.

"Mr. Steefback, sare, I would hafe you to know that Alphonse du Vinaigre is the mastare of all de known languages of Europe—ha!"

"Then Alphonse du Vinaigre will have to teach my boys German, or he'll have to find himself another place. So come with me to my study—and we will see whether I cannot tempt you with an addition to your salary."

The little Frenchman's greedy eyes twinkled vivaciously at this, and murmuring something about his poverty, and not his will consenting, prepared to follow Mr. Stiffback.

They crossed the corridor, and entered the schoolroom; but no sooner had they opened the door than a gigantic figure appeared in front of them, and beckoned them to follow.

"Mon Dieu!" exclaimed the Frenchman; "dare is de foul fiend heemself come to reproach me for my crime."

Mr. Stiffback made no reply, but seized the Frenchman by the arm, and dragged him hurriedly across the schoolroom, and into his study—then hastily bolting the door, he fell down in a state of total collapse on the floor.

M. du Vinaigre rose equal to the occasion.

At first he had been, if anything, more frightened than Mr. Stiffback.

But when the latter worthy seized him by the arm and dragged him from the room, the little Frenchman began to argue philosophically with himself.

This was the second occasion on which the apparition had been seen by him.

On the first occasion he had experienced no worse misfortune than a few kicks and scratches.

On this occasion, here he was safe in the schoolmaster's study.

He could, therefore, no longer doubt.

Whatever the mission of the demon might be, it evidently did not concern him.

But beyond this his philosophy did not carry him.

He could not pluck up sufficient courage to look at the spectre again.

So, throwing himself down on a sofa, he buried his face in the cushions, hoping, ostrich-like, that he should be safe from *whatever* entered the room.

This resolve on his part, was near causing the destruction of Mr. Stiffback, and indeed, probably, of Lake Island School.

As the schoolmaster fell to the ground with a heavy crash, in a paroxysm of terror, he wildly clutched at the table for support.

He just missed the solid help that he needed, but managed to clutch a corner of the table cloth.

In an instant all the articles on the table were shot pell-mell on to Mr. Stiffback.

Amongst them unfortunately happened to be a rather massive colza lamp.

The oil found its way into the schoolmaster's face.

The heavy stand lodged itself in that portion of his anatomy which prizefighters call the breadbasket.

But, though this was bad enough in all conscience, worse remained behind.

For the burning wick insidiously insinuated itself into his neck.

With a yell of terror Mr. Stiffback sprang to his feet, and clutched wildly at his neckcloth, tearing it from his neck, and flinging it across the room.

To his affrighted imagination it seemed as if he had been caught by the fiery hand of the demon himself.

M. du Vinaigre heard the yell, but it only made him bury his nose, eyes, and mouth more deeply in the sofa cushions, at the imminent risk of suffocation.

Poor Mr. Stiffback was too terrified to notice what he had done—otherwise he might even then have been brought to his senses.

In flinging away what he thought were the fiery fingers of the fiend he had pitched the burning lamp-cotton against the muslin curtains in front of the study window.

A blaze was the result, which only rendered the schoolmaster ten times more frightened than he was before, and entirely convinced him that he was in the presence of a visitor from another world.

"Dear Mr. Beelzebub," he said, as he sank on his knees, "I apologise for having doubted that you had appeared to Herr Kobblersvax. Do forgive me this time. I'll never scoff at spirits again."

As might be expected no answer was vouchsafed to this appeal.

But a violent shaking was heard at the handle of the door.

Then a vigorous kick.

Another kick.

The door yielded, and Sam Scarecrow dashed wildly into the room, seized the burning curtains in his arms, trampled on them, and in half a minute had extinguished the conflagration that would have rendered Lake Island school a pile of smouldering ruins.

M. du Vinaigre heard the uproar, but, considering discretion the better part of valour, he still kept his head buried in the cushions.

Sam having succeeded in extinguishing the flames, turned his attention to Mr. Stiffback, who was seated on the floor looking woefully and wonderingly at Sam.

That latter worthy said——

"Well, you've been a going on it, you have."

"Where—where—where's the spirits?" gasped Mr. Stiffback.

"Spirits!" echoed Sam. "I should think you'd busted well a-been and took 'em all yourself."

To this insulting remark Mr. Stiffback made no reply.

He turned his head round, however, and said dismally—"And where's Vinaigre?"

"Old Vinegar's a kicking up his heels on the sofiar," answered Sam, as he moved towards that gentleman, and gave him a sharp pinch.

But Sam reckoned without his host.

The Frenchman, although small in stature, had abnormally long legs, and before Sam knew where he was a vigorous kick had sent him half-way across the room, where, becoming mixed up with the schoolmaster's legs, he came to the ground.

"Blowed if that ain't a busted shame!" cried Sam. "'Ere's you two coves goes and gets thundering drunk, and sets fire to the place, and when I comes to yer rescoo blow me if you don't go and try for to kick my brains out. Bust me! I'll leave this yer place in the morning, that's what I'll do."

"Nay, Samuel," answered Mr. Stiffback, "do not give way to temper. You have found us in a very undignified position, but nevertheless there is a reason for it, with which I will not trouble."

"Reason or no reason," replied Sam, "just you look at my nose."

And well might Sam invite his master to look at his nose.

The heel of M. du Vinaigre's boot had deprived it of quite half an inch of its outer covering.

"Well, Samuel, I am sorry M. du Vinaigre should have treated you so roughly, but he was quite unaware that it was you he was kicking. Is it not so, Vinaigre?" asked Mr. Stiffback.

Ere the Frenchman could reply, Sam remarked with bitterness—

"I wish as how I was as unaware of it as you ses he was."

M. du Vinaigre had by this time removed his head from the cushions, and was looking about him as if in doubt whether he beheld the demon or only Sam Scarecrow before him, but he was half suffocated, and could not venture on a remark of any kind whatever.

"Never mind, Samuel, here is that which will make you forget your injuries, and I hope it will also make you forget what you have witnessed," and so saying, Mr. Stiffback handed Sam a sovereign, and bowed him out of the room.

* * * * * *

We do not think that any philosopher has yet remarked that at the approach of the penultimate month of the year a startling change takes place in the religion of the youth of this country, and from being (we trust) sincere young Christians, they become ardent and devout fire-worshippers.

It is on the fifth of November, popularly styled "Guy Fox" day, that this change is exhibited at the fall.

Then not the most ardent Parsee or Guêbre ever watched the rising of the sun with one-twentieth part of the devoted enthusiasm with which Our Boys watch the fiery rocket as it cleaves the blackness of the midnight air with its brilliant parabola.

It is then that the firework-manufacturer becomes a being of more importance to Our Boys than the mightiest king on earth; it is then that he even becomes false to his favourite journal, and, turning an indifferent glance upon the startling illustrations, asks for a penny squib instead.

It is then that elderly ladies and gentlemen, returning home at night, are chased into corners by a horribly ingenious firework, which leaps and darts about them like a live creature, and lets off five or six pistol-like explosions to the intense delight of the mischievous urchin who sets fire to it.

As a matter of course the boys of Lake Island school were no exception to the general rule.

For a fortnight before the great "Fifth" the conversation in the playground and dormitories had been of nothing else but fireworks, for Mr. Stiffback, wisely concluding that if he denied permission to the boys, they would certainly get the fireworks without his consent, and most probably run the risk of setting the house on fire, allowed a grand exhibition to take place on the lake under his own superintendence.

The boys all contributed according to their means, and those who contributed the most were allowed the privilege of arranging and firing the rockets and Catherine wheels—a privilege which their less fortunate brethren envied greatly.

Now, it so happened that Tommy's aunt, having been deeply moved by a charity sermon one Sunday, was touched by remorse at her general stingy conduct towards her nephew, and on Monday our plump friend was startled into frantic joy by the arrival of a post-office order for a guinea, and a recommendation from his aunt that he would invest the coin in good and useful purposes.

The recommendation Tommy instantly forgot, and in something less than an hour after its arrival the order was cashed, and the guinea invested in a sumptuous array of crackers, Roman candles, rockets, *et hoc genus omne.*

"Now, mind," said Tommy, "I'm to fire every one of 'em off, Li. Don't you let any other fellows do it."

"You shall fire all off, Tommy, and sit on 'em too if you like. You have got a shady lot after all."

"What!" ejaculated Tommy. "Why, there's a hundred and twenty separate pieces."

"It would have been a good deal more sensible if you'd been content with half-a-dozen first-class rockets, or Roman candles, or four or five magnesium balloons."

"Oh!" said Tommy, "but they would have been over so soon; now it'll take me pretty well an hour

to let all those off, and won't the Bobbles be wild, for they've only got three squibs and a sixpenny wheel between 'em?"

"And do you think, Tommy, that we're going to let you be nearly an hour letting those things off?"

"Why I couldn't do it in less."

"Oh, yes you can, Tommy," said our hero; "you see, as you've got so many little things, they will have to be let off all at once to make anything of a show, so we'll arrange 'em in the centre of the others."

"Let 'em off all at once!" gasped Tommy.

"Yes."

"How long will that take, Li?"

"About two minutes."

"Oh, Lor'!" moaned the plump youth, "only two minutes for a guinea's worth! I wish I hadn't bought 'em now."

"Think what a fine two minutes they will be, Tommy," said Lionel. "They'll look splendid, you know, when they're let off altogether."

"Do you think that the Bobbles' will be wild, Li?"

"I'm sure they will, and old Stiffback, too," replied our hero, with a wink aside to Charlie.

"Will he, though? Are you sure?"

"Pretty certain. I say, Tommy, when did you have a dose of the flogging machine last?"

"Day before yesterday, and he owes me a dozen now, but he said he'd let me off until there were some more chaps to be whacked. He don't like to bring the machine out for one—blow it! I wish he'd give us the machine for a guy, and let us burn it on the Fifth."

"Little chance of that, Tommy; but, I say, did you ever hear of spontaneous combustion?"

"Yes, I lost four places in class last week through him," grumbled Tommy. "He was a great mathematician—wasn't he?—who lived in the reign of King Elizabeth the Fourth."

"You're a bright article, you and your King Elizabeths!" laughed Lionel. "Never mind, Tommy! You wait till you're locked up in the pillory, and ready for the flogging machine next time: you'll know what spontaneous combustion is."

And so our hero and Charlie strolled away, leaving Tommy alternating between fits of joy and despair, as his thoughts fixed themselves upon the coming Fifth or the threatened thrashing.

"It must be done to-night, or not at all, Charlie," were the first words our hero said as soon as he and his especial chum were alone.

"Yes, and I don't quite see how we're to manage it," replied Charlie Drummond, thoughtfully. "It will be hard enough to get at the flogging machine, but how the dickens are we to nail the fireworks now old Soker has got 'em all under lock and key?"

"It *must* be done somehow."

"It's precious easy to say 'must,' Li, but not so easy to find out a way. We don't even know where the fireworks are kept."

"Soker's sure to have stowed them away in his own shanty," said our hero.

"That's a settler then, for we could not get into the house and back again without being noticed, Lionel."

"We must, Charlie; I've made up my mind, and it's got to be done."

"But how? That's what I want to know."

"Blow you and your 'how's,' Charlie."

"That's all very well, Li; anybody can blow a thing, but it isn't everybody who can find out the way to do it."

"Let me be quiet and think a bit," said our hero, and thrusting his hands deep into his trousers' pockets, and leaning back against the wall of the playground, he fixed his eyes upon a particular pebble, and pounced in a murderous fashion at it, which was his way of puzzling out a knotty point.

"I've got it, Charlie," he said, after an interval

of ten minutes, during which his chum had patiently awaited his decision.

"Out with it, Li."

"We must both be ill this afternoon, Charlie."

"Sham ill, you mean?"

"No I don't—the game don't pay with Stiffback; he knows too much We must be really ill, Charlie."

"I don't see it, Li."

"I'll put you up to that all right."

"But I don't want to be ill, Li."

"You'll have to be, or we shan't be able to carry out our lark."

"All right, then," grumbled Charlie "I suppose you must have your way, as you always do, but don't make a fellow too ill, Li."

"Not more than I can help, Charlie. You'll only have to drink a tumbler full of warm water and salt."

"That's cheerful," replied Drummond, with a shudder; "and what will that do?"

"Only make you 'shoot the cat.'"

"Are you going to take a dose too?"

"Of course I am; we must both be in it."

"It's an awful nasty thing to do, Li. Can't we say we're ill?"

"It won't wash, I tell you, Charlie—you can't get over Stiffback that way; but when he sees with his own eyes that we're ill, he is sure to send us upstairs, and *then*, Charlie."

"What then, Li?"

"Why the doom of the flogging machine is sealed for ever," replied our hero.

Charlie, who seemed in anything but a cheerful mood at the prospect of the festive tumblerful of salt and water he had to swallow, growled out an anathema upon the machine, and Mr. Stiffback to boot, and then betook himself to his Euclid.

"You needn't worry about that," whispered Lionel; "we shall be excused lessons this afternoon, you know."

"There's some comfort in that, at any rate," said Charlie, laughing a little. "It'll be an awful sell though, being ill directly after dinner."

"Never mind, don't eat too much. Hullo! there's the bell; come on, Charlie."

The usual uproar and scramble now took place—books, slates, pens, and pencils clashed and clattered on the desks, and a babel of sounds arose from the tongues of the boys who had been spending the four previous hours in enforced silence.

Lionel disappeared mysteriously, for what purpose Charlie guessed only too well, and he shuddered as he thought of the mixture he would presently have to swallow.

It did not spoil his appetite though, and he made such a precious attack upon the boiled beef, carrots, and plain suet pudding, which formed the chief part of this day's dinner, that Mr. Stiffback noticed him, and said—

"Really, Drummond, I do not like to check any healthy appetite, but you will surely be ill if you eat any more pudding."

"I know that precious well," said Charlie to himself; "I shall lose it all directly, so I don't care how much I eat now."

Dinner was over at the accustomed time, for punctuality was observed in that as in all things at Lake Island School, and Lionel managed to be last in, beckoning to Charlie to keep behind as well.

The moment they were alone, he brought out from his trousers pocket a flat bottle, and handed it to Charlie.

"Make haste old fellow, down with it."

Charlie made an extraordinary grimace, and then shutting his eyes, gulped down the liquid.

"Ugh! oh—ah! how filthy it is. Oh! dear me, I shall be ill before we get to the class-room!"

"Don't do that, Charlie, keep it down, old fellow."

"Have—have you had your's, Li?" gasped Charlie.

"Oh, yes, long ago. Hold up, Charlie."

But Charlie was past holding up; he leaned his head against the wall, and just as Mr. Stiffback returned to find out why the two were lagging behind, overburdened nature relieved itself. There was a rushing sound, resembling the working of a wheezy pump, and Charlie's dinner decorated the floor of the passage.

"Go upstairs to the dormitory and lie down," said Mr. Stiffback, sternly; "you feel, Drummond, the evil effects of gluttony. You go with him, Wilful, and stay with him till he is better."

This was exactly what our hero had foreseen would happen, and with a chuckle of delight he helped Charlie upstairs.

A little brandy and water, which Mr. Stiffback sent him, put Charlie to rights in a few minutes; and then gently, and on tiptoe, the two conspirators went forth, and in an hour returned, excited, but triumphant. The deed was done, and the detested flogging machine bore in its own bosom the elements of its destruction.

CHAPTER LVI.

DESTRUCTION OF THE FLOGGING MACHINE.

MR. STIFFBACK had lately adopted a formal method of dealing with culprits about to be flogged. For an hour or two previous to the execution of the sentence they were placed in solitary confinement, then a list was given to Soker, who, in the character of executioner, visited the cell, and brought them back to the class-room. There Mr. Stiffback himself, and in his most awful tones, read out their names, the nature of their crime, and the number of turns of the handle each was to have; and, finally, they were grabbed by Soker, pilloried in the machine, and tortured by the whalebone canes.

There was something about all this formality to which the boys highly objected. The pangs of suspense, doubled—which was unnecessary—the pain of the flogging, but they had to submit. There was no appeal from the decrees of the autocrat of Lake Island School.

On the morning, therefore, after the events recorded in our last chapter, and immediately breakfast was over, Soker took up his position in the doorway, and as the boys filed out, took into custody those whose names were inscribed on his fatal list.

"Blow the beggar!" said Tommy, in a fierce whisper. "I know he's waiting for me."

"Never mind, Tommy," returned Lionel. "This is the last time the flogging machine will hurt anybody."

"Eh?" said the plump youth, opening his little round eyes to their fullest extent.

"Go on—it's all right, I tell you. Don't stop now. Soker's beckoning you."

"Blow Soker! what were you saying about the—"

But before Tommy could complete his sentence our hero had given him a gentle push, which sent him into the arms of Soker, who, with the avidity of a spider pouncing on a fly, seized him, and then pulled his ears for treading on a favourite corn.

"Never see such a boy as you in all my born days," said Soker, fetching another yelp out of poor Tommy. "Now, Master Bobbles, I wants you and your brother, and then I'm complete."

"That's some consolation," thought the plump youth, as he placed himself in the rear of his traditional foes, and got a long pin ready. "These chaps are in for it, too; but I wonder what Li meant by saying it was the last time the flogging machine would hurt anybody?"

And thus meditating he thoughtfully inserted the pin just below the tail of the elder Bobbles' jacket, who gave a skip and a shriek simultaneously.

"Now, Master Bobbles," remonstrated Soker, "singin' and dancin' ain't allowed, you know."

LIKE AJAX DEFYING THE LIGHTNING, TOMMY BADE THE MUCH-BE-HATTED YOUTHS "COME AND HAVE IT OUT!"

"I wasn't singing," retorted the injured one, with a sniff, "nor yet dancing."

"The nat'ral hobstinacity o' these 'ere boys is most aggrawatin," said Soker. "I orter know what singin' is, I think, when I've been a Chrissemus wait for nigh forty years; you *was* a singin'—I knows the note well, it was O sharp."

"You're a pretty judge of music," retorted Bobbles. "Why there's no such a note in the gamut."

"No sich a note, ain't there?" said Soker. "We'll see about that."

And dextrously catching the gristly part of Bobbles' right ear he gave it a twist, which brought out of the victim a long shrill "O—o—o—o."

"There," said Soker, triumphantly. "Now will you say there ain't sich a note, or will you try agen?"

"I'll tell Mr. Stiffback, I will," sobbed the sufferer. "I'm not going to be pulled about by you."

"On'y wait till twelve o'clock comes, my young moosishun, and I gits you into the pillory; you shall have the top corner, where the double set o' whalebones is—you shall."

"That's Codlings' place—I'm not going to be put there."

"Oh, I daresay Master Codlings won't mind changing places for once."

"Not at all," replied Tommy, returning Soker's wink. "Bobbles is quite welcome—he knows that. If he could fill two places at once he should have 'em both, and welcome."

The four hours that were to elapse were passed pretty comfortably by Tommy, at least, for he had been provided with some biscuits, a couple of jam puffs, and half a pound of hardbake, by Lionel, and, stretching himself on his back in the middle of the floor, he munched contentedly the whole of the time.

Most people would have experienced some difficulty in eating dry biscuits in such an attitude, but not so Tommy; he could eat anywhere under any circumstances, and could, we believe, have swallowed his dinner upside down with a relish.

Twelve o'clock came, and punctually with the first strike Soker, the gaoler, appeared, and summoned his victims.

"Come along, young genelmen," he said. "Now, Master Bobbles, it's no good a trying to hide under that form—out you come as the pin said to the perriwinkle. Why don't you be'ave like Master Codlings? It's a pleasure to flog a boy like him."

Tommy looked rather doubtful at this compliment, but the hardbake had been very sweet, and the almonds crisp and plentiful, so that he felt more charitably disposed than usual towards his tormentor.

Arrived in the class-room they found the chief justice represented by Mr. Stiffback, who in the most solemn and impressive manner read the sentences, and handed them over to Soker.

Tommy, as usual, looked round for his chums, Lionel and Charlie, hoping to get a wink of sympathy to cheer him in the hour of tribulation, but to his dismay they were both evidently in a high state of glee, and quite ready to break out into an explosion of laughter.

"That's feeling—that is, I don't think," growled Tommy to himself. "If they were going to be whacked I should look as miserable as a cat with the mange, but never mind, it will soon be over."

It was soon over, but not in the way that Tommy had interpreted.

The culprits were all placed in position, and Soker, moistening his hands, waited for the signal.

Mr. Stiffback raised his hand, and Soker strained at the crank, but it would not move.

"What's the matter?" demanded the head master.

"Machine wants oil, I think, sir," replied Soker, almost black in the face with exertion.

"Then why did you not perform your duty, Soker? It is your business, I believe, to oil the machine."

"I give the blessed thing a pint on it yes'day," grunted Soker, "and my wages ain't good enough for me to buy ile out of my own pocket."

"Don't be insolent, sir," said the head master, sternly. "It's my belief that you have been drinking again."

"If I had," said Soker, "I could wring the blessed handle orf, but a man ain't got no strength when he's fed on slops and slush."

"If you don't turn that handle in less than two minutes I'll turn you out," said Mr. Stiffback.

Soker made another yet more desperate effort. There was a creaking, mingled with a rasping noise, like that caused by scraping a number of lucifer matches over a rough surface, then thin clouds of light blue smoke made their escape from the various crevices in the machine, accompanied by a curious hissing sound.

"Wot's that?" said Soker, pausing, and gazing on the novelty with a wondering eye.

"Who's that smoking?" demanded Mr. Stiffback, who had smelt the smoke, but without noticing whence it emanated.

His query was answered in a most unexpected and unpleasant manner, for the words had hardly escaped his lips when a squib—and a twopenny one too—burst its way out of its confinement and describing a graceful curve in the air, singed his back hair, which was rather long, and lodged between his collar and his neck.

Mr. Stiffback had long since given up the practice of athletics as inconsistent with that grave and dignified deportment which should characterise so important an individual as an instructor of youth, but there is a warmth of argument about a squib in the back of one's neck which is not to be resisted; he uttered a howl, and with one spring cleared the desks and forms in front of him and ran for the door, making frantic efforts to pull off his coat.

"Oh, my good gracious!" exclaimed Soker, who stood staring helplessly at the flogging machine, the strange conduct of which seemed to have deprived him of all powers of reason.

He was soon awakened from that state though. The noise in the interior, which was like the hissing of the steam waste-pipe of a locomotive, suddenly changed to a succession of sharp bangs; the outer case flew to pieces, and, like fragments of lava from the crater of a volcano, a burning mass of blazing squibs, crackers, Catherine wheels, and hosts of others, the names of which are only to be found in the price list of a pyrotechnist, were shot forth.

Few people are sufficiently gifted to be able to calculate with accuracy the consequences of any particular action. For instance: A man goes out for a walk and falls down and breaks a leg or two, or is run over by an omnibus—events which he neither foresaw nor desired. So in this case, our hero carefully planned the destruction of the flogging machine, but he did not foresee that the very chum he designed to rescue would be the greatest sufferer.

Poor Tommy and the other unlucky four, carefully tucked up in the pillory, were exposed to the full play of the fireworks. Soker and Mr. Stiffback could run away when they were burned a little, but not so the five unfortunates, upon every inch of whose unlucky persons a fearful rain of fire was pouring.

"Help!" shrieked Tommy. "Take 'em off. Oh, Lor! I shall be burned to death."

The others joined in the chorus, but far above the voices of his suffering companions arose the shrill yell of Bobbles senior, who gave his favourite note, "O sharp," with immense success, and doubtless Soker would have added his applause but for the fact of his being himself engaged in putting out several conflagrations which were flourishing in different portions of his person.

Luckily Lionel, Charlie, Vansittart, and a few others retained some presence of mind, or the consequence of the explosion might have been rather serious. They ran for water, and some half a dozen bucketfuls dashed over the sufferers and upon the machine soon put an end to all chance of danger.

But there was one thing that the water could not extinguish, and that was the pain of the burns that the sufferers had already received.

"Poor old chap," said Lionel, as he looked at the multiplicity of burns at the rear of Tommy's trousers, and watched the writhing of the plump little legs inside them. "I never thought of this happening, Charlie."

"Neither did I," said Charlie. "Hold still a minute, Tommy, or we shall never get you out. Dash this padlock, Li, where's the key?"

"Soker's got it I expect. Hi, Soker, hand the key, will you."

But Soker was busy just then. He had a particularly sore burn just between his shoulders where a Catherine wheel had lodged and fried nearly a square foot of him. He really couldn't attend to anything at that moment.

Time was short, and our hero impatient. A couple of blows from a poker knocked off the staple, and then Charlie and our hero lifted Tommy out.

"What shall we do with him?" said Charlie.

"Carry him upstairs. Then we'll get the sweet oil and grease him well—that's the best thing."

"Look after those others, some of you fellows," said Lionel to the boys, who were crowding round roaring with applause at what they considered a first-rate piece of fun. They hadn't been burnt, you see—so they were not prejudiced like the others

They laid Tommy carefully face downwards on one of the beds in the dormitory, and while Charlie went for the oil, Lionel counted the burns.

"Do they hurt much, Tommy?"

"Awful," moaned the plump one; "is there much of me left, Li?"

"There seems to be rather more of you than usual, for the blisters are coming up."

"How many are there?"

"Only forty-seven of any size, Tommy. There's a few more little ones, but I didn't count them."

"They're worse than the others. What a chap you are, Li, to get a fellow into this scrape!"

"I did it all for the best, Tommy. And you know, after all, the machine is bust up for good."

"I'd rather have slept with it for a month than suffer this agony. Do you think I'll die?"

"Lor, no!" replied our hero, heartily, but turning pale at the probability of such an occurrence. "A little sweet oil will soon put you to rights."

"Oh, no it won't. Oh, my, the agony! I say, Li, as soon as ever I get well I'll punch your head for this, and then I'll cut your company for ever."

"Don't say that, Tommy."

"I do, and I mean it; I'm very fond of you, Li, but somehow I've had no peace of mind since I knew you. I'm always in hot water, and it don't agree with me."

"All right, Tommy—wait till you get well, and then we'll talk about it."

At that moment Charlie came rushing into the room, without the oil, and also without a fair allowance of breath.

"What's up, Charlie?"

"Lock the door, bolt it, quick. Old Soker's gone mad with the pain, and he's chasing Frenchy all over the house with a poker, swearing he'll have everybody's life. Hark! didn't you hear him?"

The sounds they heard were indeed truly alarming. An almost incessant yelling, as of some one in mortal terror, accompanied by heavy blows, made every hair in Tommy's head stand up with fright.

"Hide me away somehow," he said. "Dash it, Li, make haste. Soker's sure to drop on me if he comes in here."

But Charlie and our hero were busy in barricading the door, and left Tommy to shift for himself, which he did by rolling off the bed upon his back, and

putting himself to such agony that he howled more dismally than the unhappy mortal who was being chased by Soker.

Nearer and nearer, with startling rapidity, the pursuer and pursued approached the door of the dormitory.

Our friends had not nearly completed their barricade when there was a louder cry of "Help!" than ever, and with a crash the better half of a huge kitchen poker made its appearance through one of the panels.

Lionel was nearest, and instinctively he grasped the weapon to pull it through, but with an exclamation he instantly let it go again.

"Oh, Charlie! It's red hot."

Charlie's presence of mind was equal to the emergency. He seized a towel, and with his hands thus protected grasped the poker, and tugged away vigorously.

Soker, on the other side, was at a disadvantage, for he had only one hand wherewith to hold his weapon, as the other was engaged in the humane occupation of throttling his employer, and so the two boys in a few vigorous tugs made themselves masters of the weapon.

"He—e—elp!" they heard Mr. Stiffback feebly gurgle, in a voice which seemed to proceed from the pit of his stomach.

"Whatever shall we do?" said Charlie. "Soker's gone mad—that's certain."

"We must try and help the governor," returned Lionel, firmly. "Help to pull away these mattresses."

"But madmen are so frightfully strong, Li. We shall be murdered."

"We'll think about that after," replied our hero. "Besides, we've got the hot poker, and even a madman wouldn't be able to stand that. Heave away!"

Charlie obeyed, but he turned pale and shuddered when his leader turned the handle of the door. Let our readers remember that he was but a boy in years, and that there are but few men who would care unarmed to grapple with a maniac.

The door was thrown back, and then a very unpleasant spectacle was before them.

Mr. Stiffback lay prostrate, with Soker kneeling on his chest and grasping his master's throat with both hands.

"Put your tongue out a little furder," he said, with grim humour. "You looks prettier so, but I must say it ain't manners for a genelman o' your perfession to stare so; but your complexing are a lovely purple, that's sartin."

Lionel did not hesitate a moment. He was alarmed, it is true, but he never lost his self-possession, and taking careful aim with the poker he gave Soker one for himself, which rolled him over, and rendered the further inspection of Mr. Stiffback's tongue and complexion a matter of perfect indifference.

"Get the towels," said Lionel, hurriedly, "and tie his legs and arms quick, before he gets round. I'll look after the governor."

In the "twinkling of an eye," to use a popular but highly exaggerated expression, this was done, and Mr. Stiffback, with his complexion restored in some degree to its normal colour, and with his tongue once more inside his mouth, gasped out his thanks to his preservers.

"Don't say a word about it, if you please, sir," said Lionel. "It was nothing. Anybody could have knocked him down when he wasn't looking."

"No—o—matter, my—boy. You shall—be—rewarded. Now oblige me by calling those rascally cowards of servants, and make them carry Soker down, and send for the doctor."

Our boys hurried away to execute their orders, but scarcely had they disappeared round the angle of the corridor than Soker, with the glare of a demon in a state of *delirium tremens*, slipped from his bonds, and, grasping the poker, stood before the horrified Mr. Stiffback, whose tongue clove to the roof of his mouth with terror.

There are certain kinds of terror so intense that the victims are for a time paralysed, and unable to speak or move. Fortunate individuals who have been pounced upon by a lion or tiger invariably record—though it reads like a genuine Irish "bull"—that they were so frightened as not to feel frightened at all; and the fascination which the snake exercises over its victims has long since passed into a proverb.

It was so in some degree with Mr. Stiffback when Soker so suddenly and, as it would seem, so miraculously, broke from his bonds and waved the murderous poker before his head.

Soker was for the time mad, beyond a doubt. His brain was inflamed and diseased by excessive drinking, and now, suddenly and completely deprived of its accustomed stimulant, had given way, and all the unreasoning ferocity of a disordered intellect was turned against his master.

Fortunately, though, he still thought that the poker was hot, and instead of cracking the top of Mr. Stiffback's skull as a man cracks the shell of an egg, he only stirred him up with the end of the poker, and roared with laughter as in his frenzied imagination he fancied that his victim writhed and screamed.

The poker was still warm enough to be unpleasant as a "pocket companion," but not so hot as to burn him seriously; still, if it had been, we doubt if terror would not have so paralysed the head master as to render him incapable of moving.

It was one of those *mauvais quarts d'heure* which does the work of fifty years in fifteen minutes, and turns men's hair white without the slow aid of old Father Time. It is more than probable that it would have had this effect upon Mr. Stiffback: but he wore a wig, on which it would have puzzled Medusa herself to make the least impression.

It was lucky for Mr. Stiffback, though, that he had despatched two such light-heeled messengers as our hero and his chum for assistance, for in less than ten minutes he heard the sound of their footsteps echoing along the corridor, and summoning up all his strength he managed to let out a feeble squeak for help.

"Hullo!" said Lionel, as he neared the top of the last flight of stairs, "there's the governor's voice, and—yes—by George! Soker's got loose. Certainly you're a pretty fellow to trust to tie half-a-dozen knots."

"I tied 'em tight, Li," replied Charlie, in an injured tone; "but madmen are so strong they can break an iron chain."

"He wouldn't have got loose if I had tied him."

"Oh, I daresay not!" growled Charlie, in an undertone. "You're mighty clever, we know. Tie him yourself next time, and p'raps you'll be satisfied."

Lionel did not hear this, or he might have replied in a stronger manner than would have been comfortable for Master Charlie. He had paused at the head of the stairs to hasten the slower movements of Mr. Bunglebottle, the butler, the footman, the classical master, and Monsieur du Vinaigre, whom he had summoned to the rescue.

"Make haste!" he called out. "How slow you are! Quick! or Soker will have killed him."

"Is—is he werry wiolent?" panted the butler, who, like Hamlet, had become "fat and scant of breath."

"Dreadful!" replied our hero. "Hurry, or you'll be too late."

Mr. Bunglebottle was naturally a nervous man, and but for the fact that he supposed his old enemy Soker to have been safely bound hand and foot, he would not have ventured there at all.

He wanted to go back now, but the footman and the valorous Monsieur du Vinaigre were pressing him from the rear, and retreat was impossible.

"Stop a bit, gentlemen," he gasped. "Let's think it over."

"Dis is not de time to sink," said the French professor. "*En avant! Au secours!* One more leetle shove and op he go."

The "leetle shove" projected Mr. Bunglebottle a couple of yards into the corridor, and before he had time to turn round or offer any resistance he was urged on—our hero and Charlie helping as a matter of course—and propelled with a crash against Soker, just as that gentleman was playfully engaged in the endeavour to bore a hole through Mr. Stiffback with the poker.

Mr. Bunglebottle weighed some eighteen stone, there or thereabouts, and the force of his impact was such as to dash Soker against the wall, and spread him out like a plaister.

"So much for Soker!" said Charlie, in tragic tones, as he misquoted Shaks—— we beg pardon, Colley Cibber.

"I think he's settled," added our hero. "Come on, Drum, and let's tie him. I'm bothered if old Bunglebottle isn't afraid of him now."

But it was not fear which caused the obese butler to retire into a corner and groan. It was the stomach-ache, for the collision had been nearly as disastrous to him as to Soker.

The valorous little Frenchman, though, no sooner satisfied himself that Soker was quite helpless than he pounced upon him, with all the energy of eight stone two, and grasping him by the collar poured forth a torrent of fluent imprecations, mingled with assurances to Mr. Stiffback that it was all right now, and that he, the chivalrous Alphonse, would die in his defence.

"It's precious easy to cackle now," muttered Lionel, in an under tone; "but if he had the poker in his fist you'd be at the other end of the corridor, Monsieur, and in double-quick time, too."

But Mr. Stiffback had not been too bewildered by fright to single out his real preservers, and as Lionel and Charlie helped him to rise, he shook them both by the hand, and said in an under tone—

"You are brave boys, and I shall not forget this."

"It's all up with us, Charlie," said Lionel, gloomily, when order and quiet were once more restored, and the chums were alone together.

"What do you mean, Li? I think we're in for a good thing. Didn't you notice what Stiffback said?"

"That's just it, Charlie. If we get into any scrape now, or play any larks, he'll feel bound to overlook 'em, and it wouldn't be honourable of us to take advantage of him that way, Charlie?'

"Oh! blow that, Li," grumbled Drummond; "you carry the thing too far. It's all very well to be humble, and all that; but now we've got him under our thumb, and can do pretty much as we like, we should be fools to throw away the chance."

"I wish I could look at it in that way, Charlie, but it seems like hitting a fellow when he's down. It takes half the fun out of a lark, too, when you know you won't get punished if you are found out."

"There's something in that," said Charlie. "Hang it, Li, I wish we hadn't interfered now."

"If we hadn't, Charlie," replied Lionel, "there would have been a job for the undertaker."

"So there would. Soker was regularly mad, wasn't he? And I say, Li, you nearly made cold meat of him. What a wipe you gave him with that poker!"

"It didn't seem to hurt that thick skull of his much, though—but that reminds me of Tommy—let's go and see how he gets on."

They hurried back to the dormitory, where the shattered panel of the door remained as evidence of the exciting scene in which our boys had taken part, but the bed was no longer pressed by the recumbent and half-roasted body of their chum.

"Why, where can he have got to?" said our hero, as he rapidly glanced round the room; "he was too sore to move."

"He must be under one of the cribs, Li, or up the chimney. Let's look."

The search was soon made, and not a corner large enough for the concealment of a mouse escaped their keen eyes, but they found neither Tommy nor any trace of him.

"This is queer," said Lionel.

"Rather," added Charlie, turning pale. "I say, Li, do you think Soker's got loose again, and has carried him off, or ——"

"Or eaten him?"

"Not likely—he's safe enough—and, besides, he couldn't have got to the dormitory without passing us, you know; there's no other way."

"Then what's become of him? Here are all his clothes, and he hasn't got a rag on him."

"He can't be far away, anyhow," said Lionel; "we'll go and look for him. Come on, Charlie."

And hastily quitting the dormitory, the chums hurried along the corridor, in the hope of coming upon the traces of their vagrant chum.

CHAPTER LVII.

TOMMY'S ADVENTURES IN THE PUNT—CAUGHT NAPPING—I'M AFLOAT, I'M AFLOAT—THE PICNIC ON THE ISLAND—OUT OF THE FRYING-PAN INTO THE FIRE.

THE ears of our old friend, Tommy Codlings, were sharp, and though he lay face downwards, his head almost buried in the pillows, yet he heard, with an unpleasant distinctness, the sounds of the strife that was taking place between Soker and Mr. Stiffback.

Then came the crash of the poker as it dashed in the panel of the door. That made Tommy's heart leap almost into his mouth, but he lay still until Lionel had mastered the weapon, and then forgetting his burns, he struggled up into a sitting posture, and glanced towards the door, every tuft of hair on his round head standing up with horror.

"Oh, my," he thought; "what did they say? Soker gone mad! They'll be murdered, and me too. Oh, Lor'! what shall I do?

He heard now the gurgling, choking sounds, which proceeded from the half-stifled Mr. Stiffback. Tommy almost fainted—then came the dull heavy thud of the poker, as Lionel floored the maniac, and he waited to hear no more, but made for an open window.

The sloped roof of an outbuilding was some eight or ten feet below, and on to this Tommy dropped, without an instant's hesitation, and from thence another drop of about the same distance landed him on the ground.

Tommy managed, though, to take away half a pound or so of gravel with him, and it was only then that he thought of the extreme impropriety of his appearance.

"My eye! if any one sees me like this, I shall get in a row. Never mind—I know. I'll bolt down to the water, and say I went for a bathe. I should think, though, old Stiffback is killed by this time."

Then it flashed upon his mind that Lionel and Charlie were also in the same peril, and his conscience reproached him for leaving them; but he consoled himself with the recollection of our hero's wonderful luck.

"It's all right—it's sure to be," he thought. "Nothing ever hurts Li; I wonder who got that domino with the poker, though—that was a nasty one."

By the time he had reached this stage in his reflections, he had also reached the edge of the water, just opposite to which point was a sort of sluice gate, through which, from time to time, the superfluous water of the lake was allowed to flow.

"I wonder, now," mused Tommy, as he stood panting and shivering in the long grass, "whether Soker's killed 'em all. I wouldn't mind if he has settled Stiffback: the man don't deserve to live who

invented that beastly flogging machine, but I hope he hasn't Li or Charlie. My! isn't it cold here, and don't I smart?" he went on, recalled to a recollection of his own sufferings by a chilly north-east blast, which whistled round him; "what's that?"

Tommy jumped a couple of feet into the air as he fancied he heard a faint shriek proceed from the direction of the school.

There was a punt, moored by a chain, floating a couple of yards from the shore, and Tommy made for it, flying head over heels through the mud and rushes, and grasping the edge of the punt as if for bare life.

He had probably never been in such a hurry before, but visions of Soker running towards him covered with gore from head to foot, and wielding huge pokers in either hand, made him do wonders, and in a couple of seconds the punt was unmoored and a dozen yards away from the land.

"I wonder if Soker can swim," thought the terrified Tommy: "I dare say he can. Madness can do anything. I'll lie down in the bottom, and then he won't be able to see me."

Now a punt in its normal condition is a particularly uncomfortable substitute for a sofa. All sorts of inconvenient angles and projections are there, which obstinately refuse to accommodate themselves to the tender body of the sufferer, to say nothing of odd bits of rope, stones and gravel, and perhaps a stray fish-hook or so.

Of course, as Tommy had nothing to protect him, he suffered considerably, but the fear of a sudden and violent death would have made him lie patiently in a bed of hot coals, for a while at least, and so he steered out, only groaning inwardly and reviling Soker for being so stupid as to go mad at all.

"He did it on purpose to spite me, I know." thought Tommy. "I hope they'll hang him. Oh, Lor, how I am suffering! There's a bit of sharp flint running right into my stomach."

Tommy ventured to raise himself a little, for the purpose of getting rid of the torturing flint, but just then he fancied he heard another yell, and he dropped as if he had been shot.

"He'll kill 'em all, and then he'll set the house afire," thought Tommy, breaking out in a cold perspiration. "I'm lucky after all in getting away. I declare I can smell smoke."

This must have been fancy on Tommy's part, for he was lying on his face, with his little snub nose flattened against a plank, which smelt very strongly of mud and tar, with just a soupçon of stale fish, but never a sniff of anything so pleasant as smoke.

For about a quarter of an hour Tommy lay in that position, wide awake, and listening intently for the yells of the bloodthirsty maniac, Soker, or the shrieks of his writhing victims, when his natural tendency to sleep when he wasn't eating came upon him, and he felt drowsy.

"I think I will have a nap," he mused. "I shall be all right out here, and when things are quiet I can paddle myself back. I'm only a yard or two away from the shore."

Poor Tommy, only a yard or two! Little did he dream that the sluice gate was open, and that, while he fondly imagined himself floating tranquilly in the lake, he was being drifted slowly but surely past the lock, and so towards the river.

He slept the sleep of youth and innocence, for Tommy seldom dreamed unless after a heavy supper. The punt bumped against the sides of the weir, and grated over the pebbly shallows, and here and there whirled round in an eddy, but Tommy slumbered calmly on.

The river was reached, and the punt launched out upon its wider current, sometimes with one end foremost, sometimes with the other, and occasionally for a change going broadwise, or turning round and round in a grave kind of waltz, until, having apparently journeyed as far as it wanted to, it bumped itself against a little thickly-wooded island, that lay conveniently in the centre of the stream, and stopped, but the shock awoke not Tommy, and he slumbered on.

Now this island happened to be a favourite resort for picnic parties of a very select sort, and on this very day, as evil chance would have it, the Misses Growlagain, with some of their eldest pupils, had come there, and were engaged in the consumption of tea, cake, shrimps, bread and butter, and other such delicacies known to picnicers, at the very moment when Tommy's punt landed him thither.

" *Such* a charming place," said Miss Growlagain, to the senior governess, " so silent, so quiet, no fear of interruption or intrusion from the vulgar herd."

" Delightful, indeed," was the dutiful reply of the governess; " no rude noisy men or boisterous boys to break in upon the delicious repose of thought, which the—er—the contemplation of Nature awakens in the mind of the reflective bosom—I mean in the bosom of the defective mind. No, that isn't exactly what I mean either—but it's very nice."

" Young ladies," said Miss Growlagain, at this juncture, " have you all had enough ?"

None of them had, for schoolgirls are very like schoolboys in the matter of appetite, and can put away an amount of food which is perfectly astonishing, but they were wise in their generation, and answered in the affirmative, all except one, who tardily preferred a request for another piece of cake.

" Miss Jones, I am absolutely ashamed of you," said the schoolmistress, severely. " You have actually brought out a rash upon yourself through eating so many shrimps already. Not a piece more, and you will have no supper to-night as a punishment for your voracity."

Poor Miss Jones blushed, and began to cry, but soon comforted herself with the recollection of a slice of seed cake done up in curl-papers, that she had hidden away.

The other girls were paired off to stroll about the island, chatting away, like so many sparrows, of coming holidays, and parties, new dresses, and old sweethearts, and a dozen other things dear to the feminine heart, from six years old to sixty.

The eldest Miss Growlagain and the governess, with two or three of the more privileged pupils, walked along by the water's edge, indulging in an animated conversation upon the beauties of Nature, when one gave a loud scream, and without a word of explanation turned and fled.

* * * * * * *

It was about this time that Tommy awoke from his nap. Under more comfortable circumstances he would have slept at least an hour longer; but lying in such a position, flat upon their faces, and upon the hard, uneven planking of a punt, would have shortened the slumbers of the Seven Sleepers by at least a couple of years.

So Tommy awoke, and fancying himself in the dormitory at school, began, as his invariable custom was, to call out to Lionel—

" First bell gone yet, Li ?" he murmured, sleepily, as he rolled over and stared up at the sky.

" Blow the— Hullo! what's the matter with the ceiling ?"

Instead of the white plaster that he expected to see, there, stretched above him, was the blue and boundless vault of heaven; the river rippled gently by, and the wind played with the tall grass and rushes on the bank.

Tommy stared at it all dreamily for a while, and fancied he understood how it was.

" Oh, oh!" he thought. " I remember now. The punt has drifted back to shore. What a lucky thing, though, that old Soker did not come back while I was asleep. I might have been pokered without ever knowing anything about it. Everything seems quiet. I'll go ashore now, and see if I can get back to the school.

And poor Tommy, little suspecting where he was, scrambled up in the punt.

The mud, caked upon his body, had acted as a kind of ointment, and though he was very stiff, yet the burns did not pain him so much. There may be some unknown virtue in mud, surpassing that of Gobbleaway's ointment. At any rate, it does not cost one shilling and a penny-halfpenny per pot—so it has cheapness to recommend it, if any of our readers care to try the recipe.

Water, grass, and mud, all bear a strong family likeness to their respective species, and Tommy never suspected for an instant that he was anywhere but at Lake Island.

There was a barge crawling leisurely along under the opposite bank, with a huge snuffy sail hung out to dry, apparently, and Tommy might have known that such a thing was never seen upon the lake, but he was not an observant youth, and would most probably have taken a whale or a rhinoceros as a natural production of the climate, if he had seen one.

Of course he managed to pick out a deep hole to wade into, but he didn't mind that, for it washed the mud off, and though the water was chilly and gave him the appearance of a statue of Cupid carved out of mottled soap, he consoled himself with the thought that he was clean again.

" What a comfort," he thought, as he once more stood on dry ground, " that our school is on an island, where there's nobody to meet. How lucky for me, now that I haven't got my clothes on ! Let me see, which is the way ? The trees don't seem quite so big as they are, and there's more of 'em, but I s'pose it's my fancy."

There was no path, and so Tommy took his direction haphazard, looking carefully before him, and listening intently at every step.

Suddenly, a little to the left, he heard the sound of youthful voices raised in laughter.

Tommy jumped to a conclusion at once—it was his only way of getting one—and he called out aloud—

" That's Li and Charlie. I know their voices. Hullo, Li, here I am !"

And before the words had left his lips he had left the shelter of the trees, and was landed in the midst of a group of—the Misses Growlagain's most select pupils !

CHAPTER LVIII.

SAM GOES FISHING, AND CATCHES MORE THAN HE BAITED HIS HOOK FOR.

SAM SCARECROW had always possessed a latent ambition to shine as a sportsman, and taking advantage of the geographical position of Lake Island School, he thought he might commence his sporting career as an amateur angler.

He had managed to save up money enough to purchase a battery of rod, lines, and hooks, sufficient to have terrified even the octopus at the Brighton Aquarium.

But, as many of my readers know, the possession of an elaborate array of fishing tackle does not always ensure a corresponding take of fish.

Sam had made various attempts at acquiring the gentle craft, but with indifferent success.

On the occasion of which we are now writing, however, he distinguished himself in a way that astonished more than it delighted him.

" It's a proper arternoon for a bite," said Sam to himself, examining his tackle with the eye of a connoisseur.

" And I'll be busted if I don't take a lot o' fish to-day."

So packing up his traps he sallied forth, bent on sport.

He chose a likely-looking spot, as he thought, for his operations, and baited his hook with a degree of nervousness that nearly caused that instrument to insert itself into his fingers more than once.

However, at last he got the worm on.

"Now, ye beggars, you only just take a bite—that's all," said Sam.

So saying, Sam seated himself on the stump of an old tree, and not having made up his mind what style of fishing he purposed catching, alternately sank his bait into the water, and then swept the horizon with it, as he had often seen Lionel do when fly-fishing.

Time sped on, and Sam's efforts were unrewarded with even a nibble.

"Bust the blessed fishes," said Sam, as he swept out his line with a little more vigour than usual.

Joy!

He felt resistance at the other end.

He had got a bite.

The obliquity of his vision prevented his discerning for the moment what sort of a bite he had got.

But his hearing being sharp enough he heard what was decidedly a female voice, cry out—

"I'm caught, I'm caught."

"Blowed if I ain't a been and copped a mermaid!" cried Sam, as he eagerly pulled his line home.

If he had caught a mermaid she certainly wore a wig, for when he got the hook and its victim into the line of sight it proved to be a lady's head of hair, false front, curls and all.

As he looked at his curious fish in open-eyed wonder, a boat, propelled by some of the pupils, shot round a corner, and seated in the stern was a stout old lady, perfectly bald-headed—and in a state of mind the reverse of peaceful.

"You——"

But, there, I will not bore my readers by recapitulating the epithets that were hurled at the head of the unfortunate Sam.

But this, to Sam, was not the worst. The boys in the boat took up the chorus, and alternately chaffed and upbraided Sam till that worthy was rendered well-nigh frantic.

He managed to unfasten the wig from the hook, and hurled it with all his might at the inconsolable nymph whom he had deprived of her headgear.

She in her excitement clapped it on hind side foremost, and as she clambered out of the boat she grabbed at Sam, caught him by the collar, and said—

"You vagabond! you scoundrel! Come with me to Mr. Stiffback at once."

'Twas vain for Sam to resist. She had the strength of a dozen Sams.

So, like a lamb led to the slaughter he was dragged into the presence of the schoolmaster.

Of course Mr. Stiffback pacified the irate fair one as best he could, and dismissed Sam to his study, to await punishment most dire for his offence against propriety—and the maiden aunt of a prospective pupil.

Sam, bewailing his unlucky lot, made his way to Mr. Stiffback's study, and in an agony of doubt and fear as to what his ultimate fate would be, awaited the coming of the schoolmaster.

CHAPTER LIX.

THE FURTHER ADVENTURES OF TOMMY ON THE ISLAND—DEFEAT OF MISS GROWLAGAIN—THE GOVERNESS TO THE RESCUE!—TOMMY GETS THE WORST OF THE FIGHT—THE ARRIVAL OF THE BOATMEN—TOMMY'S VENGEANCE.

FOR one awful moment Miss Growlagain stood speechless, paralysed by the scandalous nature of the intrusion. Then her presence of mind returned, and turning her back on Tommy she spread out her skirts, and screamed at the top of a preternaturally shrill voice—

"Run away, young ladies! Go away directly to the other end of the island, and do not look in this direction till I allow you to."

But most of the girls had gone already. A natural sense of propriety had caused them to run at the appearance of such a shocking spectacle; the rest followed, and in a moment Tommy and Miss Growlagain were alone.

If Tommy had been wise he would have run to and taken refuge in his punt. But he stayed thinking that some kind of an apology was due.

"I'm very sorry, ma'am," he began, addressing himself to the nape of Miss Growlagain's neck, for that lady's rigid ideas of decorum would not allow her to face Tommy.

"Don't talk to me, you low, bad boy!" exclaimed the schoolmistress; "but go away directly."

"If you please, ma'am," replied Tommy, "I live here."

"What!" said Miss Growlagain. "How dare you tell me such a falsehood? How can you live here when there are no houses?"

"No houses!" said Tommy, in consternation. "There was one an hour ago, and a good large one too. Why, I've been at school here for months."

This outrageous falsehood, as Miss Growlagain deemed it—for of course she was quite unaware of Tommy's adventure in the punt—exasperated her so that she turned half round, and "fetched" Tommy a back-hander that made him see stars.

"Oh!" exclaimed the injured one. "Oh, you spiteful old wretch—take that!"

And lowering his head Tommy charged her like an angry bull, hitting the poor lady just where her waistcoat would have been had she worn one.

The poor old lady went over like a ninepin, but not before she had given utterance to a "squall" which might have been heard a mile away, so shrill and piercing was it.

"Blow her!" muttered Tommy, "what does she want to make a noise like that for?"

He did not think then of the noise he made when suffering the penalties of the flogging machine or other similar tortures, but it is a peculiarity of our erring human nature to think that no one has a right to complain of misfortune but ourselves.

Tommy was still under the impression that he was on Lake Island, for when once an idea did get into his head it was extremely difficult to get it out again; and instead of making for the punt, and seeking the comparatively safe shelter of the river, he darted amongst the trees in the hope of meeting Lionel or some of his chums.

It is hardly necessary to say that he did not meet our hero, but he met the governess, who, not being quite so overcome at the sight of Tommy's primitive costume, charged him, grabbed him by the hair of his head, and began prodding him with the point of her parasol.

She was as tall as a grenadier, bony and sinewy, and Tommy, being handled in such a way, was helpless. The point of the parasol was sharp too, and flicked little bits of skin off him at every prod, and sore as he was with the burns he had already received, the torture was exquisite, and his sweet voice made the air ring again with his yells for help.

The help came, but not exactly in the shape Tommy would have chosen.

It was near the time appointed for Miss Growlagain to return to the mainland, and the watermen were at hand with the boat—two strong, sturdy fellows, who lived upon pigtail tobacco and rum—and smelt accordingly.

"Seemingly there's a row on, Bill," said one, as he shipped his oar, and jumped on land.

"It's only one of them gals as have seed a water-rat or some sich warmint," replied Bill. "They're always taking a skeer. It cannot run much," added George; "come on. We may get a pint o' beer for killing on it."

The word "beer" was sufficient to stimulate Bill into action. He was by the side of his mate in a moment, and guided by Tommy's yells they soon reached the scene of action.

George stopped short as soon as he caught sight of the little group.

"Bill," he said, "it's only the school marm a-walloping one o' the gals. We didn't orter look. I'm a modest man."

"Wot an old she-cat!" said Bill. "But let's bear a hand. George—think o' the beer!"

By this time George, who had been staring steadfastly at the interesting little combat of two, discovered that the victim was a boy, and his modest scruples being thus overcome, he went in, and laid hold of the unlucky Tommy.

"It's all right now, marm," he said, soothingly. "I've got the young warmint."

"Oh, thank goodness you came in time!" said the governess, faintly, for she thought it right to show a little feminine weakness after such an exhibition of unfeminine strength.

"Wot's he been a doin' of, marm?"

"Oh, I can't tell you! The wretch!"

"You're a nice harticle, ain't you?" said George, giving his captive a violent shake. "At your age too! Wot next?"

Here the governess gave an affecting moan, and seeing out of the corner of one eye that Bill was handy, and not so very bad-looking, she fainted away comfortably in his arms.

"Here, hold up, marm!" said Bill. "Blow it! Wot's the little game?"

"Take care on her, Bill," said George. "We shall get a quart a-piece out o' this job. Sing out for the missis. They understands wot to do with these 'ere tantrums."

"They won't come nigh while that there boy's by with ne'er a rag on him. Stow him away in the boat, George, and then come back and bear a hand. Dash it! her elbers is working right through me. She's more bony than any skillinton I ever see."

Bill's unwary expression of opinion regarding the anatomy of the governess ruined all his hopes of beer, for the governess came out of her faint as quickly as she had gone into it, and audibly giving vent to the sentiment that Bill was a "brute" and a "beast," she picked up her parasol, and marched off.

"You've done it now!" cried George, savagely. "Wot did you want to call her a skillinton for?"

"How did I know she was a listening?" growled Bill.

"You might ha' known as these women is allus ashamming. If you'd called her a dear and give her a kiss she'd a kep her eyes shut fast enough."

"There she is now, a hailin of us," said Bill. "Give the boy a clout in the head, and send him off."

George did it, and with such a hearty good will that poor Tommy reeled half-a-dozen yards away, and landed finally in a fine fresh bed of nettles.

"Oh, my! oh, lor!" he gasped. "Was there ever such an unlucky chap as me? Oh, don't I wish I could pay 'em out! I wish I had a gun or something."

Wild and desperate ideas of vengeance filled his mind, but were impracticable. At last a happy thought struck him. He scrambled up, and ran to the bank, where the boat was moored side by side with his punt. A vigorous push sent the punt whirling into the middle of the river. Then Tommy got into the boat, cast off the painter, and with one of the oars pushed off from the bank.

CHAPTER LX.

UP THE RIVER AND DOWN AGAIN—THE BOATMEN VERSUS MISS GROWLAGAIN AND THE GOVERNESS —OVERTURES OF PEACE, AND OVERTURES OF QUITE A DIFFERENT NATURE.

TOMMY'S push was quite vigorous enough to send the boat some five or six yards from the bank, and hardly was this feat accomplished than Bill and George put in an appearance, red and wrathful.

"Here, come back, will you?" roared Bill.

"Dash your young carcase!" shouted George. "Bring that there boat back, or I'll smash you."

"Not to-day, baker!" replied Tommy, cheerfully. "I'm going for a little row. Don't wait for me."

"Jump in, and swim arter him," said Bill.

"I can't swim, worse luck!" growled George, "or I'd soon overhaul him. Do'ee try."

"I can't ayther," replied Bill.

"Eave a brick!" said George.

"There bain't none, nor yet no stones, or I'd fetch him a crack which 'ud stop his larks for a while," said George, vengefully.

"Wot's to be done?" said Bill.

But before his companion could offer any reply to this question, Miss Growlagain appeared upon the scene.

"Boatman," she said, "we will go away directly."

"Werry well, marm," said George, sullenly. "I'm werry glad to hear it, and I hopes you'll take Bill and me with you."

"No impudence!" said the schoolmistress, sharply. "Get the boat directly."

"That's impossible," replied Bill.

"How dare you say so? Where is it, you low men?" chimed in the governess, who had by no means forgotten the uncomplimentary allusion Bill had made to her angularity.

"Out theer," said Bill, pointing to the river, "and unless you can persuade your young man to bring it back I don't azactly see how we're to make him."

The governess and Miss G. went to the edge of the bank, and there sure enough was the naked and shameless Tommy standing in the stern, and kissing his hand to the ladies with a studied grace.

"Oh, the little beast!—the disgraceful young scamp!" said the governess, shaking her parasol at him. "I wish I had him here, I do!"

"Call him back, marm," said Bill, who did not care what he said now that all hope of beer was gone. "He'll come back if you calls him. You was a werry lovin' together a while ago."

"Oh, you bad wicked man! How dare you say such things?"

"Well, George see it as well as me. You had him round the neck, and was a tickling un with your umbreller."

There was a very audible tittering amongst the girls, who, urged by curiosity, had approached near enough to hear the remarks of the boatmen; and the governess, looking unutterable rage and scorn at her insulter, audibly expressed a wish that she had the "tickling" of them even as she had tickled Tommy.

"Enough of this," said Miss Growlagain, who found it necessary to assert the dignity of her position. "Boatmen, you will row us across the river at once, or take the consequences."

"I doesn't know wot the consekences may be, marm," said George; "but if they're anythink to drink we'll take it, and thank you kindly. Likewise we'll row you ashore—if you'll find a boat to do it in."

"And in course," added Bill, "the lady'll pay for our boat, as her young man's took it away."

"In course," assented George. "We stands on our rights."

"But, my good man," said Miss Growlagain, whose civility increased as she saw the desperate state of the case, "that low-minded wretch had nothing to do with us. We don't know him—we would scorn it."

"I don't know nothink about that," said Bill doggedly. "That there boat was our livin', and we've got to be paid for it."

"That's the way to talk," added George; "and if we gets ashore afore we dies o' starvation we'll have our rights afore the judge."

"I'll give you," said the schoolmistress, aghast at the liberality of her offer, "I'll give you sixpence extra if you'll take us over at once."

"There's generosity!" exclaimed Bill. Sixpence! —only fancy!—and all at once too."

"I'll make it a shilling, then!" said Miss Growl-again.

"You'd better hail that there boy, and offer him a pound to come back with the boat," growled Bill.

"And then," said George, struck with a bright idea, "when he's got it we can take it away from him."

This was a notion after Miss Growlagain's own heart, and extracting a sovereign from her purse she held it out towards Tommy, who had not got very far away, for the tide was slack.

"If you come back," she squeaked, in her shrillest tones, "you shall have this."

"Ay, and sumut else besides!" growled Bill.

"What's the old girl doing, I wonder?" said Tommy, as he saw the schoolmistress going through a species of gymnastic performance on the bank. "What's that she said? 'Come back'? Oh, ah! precious likely, that is! Besides, I don't know that I could if I wanted to. These oars are precious heavy. I can only manage one at a time."

The tide, as we have said, was slack, and in a little while it began to ebb, and Tommy by slow degrees drifted back the way he had come.

"Hullo! What's up?" thought the plump youth. "I'm going back again. There's something the matter with the boat. Perhaps it's sinking."

But a little examination proved that she was as dry as a bone; and then Tommy began to fear that there was some hidden machinery in the boat which was urging it back towards its masters, and sitting down in a hurry he seized the oars, and went through some very complicated manœuvres with those implements.

In the course of Tommy's complicated manœuvres he knocked out a tooth, gave himself a black eye, made his nose bleed, and finally, catching a crab, dashed all the temporary supply of breath out of his body with the butt of the oar, and lay in the bottom, a melancholy example of misdirected genius.

He was soon up again, though, gasping for breath and pale with terror lest he should fall into the hands of his foes.

"Dash it!" muttered Tommy, after a moment. "It's only the tide, after all! What an ass I was to be in such a funk!"

As his fears vanished so his "cheek" returned, and now that he was within hail of the island again he uttered sundry taunts and pleasantries which, as Bill said, made his "blood bile."

To do Tommy justice, though, he was now aware of his indecent want of costume, and as Bill had left a spare coat in the boat he arrayed his form therein, and as there was enough of it to have made him a complete suit, the modesty of Miss Growl-again and her pupils was no longer likely to be offended.

"Come ashore with that there boat, you young warmint! Come ashore!" roared Bill.

"Come and fetch me!" retorted Tommy. "It's a beautiful day for a swim."

Bill had found a stone, after a long and laborious search, and taking careful aim he hurled it with a vicious intent at the plump youth.

Unfortunately he stood too near the edge, and the force with which he threw the missile caused him to lose his balance, and in an instant he disappeared into the water.

It was not very deep just there—not more than two feet, but there was a good three feet of nice soft, slimy mud, and into this Bill had dived head first, and there he stuck.

The soles of his boots were visible above the water, and these were being jerked about with such energy by the legs inside them that proved far more strongly than words Bill's disapproval of the flavour of the mud.

George watched for a few moments, and then roared, in an encouraging voice—

"Come up, Bill."

It is doubtful whether Bill heard him, and if had he couldn't have obeyed; and as the jerks of legs became weaker and more convulsive, Geor began to think that he had better fetch him out.

For this purpose he lay face downwards on bank, and leaning over laid hold of the boots, a hauled away.

But in that position he could not exert streng sufficient, so, getting up again, he planted his hee as firmly as he could on the slippery grass ai weeds, and taking a fresh hold tugged away wi all his might.

The result was startling. Bill's boots were n a tight fit—they came off with a jerk. Geor slipped, made a few wild grasps at nothing in pa ticular, and then fell over into the water by the sid of Bill, going in as straight and clean as the mo practised diver.

Tommy was in ecstacies. He danced and cheere as if the whole affair had been some entertainmei got up for his special amusement.

It was not so very amusing, though, to the partie principally concerned, and another thirty second would certainly have settled Bill; but, luckily fc him, the sudden arrival of George stirred up th mud, and with a last desperate wriggle he cor trived to get his head above water.

George followed suit, and there they sat, thei heads alone visible, covered with black mud, thei mouths shutting and opening like that of a strande fish, but emitting no sound whatever.

At last Bill made the remark—

"Oh, Lord!"

To which George added an observation which w resolutely decline to print, but it was very expres sive, and it related to the mud.

After a few moments George managed to get u and scramble ashore, whither he was followed b Bill, both wearing a savage and gloomy expressior which was not improved by the streaks of mu which the water had not entirely washed off.

"Bill!"

"Well, George."

"If ever I gets a holt of that boy I'll flay hin fust, and then I'll roast him."

"And I will eat him," added Bill, with a tremen dous oath of so violent and bloodthirsty a natur that Miss Growlagain gave a little jump, and nearl pushed the governess into the water.

"Look at the young warmint!" suddenly ex claimed George. "Blow me if he ain't found ou our grub in the locker. Look! he's got the bottl o' beer."

Bill gave a groan, but the next minute he was on his feet, waving his arms and shouting excitedly.

"Hi! There's Tom Chiffery in his wherry. Hi Tom! board that dashed young pirate, and bring him here. Tom, ahoy!"

Tom was a long way off, but Bill had the lungs of a Stentor, and when he sang "Homeward Bound' or the "Death of Nelson," his audience generally stood a mile off to listen.

So the very first "Ahoy!" reached Tom, who stopped rowing, and looked round.

"Hillo, Bill! What cheer, mate?"

"Stop that young warmint, Tom, and bring hin and the boat over here."

"Ay, ay!" replied Tom Chiffery, and pulling his wherry round with one sweep of his starboard scull, he headed for the unlucky Tommy, who by this time was fully aware of his danger.

"I'm in for it now!" he thought. "Oh, lor! they'll drown me. What shall I do?"

Apparently there was nothing to be done. Chif fery was coming up hand over hand, and Tommy had already tested and proved his incapacity to use the heavy oars. He was a victim, and there was nothing to be done but to submit to his fate.

Nearer and nearer came the light wherry, urged through the water by the powerful arms of Chif fery, and Tommy watched his approach even as the bird fascinated by a serpent awaits the coming of its destroyer.

The bow of the wherry was within a yard of the boat, when a desperate idea occurred to the plump youth. He grasped the heavy stone jar, and raising it above his head, hurled it with all his might at the waterman.

Fortunately, it did not hit him, or that jolly young waterman would have feathered his oars with skill and dexterity for the wherry last time; but it did what, under the circumstances, was quite as effectual for Tommy's purpose. It struck the side of the boat below the middle thwart, and crashed through the thin planking as if it had been so much paper.

The wherry filled and sank in an instant, and before Chiffery had time to do anything but swear one extremely strong oath, he sank too.

"Hooray!" shouted Tommy, not thinking in that moment of triumph that he ran a very excellent chance of being tried at the bar of a criminal court for murder. "Hooray! That's settled him."

And so it had very nearly, for by a peculiar dispensation of Providence it is provided that the very men who pass three-fourths of their lives on deep water shall be ignorant of the only art whereby their lives can be saved in case of a "spill."

Chiffery was a waterman, and of course he could not swim; but luckily for himself and Tommy he came up close by one of the sculls, and, grasping that, was just able to keep his own skull above water

"You dashed young warmint!" he gasped, as soon as he was able to find breath enough for speech. "Only let me get hold o' you!"

"Thank'ee," replied Tommy, cheerfully; "but I'm very comfortable where I am. How do you feel?"

Mr. Chiffery's reply was far too strong to be rendered in print. We can only hint that it recommended Tommy to a place of so warm a nature that there would be little chance of his ever catching cold.

"You're extremely polite," replied Tommy, "but I think the situation would suit you best. Don't you find it rather wet down there?"

But Mr. Chiffery, holding on to the scull very tightly, was too busy in making his way to the island to reply to Tommy's inquiries; besides, his vigorous kicks sent his head under water every moment, and he really had no breath to spare.

Tommy watched his progress with easy indifference, and as the tide was carrying him along without any trouble to himself, he thought that the best thing to do under the circumstances was to sit down and consume the remainder of the provisions which Bill and George had left in the locker.

Meanwhile, Chiffery had made his way to the shore, his bosom full of hatred, malice, and all uncharitableness towards mankind, but especially towards Tommy. If he could have laid hands on that youth it would have gone very hard indeed with him, but as he was not to be got at just then Chiffery resolved to have it out with Bill and George, the primary causes of his misfortunes.

"You're a nice set o' chaps, you are!—I don't think!" he gasped, as soon as he was safely landed. "Wot d'ye mean by it?"

"Mean by wot, Tom?" said Bill.

"Here," continued the injured Chiffery. "Here am I nigh drownded—my boat sunk, and all through you! I'll have it out on you, though! You'll ha' to pay for it!"

"I likes that!" said Bill. "'Twarnt our fault."

"Whose was it, then?" said the exasperated Chiffery. "Who set me on to go arter that dashed young himp? Fifteen pound won't square damages."

"Take it easy, Tom," said George, soothingly.

"'Take it heasy!' You take that heasy!" said Chiffery, as he applied his right fist to the left eyebrow of George, and laid that unlucky waterman prostrate on the grass. "And if yer want any more get up and I'll give it yer."

Bill was not a man to see a friend assaulted without going to the rescue. He promptly closed with Chiffery, and hammered away in front, while George, as soon as he could scramble up, peppered him in the rear.

Miss Growlagain, the governess, and the young ladies screamed, as was only proper and natural, and the dull little island was the scene of more excitement than it had witnessed since the first day when it became dry land.

Tommy could not see what was going on; he had drifted too far down the river, but he heard the screams of the females and the shouts of the combatants, and chuckled in his joy. For once he was in luck, and had defeated his enemies. But what was to be the end of it all?

Meanwhile Lionel and Charlie, sorely puzzled at the disappearance of their chum, had made a hurried search for him all over the house and grounds, but of course without finding any trace of the plump one.

"He must have got into the water," said Charlie, at last. "Poor chap! I'm afraid he's settled, Li."

"Not a bit of it," replied our hero. "Tommy's sure to turn up somehow or somewhere."

"But where and how, Li? Do you think he's taken one of the boats, and rowed across as he did before?"

"No, all the boats are in the boathouse. I counted 'em."

So he had, but neither of the chums thought of the punt, and as they were getting seriously alarmed at the mysterious absence of Tommy they thought it best to report the matter to the head master, and get the benefit of his experience.

"Confound that boy!" said Mr. Stiffback, angrily. "I never have a moment's peace because of him. What do you say—he had no clothes on?"

"Not a rag, sir," said our hero. "He had stripped so that we might oil him where he had been burnt, and then Soker went mad, and while we were helping you Tommy vanished."

"It's very strange, but he must be about the house somewhere. Tell the servants to search."

"We have done that already, sir. We have looked everywhere."

"Then he must have got across the lake."

"He can't have done that, sir. All the boats are in the boathouse."

"Look again," said Mr. Stiffback. "He must be somewhere, and he must be found."

A second search was of course equally unavailing, but it led to the discovery of the punt pole and the stake to which the chain was fastened.

"That's it!" said Lionel, hitting at once upon the truth. "What an ass I was not to think of the punt before! And see, the sluice opposite is open; he has drifted through there. Run for the key, Charlie. We'll get a boat and go after him."

Charlie was off like a shot, and in less than ten minutes the boat was out, manned by our hero, Charlie, Vansittart, and Pryce, with the smallest of the Bobbles family for the coxswain. He was the first small boy they came across, and was pressed into the service much against his will.

"Hurrah!" said Lionel. "Pull away, boys. We'll soon find Tommy now."

And so they did, but in a way they little expected, and to the narration of which we must devote a fresh chapter.

CHAPTER LXI.

THE GRAND "BREAKING-UP" AT LAKE ISLAND SCHOOL.

THERE is nothing equal to a touch of adversity for banding people together in one common cause, and so Bill, George, and Tom Chiffery found it when their first temporary disagreement was over.

They had each received a pretty equal share of punishment, so that there was no jealousy on that point. Bill's right eye was blackened, and George's left was ornamented in a similar way, while Tom had lost a front tooth, and possessed a swelling on his forehead, very like a diseased potato.

"Now, the great thing is, how are we going to get out o' this?" said Tom Chiffery.

"Ah! that's wot I'd like to know," was Bill's comment, "and so would those 'ere ladies. Blowed if I don't think we'd better chum in and make a night on it."

"Wot!" said George; "with ne'er a drop o' beer, nor yet a bit of backer. Not for me, Bill."

"Well, then, if so be as you ain't inclined to stop, George, you'd best stir up that thick 'ed o' yourn and hit on a idee for getting away."

"Thick 'ed," growled George, "I likes that. You're a nice party to talk about thick 'eds, when I've seen you knock a couple o' bricks out of a nine inch wall by fallin' up agin it."

"Blow bricks, and walls, and thick 'eds too," observed Chiffery. "We've got to git away, and if somebody don't bear a hand we shall have to stick here."

"We know that as well as you, don't we?" said Bill, whose eye was still extremely painful.

"Well," continued Chiffery, "my plan is this 'ere—you, Bill, go to one end o' the island, George take his station at tother, and I'll stay here. Then we must all three holler, and if the ladies put in a scream now and agin, we are sure to be heerd."

This was extremely likely, as a combination of such lungs as the watermen possessed, and the shriller voices of the ladies, young and old, must have been audible nearly as far as the explosion of the eighty-one ton gun.

They tried it, and the second hail woke up the captain of a coal barge, a mile and a quarter off, who was coming up with the tide, and after swearing a few strongly-flavoured nautical oaths, he ordered all hands to keep a sharp look-out, and stowed a pint of rum in what he called his "hold," but which ordinary mortals style the stomach, to make him equal to an emergency.

"It's a revylution," muttered the captain of the coal barge, as the roars of the watermen, mingled with the shrieks of the young ladies, became louder and more frequent, "or p'raps some o' the Turks has landed, and is doin' summat in the Bungling atrocity way."

But in a few minutes he caught sight of George, who was standing on the very verge of the island, and, with a hand clapped to either side of his mouth, was howling in the most hideous manner.

"Hillo, mate!" hailed the cap'en.

"Run your barge in, cap'en, or send a boat ashore," roared Bill; "we've been captured and stove in by a ——"

We cannot repeat the complimentary epithets bestowed upon Tommy, but George may be excused on account of the excitement and the strong sense of injury under which he was labouring.

Men of that class are generally ready to oblige one another, and the cap'en readily brought his craft to an anchor by simply running her into the mud.

"Now, make haste, mum!" shouted Bill. "All as wants to come aboard show a leg there!—show a leg!"

"The horrid rude wretch!" said Miss Growlagain. "He shall pay dearly for that insult. Show a leg, indeed!"

There was no time then to resent the offence, for the cap'en, aided by George, was already tugging at one of the long sweeps to get her head off shore, and Miss Growlagain unwillingly obeyed the rude order of the waterman—and not only showed one leg but two, as she fell over the low gunwale and pitched head first into the bottom of the barge.

There was a good deal of tittering amongst the pupils, and some very expressive winks were exchanged between the two watermen, Bill and George; but long before Miss Growlagain had recovered from her confusion the barge had swung out into mid-stream again, and Chiffery, with a vengeful eye, was in the bow looking out for Tommy.

If that young gentleman had been content to let the boat drift he would have been in safety long before his pursuers could have reached him, but, in the insane belief that he was facilitating his movements, he tried to use the oars, and the boat, naturally resenting this interference, tacked across from one side of the river to the other, turned round and round, and, in short, did anything but proceed in a straightforward manner.

As a natural consequence he was not more than five hundred yards distant when Chiffery sighted him.

"There he is!" he said, in tones of the strongest excitement.

"Hooray!" said George. "So it be. We'll nab the young swab now."

"Here's a boat astarn," said Bill. "We can drop into that and board him."

"Not me," was Mr. Chiffery's cautious reply. "I've been swamped that way a'ready. The cap'en can steer the barge close on, and we'll grapple the beggar with this here hook and rope. Then one on us can jump in and chuck him aboard."

"That's the plan, Chiffery," said Bill; "but spose the young beggar sees us and pulls out o' the way."

"He can't do it. I've bin a watchin on him, and he knows no more how to handle a boat than I know how to play the violentceller."

As Bill foretold, so it happened. The unlucky Tommy, perspiring freely in his vain endeavours to row the boat, took no heed of the barge until it was abreast of him. Then uprose the grinning faces of Bill, George, and Chiffery, a couple of huge iron hooks grappled the thwarts, and before he had time to realise the fact he was a prisoner.

"Hold him tight, George," said Chiffery, with a vengeful gleam in his eyes.

"Aye, I'll hold him tight!" replied George, squeezing Tommy in a hug compared to which the grip of a grizzly bear would have seemed a playful caress. "One—two—three—hup!"

And with the last word George pitched Tommy aboard the barge, and followed with very little loss of time.

"That's my coat he's got on," said Bill. "Come out o' that, you young beggar."

"Consider the gals, Bill," said George. "They'll all go orf in sterricks if you undresses him agin."

"I'll find him a suit," said the captain of the barge, who had made a voyage or two to the Southern States of America. "I've got a lot o' tar aboard, and some cotton waste—that'll keep him warm, comfortable, and decent till he gits home."

The watermen took the joke at once. It would be some revenge for what they had suffered, and it was unanimously agreed that Tommy should be "tarred and feathered."

Some pitch was very soon heated over the cabin fire, Tommy was spread-eagled on the deck, smeared with warm tar by Chiffery, while George stuck the cotton waste all over him with a liberal hand.

Then he was stowed away in the stern of the boat he had so wickedly appropriated; the picnic party followed—the mistress particularly careful of her ankles this time—and the watermen, roaring an adieu to their friend the captain, pulled ashore.

"YOU'D BETTER BLOW YOUR BRAINS OUT FIRST," SAID SAM; "THEY CUT YER THROAT; ARTER THAT YOU CAN 'KICK THE BUCKET

No. 30.

They set the unlucky Tommy down at the very entrance to the sluice through which the punt had drifted with him, and then, giving him a playful kick apiece by way of souvenir, departed, leaving him half-blind with the tar, and wholly bewildered at the unpleasant novelty of his new clothes.

It was about this very time that Lionel and his chums put off from Lake Island in search of the lost one, and paddling up the sluice with a slow stroke, Lionel, who was in the bow, kept a sharp look-out around him.

"Hullo, I say," he said to Charlie, who was pulling the bow oar, "what's that on the bank yonder?"

Charlie looked, and saw something resembling a bloated gate-post which had been newly white-washed.

"I don't know," he replied, after a long stare. "It's moving, isn't it?"

"Yes; and now we're nearer it looks something like a sheep walking on its hind legs. Pull into the bank a bit, boys. Not too close. Steady—so!"

"Bother me!" he said again; "if I don't believe it's a human creature. But what an extraordinary suit of clothes it has on!"

It had indeed, for the strange apparition was none other than our old friend Tommy, in his new suit of tar and feathers, or, to speak more exactly, tar and cotton.

"Easy all," said Lionel; "we'll go and see what this is. Some strange animal escaped from a menagerie, I fancy."

In a few moments the boys were all ashore, and advancing with cautious steps towards the strange apparition, which was turning slowly round and round, and giving utterance to curious sounds, something between a wail and a groan.

The boys halted at a distance of six or eight yards, and watched it narrowly. Not one cared to go too close to such a curious animal, the like of which they had never seen before.

"I wonder if it bites?" said Charlie. "Can you see any mouth, Li?"

"No, that long wool, or feathers, grows so thickly all over it."

"It must be some kind of monkey or baboon," said Vansittart.

"What a queer noise it makes!" said Charlie. "It can't be human, and yet there's something about it that I seem to know."

"It seems familiar to me too," added Lionel, who drew cautiously nearer and nearer as the strange animal showed no signs of hostility.

All at once he uttered a cry, something between a shout and a laugh, and, darting forward, caught hold of the monster by the arm.

"Look out, Li—it'll do you a mischief."

"It's Tommy Codlings," was our hero's startling reply; "somebody tarred and feathered him."

In an instant the boys were crowding round him, full of sympathy for their unlucky comrade.

"Poor old Tommy," said Lionel. "How do you feel, old fellow?"

But Tommy was gagged, his mouth was full of tar and cotton fluff, and all that he could say was—

"Um—um—mum—mum—mum—yum—yum."

Which is a language the boys could not understand.

They understood one thing though, and that was the necessity of getting Tommy back to the school at once.

Mr. Stiffback was a man of science, and it would be an easy task for him to clean Tommy with one of his wonderful inventions.

But Mr. Stiffback was of a different opinion; he had never lowered his genius so far as to invent a specific for the cure of tar and feathers, and so Tommy had to undergo the slow and unpleasant process of being oiled all over three times a day; and so thickly had the tar been laid on that the head master declared that a week would be necessary to remove it.

"And a great nuisance it is," said Mr. Stiffback to the second master, "for I had arranged that all the boys should have two days' holiday at the end of this week, under your and the professor's care, as I am about to test an invention, which I would rather not attempt with so many mischievous boys in the house."

"Indeed, sir!" said the second master, with a doubtful interest in the subject. "And may I ask——"

"It," continued Mr. Stiffback, "is a new explosive material, surpassing picrate of potash five hundred times in strength, and as readily explosive as the iodide of ammonia; but so completely under my control that I can at will explode it by the touch of a hair, or render it so innocuous that the steam hammer at Woolwich Arsenal would have no effect on it."

"Indeed, sir!"

"I am now," added Mr. Stiffback, "in process of manufacturing about two pounds weight, and that quantity, according to my calculation, if placed under the most powerful and largest ironclad in the world would, when exploded, leave not a fragment so large as a tin-tack visible."

"Lord bless my soul!" exclaimed the second master. "It—it isn't made yet?"

"No, I do not intend to complete the process until all the boys are out of the way; then I have invited a select party of scientific gentlemen to witness the effect of a torpedo sunk in the lake. Codlings will have to remain of course—he can't leave the house in that state; and you, if you particularly desire it, can also witness the experiment."

"N—not for worlds," stammered the second master, who had become alarmingly limp and pale. "I—I have a—a little business in Deliverham to-night, could I have permission to go over at once?"

"How can you think of such a thing?" said Mr. Stiffback, evasively; "you will be going with the boys to Deliverham to-morrow, and you can transact your business then."

"Oh dear me," moaned the second master, "how shall I rest to-night with all that horrible stuff in the house? Why if—if it went off, we—but there I dare not think of it."

Such a strict watch had never before been kept over the boys since the establishment of the school. The second master would have had them all handcuffed and chained down to the forms if he could have had his way, and he was in such a state of perspiring nervousness that he had to change his shirt three times the next day.

The boys were heartily glad when the time came for their holiday, but all their gladness, counted in one bundle, could not have equalled that of the classical master with that awful secret on his mind.

The picnic took place in a park some twenty miles away from Deliverham, and the boys were to be lodged for the night at the hotel, much to the delight of the proprietor, who was an innocent, and had not had much to do with boys before.

The first day passed off beautifully, as did the first night, but in the morning the proprietor of the hotel anxiously wanted to know if the boys were going to stay any longer.

"No," was the reply.

"I'm glad of that," was the proprietor's grim reply, "for if they stayed another night you'd have to order a funeral for the lot. I'd get the corpses ready."

The second day was also spent in the park, the afternoon was drawing to a close, the masters were busily ranging the boys in rank, when there came a sudden shock in the air, a sound which was more felt than heard. It was as if each one there present had received a blow from an invisible hand.

The boys looked at one another in alarm—the second master alone seemed to understand the cause.

He staggered back against a tree, and, pallid as death, said in a faint voice——

" It's gone off."

*　　*　　*　　*　　*　　*

And so it had. Mr. Stiffback had so completely proved the wonderful power of his new invention in explosives that on the spot where Lake Island School once stood only a deep hole, like a disused gravel pit, remained. Never before was the breaking up of school so effectual or so complete. Mr. Stiffback's last wonderful discovery had raised him so high above his fellow-men that he disdained to come down again. As for the scientific gentlemen who had been invited to witness the experiment they were dispersed over so wide an area that for weeks after the explosion the coroners of half a dozen distrcts were engaged almost night and day in the endeavour to get identified the various fingers, toes, and odd buttons that were brought to them.

But what of our old friend Tommy? Lionel, Charlie, Vansittart, and Sam were in deep grief, for they had no doubt but that he had shared the fate of Mr. Stiffback, and they mourned for their plump, good-humoured, ever-unlucky chum.

Some three days after the explosion an elderly clergyman, passing through a lonely part of a wood situate about a mile and a half from Deliverham, distinctly heard a feeble wail, like the cry of a child.

He looked round him and listened; the cry was repeated, and seemed to come from above.

He looked steadily, and at last made out some object, perched on the topmost branches of an immense elm tree, and from thence the sound certainly proceeded.

He was too old to climb himself, but he was certain that the cry was human, and marking the spot he ran for help, and soon returned with half a dozen active men, with ladders and ropes.

They scaled the trunk, reached the topmost branches, and there was Tommy, lying in his little bed almost unhurt, but dreadfully weak and faint from exposure.

He had had a wonderful escape, but one which has its parallel in many an authentic record of mighty explosions.

His friends were written to as soon as he was well enough to tell his tale, and how he was welcomed by his chums, and what a hero the papers made of him we will not dwell upon here. Even his aunt, that stern and unbending woman, was distinctly seen, by several people, to shed a real tear, for the first and only time in her life.

And here—for a few short weeks—we take leave of our readers, and close the second part of our story, and when our hero and his many friends make their appearance once again, the author trusts that they will receive as generous and hearty a reception as that which has already been extended to them in the past.

END OF PART II.